BLIND
DOG
CANYON

Published by Kensington Publishing Corp.

BLIND DOG CANYON

•A WIDOWMAKER JONES WESTERN•

BRETT COGBURN

PINNACLE BOOKS
Kensington Publishing Corp.
www.kensingtonbooks.com

PINNACLE BOOKS are published by

Kensington Publishing Corp
119 West 40th Street
New York, NY 10018

All Kensington titles, imprints, and distributed lines are available at special quantity discounts for bulk purchases for sales promotion, premiums, fund-raising, and educational or institutional use.

Special book excerpts or customized printings can also be created to fit specific needs. For details, write or phone the office of the Kensington Sales Manager: Kensington Publishing Corp., 119 West 40th Street, New York, NY 10018. Attn. Sales Department. Phone: 1-800-221-2647.

PINNACLE BOOKS and the Pinnacle logo Reg. U.S. Pat. & TM Off.

First Printing: November 2023
ISBN-13: 978-0-7860-4815-1
ISBN-13: 978-0-7860-4816-8 (eBook)

10 9 8 7 6 5 4 3 2 1

Printed in the United States of America

*This novel is dedicated to my daughter, River Grace,
a girl brave enough and smart enough to survive such a
tale as this and come through stronger than she began.*

CHAPTER ONE

Del Norte, Colorado, 1886

Newt Jones sat at a table in a far corner of the dance hall with a half-empty whiskey bottle on the table before him. He was gloriously drunk, although anyone watching him might not have realized his condition. He hadn't said much, hadn't danced, and might have gone unnoticed among the crowd if he hadn't been the kind of man that stood out even when he tried not to. He was tall, true, sitting there in a sheepskin coat and a big black hat. But that was only a part of what drew the eye to him. Beneath that hat brim and tucked down into the wooly collar of his coat was a face that was hard to forget.

The three-piece band on the stage at one end of the hall was currently playing a slow and fiddle-heavy rendition of "My Bonnie Lies over the Ocean" for the third time in less than an hour, and the dance floor was almost unoccupied due to that. It was not an upbeat song to please would-be dancers, especially not the current crowd of railroad men, freighters, ditchdiggers, and the other hard-living, booted sorts who had imbibed more spirits than Newt had. Those men wanted to stomp on the wood floor with a pretty lady and swing her to the ceiling, not stand around and listen to some sad, melancholy song over and over.

The house was selling more liquor while the majority of the crowd stood at the edge of the dance floor waiting, but there was also grumbling, both among the men who had spent their hard-earned money to rent a dance partner and the others who wanted their turn to do the same. Among that crowd were two young men who either had more money or more enthusiasm than their peers, for the two of them had stayed paired up with the same girls for the last hour. They danced to every fast song, and what they lacked in technique they made up for in energy. When they laughed, it was loud enough to be heard above the crowd and the music. One of them let go of the tall, blonde-haired German girl he clutched around the waist, tossed down the mug of beer he held in his other hand, and came across the room to stand in front of Newt's table.

"Somebody said you are the one that keeps tipping the band to play that song," the young man said in a chopped, twangy accent that caused one of Newt's eyebrows to lift slightly.

Newt poured himself more whiskey. It took all of his attention to make the liquid land in the glass.

"I said, Was it you?" the young man asked in a louder voice.

"Something bothering you?" Newt's face cracked into a grin. He wasn't a man normally given to grins or smiles, but the liquor was working hard on him.

"You sitting there grinning like a possum eating persimmons, that's what's bothering me," the man said. "And you paying that fiddler a whole ten dollars to keep playing that awful song bothers me worse."

Newt took another sip of whiskey and watched the fiddle

player as if he hadn't heard the young man standing in front of him.

"Mister, you see that pretty lady over there watching us? I spent my last three dollars to dance with her."

Newt threw back his head and sang, "Oh, bring back, bring back, bring back my Bonnie to me."

His voice, while not good, was at least somewhat on key, and what he lacked in style, he made up for in volume. The fiddle player gave him a tolerant nod from the stage.

The other young man still back with the girls took a step closer. "What's the matter, Tandy?"

"Trying to talk some sense into this 'un," the one at Newt's table called back to his partner.

They looked enough alike to be brothers, lean and about the same height, with sandy brown hair that curled out from under their hats. And both of them had that same accent.

"Listen, friend, I don't want to fight," the one by Newt's table said. "Ol' Tully over there, he's got a temper finer than a frog hair split three ways and tapered on both ends. What say you quit tipping that fiddler so we can have us some real dancing music?"

"Fight?" Newt slurred, as if that was the only word he had heard, and reached out and wrapped a big hand around the whiskey bottle.

Even in the poor light of the dance hall, the young man could see the battered and scarred knuckles on the big hand that gripped the bottle. And the scars on Newt's face were more noticeable than those on his fists. The marks on his cheekbones, chin, and eyebrows stood out on his suntanned skin like little cracks and seams in the fault vein of some hard rock mine shaft. His nose had been broken badly sometime in the past, perhaps more than once, and one cauliflower ear told that he had been clubbed there, as well.

Two things happened at that very moment. First, the

band finished the song and broke straight into a fast-tempo banjo version of "Camptown Races" that caused the crowd to whoop with joy and sent many couples back out on to the dance floor. Second, a man even bigger than Newt came through the front door at the far end of the hall. He waded through the crowd toward Newt's table, and in the process accidentally bumped into a man near the bar.

The big man coming Newt's way took hold of the man he had crashed into in order to keep that one from falling. Words were said between them that Newt couldn't hear. Then the big man continued on his way until he stopped to stand behind the young man who had, until then, been talking to Newt and making his complaints about music choices known.

"Have a seat," Newt said, and jerked a chair beside him out from under his table.

The chair fell over, but the giant newcomer sidled past the young man in his way, stood the chair back up, and sat down. The wood creaked beneath his weight.

The young man looked from one of them to the other, then turned on his heel and went back to the dance girls and his partner. He was shaking his head as he walked away.

"Did you see the size of that Indian?" he said to the others when they were reunited.

Newt heard what the youngster said and gave the man in the chair beside him a cursory glance. The kid was right. Mr. Smith was definitely the biggest Indian that Newt had ever seen or known. To say the Mohave was big was an understatement. Newt stood six feet three in his socked feet, yet Mr. Smith was taller. And it wasn't only the height that made him seem like such a giant. The man's upper arms were the size of most men's thighs. He was so large at the chest and shoulders that he had a hard time finding warm winter wear that fit him, finally settling for a buffalo coat he had bought from a Ute woman on their way up through the mountains. That bulky, incredibly heavy coat, with its curly buffalo hair and hanging to the back of his knees, made Mr. Smith's bulk seem even more expansive.

Mr. Smith took off his bowler hat, brushed a light dusting of snow from it, and set it on the table. His long, crow-black hair was bound behind his neck with a leather thong. He shrugged out of his buffalo coat and let it lie on the back of his chair. While the dance hall was a bit drafty and almost chilly in places, that heavy robe would see a bull buffalo through a blizzard. Newt didn't know how Mr. Smith could stand to wear it, either inside or outside. The thing must have weighed thirty pounds.

Newt blinked and watched the big Mohave carefully straighten the black suit coat he wore under the buffalo hide. The silk tie around his shirt collar was knotted and arranged as neatly as ever. Newt chuckled for the thousandth time at Mr. Smith's fastidious, odd ways.

"Have a drink." Newt shoved the whiskey bottle toward his friend.

"I do not want your whiskey." Mr. Smith's somewhat guttural accent may have been different, but his attempt at concise diction and his careful choice of words when speaking his second tongue would have done an English butler proud. It didn't fit with the rest of him any more than his fancy black suit.

In Newt's opinion, Mr. Smith was a conundrum, but that's what he liked about the man, at least sometimes. Newt pushed the bottle toward him again.

Mr. Smith looked at the bottle and then at Newt. "You're drunk."

"Highly," Newt said, with another grin.

Mr. Smith began to watch the dancers and sat that way while Newt finished his current glass of whiskey. The

Mohave's tattooed face was oddly tranquil and without expression, and it was hard to tell what he thought of the proceedings.

Newt had long since grown used to the tattoos, as well as Mr. Smith's stoic approach to life. The Mohave's face, like much of his upper body, was inked in blue-black symbols that perhaps only another of his tribe could interpret. Chevron-like bars lay across the breadth of his forehead, and T-shaped designs of dots and lines ran down from both cheekbones. Swirled designs decorated his broad, blunt chin.

"Why do you not dance like the other men?" Mr. Smith asked.

"Never was much of a dancer," Newt replied.

"Then why did you come here?"

"I like listening to the music."

"The man you seek is at the hotel waiting to talk to you," Mr. Smith said.

"Is he, now?" Newt answered. "If you're worried about him, why don't you go back and tell him I'll talk to him when I'm through here."

Mr. Smith gave a deep grunt. "You have a strange way of dealing with a man who you expect to hire you."

"I'm having fun. Try to have some yourself."

Their conversation was interrupted when three men came to their table. The one in the middle was the same one whom Mr. Smith had bumped into earlier, and he pointed a finger at the Mohave.

"We don't allow Indians in here," the man said.

"That's right," one of those beside him said.

Newt blinked twice and waited for the men to come into proper focus. He wanted to make sure there were actually three of them. "Who do you mean by *we*? All of you, or just you?"

"What?" the man in the middle asked.

"That's what I thought," Newt slurred.

"Listen here," the same man said.

"No, you listen here." Newt jerked his head at Mr. Smith beside him while he gave the men before him another goofy grin. "I'm going to do you a favor."

The man in the middle of the three smirked. "And what favor is that?"

"I'm going to whip you before he can." Newt's head almost rattled the lantern hanging over his table off its hook when he stood, and his thighs caught the edge of the table and knocked it back several inches. The whiskey bottle fell over, and what was left of its contents slowly trickled out onto the tabletop.

The man in the middle drew back a fist to hit Newt, but in doing so his elbow struck one of the two young men standing behind him, the same one that had come to Newt's table earlier to complain about the music. That elbow also almost knocked down one of the dance girls and spilled a drink all over her pretty dress.

"Watch it!" one of the two youngsters said, and then promptly planted a straight right on the gentleman's nose.

From there, the fight was on. Newt swung a haymaker from well back behind him at the man remaining closest to him. The blow was surprisingly fast for someone almost too drunk to stand. However, Newt's aim was more affected by the whiskey than his speed was. His punch missed badly and went right over his intended victim's head. The follow-through put him off-balance, and he crashed across the table and eventually rolled up under what was now a full-fledged brawl between the two youngsters and other men in the crowd.

He almost got back to his feet, but the German girl chose that moment to take a wild swing with the thick glass beer mug she held. Instead of striking her intended victim, she hit Newt in the back of the head. She was a strong, buxom lass, made stronger by helping her father at his brewery outside of town when she wasn't dancing and pushing drinks for a living. Besides being able to curse quiet loudly in her parent's native tongue while she fought, she also packed a wallop. Newt's felt hat cushioned some of the blow from the beer mug, but it was still enough to tip him over onto his face.

Somebody stomped on his fingers while he was down, then somebody else kicked him in the belly. Next there came the sound of another woman screaming, the grunts of straining men, and the dull, fleshy thuds of landing blows, all mixed with the shatter of breaking glass and the scrape of overturned tables and chairs on the wood floor.

The fight eventually moved away from Newt for some reason and gave him standing room. He managed to get his legs under him, but the world was spinning too fast to find his balance. He toppled again like an axe-cut tree, though he hardly felt any pain when he crashed back to the floor.

Hands took hold of him, big hands, and then there came the sensation of rising into the air as if by magic. He was still pondering on how that happened as Mr. Smith tossed him belly-down over one shoulder and started carrying him out of the dance hall.

"Let me down. I'll take the big ones and you take the little ones," Newt said.

He tried once to lift himself from the waist to better see what was going on around him, but he couldn't manage that feat and slumped head-down again with both arms dangling down Mr. Smith's back. He was still being carried that way when Mr. Smith went out the door and onto the dark street.

Behind them, the two young men who didn't like Newt's music backed out the door. A beer bottle thrown at them from inside barely missed them and struck the cold, hard street and ricocheted away.

"Get 'em!" Somebody shouted from inside the dance hall.

"Put me down," Newt mumbled as he came to life again and squirmed on Mr. Smith's shoulder.

Mr. Smith kept walking without complying with his request.

A pistol appeared in one of the young men's hands. The roar of that revolver was the last thing Newt remembered because it was at that very moment he passed out.

CHAPTER TWO

The old boar grizzly wasn't big as such bears went, but the grizzlies in the San Juan Mountains had never achieved the scale of their cousins farther north. Perhaps seven feet long from his nose to the tip of his stub of a tail, he might have weighed six hundred pounds. He would have been heavier if he hadn't been so shockingly thin. So thin, in fact, that his emaciated rib bones showed even through the shagginess of his winter coat. And that brown fur, tinted with silver on the tips along his back and neck, was matted and tangled. On one shoulder there was a seeping wound that had left a dried crust of old blood and serum and pus.

The hunger and the pain had almost driven him mad, and that madness had him on the move. His broad, massive head swung left and right as he lumbered and limped slowly out of the edge of the timber into the morning sunlight and onto the bare slope of the mountain leading down to the river. The pads of his giant feet hardly made any sound at all on the thin dusting of snow beneath them.

He moved with the wind in his face, and his keen nose searched for the scent of food. Twice he stopped to turn over rocks and search for grubs or insects he might find hiding. Some of those rocks were very large and heavy, but the great hump over his shoulders gave him power, even in his weakened condition, and he hooked his five-inch front claws under those rocks and flipped them over with ease.

The few grubs he found did little to satisfy his hunger, and he gave a low, rumbling growl of frustration. Adding to his torment was the certainty of the coming winter. It was going to snow soon, and snow a lot. With the snow would come the bitter cold, but how he knew that was a mystery. Maybe it was instinct or some magical foresight, or maybe the shortened daylight hours and the dropping temperatures of the past few days and nights triggered some chemical or physiologic working within him that acted like a sixth sense for the seasons. Whatever it was, it told him he should already be curled up inside his den high up on some north-facing slope and starting the long sleep to spring. Normally, he would have been.

The summer berries and tubers and roots and grasses should have seen him prepared. Perhaps some squirrel's stolen hoard of seeds and nuts, a nice fat trout plucked from some stream, or the occasional elk calf caught and devoured would have added to his fat layer and made him well-prepared to live on those reserves through hibernation. But the warm seasons had come and gone, and nothing had been easy.

Twenty-five years he had reigned as the king of the food chain along the headwaters of the Rio Grande, but now he was coming to the end. Age, aching joints, and the bad teeth in his mouth had something to do with that, however, it was his wound that sped the ravages of time.

It was the man creatures who had hurt him, the strange, noisy, two-legged beasts he occasionally came across. There had been few men in the mountains in his youth, but there came more and more of them with each year. They were men with pale skins, and they made bigger fires and more noise than the brown skins who had come first. It seemed their scent trails were everywhere except the highest, roughest places. And in his later years, as he became slower and less nimble, he had learned that where men camped there was likely to be easy food. Taking it from them was no different from taking a kill away from wolves or coyotes, or any other predator smaller than himself.

But he had not been raiding one of their camps when he came across the men who wounded him. He had found an especially heavy-laden and delicious patch of buffalo berries among a thin stand of quaking aspens one morning and had been so busy eating the juicy, orange-red fruit that he didn't notice the approach of the two men and the horses they rode up on. They were almost on top of him before he rose up on his hind legs to peer at them over the low brush. Then there had come a loud sound like the crack of thunder and a puff of fire smoke, and something struck him hard in the shoulder, tearing a hole in his flesh and staggering him. Another of those loud noises came and there was a buzzing in the brush beside him like the passing of an angry bee. By then he was already charging the men. They fled from him and their horses were swift, even over the rough mountain trail, but he did manage to rake his claws across the hind-quarters of one of the horses before they escaped him. He stood again and roared his victory as they disappeared down the mountain.

Then the pain had hit him as his adrenal gland quit pumping battle rage, and one of his front legs wouldn't work right. Limping and in shock, he found a thicket to rest in, and there he lay for days, hot and feverish and with his wound aching horribly. Only his thirst and hunger finally drove him from his bed. Though he lived, he was not the same. The bullet wound in his shoulder would not heal, no matter how much he licked it. It stank of dead flesh, and the blowflies followed him.

Then the elks' calving season came and went, and he caught not a single new calf. Nor did he catch any deer fawns where they tried to hide in the grass. Finding food had always taken much traveling, but he traveled less than ever.

The old bear squatted on his rump and lifted his nose higher. There came a tantalizing smell, only a small whiff. It was a scent he knew from before, though it was something he had only fed upon on a few occasions, all of them in his later years. It was the smell of sheep. The thought of ripping greasy, fat mutton off its bones caused him to run his tongue over his lips.

Though his sense of smell was keen, the old bear's eyesight had grown worse as he aged. No matter, he had always trusted his nose more than his eyes. He moved down the mountain, pausing often to smell the wind and searching for the sound or sight of the sheep he knew were close to him.

He heard the bleating before he saw the sheep. They were grazing not far below him. They must have seen or sensed his presence because they quit grazing and began to form a tight flock, milling about with their white, wooly bodies crammed together.

A great strand of drool slid from the old bear's mouth as he stalked closer. Experience had taught him that where there were sheep there were men, but he was too hungry to remember that detail or care. Sheep were easy to catch. Easier than any of the prey he knew. Even easier than digging marmots out of their holes when he could find some for a quick snack.

An alder thicket screened his movements and gave him cover to stalk from. His round little eyes peered through the limbs of a small bush, waiting for the right moment. By then, he was within sixty yards of the sheep. He was so focused on his prey that he didn't notice the sheepherder sitting on the shaggy little pony uphill from the herd. He also didn't notice the sheepdog, but the collie was no bigger than a coyote and could not stop him. Even had there been five men and as many dogs, it would not have changed what was about to happen, for nothing then and there could have distracted him from the urge to kill and feed.

He burst from the thicket and charged toward the flock. For a moment, his limp was all but gone, and he was as fleet-footed and horrible in a charge as he had been in his youth.

CHAPTER THREE

Newt rested his temple in one hand and squeezed slightly against the throb of the headache that he had woken with. He closed his eyes for a moment and then opened them to look again at the fellow across from him over the mug of steaming coffee he was nursing.

"There'll be a fellow waiting for you at Wagon Wheel Gap," the one across the table said. "People around these parts call him Happy Jack. He's an old prospector that knows these mountains like the back of his hand. He'll show you to the claim."

Newt closed his eyes again and let the coffee steam waft across his face. The dining room in the Windsor Hotel was sparsely populated that morning, and Newt had hoped to have his coffee in peace and recover from the previous night's debauchery.

"Are you listening to me?" the man asked.

"Saul, would you quit talking so loud?" Newt asked back.

Saul Barton was old enough to have gone white-headed, but still young enough that he hadn't lost his edge or his physical strength. He looked less like a man who had made a couple of fortunes locating silver and gold lodes and then selling them to the big mining interests. That morning he was wearing a plain white shirt tucked into plain brown wool pants, in turn tucked into a pair of plain, sturdy lace-up work boots that were scuffed and scarred enough to show they had been somewhere. The only things that hinted at his success were the gold cigar case lying on the table in front of him and the big, gold-nugget ring he wore on his calloused right hand.

He was a short man, yet his serious nature and the intensity of his gaze were far bigger in scale. And he had never been known as a patient sort, not since his first days out in the gold fields when Colorado was nothing but a territory, before the war, and when he had been just another fortune seeker panning away on a hard-luck placer claim like all the rest of the fools. But his persistence had paid off, no doubt largely due to his eternal optimism and a work ethic that would put beavers to shame. It had been a common saying back in the first mining camp Newt had lived in that Saul thought working only twenty-four hours a day was pure laziness.

"I'd say you were suffering from one hellishly bad hangover, but knowing you, you're still half drunk," Barton said.

"Let it be, Saul," Newt said. "I came just like I said I would."

"You're late," Barton replied. "I should have left for San Francisco two weeks ago."

"It was a long ride from Yuma."

"Never cared for that desert."

"I'm not partial to it myself, now that I've been there," Newt said, then gave a quick look around the room that made his head hurt worse. "Where's Mr. Smith?"

"Is the Mr. Smith you speak of that big Indian who carried you to your room last night?"

"He's working with me."

"I gathered that," Barton said. "Odd name for a Mohave,

but I suppose we couldn't even pronounce his real name. Never seen any of his kind up this way. Peculiar tribe is my impression, and that's putting it mildly."

"Oh, he's peculiar, but he's the kind you want to ride the river with," Newt said.

"I imagine those tattoos on his face take some getting used to."

Newt shrugged but gave no reply.

Barton played with his cigar case, spinning it around on the table instead of drinking his own coffee. After a while he looked up at Newt again. "I told you I wanted you to bring at least three men with you."

"I've got me and Mr. Smith, so far."

Barton leaned back in his chair. "This town's overpopulated with winter coming, and there are plenty of men down from the high country to lay up and wait for spring. I'm sure you can find a couple who will do."

"I'll see about it."

Barton pointed at a scrape on Newt's forehead and then at the swollen pointer finger on Newt's left hand. "I understand you got in a little ruckus over at the dance hall last night."

Newt sat up straighter without the movement causing his head to hurt much worse. "I wouldn't call it a fight. More of a misunderstanding."

"The city marshal is looking for two men who shot up the place."

"We never fired a shot," Newt said, and then gave a thoughtful grimace. "At least I don't think we did. To tell you the truth, I don't recollect much about it."

"Still the hardheaded scrapper you always were, aren't you? Do you still step in the prize ring when you get the chance, or is brawling in taverns and whiskey dives the only fight you can find?"

Newt wrinkled his face and avoided the question. "Your telegram said you would pay an advance."

Barton produced a yellow paper envelope and pushed it across the table to Newt. "There's money in there to pay you and three more men your first month's wages. Three dollars a day, like I promised. You'll get the rest of it when I come back in the spring."

"Have you already filed the claim?"

"I have."

"You're worried or you wouldn't be paying the money you're paying and needing so many men."

"There were two other parties working the area this past summer. And I got the distinct impression they were spending more time following me than prospecting."

"That's what happens when you're the man with the supposed magic touch for finding the next big strike."

"Maybe, but I have a suspicion that those prospectors were backed by one of my competitors," Barton said.

"And you're worried one of those competitors will try to move in on you?"

"I'm simply buying some insurance."

"You must think you have a real wing-dinger of a strike."

"Let's say it shows some promise," Barton said. "You're to let nobody on that claim. Nobody. I don't want anyone snooping around or maybe getting ideas that I can't hold what's mine."

Newt studied Barton. "If you're so sure about this one, why are you going to San Francisco instead of staying here to see to this yourself?"

Some of Barton's temper showed itself them, just a slight hint of irritation before he smothered it and hid it away. He wasn't a man who liked to be questioned. "Developing a mine is not a cheap matter, and I need to gather investors."

Newt weighed what Barton had said against what he hadn't said.

Barton waved a hand in the air as if that alleviated all concerns. "If I had to guess, I would say you and whoever goes with you will make a tidy profit for doing nothing other than lying around all winter and getting fat."

"How far away is this Willow Creek? How big of a town is it?"

"No town there."

"No tent city?"

"I'm the first one there."

"What about supplies?"

"There's already a cache at the claim, and Happy Jack will have more for you when you get to Wagon Wheel Gap."

"That all?" Newt asked.

Barton got up from the table. "Except to wish you good luck."

"Same to you." Newt stayed seated.

"I've already seen to your hotel bill," Barton said.

"That's kind of advertising that I'm working for you, isn't it?"

Barton brushed off the question simply by not answering it and started out of the dining room. "I've got a train to catch."

Newt finished his coffee, refused another mug from one of the waitresses, and went up to his hotel room and packed his belongings. It took him longer than it should have because he was pondering the job he had just taken.

The thermometer mounted outside the hotel door read twenty-nine degrees when Newt went outside, and there was a light dusting of snow. He bunched his wool coat collar up around his neck and trudged toward the livery barn and corrals on Fifth Street.

Mr. Smith was waiting there with their horses already

saddled. Newt held out a hundred dollars in greenbacks he had taken from the envelope Saul Barton had given him.

"You keep it," Mr. Smith said, with a shake of his head.

"Take it, it's yours. Start a fire with it if that's what suits you," Newt replied. "Or give it to pretty girl or tip a blind piano player. I don't care."

Mr. Smith took the money but muttered something in his native tongue. Newt had no idea what the Mohave said.

"Speak English if you're going to argue."

Mr. Smith ignored him and tightened the cinch on the big, black gelding standing tied to the corral fence. The horse had hooves the size of dinner plates. The amount of feathering above those hooves and the build of the horse testified that it had a good dose of draft blood, or what horsemen referred to as being cold-blooded. The black wasn't much for speed, but a lighter-built horse wouldn't hold up to the Mohave's bulk over a long haul. And such a horse might be a plus in snow country when the drifts got high.

Newt went over to his own horse. The short, stocky brown gelding might have appeared black from a distance when the sun hadn't faded his hair coat or when you weren't close enough to see the lighter brown tinge mixed in with the darker hairs, especially around the muzzle and lower legs. There was no white mark on the horse except for a single star between its eyes. An unusual brand was on one of the gelding's hips. It was a simple circle with a dot in the middle.

A plain-colored horse, yes, and a horse that didn't draw the eye of most on first glance. But the same horseman who could have spotted the cold blood in Mr. Smith's black gelding would have appreciated the Circle Dot horse's build, from his clean head and neck and the soft and intelligent eyes to the powerful hindquarters on the other end.

He was a close-coupled gelding, short of back and long underneath, with short and substantial cannon bones running down into dark, sturdy hooves.

Newt made sure his saddlebags and bedroll were tied tight behind his saddle and checked that his Winchester was in his saddle boot. The Circle Dot horse bent its neck in to look at him and yawned and shook its head.

"Quit complaining," Newt said to the horse. "I could have used more sack time myself."

He tightened the cinch, led the horse a few steps away from the corral fence, put a boot in the stirrup, and swung up into the saddle. Mr. Smith was already up on his horse and waiting. They moved down street riding side by side. They hadn't ridden far when they saw group of riders coming up Columbia Avenue two blocks away.

All of them were heavily armed, but that in itself wasn't unusual for men arriving in town off the range. They were a rough-looking lot, and even a fool could tell that they weren't miners come down from the mountains. Nor were they freighters or farmers, or cowmen or sheepmen, or loggers, either, for there was that dangerous air about them that told Newt as much about them as their looks. It wasn't only the sullen and cold bearing of a couple of them but also the cautious way they took in their surroundings. It was the way men looked when they were used to being hunted or doing the hunting themselves. Hard cases. Newt wondered if the locals he passed on the street looked at him and saw him the same way.

The riders pulled up in front of one of Del Norte's saloons. One of those men, a short fellow wearing a trade blanket capote coat with its hood pulled up on his head, moved a few steps away from his horse and looked their way like he saw something that interested him.

Newt and Mr. Smith moved on across the intersection and rode out of sight of the saloon.

"Do you know them?" Mr. Smith asked.

"No, but I guarantee you they didn't ride in to pay their respects to a church house. Rough bunch if I ever saw one, and you don't see that many of their kind together for no reason."

Mr. Smith nodded. "Anyone can see that they are *kwanamis*."

Newt had learned over their months on the trail together that the word Mr. Smith used was his tribe's way of referring to brave men and those of the warrior class. *Fighting men.*

"Like Saul said, we're only insurance. Odds are, we'll have an easy winter. Nothing to worry about," Newt replied with more than a touch of irritation in his voice. "Nothing at all."

"I do not worry. All any warrior can hope for is a good death, and last night I dreamed—"

Newt scowled at the Mohave and interrupted him. "I don't want to know what you dreamed. Keep that medicine man stuff to yourself."

"I think it might have been a power dream." Mr. Smith continued as if he hadn't heard Newt.

"I said I don't want to know what you dreamed." Newt took his canteen from where it hung off his saddle horn and took a slug from it. The water was so cold it hurt his teeth. "No, what I want is to spend a winter laid up in a nice, cozy camp with plenty to eat and a nice hot fire to sit around. I've brought three good decks of cards with me, and come spring I expect us to have worn them out. We'll laugh at Saul for paying us so much for hibernating and eating his food."

"You do not wish that. 'Ride, boldly ride.' Is that not what Poe wrote?" Mr. Smith asked.

"What are you talking about? Who's Poe?"

"Edgar Allan Poe, one of your men of words, a poet."

"Never heard of him."

Newt had never read so much as a single poem himself. Oh, there were a few children's rhymes he had learned as a boy and a handful of lines and bits and pieces that he had picked up over the years in theaters and watching traveling shows. But little of that had stuck with him, and the best he could do was paraphrase a few of them. On the other hand, while Mr. Smith might take spells where he didn't talk for a full day or more, when he did talk the first words out of his mouth were just as likely to quote some famous poem or bit of European philosophy as they were to be about some random Mohave custom or religious practice. He was sometimes irritatingly odd, even for a Mohave.

"'Over the mountains of the moon, down the valley of the shadow, ride, boldly ride,'" Mr. Smith said. "I still do not know all of how you white men think or the things you speak of, even after so many years among you, but those are words of power that I can understand."

"They do have a ring to them," Newt said. "Mother Jones, she always loved the sound of a fine turn of phrase. Used to recite of a bit of poetry herself, though mostly she was given to quoting scripture from the Good Book."

"Do you remember the words she taught you?" Mr. Smith asked. "My people have no books or writing."

"Ah, most of what she said I forgot as soon as she said it, but the older I get the more I regret that."

"Few remember my people's words and the power that went with them. The old ways are no more, and when the words are gone we will be no more."

"By golly, but you're gloomy this morning. You're making my head hurt."

"No, that is the whiskey poison eating you from the inside like a bad snake swallowing its tail."

Newt squinted at the sun glaring off the dusting of snow and rubbed at his temples. "You've got a point. Remind me to stay off the firewater next time."

"'Quoth the Raven "Nevermore,"'" Mr. Smith said, and lifted his chin a little higher, almost smugly.

Newt shook his head and growled from the pain that movement caused. "I'm not even going to ask."

As was their habit, both men soon fell into silence, and the only sound was the wind over the high desert and the plod of their horse's hooves. The headwaters of the Rio Grande River were somewhere up in the mountains ahead of them. There in that same country was a mountain stream of little consequence called Willow Creek where Saul Barton had a silver claim that he was paying them to guard.

CHAPTER FOUR

The grizzly charged downhill toward his prey. Despite his injury and despite his age, he was hitting speeds in excess of twenty-five miles per hour by the time he reached the edge of the flock—six hundred pounds of fur-wrapped muscle and bone barreling forward with all the force and inertia of a runaway mine car. The low brush parted before him in a wave, with alder limbs snapping and crackling like pistol shots in the crisp, high mountain air.

Most of the flock scattered before the bear and made an attempt to avoid him, but one of the sheep, a ewe with a late-born lamb huddled close to its flank, froze in terror. A swipe of the bear's paw broke her spine, and claws the thickness of cigars ripped hunks of wool and flesh from her body. The bear's momentum carried him over her in a cloud of snow and dust, then he doubled back and sunk his teeth into her neck at the base of her skull and the bones crushed under the force of his jaws.

The lamb was more confused than afraid and did not run. It bleated twice before the bear ended it with another swipe of a paw. Then the dog barreled into the fray, yapping and barking and with the hair on its spine standing straight up. It nipped once at the bear's rump, then darted away and barely avoided a snap of the bear's jaws aimed for it. Again, it darted in when the bear clamped its mouth over the ewe for a second time, although this time the dog's timing wasn't so perfect. Without even letting go of the ewe, the bear gave another nonchalant sweep of his paw and caved in the dog's ribs. The dog whimpered and went flying, another victim of the brown fury that had descended upon them.

The bear laid down on top of the ewe, pressing her body under his weight. He was posed over her that way when he became aware of the sheepherder shouting at him from up the hill. He craned his neck around, bared his teeth, and gave the man a low, warning huff.

The sheepherder was having a hard time keeping the terrified horse he rode from bolting. The horse scrambled on the rough slope and reared against the pull of the bridle bit. The sheepherder kept his seat in the saddle and fought his mount to a quivering standstill, where it stood low in the front end with spraddled front legs and with its eyes wild with fright and its nostrils flaring and blowing.

The old bear understood nothing about guns, so he did not recognize the rifle the sheepherder pulled from his saddle boot for what it was. But he did take that movement as a threat. He popped his jaws together and gave a woofing bark of warning. He started to charge, but the desire to eat the ewe was greater than the threat of the puny man on the horse, especially since the man was so far away.

The sheepherder was a short, stocky Basque. He knew as little about grizzly bears as he knew of speaking English, for he had been born in the Pyrenees Mountains of Spain and had only been in America two years. Also, there were few such bears in the San Juans, and he had never come across one. But he did know the mountains, and he was devoted to taking care of the sheep he was contracted to tend. He shouted at the bear in hopes of scaring it away.

"Get out of here!" he screamed in his native Euskera language. "*Irten hemendik!*"

The Basque had been trusted to manage the herd's summer grazing and to see to it that the lambs grew heavy and strong before driving them back down to the desert for winter. His only pay was a small percentage of the wool and the lamb crop, which he one day hoped to turn into a herd of his own. The bear had already killed one of those lambs, plus its mother, as well as wounding his dog.

"*Irten hemendik!*" he screamed again.

The old bear rose and stood over the dead ewe with blood dripping from his mouth. The Basque raised his rifle. He was a brave man not to have fled, but still, his hands and arms shook so badly that he had trouble finding his aim. His rifle's front sight somehow found the bear's chest, and he fired.

Overcome by fear and a host of spinning emotions, he jerked the rifle's trigger instead of squeezing it. That threw off his aim and he missed badly. The bullet that should have struck the bear went harmlessly past it and kicked up snow and earth to one side. The gunshot didn't scare the bear away. On the contrary, it caused the bear to charge him.

The old boar heard the roar of the rifle and saw the cloud of powder smoke, and he instantly associated it with the day he had taken the wound in his shoulder from the other such men—maybe the same man. He started up the hill as fast as he could go, intent on destroying the source of his pain and the pale-skinned two-leg who threatened to take his kill.

The rifle the Basque carried was an old single-shot, trapdoor Springfield. It was army surplus and had seen better days. His employer had loaned it to him to kill coyotes and wolves and mountain lions, or whatever other predators might stalk his herd, and to hunt and keep himself in camp meat. The rifle's chamber was rusty and pitted from years of black powder corrosion, and it was prone to swelling spent cartridge cases so badly that they were hard to extract, and the extractor sometimes didn't working properly. That was a problem common in many of the guns of that model, and reloading such a weapon and preparing for another shot was not a quick process, even in the hands of a calm, cool expert marksman used to the gun's quirks.

The slow-reloading rifle played in the bear's favor, that and the sheepherder's panicked horse. The horse whirled uphill to flee from the bear, and in doing so caused its rider to drop the fresh cartridge he was trying to poke into the rifle's chamber. Then it threw him from the saddle and ran up the mountain.

The Basque disappeared from the bear's sight beneath the bushes ahead, but he stood again before the bear had run ten more yards. There was now only a short stone's throw between them, and the bear ran faster.

The Basque turned and tried to run, but he couldn't manage the speed necessary to save his life. Part of that was because the bear was too fast, and part was because, like the bear, the sheepherder had a bad leg, a sprained ankle that he had incurred clambering along a rocky slope two days before while in search of some missing sheep that had strayed from his band.

Running up the steep slope slowed the bear some, but the Basque realized it was a footrace he could not win under any conditions. He turned at the last second and faced his attacker with the rifle held in both hands and reared back like a club. He screamed again. His words were too wild to be understandable, but they sounded like a defiant challenge, like an Iberian war cry of ancient times. Then he swung the rifle with all his might, aiming in a downward stroke for the bear's skull.

The rifle stock splintered and broke on the crown of the bear's head, but it did not stop him. Some of the sheep-herder's bones cracked and broke on impact as the bear drove him down to the ground. His next screams were caused by pain and torture, and they were not defiant at all.

And that was how the bear killed his first man.

CHAPTER FIVE

Newt and his Mohave companion made the first five or six miles upriver easily and in good time, with Mr. Smith seemingly enjoying the solitude and the scenery while Newt nursed his hangover and scowled at his horse's ears. By late morning, the sun was shining bright and warm and the thin dusting of snow had melted away. They stopped once to shed their coats and then moved on.

The old stagecoach road they followed led up the Rio Grande into the San Juans. It wasn't really a true road, not graded and smoothed, instead being nothing more than a well-defined set of wagon ruts running before them like parallel claw marks gouged in the earth. The river valley was flat and all but treeless, and their traveling was easy. Other than the scattered farmsteads, a few cattle dotting the slopes, and a big mule deer buck that bounded away from them, they encountered little in their passing to break the monotony. They kept their horses to a long trot, and by noon they had covered ten miles and rode into sight of the settlement of South Fork. There wasn't much there, other than a Denver & Rio Grande Western Railroad water tower for the trains, a depot, and a few other scattered farm or ranch buildings dotting the valley around it.

Beyond South Fork, the river valley began to narrow even more until it became more of a canyon, and the countryside changed as they left the San Luis Valley behind and began to climb into the mountains proper. Dark green, scattered stands of conifer timber dotted the rocky, steep peaks and bluffs to either side of them, and the road they followed and the D&RG tracks ran almost side by side. The river was shallow and the water was crystal clear.

The canyon soon narrowed more, and both the road and the train tracks crossed the river and hugged close to the foot of the mountain on the north side. Newt stopped his horse midstream to watch the speckled back of a brown trout showing out of the water as it muscled its way over the rocky shoal. Another fish splashed in the dappled shadows beneath a clump of willows not far from him, and he was watching it when Mr. Smith suddenly stopped his horse short of climbing up the bank and out of the river on the other side. The way the big Mohave was looking up the valley told Newt that something was wrong.

"We've got company," Mr. Smith said.

Newt rode the Circle Dot horse beside Mr. Smith's horse and peered over the lip of the riverbank. Less than a quarter mile upstream, at a point where the river passed through a tight gap between the mountain on the north and a long finger of timber from the opposing mountain on the south, there were two saddled horses standing in the trail.

Newt and Mr. Smith shared a look between them, then the Mohave rode back across the river, used the cover of the willows to mask where he climbed out of the channel, and soon disappeared into the timber. Newt waited a while to give Mr. Smith time, then he adjusted the lay of his pistol holster on his right hip and nudged the Circle Dot horse out of the river and up the trail.

The Circle Dot horse was a fast walker, but Newt held

him back with a light feel on the bit. He kept watch on the slope above him and the timber on the other side of the river as he rode. Ahead of him, he could see that there was only one man with the two horses. That man was bent over with one of the horse's front hooves between his knees as if he was checking the condition of a horseshoe or cleaning that hoof sole. If there was another rider for the second horse, he couldn't be seen.

The man Newt could see put down the horse's front leg, straightened up, and looked Newt's way with the flat of one hand held up to shade his eyes. Newt kept coming and finally stopped the Circle Dot horse twenty-five yards from him. There was something familiar about the young man standing before him, but it took several silent seconds for it to come to him. It was one of the youngsters from the dance hall the night before.

"Having trouble?" Newt asked.

"You wouldn't happen to have any horseshoe nails, would you?" the kid asked.

Newt noticed that both horses with the man were of good stock, with one of them being a flashy strawberry roan of exceptional quality. He also noticed that both of those horses were matted with dried sweat and salt marks. It was obvious they had been put to hard use, just like the empty rifle scabbard hanging from the saddle on one of the horses was obvious, if one paid attention to that sort of thing.

"My horse has got a loose shoe," the kid added.

"I've got a sack of nails in my saddlebags," Newt answered.

"I'd sure appreciate the loan of a few."

Newt saw the kid make a quick flick of his eyes toward the trees on the other side of the river. He didn't have to look that way himself to understand that whomever the other saddled horse belonged to was likely over there and up to no good.

Newt pressed his spurs against the Circle Dot horse and stepped the gelding quickly forward to close the distance between himself and the kid in front of him. He purposely reined the horse to place the kid between himself and the timbered ridge across the river.

The kid had to move to get out of the way of the Circle Dot horse, and in doing so, his right hand moved toward the nickel-plated Merwin & Hulbert revolver riding in a holster flopping at a cross-draw on his opposite hip. Maybe it was an accidental move of his hand, or maybe it wasn't.

The Circle Dot horse had a fine, light handle, and Newt reined him around to bring his right side to the kid. There was a quick rasp of holster leather, and Newt's Smith & Wesson No. 3 was suddenly in his fist and pointed at the kid. The clack of the cocking pistol hammer was loud in the brisk air.

"Kid, I'd keep my hand away from that hogleg if I was you," Newt said.

The young man lifted his hands away from his sides. "Easy there, mister. You got me all wrong."

"Tell whoever it is up in the trees to show himself," Newt said. "Do it quick."

At that moment Newt caught the flash of movement across the river. Mr. Smith was splashing through the shallows toward him with the kid's partner marching in front of him. Both the Mohave and his prisoner were wet to the knees when they came out on the near bank. That prisoner was another kid from the dancehall, and he also had a trickle of blood running out from under the wool cap he wore and down one side of his face.

Newt also noticed that Mr. Smith had a Winchester carbine in his hand that wasn't his. His prisoner had no holster on his belt, and Newt trusted that Mr. Smith would have checked him closely for a sneak gun. The Mohave was thorough about such little details.

Newt gave Mr. Smith a slight nod. "What have you got here?"

"He was over there with his rifle pointed at you." Mr. Smith jerked his head back over one shoulder in the direction of the timber across the river.

"Now, that ain't real friendly, is it?" Newt asked.

"It ain't like what you think," the one who had pretended to work on his horse's hoof said. "You all right, Tully?"

"He hit me with a stick," the other answered and lifted his checkered wool cap gently away from his head to probe his wound with his fingertips. "Injuned up behind me and whacked me with no warning."

With the cap out of the way, Newt could see that the wound was a nasty one. Not life-threatening or bleeding badly, but the laceration just above the kid's temple was enough that it could use a couple of stitches that it likely wasn't going to get.

"You two are about the poorest pair of road agents I've ever come across," Newt said.

"We ain't stickup men," the one with the bleeding head said. "I'm Tully Hudlow, and this here is my brother, Tandy."

"I remember you two from the dance hall last night," Newt said.

"You were so drunk I'm surprised you remember anything," the one called Tandy replied, the one without a knot on his head. "Listen, Mister, we ain't out to rob you. Our horses are all tuckered out is all, then we look back and see you two coming. Thought you was a posse on our heels because of that little fracas back there in Del Norte. We had to burn a little powder to keep those old boys from getting the best of us, but we didn't hurt anybody."

"Thought you'd get the drop on us? That it? Or maybe you were thinking on swapping horses with us?" Newt asked. "Sound about right to you, Mr. Smith?"

The Mohave gave no answer and only continued standing there staring at the two young men like a big silent boulder that might have rolled down the mountain and landed there.

"There you go again, getting it all wrong," Tandy said. "We were worried, is all. We've come a long ways and ain't exactly wishful of being caught by those city dudes back yonder."

Newt had caught their names, but he was still trying to get the pair of them sorted out in his mind. Both of them somewhere in their early twenties or late teens if he guessed right. And both of them didn't exactly look prosperous. Their clothes were worn and stained in places, and the broad-brimmed hat the one called Tandy wore was so sweat-stained and old the brim of it flopped down over his eyes like a sagging tree limb.

He tried to sort them in his mind. Tandy was the one in the floppy hat, and the taller of the two, if only by a little bit. He had a wispy boy's mustache sprouting from his upper lip and a peach fuzz, patchy set of whiskers on his jaws and chin that should have been shaved off days before.

Then there was Tully, the one in the wool cap that Mr. Smith had dragged out of the woods. Clean shaven, but with a pale complexion like his brother, a scald of sun or windburn on his nose, and the cool morning making his cheeks almost as red. Instead of the pair of brogan work shoes like his brother wore, Tully had his pants legs tucked into the tops of a pair of boots with mule ear tugs that flopped when he moved. Both of them were as nervous as they were green.

"Yeah," Tully said, "What was that word that book peddler on the train kept using when we were coming through Kansas?"

"*Discombobulating*, that was it," Tandy replied.

"Yeah, *discombobulating*," Tully said. "Both of us were a little discombobulated about that city marshal making such a big deal of that little set-to back there. We wasn't gone half an hour before he was after us. Hounded us half the night."

The faint hint of a wry grin showed on Newt's mouth. There was something about the pair of them that made it hard to keep down a smile, no matter what shenanigan they had intended to pull on him and Mr. Smith.

"I'd appreciate it if you put that pistol away," Tandy said. "You pointing it at my noggin that way really puts a damper on friendly conversation."

Newt kept his revolver pointed just the way it was and nodded at Tandy. "Where are you two hilltoppers from?"

"Who you calling hilltoppers?" Tandy asked.

Newt went on like he hadn't heard him. "I recall some Hudlows that ran back on Turkeypen Ridge."

Both of the young men cocked their heads the same way as soon as Newt said that.

"What do you know about Turkeypen Ridge, and how do you know any Hudlows?" Tully asked.

"I always heard Hudlows were no good for anything but making cat whiskey, coon hunting, and stealing hogs," Newt said.

"You put that pistol away and get down off that horse and we'll teach you a thing about slandering the good name of a Hudlow," Tandy said.

Newt let out a deep, gravelly chuckle.

"Who the hell are you?" Tandy asked. "I'm beginning to guess I ought to know you."

"Name's Newt Jones. And my friend there is Mr. Smith."

"Jones? There's some of them back home. You one of them from over on the other side of Roundtop? One of them Tuckaleechee Joneses?"

"I might be."

"Hell's bells," Tandy said. "You've been funning us all this time, ain't you?"

Tully gave Tandy a questioning look.

Tandy nodded at Newt. "Meet your kinfolk and say a howdy."

Tully dabbed at the cut on his head again, squinted against the sun or the pain, and gave Newt a closer look. "Kin? You ain't one of old Kinch Jones's sons, are you?"

Newt's answer was only a subtle nod of his head.

Tully scuffed the dirt with the toe of one boot and let out a long exhale. "Shoot, Kinch passed on before we were big enough to know him, but our pappy used to talk about him all the time. Said he was the toughest man and the finest rifle shot in Tennessee. Said he was raised by a she-cat in a limestone cave and growed out to man-size on nothing but bear fat and white oak acorns. I don't believe all that, but I reckon he was a legend in those parts as much as anyone."

Tandy nodded his head in agreement and set in where his brother left off. "Old folks still like to tell how Kinch went west to the far mountains a-trapping and a-hunting for beaver. Didn't come back for three years, and when he did he was riding a hundred-dollar black mare and wearing a fine suit of clothes. All the ladies from Pigeon Forge to Gatlinburg were hoping he'd spark them so's they could latch on to all that fortune he'd made selling his furs."

Newt's laugh was a short, scoffing bark. "Fortune? He barely made enough to build a good cabin and clear him some land. Told me once that the only thing he brought back after all those years was three hundred dollars and a Blackfoot arrowhead in his hip. But I guess he did catch Ma's fancy. She used to tell the same story about him on that black mare and what a fine figure he cut."

Mr. Smith nodded at the Hudlow brothers, seemingly confused at the social turn the gathering had taken. "They are your people?"

Newt didn't answer, but Tully Hudlow chimed in for him. "We be kin. Our ma was his daddy's half sister."

Mr. Smith looked a question at Newt. "This *kin*? It is like a clan?"

Newt shrugged. "Family, clan, either one."

"So, we don't shoot them?" Mr. Smith asked in the same flat tone, the same tone he would have used to ask Newt to pass the coffeepot or something.

"Now, you need to talk to that savage," Tandy said.

Tully Hudlow backed a step until he was beside Tandy and turned slightly so that they were almost back-to-back. The two brothers seemed to adopt that defensive position without even having to think about it and as if they had taken it many times before.

"I'd speak more politely to Mr. Smith if I were you," Newt said.

"We've done told you we ain't no robbers," Tandy said. "We ain't nothing but two Tennessee cousins on our way to Lake City."

"What's in Lake City?" Newt asked.

"We were told about a mine job there where we might get hired," Tandy said.

"I hear those passes up to Lake City and Silverton are all but blocked come winter."

"We'll make it," Tully replied.

"This your first winter out here?"

"We've seen snow before."

"You've never seen snow like it falls here," Newt said, as he uncocked his revolver and holstered it. "Up in those mountains it can get so deep you could bury a freight train."

The brothers seemed to relax a little once Newt had holstered his pistol, but they both kept casting wary looks at Mr. Smith.

"Say what you want, but we're going. Got no choice," Tandy said.

"You broke?"

"When ain't we been?" Tandy said. "But the truth is, what little spending money we had we left back there in Del Norte."

"Spent all your money on dancing girls and liquor, and now you don't have the price of a meal in your pockets. Is that it?" Newt said.

"We didn't spend it all on girls and whiskey," Tandy replied with a slow-forming grin. "We spent some on unimportant stuff."

"Keep an eye on them while I go get your horse," Newt said to Mr. Smith.

The big Mohave pointed the Winchester he was carrying one-handed from the hip at Tully Hudlow's belly. The short-barreled carbine looked almost like a toy in his grasp.

"This ain't no way to treat kin folk," Tandy said, all the while keeping his hands wide of the Merwin & Hulbert in his holster. "You don't seem to set much store by family."

"I've never had family try to rob me," Newt said. "Kind of puts a different twist on things, doesn't it?"

He rode across the river and into the timber. It didn't take him long to find the horse where Mr. Smith had left it, and he led the black back to where the Hudlow brothers and Mr. Smith waited.

Newt handed one of the black's bridle reins to Mr. Smith,

then looked at the brothers and then at their horses. "That roan horse there really got a loose shoe?"

Tandy gave what was likely meant as an apologetic grimace and rubbed at the scraggly whiskers on one side of his face. "Might be I was pulling your leg about that."

Newt nodded, already knowing the likely answer before he had even asked the question. "Now that might be the first honest thing you've said so far."

"We might be a lot of things, but we ain't liars," Tully snapped back at him.

"A Hudlow stands by his word," Tandy added.

"What say you ride with us as far as Wagon Wheel Gap?" Newt asked.

"You aim to hand us over to the law?" Tully asked, with a creased furrow appearing over his eyebrows.

"Doubt there's any law there to hand you over to," Newt replied. "You come along now. Maybe we give you two the benefit of the doubt, but if we're going to be on the same trail going the same direction, I'd as soon you be where I can see you. No more *misunderstandings* that way."

"Fair enough, but we ain't waiting on you if that Del Norte marshal shows himself," Tandy said.

Tully nodded at Mr. Smith, and from the set of his jaw it was plain he was getting mad. "Seeing's how it's all straightened out, tell him to give me back my rifle gun. Cost me thirty-eight dollars back in Missouri. First good gun I ever owned."

Mr. Smith made no move to hand over the Winchester, and the muscles and tendons in Tully's jaws popped out against the clench of his teeth and his face began to flush. He stretched out an arm and pointed a finger at Mr. Smith and started to say something, but Tandy pushed his hand down.

"Don't mind him. He's just partial to that gun," Tandy said. "First new rifle he ever owned."

Newt nodded at Mr. Smith, and the big Mohave read his
intention and uncocked the Winchester and pitched it to
Tully. The kid caught it deftly and gave the Mohave a nod
of truce.

"Get on your horses," Newt said.

The brothers did like they were told. Soon, they all
started upriver with the brothers riding in the front and
Newt and Mr. Smith coming behind. They hadn't ridden
far when Newt noticed Mr. Smith glaring at the brothers'
backs.

"You cold?" Newt asked the Mohave. "We can stop and
build a fire to dry your feet out."

Mr. Smith shook his head. "The cold does not hurt."

"Why are you looking so sour, then?"

Mr. Smith's lips tightened. "My shoes are wet. I should
have taken them off before I crossed the river."

Newt grunted instead of outright laughing. Mr. Smith
had been wearing that suit of his when they had first met in
California, and despite the impracticality of such clothing
on the trail, he continued to wear it. The black garments
were beginning to show spots of being threadbare, but the
Mohave was fastidious about their care, often brushing
the wool fabric free of dust and debris at night in camp.
And Mr. Smith took equally good care of his shoes.

"You will hire them to go with us?" Mr. Smith asked,
without looking at him.

Newt gave him a scowling glance. "Those two are about
as green as they come. Nothing but fool kids."

"But they will go with us?"

"Why would you think that?"

"You said they are . . . How did you say it? Your kin?"

"I've never laid eyes on those two in my life."

"But they will go with us?"

Newt scowled at him again. "I don't know why I travel with you. All you want to do is argue."

Newt made a point of not looking at Mr. Smith again, pretending as if he weren't riding there beside him. Mr. Smith also pretended that he didn't notice Newt's stubborn reaction. However, unreadable though his expression usually was, the Mohave could not help the flick of his eyes toward Newt a couple of times nor the tiny quirk of a smile that lifted one corner of his mouth and disappeared just as quickly as it formed.

They said nothing else to each other for a while, riding along with a careful watch on the brothers and the river pass through the mountains that led toward Wagon Wheel Gap. Neither man had been there before, but from what they were told it was another ten miles or so ahead. The sunshine that had somewhat warmed away some of the previous night's chill was disappearing, and the cloud cover moving in overhead was steel gray.

"Do you think it will snow again?" Mr. Smith asked after he noticed Newt studying the sky on several occasions.

Newt shrugged and shook his head. "Who knows? But a fellow I met back in Del Norte said all the signs this year say it's going to be a bear of a winter."

CHAPTER SIX

The little girl's name was Zuri Altube. She was the sheepherder's daughter, and she was only eleven years old. She was normally a bubbly, inquisitive, happy child who had held on to those attributes despite already having known loss in her short life, but everything inside her shattered into a thousand pieces when the grizzly came.

The sheep were grazing on the mountain ridge several hundred yards above camp, and her father had gone to check on them. She was playing with her only toy, a ragged and worn stuffed doll, inside their tent when she heard the commotion.

At first it was the bleating of a few of the sheep, then a crashing of the brush not far uphill, followed by the barking of the dog. She barely had time to run out of the tent and stand with her doll dangling at the end of one arm before the entire band of sheep came charging downhill toward the camp in a panic.

Her father's two pack mules were across a small stream from the tent, and they had stopped grazing and were staring up the mountain with their long ears perked and their heads held high. When the sheep came, both of the mules tried to bolt and flee in the same direction, but the rope hobbles tying their front legs together hindered their flight.

They both leapt and lunged forward in the peculiar way that hobbled mules or horses sometimes learned to move, and one of the mules was so frantic that it fell and flipped end over end. The other mule fought so hard to get away that it busted its hobbles and took off in a dead run, braying like it had gone mad.

The sheep veered at the last second at the edge of camp and kept running, right into the dense stand of white-barked aspens on the other side of the stream. The quakies' leaves had already turned with the changing season, and the sheep and the mule crashing through the trees sent a shower of yellow leaves falling and floating on the air.

Zuri took in all those impressions as if in a dream, and she wasn't sure what was going on, other than something had gone wrong. Badly wrong. Then there came the sound of a gunshot, and moments later her father screamed.

She looked up the mountain, trying to spy him. Then he screamed again. The sound was awful, like the sharp point of a knife stabbed into her brain. She didn't have to know exactly what was going on to know that he was in pain and suffering some horrible fate.

She was still standing with her mouth hanging open and her heart hammering in her narrow chest when her father's horse ran through the camp with its saddle stirrups flopping and its eyes wild with fright. Both bridle reins were broken off short, and its mouth was bloody from the snatch of the bridle bit when it had stepped on those dragging reins and jerked them in two. She held out a hand to stop the horse, but it was running so blindly in panic that it almost trampled her. She ducked inside the tent's doorway and felt the throb of it hooves and the rush of its weight going past her.

When she came back out of the tent, the horse was gone and her father had quit screaming. Again, she searched the mountain for signs of him. It felt as if she couldn't breathe.

She wanted to call out to him, but the pressure in her chest and the knot in her throat wouldn't let her make a sound. She closed her eyes.

What do I do? What do I do? she thought. *Be brave. Be brave.*

She opened her eyes again and guessed at what could have happened. Had he been thrown from his horse? *No, it was something worse than that. Far worse.*

He needs you. Still, for some reason, everything in her body was demanding that she run as fast as she could and as far away as she could, though she didn't know why. She started to walk up the mountainside but hesitated. The fear in her was growing and growing until it weighed her down and threatened to smother her.

She saw the knife lying in the skillet beside the fire. It was a small butcher knife, barely as long as her forearm. Her father had been using it that very morning to cut up sausage for their breakfast.

She walked toward where she had last seen the sheep grazing on the mountain with the little butcher knife in her hand. Even at her age, she knew that it was a ridiculously puny weapon, but holding it made her feel better. Something horrible had happened to her father, and whatever it was waited for her. Tears streamed down her cheeks, but she kept walking.

The slope was steep and the leather soles of her shoes were slick. She almost fell once, went down to one knee, but righted herself. The slushy, mostly melted snow and mud left a kneecap mark on her red skirt, but she didn't even notice.

If only they had gone down to the desert earlier this wouldn't be happening, she thought as she walked. The year before, their first year herding the sheep, they had taken the band to the lower country long before now, partially out of

fear of being caught too high up when winter came. There
was no way not to notice that the temperature had been
getting steadily colder for the past week and the vegetation
had been changing, yet her father wanted to take advantage
of what grass remained and graze their way back downriver.
He told her how the lambs would be the fattest brought in
to headquarters and how his share of their sale the next
spring and his cut of the sheering would add to their sav-
ings. The ewe lambs he chose to keep would be stronger,
and one day they could build a sheep band of their own so
that they didn't have to tend another man's property and
could work for themselves. It was a nice dream, but she also
knew that he was a stubborn man. It was something her
mother used to chide him about.

But the light dusting of snow that had fallen the night
before showed him that he might have waited too long to
get back to the lower country, and he had told her that very
morning that they would pack their things and drive the
sheep down out of the mountains as soon as he got back
from checking on the flock.

Halfway up the bald, grassy portion of the ridge she
climbed, there was a strip of alder bushes where a spring of
water had created a seep of sorts. It was a damp, muddy
place, and the alders and other brush had taken hold there
and grown into a short belt of thicket. The sheep had been
grazing on the other side of that thicket before they fled
past camp.

She was not quite five feet tall, and the closer she came
to the thicket the less she could see of what was on the other
side. And she was already cold. The canvas, flannel-lined
jacket her father had bought her helped some, but she had
forgotten her mittens and her stocking cap.

She looked for the best way through the alders and saw
a path beaten with sheep prints and her father's horse tracks.

It was half mud and half frozen slush, but it offered a way through. She ducked into that narrow alleyway and fought off the limbs that tugged at her with her free hand held before her face.

She wasn't quite out of the thicket when she stopped, frozen in place, and a tremble of almost uncontrollable fear coursed through her body. Ahead of her in the distance was a bear. It was standing with its rump toward her and was very intent on something at its feet. She couldn't see what that was, for the bulk of the bear blocked it from her sight.

It was a large bear . . . fantastically large with a great hump over its shoulders. It took her a while to look away from it, and only then because she saw the dead ewe and its lamb that lay not fifty yards away and closer to her. The ewe's neck and one shoulder were torn and bloody, like the bear had ripped it almost apart in one single bite.

She was a small, petite girl, even for her age, but never had she felt more minuscule and helpless in her life. She was raised a Catholic, and she began to pray to Jesus and Mother Mary as she forced herself to look at the bear again. As she considered the worst, that it was likely her father's body the bear was standing over, she prayed even harder. Her body wracked, but she fought down the sob that almost gushed from her.

She wanted to call out to him, but didn't . . . couldn't. She clutched the knife so tightly that her knuckles and the joints of her fingers turned fish-belly white. Again, the knife seemed so silly and stupid as a weapon. Her father had a gun, and she had heard him shoot. But even that had not been enough to stop the monster standing over him, much less a pitiful little knife.

The bear is going to come for you if you take another step. It will hear you or it will see you. And then it is going

*to come and rip you with its teeth just like it did the ewe and
her baby.*

A tremble coursed through her body. *Be still. Be a quiet
little rabbit just like Papa calls you. His little* untxia. *Not so
much as a squeak or the twitch of a whisker or the flick of
an ear. Little furry feet that make no noise.*

It was almost as if the bear had read her mind. She had
not moved, nor had she made a sound, yet it raised its snout
and sniffed the air. Then it turned on its haunches and rose
halfway up with it front paws curled before its chest, still
seeking to interpret some scent, quite possibly hers.

At least eighty yards separated them, but even at that
distance she could see the bear's little round eyes peering
straight at the spot in the thicket where she stood. She knew
she must be hard to see, screened by the alders as she was,
but it was looking right at her.

Oh Lord, please don't let it kill me.

The bear gave a strange grunt and chopped it jaws and
then it started walking. Not straight for her, but arcing like
it was about to circle the dead ewe. It carried its nose
high—smelling, smelling, and searching for whatever it
had caught a whiff of. Her father had always told her what
keen noses bears had. They saw many black bears in the
days of their wandering through the mountains. Not all of
them black of color, but some brown and some reddish
brown. And most times those bears fled before they even
got a good look at them. Her father said it was because
bears were shy of humans and because their noses were so
good they could smell somebody even before their eyes
could see them.

But the bear coming her way was not shy. No, far from it.
It was a killer, and it was hunting for something else to kill.

There had been not a hint of wind that morning, but it
came then. It was only a small tickle of a breeze like icy

feathers brushing her skin, but it grew slightly, not at her face but angling from behind her. Angling straight to where the bear's circling was going to carry it. *It was going to smell her as soon as it took a few more steps. It had already smelled her.*

The bear made another strange noise, almost like a groan, then it gave a huff out its nostrils. She glanced at where she thought her father lay. *Why didn't he get up and help her? Was he hurt so bad he couldn't? Was he dead?* The bear took another few strides, closer to her now.

Her first instinct was to turn and run for camp, but some bit of common sense overruled her fear and she knew she would never make it. And what was there at camp that could stop such a thing from finding her or getting her? If she ran, there was no way the bear wasn't going to hear her. It would catch her before she made it halfway back to camp.

At one end of the alder thicket was nothing but open ground, half a mile of grassy mountainside, but on the other end, to her right, was a stand of fir trees. Not many of them, but a narrow finger of forest running down from higher up the mountain. Her father liked to point at things in the distance and try to guess how far away they were. He had often tried to get her to guess with him, but she had no aptitude for his game. She looked along the edge of the thicket and tried to calculate how far away the forest was and if she could make it there before the bear caught her.

She heard the bear walking, and she did not even bother to look to see where it was by then. She simply bolted for the timber as fast as she could go. A limb slapped her in the face before she was free of the thicket, and the sting of it was like a hot lash across her cheek. She used her free hand to grab a handful of her skirt and hold it higher above her ankles to aid in her speed. She thought she heard the bear coming behind her, and suddenly those trees ahead looked impossibly far away.

She dared not look behind her, afraid of what she would see. The trees were closer now, oh so close. But she could hear the bear racing after her, and at any moment she expected to feel its hot breath on her neck. She tripped once, almost fell, but her legs kept churning and she didn't go down.

The first few trees she came to all had limbs too high up for her to reach. She zigzagged through the forest like a field mouse sensing the looming shadow of a hawk overhead, came to a rocky little streambed, and hopped across it in two wild leaps from the top of one rock to the other. Out of the corner of one eye she glimpsed the bear. It was so close she wanted to scream like her father had.

Finally, she spied what she sought, a tree with limbs within her reach. It was a young tree and not very tall. She ran to its trunk and then looked behind her. The bear was just on the other side of the streambed. She gripped the knife blade sideways between her teeth to free both her hands and jumped to grab the lowest limb. Her fingertips only brushed it, and she fell back to the ground. The bear was coming across the creek by then, running faster than she would ever imagine such a beast could, a brown blur of motion.

There was only time for one more try. She bent her knees and swung her arms and jumped again. The limb she reached for slapped her palms, and she grabbed hold of it. A rush of triumph filled her, but it was short-lived. She scampered frantically to pull herself up. She managed to get on top of the first limb, little more than six feet off the ground, and was reaching for the next one above her when the bear reached the trunk of the tree. It pawed at her legs as she pulled higher, and one of its claws nicked the heel of her shoe and scratched bark from the tree below her. She imagined those claws ripping her legs from her body, and that fear strengthened her.

She climbed as fast as she could. Her skirt snagged on something, but she didn't stop. There was only a moment's resistance and then the fabric tore against her pull. She had only managed to climb a few feet higher when a limb snapped and gave way under her foot. The sensation of falling and the thought of the bear's open maw of teeth waiting for her at the bottom only lasted an instant, then she caught herself with a wild snatch of her hands. There she dangled, held only by her grip on a thin limb she had managed to grab on her way down.

The bear was so close she could smell him, musty and bloody like old meat left out too long, mixed with the smell of something like a wet dog. The bear rose up on its hind legs and to its fullest height and clawed at her again. Bark flew and branches snapped. She pulled herself a little farther up until she was fifteen feet off the ground and the limbs were becoming so tight together and the trunk so small she could go no higher. She wrapped both arms around the trunk and huddled there in the treetop with her breathing coming in ragged gasps. It was then that it dawned on her to wonder if the big bear could climb trees, and it was also when she remembered her father saying black bears were exceptional climbers.

Below her, the bear was so enraged it was biting the bark from the tree. As if in answer to her question, it began to climb, or at least to try. She took the knife from her teeth, almost fumbled it and dropped it, but didn't.

Like the rest of its kind, the old boar grizzly was not a tree climber, nor was it built for such. Its extra-long claws, good for flipping rocks and tearing apart dead logs, digging or slashing, were not made for gaining purchase on a tree trunk, especially not one so small in diameter. Its weight and those close claws made climbing almost impossibly hard, but the fury driving it was making up for those hindrances.

It took it three tries before the bear managed to get a purchase. It was big enough that it wasn't going to have to climb very far before its length would allow it to reach Zuri. However, the tree's young limbs were small and flexible. They continually bent away or snapped under its weight, thwarting its ascent. The tree shook violently, swaying her wildly back and forth.

The bear could go no higher, but it was already high enough that it felt as if she could reach down and touch it. Its mouth gaped open and it growled, and its hot, rancid breath washed over her. She slashed with the knife at its nose, and felt the edge bite into soft tissue and cartilage.

The bear lost its hold and fell back to the ground. It did not try to climb again, but instead, it placed both paws against the tree and began to shove, bouncing and rocking its weight against the trunk. The treetop swayed so badly that she feared she would be flung out of it. Yet, somehow, she hung on. However, when she looked down again she saw the roots of the tree bulging up out of the ground, and the tree leaned like it was about to be uprooted and fall over.

But the tree held fast, and the bear gave up after a while. He paced a circle around the base of the tree, once one way and then the other, all the while looking up at her. She could see the bloody cut on its nose where her blade had sliced home. And she saw the wound in its shoulder and wondered if her father's gunshot had done that.

The bear acted as if it would walk away once but then came back. Again, it circled the tree making low, grumbling sounds.

"*Utzi nazazu bakarrik!*" she screamed at it. "Leave me alone!"

She found a way to wrap her legs around the trunk with the support of a limb beneath helping to hold up her weight and take some of the strain off her. She hugged the tree tightly and closed her eyes. It was a long time before she opened them again, so long that her body was aching and trembling.

The bear was gone, and she sobbed with relief and said a prayer of thankfulness for such mercy. After she had some time to gather herself, she looked through the treetop hoping to see her father. She held out some hope that he was still alive, and the more she thought about it the more she thought he might have taken the opportunity of the bear being distracted with her to get away. Perhaps he, too, was now hiding out of the bear's reach.

The bear appeared again, not beneath her but back near the edge of the alder thicket. The height of the treetop gave her an elevated vantage point, but other trees between her and the open ground screened her view somewhat.

The bear went down on its belly, and she could see its head jerking and hear its straining grunts and its smacking jaws. She realized it was feeding and, worse, what it might be feeding on. *No, please no!*

Then she noticed the chunks of wool the bear had ripped free and spat aside, and she knew it wasn't her father being eaten. It was the ewe or its lamb.

Please let him be all right. Please make the bear go away.

The bear fed on the ewe for the better part of an hour. By then Zuri's muscles were cramped and stiff, and she didn't know how much longer she could stay in the tree. What's worse, there was still no sign of her father. She thought for a while that she could see something where he likely had

gone down, an indistinct shape lying in the grass and behind
a little bush. But she doubted that now and continued to tell
herself that he was only wounded and had gotten away
when he had the chance.

Then she shifted to imagining that someone would come
to help them. Men with dogs and guns would show up and
drive the bear away. They would help get her father down
to a town where a doctor could see to him. Everything was
going to be all right.

But that dream was only a dream, and she couldn't hold
its vision very long. She and her father had been alone all
summer, except for a roving man with a string of pack
mules who showed up every two weeks to drop off supplies
for them and other herders scattered throughout the mountains. During the two months and more roaming with the
band of sheep, the only human they had come across in
their travels other than the supply man had been a single
prospector they had crossed paths with one morning. He
was a strange old man, walking and leading a mule. And
he had a half-blind dog following at his heels. Her father
had said the man was a prospector, though she wasn't quite
sure how he knew that. The old man had only spoken a few
words to him and then had gone on his way like he was
bothered by having to talk to someone.

The supply man wasn't due to come again, as they
were supposed to be already back down on the desert with
the sheep by now. She couldn't guess how long it would be
before the sheep manager or the owner decided something
had gone wrong and came looking for them and the flock.

*Nobody is going to come. Not soon enough, and maybe
not at all. There is no one. Not in this lonely place.*

Even the sun coming out from behind the clouds and
warming her body couldn't help her grief and her fear. She
wanted her father, wanted to know that he wasn't dead. And

she wanted her mother to hug her close and rock her and mutter soothing words close to her ear, even though her mother had died three years before.

The bear got up, and that movement brought her back to reality. It went out of her sight for a moment, she caught a glimpse of it again, then it disappeared. She had the impression that it had lain down. She watched closely, peering through the tree limbs, straining her vision for signs of the monster.

She shifted her position slightly and leaned out from the tree. The bear was, indeed, lying down, and it appeared to have gone to sleep. It was not far from what remained of the ewe in the edge of the alder thicket. It dawned on her that it had chosen a spot where it could still see the carcass. Even in sleep, it was guarding its kill.

She had hoped that when the bear's belly was full it would leave. Thinking that had given her the strength to hold on, no matter how badly she hurt and no matter how hard it was to stay in the tree.

It was impossible for her to tell how long the bear slept. Was it hours? The sun had climbed to almost straight over her head. She had to adjust her position in the tree more and more often, changing grips and moving her legs to different places. There was no comfortable position she could find, nor one where she could relax. She didn't think she could stay there much longer. Fatigue was beginning to defeat willpower.

The bear finally woke, but instead of leaving it went back to the ewe's carcass. Zuri couldn't see it well, but she could hear it crunching or gnawing at a bone.

The bear didn't take as long to satisfy itself that time, but the sun was tilting over to the west when it moved away. When she saw it again it was carrying the lamb's body in its mouth. It carried the poor little thing into the thicket and went out of sight. It wasn't long before she heard what sounded like the bear was digging. Did bears use their claws to rake up grass and other debris to cover the portion of their kill that they couldn't finish eating? Her father had once showed her the half-eaten body of a deer they had found covered in pine needles and had told her that it was the work of a mountain lion. He had also said that he had found several such lion kills where the deer was almost rotted away and that he believed that many times a lion did not ever come back to finish its meal, as if it might have killed something else and forgotten about its past work.

Would the bear leave and not come back? Was that really what it was doing in the thicket?

The bear didn't reappear. She tracked the sun as it inched across the sky, and she wondered if she dared climb down. But just because she couldn't see the bear or hear it anymore didn't mean it wasn't close by. Even a slight chance of its presence was too much for her.

It was almost dark before she decided to come out of the tree. She was shaking cold by then. And one of her legs had fallen asleep to the point that it was unresponsive. Not to mention that her arms and hands were so tired that it was all she could do to climb down. Somehow, she managed it and was almost to the ground when her arms wouldn't obey her any more. Her grip slipped and she fell. She landed on her feet, but her dead leg gave way and she crashed in a heap against the foot of the tree.

She tried to get up, but her leg was so numb that it was like a heavy, flopping thing that didn't belong to her at all. She fell back down and lost the knife in the process.

"It's going to be all right," she said to herself. "It's going to be all right."

She didn't really believe that, but it felt good to say it. She got to her feet, leaning all of her weight on the leg that would hold her up. The feeling was coming back in her other leg, but with that return to life came an awful tingling and stinging, like needles of fire working from the inside out. She leaned against the tree and waited for the pain to subside and for her to be able to trust her leg enough to walk on it and find the knife.

When she did move, she went slowly, partly because her leg wasn't fully awake yet and partly because she didn't take a single step where she wasn't expecting to hear the bear or for it to loom up out of the night. And she was torn about where she should go. She wanted to go look for her father, but going that way meant going by where the bear had killed the sheep. That would be guaranteed trouble if the bear was still around.

She considered that her father might have made it back to camp, and perhaps that was where she should go. She would stay away from the alder thicket and stick to ground with a better chance for her to run uninhibited. Even in the dark, it would be easier to detect the bear if it came for her again. She tried to think like her father would have thought. There was food in the camp, and she could build a fire so big that no bear would dare come close to it. There would be warm blankets there, and the tent, and her father would be in that tent, worrying about her and trying to tend to his wounds. It was going to be that way because that was what she prayed for. God would hear her and wouldn't let any more bad things happen.

She kept walking. *Don't be afraid. It's going to be all right.*

CHAPTER SEVEN

The sky was a shade of even darker gray by the time Newt and his party rode into sight of the D&RG depot house at the end of the tracks. The settlement that had grown up around the depot lay on a small bench of land on the north bank of the river just east of a narrow pass that led on upstream. That gap, barely a hundred yards wide, ran between a high, sheer rock wall on the north and a bald pinnacle on the south. There was barely enough room for both the river and a trail to pass through it. The location was as picturesque as it was forlorn and removed.

The depot was a framed lumber structure painted a bright shade of yellow with brown trim. Several other buildings, all built of logs, stretched in a line beyond the depot. Other than those buildings, a water tower for the locomotives, and a couple of cabins scattered about close by and downriver, there was not much else to Wagon Wheel Gap.

A little more than a mile downstream was the Hot Springs Hotel, half the reason the D&RG had built tracks to the Gap, the other half being the growing number of mine operations in the high country to the west. The supposed curative powers of the hotel's steaming, sulfurous mud baths drew many a lunger and other infirmed people up-river, as well as sightseers and trout fisherman, but those travelers usually spent no more time in the settlement than it took them to get on or off the train.

One of the narrow-gauge trains was about to leave, having been unloaded and turned around. The stack on its locomotive poured smoke, and steam vapor floated alongside the short hitch of cars behind it. The handful of passengers in the single passenger car stared out of the glass windows for a departing look at the gap, and no doubt many of them were the last of the Hot Springs Hotel's visitors of the season.

Newt and the other three reined their horses farther from the tracks to avoid some of the worst of the noise and commotion as the train chugged and churned to gain momentum and passed them by on its way back to civilization. The Circle Dot horse shied sideways and blew out its nostrils at the locomotive, but it never had liked trains and Newt ignored its antics and urged it on past the train.

Several men were in front of the depot handling freight, and a single buggy was parked there for the load out. A few of the men working there took note of Newt and the others with him, but that assessment was brief and they soon went back to work.

Newt did not stop at the depot. Instead he led the others toward the end of the line of log buildings and farthest away from the depot. There, close beneath the spreading limbs of two large cottonwood trees was a plain, square log cabin with a sign above its door with a simple advertising proclamation, SALOON.

There was a long set of hitching rails under the trees and some stock corrals and some kind of barn not far away. Newt and those with him chose the hitching rail, dismounted, loosened cinches, and secured their horses among a few other mounts already tied there.

Newt placed both hands on the small of his back and

stretched the kinks out of his muscles. He eyed the saloon while he waited for some of the stiffness to leave his body.

Mr. Smith came to stand beside him and saw where he was looking. "No firewater. That is what you said."

"I was just looking. What I really want is something to eat."

Tandy Hudlow heard what Newt had said. "I'll second that. I'm as hungry as a starving bitch wolf with pups."

"Yeah," Tully elbowed his brother in the ribs. "Let's go see if we can scare up some vittles."

Newt's intent had been to leave the brothers as soon as they made it to the Gap, but the effects of Newt's hangover had left him over the course of the day, and he found himself almost as hungry as the two brothers claimed they were. It had been a long time since breakfast back in Del Norte. He fell in behind the Hudlows, and Mr. Smith did the same.

There was no boardwalk along the front of the row of buildings, and the recently melted snow had left the ground slick with mud. Newt was carefully making his way along that treacherous footing when he smelled woodsmoke and the wonderful scent of food cooking. Ahead of him, a man opened the front door into one of the log buildings, and the tantalizing smell of food was stronger. Then Newt spied a tiny sign proclaiming the place as some kind of eatery. The Hudlows figured out the same thing before he did.

Newt stopped and pointed at the pair's backs as they disappeared inside. He said to Mr. Smith, "If they had wagging tails they'd look like a pair of hound pups."

"The young run even when they do not need to," Mr. Smith answered. "You and I did the same."

"Were we ever that young?" Newt asked.

"You talk as if you are an old man," Mr. Smith said.

"Sometimes I feel like it."

Newt pondered his own answer and didn't like most of the conclusions he came to. He was only thirty-six years old, yet there were times when he felt twice that age, in mind if not in body. And watching those two foolish kids made that feeling of having long left his youth seem all the stronger.

Newt tried to guess, not for the first time, how old Mr. Smith was. It was hard to tell. From some of the things the Mohave had said, he had to be well past fifty, and maybe more, though he didn't look that old.

He held the door open for Mr. Smith and went in behind him. The cabin that was the café or restaurant was small, and the inside of the room was barely big enough to house a long table with a bench down each side of it. Newt could see another doorway in the back that likely led to a kitchen. He guessed the place was only intended to feed the railroad workers and whatever few of the more rugged travelers passed through the Gap. Accordingly, it was a humble affair.

There were two other men at the table. The Hudlow brothers were already on the bench beside those two men, and Newt and Mr. Smith sat down on the opposite bench across from them.

One of the two strangers, an old man in a red-checkered flannel shirt and with a grizzled gray beard that hung almost to his chest, stared at him but said nothing. After a time he gave Newt a nod of his head in greeting. Newt nodded back.

The other one beside the old man looked like an Indian, but it was hard to get a good look at him. He was too busy eating to look up or pay much attention to the new arrivals.

The cook came out of the kitchen carrying several bowls of something on top of a baking pan that he used as his serving platter. He began setting a bowl in front of each of them. His touch was heavy and good portions of the soupy liquid in the bowls slopped out onto the tabletop. The light-colored wood the table was made from was scarred and nicked from rough usage and showed many such stains from other spills.

"We ain't even ordered yet," Tandy said to the cook.

The cook was a middle-aged fellow with a three-day growth of black whisker stubble on his face and a cigarette dangling out of one corner of his mouth. The top of his head was bald and wet with sweat dew from standing over a cookstove's heat, and the only hair he could claim was on the sides and the wiry fuzz growing out of both ears. An apron so stained that it was hard to tell it had once been white was tied on over his clothes, and the sleeves of his shirt were rolled up to the elbow.

"You see any menus?" the cook growled. "We got one thing today, and one thing only. And that's stew. You either eat it or you don't."

Tully poked around in his bowl with a spoon and stared at the stew. "What kind of meat is that with the taters?"

"One of those picky sorts, are you?" the cook growled again and wiped his hands on his apron.

"I ain't picky, but I like to know what I'm eating."

"Venison," the cook said. "Fellow that hunts for me said the deer and elk are already moving down from the high country. Always that way before the first big blow. Pushes them down out of the hills."

"I like deer meat," Tandy said, and made as if to scoop up a spoonful.

"Good you do if you stick around here," the cook replied. "Chickens already quit laying, and we'll have the last of the ham and beef ate up in another two weeks or so. Spuds and turnips will likely go to rot or freeze so bad they ain't fit to eat. After that, nothing but deer meat and biscuits and gravy. And when the flour runs out there won't be nothing but deer. Me, myself, I get sick of it."

Tandy cocked an eye at the cook. "We ain't sticking around here through the winter. Headed up to Lake City."

The cook snorted, and that caused the long ash on the end of his cigarette to fall on the table. He didn't seem to notice. "Don't matter. You ain't getting to Lake City. Not this late, and not over Cinnamon Pass or Stony Pass, either. They say there's already snow on the mountains above Baker's Park. Big fall two days ago."

Tandy took that news and made as if to eat again.

"That'll be two bits," the cook said, stopping him. "Coffee's free."

"Two bits for nothing but a few pieces of taters, some deer meat, and a little salt and pepper?" Tandy asked.

"Two bits," the cook repeated. "And you pay before you eat or I'll pour it back in the pot. You wouldn't be the first to try and short me."

Tandy scowled back at the grouchy cook, but he slapped a silver dollar on the table. "That's for me and my brother here. Make sure you fetch my change. You wouldn't be the first to try and short me."

The cook grunted and gave him his change. The rest of them paid for their meals, and the cook headed back to the kitchen. As he was leaving, Newt saw a flour-dusted impression of a handprint on the seat of the gruff pot wrangler's pants where he had been scratching himself.

Tandy scooped a spoon of stew into his mouth and then another. He was reaching for the plate of cornbread on the table before him when he saw Newt watching him. "What are you looking at?"

"Nothing," Newt answered and then retrieved his own piece of cornbread. The bread was hard and lifeless, and he guessed it had been made the day before. He also couldn't help but look for cigarette ashes in the stew before taking a bite of it.

When he looked up again, Tully was looking back at him.

"Not bad, is it?" Tully said, around a mouthful of stew. He was one of those who could grin while he ate.

"No, not bad at all," Newt replied and managed to keep a straight face.

Sopping the cornbread in the stew juice made it a little better. He was almost finished with his bowl when the old man with the beard sitting beside the Hudlow brothers cleared his throat to get his attention.

"Were you ever at Cherry Creek?" The old man asked.

"Before my time," Newt replied and reached for the coffeepot at the center of the table.

"Maybe it was Buckskin Joe," the old man continued. "No, no, you're likely too young for that one. But I got you now. It was at Tin Cup. Yes?"

Newt shook his head. "You got the wrong fellow."

The old man gave a perplexed frown. He must have been hard of hearing, for he talked overly loud and had that way of intently studying your face like a man trying to match the shape of words on your mouth with what he thought he heard.

"I know you from somewhere. You see, I never forget a face."

Newt poured himself a mug of coffee and looked up at the old man through the steam. "I doubt you know me."

The old man pulled a pipe from his person and began filling it with tobacco from a drawstring pouch. He tamped home the tobacco with a thumb while he studied Newt with twinkling, watery old eyes. The liver-spotted skin on his cheeks and nose was flakey and chapped from years of wind and weather.

"Maybe not, but if your last name isn't Jones, then I'd best be getting gone," the old man said. "Done waited too long as it is."

Newt gave the old man more of his attention. "You do a lot of guessing."

The old man smiled and revealed that he had two missing teeth on one side of his mouth. "Saul sent word on the train that you were on your way. That is, if you be Jones."

"And you are?"

The old man held out a hand for a shake. "Jack Henson, but folks call me Happy Jack."

Newt took the offered hand and shook it. The old man's paw was as hard and calloused as rawhide and buffalo horn.

"Newt Jones," he offered. "Glad to meet you."

"These here gents with you?" Happy Jack asked, taking in the Hudlow brothers and, with a lingering gaze, Mr. Smith.

Newt tipped his head toward the Mohave. "He is. These other two are a pair of strays we picked up on the trail."

Happy Jack gestured at the brown-skinned man beside him. "This here is Jose Vasquez."

"You coming with us, too?" Newt asked.

Happy Jack answered when his friend didn't make any effort in that regard. "Jose has been making a start on proving up the claim. "

Jose finally looked up from his meal at Newt. He didn't speak a greeting, but he did give a nod of his head. He was a petite man, small-boned and lean, with his black hair bobbed off at shoulder length and framing his square jaw.

"Saul mentioned you," Newt said to Happy Jack, and then tilted his head toward Jose, "but he didn't mention anybody else."

"Saul can't remember where he stuck the last dollar he made. And don't mind Jose. He's half Ute and the other half Mexican. Doesn't say much but he's steady. And he brings in plenty of meat to camp," Happy Jack answered.

"I'm supposed to pay you?" Newt asked.

"No, me and Jose got our own agreements with Saul."

Newt took a sip of the coffee. It was strong and bitter. "He said you'd have supplies enough here to winter us over."

Happy Jack nodded. "Jose unloaded the last of them off the train this afternoon."

"You satisfied with what we've got?"

"Doesn't matter. That train that just left was the last one until maybe June or so. Snow gets too deep, and then the spring thaw washes out the river bridges."

"I see."

"No, if you saw you'd have been here sooner." Happy Jack got off the bench and paused long enough to light his pipe with a match. He shook out the match and peered through the smoke puffing out of his mouth as he drew the pipe to life. "Best we be going instead of sitting here palavering."

"Figured we'd lay over here for the night and move on in the morning," Newt said. "Thought maybe I'd give that resort hotel we passed on the way a try."

"Suit yourself. Me, I'm leaving."

The old-timer went to the door. His stride was uneven and listed him to one side and then the other, like his knees were bad. And there was a slight hump to his back that bent him over and made his arms seem longer than they were for a man his size.

Newt frowned slightly, wanting to finish his coffee. Jose got up from the table and followed the old man. Newt and Mr. Smith weren't far behind.

They were only a few steps outside the eatery and following Happy Jack and Jose toward the depot when the Hudlow brothers came out the door behind them. Newt stopped and looked back at them.

"I guess it's dawning on you that you probably won't make it to Lake City," Newt said, when they couldn't seem to say anything.

"Seems like you've got a job," Tandy said, "and we were thinking maybe whoever is paying you might have some work for us."

"What use would you two be?"

"We're both hard workers," Tandy replied.

"How about I loan you some money and you ride back down to the low country and find you something to tide you over until spring?"

"We don't want your charity," Tully said, with the color once again creeping across his face. "What we want . . . what we need is a job."

Newt looked at Mr. Smith and thought he saw a bit of I-told-you-so on the Mohave's face.

"You don't fit the requirements," Newt said.

"We can learn," Tandy replied.

"Only thing you'll learn where I'm going is bad habits."

"Try us," Tully said. "What's the job?"

"Guarding a mining claim until spring."

"And you think we can't handle that?" Tandy asked.

Newt looked back at Mr. Smith. "You explain it to them."

Mr. Smith simply shook his head.

"Pa always said blood is thicker than branch water," Tandy said.

"I never even laid eyes on you two until today," Newt replied.

Tandy gave a somber shake of his head. "Family is family, and when family needs help, you come running. But maybe you don't set store by your kin like we do."

Newt threw a glance over his shoulder and saw that Happy Jack was getting farther away. "Nobody's going to nursemaid you."

"We're just fine taking care of ourselves," Tandy said, with his usual grin returning. "That mean we're hired?"

Mr. Smith cocked one eyebrow at Newt.

"Don't say it. Not one word," Newt said to him.

"Young warriors must have a chance to learn," Mr. Smith answered.

"Young warriors? Wet-behind-the-ears kids is what they are."

"Who are you calling kids?" Tully asked. "I turned twenty last week."

"You said this would be easy," Mr. Smith said, ignoring Tully like Newt was. "Play cards, sleep, and sit by the fire. That is what you said."

"You don't have to remember everything I say, you know," Newt grumbled.

Newt was about to head off in pursuit of Happy Jack when he saw a man walk out of the saloon three buildings down the row. The sight of that man was enough to stop Newt.

He was tall like Newt, though a little heavier, older, with a thick walrus mustache and sideburns tinted with gray that ran down to the turn of his jaw. He had on a black bowler hat like the one Mr. Smith wore. He could have been a lawyer or a banker in a bigger town, but that was likely ruled out by the pair of bird's head–gripped pistols hanging in shoulder holsters strapped over the top of his striped vest.

Newt was suddenly very aware that the keeper thong on his holster was in place over his pistol hammer. Mr. Smith was watching the man also, and he recognized him the same as Newt did.

The man who had come out of the saloon was walking toward them.

"Easy. We're not looking for a fight," Newt said quietly to Mr. Smith.

"No, but he might be," Mr. Smith answered.

CHAPTER EIGHT

"Why, if it isn't the Widowmaker in the flesh." Kirby Cutter, for that was the man's name, though most simply called him the Cutter, stopped ten feet away from them. He leaned against the wall beside him and crossed one foot over the other while he whittled at his fingernails with a little pearl-handled pocketknife. "Fancy finding you here. Long ways from California."

"I could say I'm just as surprised, Kirby."

The Cutter shook his head without looking up, as if his fingernails required all of his attention. "Let's don't play any games we don't have to. You turned me down when I offered you a job, and now here you are."

"Up here doing a little hunting," Newt said.

The Cutter gave what was meant to be a smile but was nothing more than a slight widening of his mouth. Instead of easing the tension, it only made him seem more dangerous, and Newt was very conscious of the feel of his holstered pistol pressing against the inside of his right elbow.

Newt and Mr. Smith had briefly crossed paths with the Cutter the summer before in California while they'd been venturing out on a little desert treasure hunt. The Cutter had been hired by one of their former partners, a lady gambler, to protect her interests and serve as her personal bodyguard.

It was the only time Newt had met the man, but you didn't have to know the Cutter to know of him, not if you spent any time in the mining camps and boomtowns up and down both sides of the divide. And Newt, like most, had heard plenty of stories, not to mention that their California encounter hadn't necessarily been a friendly one.

The Cutter was said to have killed several men, although the number varied according to who was doing the telling. He had spent time in Colorado and the New Mexico and Arizona territories, and in E-Town, Leadville, and Silver City and all up and down the mountains as the finds came and went. And there were stories that his history went as far back as the early days in Julesburg and Central City, where he and a few of his cronies specialized in jumping claims or waylaying travelers and robbing them.

But the Cutter was mainly known for working for the big mining interests. Not the men who made the strikes or proved up their claims, but the big money sorts who came in later and bought them out or forced them out. The Cutter specialized in the rough stuff and doing the behind-the-scenes *negotiations* for those kind of deals. One of the sayings that went around was that when the Cutter showed up and told you how things were going to be, you either listened or you wished you had, right before you disappeared or somebody was digging you a grave.

"I wonder what the odds are of us running across each other twice in such a short time."

"It's a small world. Isn't that what they say?"

"I guess so."

"Like I said, we're just up here doing a little hunting."

The Cutter folded his little pocketknife closed and straightened. He cocked his head slightly to one side and made a show of looking Newt up and down. Then he took in Mr. Smith, and finally, his eyes landed on the Hudlow brothers. "I remember the big Indian but don't recall those two. They with you?"

"They are."

The Cutter's face hardened almost imperceptibly, like the slow freezing of winter ice. His expression was as calculating as it was controlled. "Quite the hunting party you've got there. You turned market hunter?"

"They say the elk are thick this year."

"That so? I'd say you're getting a late start."

"Maybe so, but I intend to be back down to Del Norte to sell my haul before winter comes on strong. Then I'm going to spend a little of my money and get good and drunk before I try to find me some place warm to lay up until spring."

"That's a reasonable plan."

"What about you?" Newt asked, tired of being questioned and tired of lying.

"Me?" the Cutter asked as if he weren't the only one standing in front of Newt. "Oh, I've got a little job to do. Shouldn't be much trouble."

The Cutter's calm, cocksure demeanor was getting the best of Newt and wearing on his patience. "You never know. Like you said, winter can be a hard bite to chew in this country."

The Cutter again cocked his head to one side, as if weighing something in his mind or looking at something from a different angle, then he smiled again. "You can tell the Indian to quit glaring at me. I just came over to chew the fat with you friendly like. Maybe I ought to have some hard feelings over what happened in California, but I don't."

"Glad to hear it."

The Cutter nodded at something behind Newt. "Now, that man coming yonder might not share my goodwill."

Newt was slow to take his attention off the Cutter long

enough to take a look at what he was nodding at. If the Cutter was half as good as some said he was, then he wasn't a man you took your eyes off of when he was standing in shooting range. Newt's quick glance, when it finally came, revealed two riders crossing the tracks down by the depot. One was a Mexican in a great big sombrero hat and leather leggings below his knees with a row of hammered silver peso conchos decorating them. He also wore a bright red wool serape wrapped around him for warmth and against the increasing chill of the coming evening, and it was secured in place by a leather bandolier buckled across his chest with its loops full of brass rifle cartridges.

The other man was a thin gringo with a stooped, slumping seat in the saddle. He wore an old, stained buckskin coat that hung halfway down his thighs with fringe across the chest and on the sleeves. Both men were making a beeline toward Newt and the others.

"Friends of yours?" Newt asked the Cutter.

"You might say that," the Cutter answered.

Newt and Mr. Smith turned slightly so that they could see both the new arrivals and the Cutter at once.

"*Buenas tardes,*" the Mexican called out to the Cutter as he reined his horse up.

The man beside the Mexican said nothing and kept his sour expression aimed at Newt and Mr. Smith.

"Where are the rest of the boys?" Cutter asked.

"They stayed Del Norte to have a little fun," the Mexican answered. "They come before long."

The man wearing the buckskin coat was slightly bucktoothed, making his cheeks seem even more hollow and his face as narrow as a knife's edge. And his eyes were only tiny pinpricks in the shadow of his hat brim.

He leaned slightly out from the saddle and spat a stream

of tobacco juice on the ground between his horse and where Newt stood. "Who be you?"

Newt looked at the splatter of brown juice on the ground at his feet and then back up at the man. He gave hard look for hard look but didn't answer.

The Cutter broke the silence. "Well now, Johnny, old son, you're looking at the living legend himself. Don't you recognize him?"

The man in the buckskin coat that the Cutter had called Johnny wiped at the tobacco juice that glistened on the whiskers of his narrow goatee with the back of his hand. "Don't believe I do. What kind of game are you playing, Kirby?"

Newt knew exactly what kind of game the Cutter was playing the very instant he heard him mention that last name, *Dial*.

"Where are my manners? Perhaps you two have never been properly introduced," the Cutter said, then gave a grandiose wave of his hand at Newt. "Johnny, you're looking at none other than the original Widowmaker Jones."

Johnny Dial's slumped spine straightened slowly, and he worked the chew of tobacco in his cheek as methodically as a cow chewing its cud. The sudden hatred on his face was as recognizable as it was livid.

"Is that a fact?" Dial asked.

"Bareknuckle pride of the Rockies in the flesh, I kid you not," the Cutter said, and smirked at Newt. "How many rounds did you go with Butcher Joe in Silver City? Forty-five? Hard to believe, but that's what they say. Wish I had been there to see it. They say it was quite a brawl."

Newt didn't answer him. Most of his attention was now on Johnny Dial, and he fully expected things were about to get worse. Way worse.

The Mexican gave the Cutter an incredulous look and nodded at Newt. "*¿El es un pugilista famosa?*"

"Oh, he's more than that, Cholo," the Cutter said. "Why, you're looking at the man that tamed Shakespeare. Pure poison with his fists or a gun, they say. Take your pick."

"*Este hombre?*" the Mexican asked with an incredulous look, again giving a nod of his sombrero brim toward Newt.

"The one and only," the Cutter said.

The Mexican gave a scoffing chuckle. "*Yo pensé el serà mas grande. Un gigante.*"

"He says he thought you would be bigger. A giant, even," the Cutter said to Newt.

"I speak passable Spanish," Newt said, with his focus still on Dial and making no attempt to hide his irritation.

Newt glanced at the Cutter out of the corner of his eyes. The man was obviously enjoying himself, and that said a lot about the mean streak in the man, despite his civil act. For the Cutter knew good and well what had happened back in California and how it would set off Johnny Dial once he found out. The Cutter had been there and had seen the whole thing, yet despite that, he was egging on Johnny and Newt like a mean kid throwing two tomcats in a sack and shaking them just to see them hiss and growl.

Newt, on the other hand, was trying to figure his way out of the bind he was in. He had the Cutter on his right shoulder and the Mexican and Johnny Dial in front of him. Mr. Smith would know what to do, but the odds were still against them. And the Hudlow brothers were staring at the whole proceeding like they were lost and oblivious to what was likely going to happen.

"Bobby Dial was my brother," Johnny Dial said to what Newt, ignoring the Cutter. "He was a good man. The best."

Newt let the irony of the man making such a statement

soak in. Bobby Dial had been nothing but a two-bit badman and killer. Just another mean Texas outlaw reject like his brother sitting there on that horse.

"Now, Johnny, that's no way to introduce yourself," the Cutter said in that same chiding, mocking tone.

Dial was wearing his gun belt over the outside of his coat, and the butt of a big Model 1878 double-action Colt revolver stuck out of his holster. He took a deep breath, working himself up to what he was obviously about to do.

The Cutter's tone changed, and all his devilish manners and flippant behavior were suddenly gone. "I said let it be."

"None of your affair," Johnny answered.

"You ride with me, and that makes it my affair," the Cutter answered.

At that moment, Newt heard the sound of a rattling wagon. When he looked he saw it wasn't a wagon, but instead a red buggy with a double bench seat and a fold-away top. Painted on the side of it were the words WAGON WHEEL GAP HOT SPRINGS HOTEL. The driver and another man with him were likely headed back to the resort, but both of them were watching Newt and the others standing near the saloon. And Newt noticed that several of the men down by the depot, including Happy Jack and Jose, were also watching, likely curious to know what was going on.

The Cutter had noticed all the attention on them, as well, and apparently wasn't liking it. Such caution was possibly why he had lasted so long in his business. Newt realized then that the Cutter was not only tough, but he also had smarts to go with it. That made him all the more dangerous.

"Me and the Widowmaker were having us a friendly talk, Johnny. Now, why don't you and your buddy Cholo go to the saloon and have a drink on me?" the Cutter said.

The Mexican didn't argue and reined his horse behind

Johnny's and started toward the saloon. "Come on, Johnny. *Vamonos.*"

Dial took his time, glaring at Newt, but he eventually rode away with the Mexican.

The Cutter watched them for a moment and then looked back at Newt. "You know, I don't think Johnny likes you."

"I can tell that really bothers you," Newt replied.

"Best of luck to you, Jones," the Cutter said, with a tip of his hat brim.

"I guess you'll have to forgive me if I don't wish you the same."

The Cutter let that dig slide past him as if it were nothing. He started for the saloon but stopped and looked back before he had gone two steps. "Oh, I almost forgot. Give Saul Barton my regards the next time you see him."

Newt wondered how good of a job he did keeping a poker face after the Cutter's last words. And he was still wondering that and hating the fact that the Cutter had gotten in the last lick when the Cutter disappeared inside the saloon.

"That's a bad bit of luck," Newt said to Mr. Smith.

"He told you he was coming to Colorado for a job when we met him in California," Mr. Smith replied.

"I was kind of hoping he would change his mind, and I sure didn't think he would beat us here or bring Bobby Dial's brother with him," Newt said.

"It does not matter."

"To hell it doesn't."

"So, we are going back to Del Norte and you will tell Saul Barton that you've changed your mind?"

"I wish I had that much good sense." Newt turned on his heel and started toward the depot.

Mr. Smith was willing to lag behind and take a more leisurely pace, but the Hudlow brothers fell in beside Newt.

"That man back there, the skinny one in that fringed coat, he hates you," Tandy said.

"Yes, he does," Newt answered without stopping.

"How come?"

"'Cause I killed his brother, that's why."

Tandy gave that news a moment to sink in, only long enough for a quick rise and fall of his eyebrows and a slight stutter in his step. "Well, that can tend to make a fellow surly, yes indeed. But what about that other fellow, the big one wearing that shoulder rig? I don't think he likes you much, either."

"You're a genius. You'll go far." Newt quickened his pace as a hint to get Tandy to leave him alone, but it didn't work.

"How come he called you the Widowmaker?" Tandy asked before they had gone more than a few steps.

Newt stopped and turned on the pair of them. "It's a damn fool name, and don't you ever think you can call me that. Hear me?"

"We hear you," Tully answered. "No sense in getting riled at Tandy for asking."

Newt realized that he had raised his voice and that all the tension of the encounter with the Cutter and Johnny Dial had him wound too tight.

"Just don't go nosing in my business," he said in a quieter, calmer tone.

"We only wondered what that back there was all about. Figured we had a right to know," Tandy said.

Tully nodded in agreement. "That's only fair if we're going to be working together. Any trouble you've got is likely to end up our trouble."

"Working together?" Newt asked. "You two aren't going with me."

"You said we had the job," Tandy said.

"I changed my mind."

"That ain't right," Tandy threw back at him.

"You said you wondered what that back there was about," Newt said. "Well, I'll tell you. It means that the job has probably changed and got a whole lot harder, and believe me, you don't want any part of it."

"Try us. We don't run from a fight, and those men didn't impress us much," Tandy said.

Newt shook his head, felt the anger rising up in him again, turned, and once more started for the depot, leaving the brothers in his wake.

"Are we still hired?" Tandy asked Mr. Smith.

"I do not think he will stop you, but you would do well not to ask any more questions of him," Mr. Smith answered. "When he is troubled he always wants to hit someone."

"Seems like a fellow that's hard to get along with, but Pa always said those Joneses were like that."

"On the contrary," Mr. Smith said. "It is a trait I find most admirable in him."

"You talk funny for an Indian," Tandy said.

"And you talk funny for a white man," Mr. Smith replied.

The brothers shared a private look between them that only they could interpret, but they gave no voice to whatever it was they were thinking on the matter. When they got to the depot they found Happy Jack and Jose packing four little mules. Newt was already joining them, and the Mohave and the brothers did the same.

Newt heaved the last of a pair of flour sacks into a pannier on one of the mules, then began helping Jose secure the top load, cover it, and lash it down with a diamond hitch. He didn't say anything when he saw the Hudlow brothers were still with Mr. Smith, but he did scowl at them and mutter something under his breath.

Happy Jack was working by himself on another mule

with his back to Newt. The Hudlow brothers tried to help the old man.

"No, no. Don't you know one thing about packing?" Happy Jack said. "You load that mule that heavy and you'll break his back."

Newt listened to Happy Jack's ravings. He could already tell the old man was more bark than bite and that he was more a man who liked to hear himself fuss than he meant anything by it.

"Good grief, son, hasn't anyone ever showed you how to tie off a pack?" Happy Jack said, as Newt and Jose finished with their mule. "Here, just rig a squaw hitch. That ought to be simple enough for you to figure out . . . Damn! Watch that john! You're going to get your fool head kicked off! Where in the hell did he find a pair of shavetails like you two?"

"Listen, old man, you surely are trying me," Tandy said. "We ain't your sons, and we ain't partial to how you're talking to us."

"Yeah, we've already had enough of him lecturing us about this an' that." Tully nodded at Newt. "So don't you set in on us or me and Tandy here are liable to notch your ears."

Happy Jack scowled at Tandy, then walked away muttering something about obnoxious kids, and when he returned carrying an armload of items that needed packing he was still mumbling under his breath. The brothers watched him for a moment, then grinned at each other.

In less than a half hour, their supplies were loaded. By then, the sun had sunk close to the top of the bluffs above the gap. A cold hint of wind cut around the corner of the depot from the north, and Newt was already wishing he hadn't left his sheepskin coat on his horse.

Jose left and came back riding a scrawny, hammer-headed, black-and-white paint gelding. His saddle must have weighed close to what that ugly little nag weighed. And the gray horse he was leading wasn't a much better specimen of horseflesh. Happy Jack took the gray and climbed up on it.

"Get your horses and let's be gone," Happy Jack said to Newt and the others.

"How far is it to the claim?" Newt asked.

"Three hours, maybe less if everything goes right," Happy Jack said. "Easy going most of the way. You coming?"

Newt had his own reasons for getting out of the settlement, but Happy Jack seemed even more anxious to leave. Newt surmised that the old man's reasons had little to do with fear of a snowstorm or a norther blowing in. "Gonna be dark in a couple of hours."

Happy Jack turned around and frowned at him. "If I was you, I'd worry about the dark a lot less than that man you were talking to down there by the saloon."

Newt studied the old man, trying to guess how much he knew.

"Don't look at me like that," Happy Jack said. "I might not know who he is, but I know what he is. Loafing around here since yesterday trying to hide what he's about, and now I see two more of his kind with him. He's sniffing around for something, and that something means trouble. You hang around here if you want to, but my mother didn't raise any foolish children."

Jack took the lead rope on one of the mules and started toward the gap in the bluffs. Another of the mules was strung behind the mule he led, and Jose took up the other two.

Newt and the others headed for their horses. They were almost there and passing in front of the saloon when the door opened and the Cutter stepped in the opening, holding a bottle of beer in one hand. Dial and the Mexican must have been somewhere inside and out of sight of the open door, and that was a good thing.

Newt kept on walking. The Cutter said nothing to them, only lifted his beer in a mock toast, then went back inside and closed the door behind him.

The Circle Dot horse wasn't at the hitching rail with the other horses and was instead standing farther under the cottonwood trees with his head down and picking at the wispy brown grass there. Most broke horses had the good sense after a hard day's ride to make use of the opportunity to take a break and stand quietly at a hitching rail for as long as they could with no more than a wrap or two of a bridle rein around the rail or a halter lead rope tied to it. But the brown gelding wasn't most horses. Newt frowned but wasn't really bothered. He had long since grown used to the horse's traits, and sometimes he thought it had been put on earth to develop his patience.

By the time he reached the horse, the Hudlow brothers were already up on theirs.

"Go see if you can help Happy Jack get that fool mule moving," he said to them.

One of the mules was balking and set back at the end of its lead. Happy Jack was cussing and trying to pull it out of its tracks, and the half-breed Ute was behind it whipping at its rump with the tail of a rope and barely avoiding getting kicked. So far, the little pack mule was getting its way. The Hudlow brothers laughed and spurred their horses to go help.

Newt caught the Circle Dot horse and adjusted his saddle and tightened his cinch. "You're about as much trouble as that mule. I don't know why I put up with you."

He talked more and more to the horse over the years. It had become a habit, though one that he didn't recognize about himself. Furthermore, there was no one other than

Mr. Smith to point out that peculiarity, and the Mohave kept most such observations to himself.

Newt untied his sheepskin coat from behind his saddle cantle and was trying to tug it on when he sensed someone near him. It was nothing more than a slight flicker of movement out of the corner of one eye and the sound of a boot sole grating on the ground that made him turn and see Johnny Dial step out from behind the trunk of one of those big trees with a pistol pointed at him. Even with that slight warning, Newt almost took a bullet in his chest.

CHAPTER NINE

There wasn't more than a body length between Newt and the skinny Texas badman, and Newt was caught with both arms all but pinned, half in and half out of the heavy coat. Dial's finger tightened on the trigger.

Newt kicked out and missed the gun, but his bootheel struck Dial in the chest. Dial's pistol roared and flamed, and Newt felt the tug of the bullet passing through one side of his coat. Dial was knocked back with his gun arm flung wildly over his head, and that gave Newt time to get the rest of the way into his coat. He bulled forward and drove a shoulder into Dial and pinned him against the trunk of the tree.

Dial groaned with the pain of the impact, and all of the air gushed out of him. Newt pushed away enough to cock a fist, but Dial struck down with the pistol and hit him a glancing blow on the temple. Buffaloed and half stunned, Newt managed to headbutt the smaller man squarely in the nose, and he felt the crush of cartilage and soft flesh give against the hardness of his skull.

Newt staggered back a step, still half blind from the pistol being fired almost in his face and with this ears ringing from the report and the blow he had taken to the head. Another gun bellowed, and a bullet splintered bark from the tree. He turned and saw the Mexican standing about ten yards away with a Winchester pointed at him for a second shot.

Before Newt could react, Mr. Smith entered the fight. The big Mohave was up on his horse, and he charged the Mexican, leapt from the saddle, and tackled him. Both men rolled across the ground, punching and gouging and struggling for a hold. They finally came to their feet, and the Mexican used the moment to draw a big knife from his belt. He slashed once at Mr. Smith's throat and then made a backhanded swipe lower down. Mr. Smith gave ground to avoid the cuts aimed for him, and both his hands disappeared inside his dress coat. When those hands came back out, they held not pistols or knives, but a pair of wooden war clubs instead.

The Mexican lunged with the tip of his blade but found nothing but empty space. Mr. Smith parried the knife with the longer of the clubs he held, knocking it wide of him, and stepped to the side. The movement was so easily performed that it looked effortless.

The Mexican was left off-balance and with one side exposed. He tried to recover and buy time by aiming another backhand slash at Mr. Smith's face, but the Mohave's other club cracked against his elbow. The Mexican cried out in pain and dropped the knife, but that cry was cut off by another club blow slapping against his mouth. Mr. Smith's war clubs moved in a blur of complex attack patterns that were almost too fast to follow. The Mexican was hit twice more as he was falling and before he landed flat on his shoulder blades on the ground.

Newt glanced down at Dial, who was hunkered at his feet. The Texas outlaw's eyes were pouring tears, and his bloody nose was bent horribly to one side.

"Damn you," Dial swore.

Newt spotted Dial's pistol on the ground and bent and picked it up. He pointed the revolver at the downed man and then glanced over at Mr. Smith. The Mohave was standing over the Mexican as if daring the Mexican to move or so much as twitch again.

The Hudlow brothers came up on their horses at a run. When the wind carried away the dust they caused, Newt saw that both of them had their guns in their hands. He nodded his approval at them. They might be green, but at least they weren't cowards.

"Keep an eye on the saloon," Newt said to them.

He motioned with the pistol for Dial to get up. "On your feet."

"To hell with you," Dial said, and spat at him.

Newt took hold of him by the shoulder of his coat and jerked him upright. He shoved him toward the saloon and came behind him with the pistol at his back. Dial tried once to stop and turn on him, but Newt gave him another shove.

Surprisingly, the Mexican wasn't dead. Newt had assumed he was from the hard cracks the clubs had made when they struck him and by the way he lay there. Mr. Smith tucked his war clubs back inside his coat and kicked the Mexican twice in the ribs. The threat of a third kick was enough to motivate the Mexican to get up. He swayed and looked about to fall again, but Mr. Smith took hold of him and started him alongside Newt's prisoner. The Mexican couldn't keep up, and Mr. Smith all but dragged him along.

The saloon front door opened when they neared it, and the Cutter stood there once again. Newt gave Dial another shove, and the Cutter had to move out of the way to avoid the flailing, staggering man. Mr. Smith followed suit and threw the Mexican down in front of the door.

For all the hard things said about the Cutter, it couldn't

be denied that he had courage, for it was on full display then and there. He took in Newt and Mr. Smith before him, then the Hudlow brothers behind them. He was outnumbered four to one, but he hardly batted an eye.

Johnny Dial pulled at the Cutter's pants' leg trying to hoist himself up. The Cutter kicked him away. He looked down at Dial and then at the Mexican with disgust and anger.

"Damn fools," he said.

"Give me a gun," Dial pleaded with him, reaching up with an open hand.

The Cutter ignored Dial and met Newt's hard stare.

Newt's breath was coming fast and heavy. He pointed a finger at the Cutter. "You want me, then you'd best send better men than trash like this."

"That was no doing of mine," the Cutter said in a strained voice that he was doing everything he could to control.

"You heard me," Newt said, then flung Dial's pistol away.

He turned and stalked away before the Cutter could say anything else. Mr. Smith backed away a few steps, then turned and followed him. The Hudlow brothers stayed in front of the saloon watching the Cutter while Newt and Mr. Smith mounted their horses and only then backed away to their own mounts. All four of them caught up to Happy Jack and Jose not a hundred yards out of the settlement.

Newt was still breathing heavily, and the battle rage hadn't yet died down in him. He caught Happy Jack staring at him. The old man looked like he wanted to ask some questions but must have thought better of it and didn't.

They rode on toward Wagon Wheel gap. Tandy Hudlow looked back at the settlement when they were almost out of sight of it, and he saw the Cutter still standing in front of the saloon.

"I reckon you put the fear in him," Tandy said.

Newt turned his head and glared at Tandy. "Like hell, I did."

CHAPTER TEN

Zuri woke beside her fire. She had kept that fire mounded with wood throughout most of the night, both for warmth and to keep the bear away, but it had burned down mostly to nothing more than a smoking mound of coals and ashes. She rubbed her eyes and stared at the sun and was shocked that it was already daylight. She didn't even remember falling asleep.

She glanced at the tent with its top sagging where the stampeding sheep had snagged some of its stake ropes and jerked the pegs out of the ground. Her father wasn't in that tent, and he wasn't anywhere else. She had hoped if she sat by the fire long enough he would see its flames and come walking into camp. She would simply look up and there he would be, but there was no sign of him.

She fed more wood on the fire and watched the heat of the coals slowly take hold and the smoke and little flames feathering out from between the sticks. She had used up the last of the larger firewood her father had sawn and chopped, and she knew that her poor little new fire wasn't going to last long. He had never allowed her to use the axe or his saw, but she was going to have to use them if she had to stay there another night. But first she needed to find him.

That's what she needed to do, but still, she sat there in a

daze, hunkered before the heat of the fire, trying to clear her foggy mind and to find some point of balance and cohesion where she didn't feel like she was falling apart. She needed to act, to move, but she was uncertain as to what exactly she should do. And that uncertainty added to her fear. She looked up the mountain and wondered if the bear was truly gone. Was it only her imagination that gave her the feeling that it loomed nearby, waiting to get her?

She was so hungry she was sick to her stomach, but up until that moment she had not even thought of eating. But her body would be denied no longer, and she went to the grub boxes beside the tent and dug in them until she had found a tin of canned peaches. The tins were always hard to open, and her father had usually used a knife to hack the top away, but she had no knife, having lost the butcher knife the night before. She hurled the tin of peaches on the ground, about to give up, but then she thought of the axe again. It was stuck in the trunk of a tree nearby where her father had left it. She took hold of the handle and tugged, but it was too high up for her to get enough leverage to pry it from the wood. Placing a foot against the tree trunk, she tried again with a heave and a little grunt of exertion. The axe head came free with a pop, so quickly that she staggered back.

Once she had regained her balance, she took the axe back to the fire. There, she stood over the tin of peaches and studied it carefully in an attempt to aim the stroke from the axe she intended. She had to readjust her feet when she lifted the axe over her head due to the long handle and the weight of it, but she found her balance and chopped down with all her might. The edges on the double-bit blade were sharp and her aim was surprisingly true. The can parted in a spray of water and peach juice. Closer examination revealed that her blow had not cut the tin enough to get to the peaches, so she used the axe a second time. That cut missed badly, but a third swing hit her mark again. The result of her chopping was that the tin was mangled and smashed, but she had managed to sever the can all but in two. She bent the tin with her fingers enough to gain access to the fruit inside it, careful not to cut herself on the sharp edges. Then she sat down and ate.

Her hunger was such that opening the tin took far more time than finishing off its contents. The peaches seemed no meal at all and only increased her appetite. She had lost most of the juice by using the axe, but she tilted the tin over her mouth and swallowed what few drops fell out. Then she licked her fingers, savoring every bit of the sweet, syrupy liquid. She was tempted to go search the grub boxes for something else to eat, but she resisted the urge and tried not to think about how good her meal had tasted.

It was not as cold as it had been the day before, but she wasn't about to be caught out again so ill-prepared. She went inside the tent and pulled her legs into a pair of wool stockings. Once she had her shoes back on, she found her wool cap and tugged it down over her head and tucked a few strands of her brown hair under it and out of the way. Around her neck she wrapped the scarf her mother had once knitted for her, and her mittens were the last thing she grabbed before she went outside again.

She considered taking the axe with her, but it was so heavy that she couldn't imagine wielding it with any speed or the accuracy needed to defend herself. She cast it aside and searched for something else. There was nothing, and she gave a bitter little laugh. The axe or the lost knife didn't matter. Neither would stop the bear if it was still around. Yes, she had cut the bear's nose, but she had simply been lucky. She couldn't count on that again.

She looked up the mountain for a second time, trying to build up her nerve. Leaving the camp felt akin to leaving the safety of some castle's walls, even though she knew that feeling was false. Abstract boundaries offered her no real protection, and the bear could come and get her there as easily as anywhere.

She was drawing from her well of courage and steeling herself to go in search of her father when she heard something behind her. When she turned she saw it wasn't her father's horse as she had hoped, but instead it was one of the pack mules. Not the one that had broken its hobbles and escaped, but the other one, the little gray jenny. It stood on the far edge of the stream and looked at Zuri as if expecting something.

She found a halter and lead rope and walked to the animal, moving slowly so as not to scare it. The jenny was always troublesome and was acting especially spooky. It eyed her carefully but let her cross the stream and put the halter on its head. She checked it for injury and found that it seemed unharmed. After untying the hobbles from its front legs, she led it back to camp.

Her father's saddle horse was the only horse they had, and she had often rode double with him when they traveled. But there had also been times when he had set her on top of a pack on one of the mules when they traveled to new grazing grounds, although it was always on the other mule, the gentle sorrel john with the white blaze down its face and never the jenny. Her father had often warned her to watch out and be cautious when working around the fractious little beast. She was prone to kicking and had bit at Zuri's father on several occasions. Once the jenny had become frightened by something on a steep narrow trail and had jerked away from his hold and fallen down a cliff, losing its pack and damaging some of their gear in the process.

But if she was up on the jenny's back, she would have a higher point of view while searching for her father, could cover more ground, and could possibly stand a better chance of outrunning the bear should it come after her again. She remembered how fast the big brown bear had been, and she didn't know if even a swift little mule could outrun it.

She led the mule to the where the packsaddles and other gear lay in a pile beside the tent. First, she put the saddle blanket on the mule's back. The jenny cocked one ear back at her on the side she worked from but didn't give her any problem. The sawbuck packsaddle was a different story. Zuri was strong enough to heave it in place but not strong enough to do it gently. The jenny jumped sideways and dumped the saddle on the ground the first time she tried, startled by the saddle landing on her back and the girt and cinches flopping against her ribs on the off side.

"Good girl." Zuri rubbed and petted the jenny on the neck until it seemed calmed, put the blanket back on its back, picked up the saddle, and tried again.

The jenny stood still, and she got the saddle on its back that time. She ran the girt under its heart girth and ran the latigo through the cinch ring and the saddle ring a few times and drew it tight like she had seen her father do, but she couldn't remember how he tied off the latigo. But whether she knew it or not, she had inherited a certain degree of her father's stubbornness, and she stuck to it and improvised a tie. It didn't look like her father's, but she thought it would work.

The packsaddle was not made for riding, but she retrieved one of her sleeping blankets, an old wool army blanket, and folded it and set it on top of the bare wooden tree bars for padding. She was about to get on the mule when she thought of all the things she was forgetting. She fetched her father's canteen from where it lay by her fire, and she rolled another blanket. Both of those things she secured to the saddle.

When she was finished, she led the mule to a waist-high

rock beside the stream. The jenny was barely thirteen hands high, and she probably could have jumped on its back. But she didn't think it would stand still to try that technique. She tied the end of the lead rope back into the halter to create a single rein and then got up on the rock. Surprisingly, the mule stood quietly while she crawled onto its back. It did turn its head and look back at her when she adjusted her red skirt, but it didn't try to throw her or run off.

The packsaddle, even with the blanket padding she put in place, was uncomfortable, and she felt awkward perched there and unsure if she could stay on if the mule decided to be skittish. But the forks of the saddle gave her something to hang onto with her hands if she needed that help, and that made her feel more secure. She took a deep breath and made a clucking sound in her cheek and nudged the jenny with her heels. Expecting anything, she was surprised when the jenny walked off calmly.

She stopped the jenny just downhill from the alder thicket and took a deep breath. The little mule must have sensed her anxiety, or perhaps it, too, was remembering the bear or smelling where it had been. It perked its comically long ears upright and forward and held its head high.

Zuri could already feel her own heart beating faster. *Be strong like Mother. Be brave like Father.*

She pushed away thoughts of riding back to camp but couldn't quite bring herself to continue. But the jenny made up her mind for her and moved on without being asked. The little mule's bravery gave Zuri courage of her own, and her determination to find her father returned as strongly as it had been before. But she did rein the jenny wide of the alder thicket.

Up the mountain they went. Three ravens flew up from the remains of the dead ewe as she neared it, her arrival having disturbed their scavenging. Their fluttering wings caused the jenny to shy and almost unseated Zuri. She got the mule back under control, righted herself, and took stock of the kill site.

All that remained of the poor sheep were shredded bits of wool and a part of the skeleton. She rode on, searching the ground ahead closely and ready to get as far away from the remains of the ewe as she could. She guided the jenny toward the place where she believed the bear had attacked her father, the place where she thought she had seen him on the ground, scanning the short grass all around her. She was certain she was at the right place, but he was not there. But the more she looked, the more she saw signs of a fight. She was no tracker, no scout or Indian, and she had never lived anywhere but in town until the last two years with her father herding sheep. But even she could see the torn-up ground, the hoof prints of her father's horse, and places where either the bear or the horse had ripped the grass loose. And it was not hard to guess what those signs meant.

Zuri looked beyond the place and wondered if he had fled farther up the mountain. She rode higher. A shallow depression in the ground appeared ahead, the start of drainage that got deeper and wider the farther it went down the mountain until it turned into a shallow draw or wash. The gray jenny had only taken a few steps before one of its hooves clicked against something in the grass. She looked down and saw it was her father's rifle that the mule's hoof had struck.

Then the jenny shied again and tried to wheel and run away, but she managed to keep it in place. When she looked at the shallow fold of ground in front of them, she saw what had frightened the jenny. It was the soles of her father's boots. The rest of his body was hidden down in the depression.

CHAPTER ELEVEN

Beyond Wagon Wheel Gap, the countryside opened once again into a narrow valley that widened the farther upriver they went and curved slowly toward the south in a great horseshoe bend. The grassy banks of the river, the setting sun reflecting off the crystal clear water, and the mountains rising all around was a scene of beauty worth seeing.

"Pretty country," Newt said to Happy Jack. "Pretty as I ever saw."

"Wait 'til you're freezing your tail off this winter, and then tell me how pretty it is," Happy Jack replied.

But the old man, despite his cynical words, was soaking it all in the same as the rest of them were. It was written on his face and in the gleam of his eyes as he looked toward the far mountains and farther still into the distance.

Newt thought no man could lay eyes on such and not be affected by it. After all the years of traveling the wild country, the grandeur of certain places still hit him like the first time. Some of the Indian tribes would refer to those places as big medicine, and Mr. Smith would have called them places of power. Newt was not a man who shared many of his thoughts, but in the core of him, the rock of his making, was a belief that the Indians were right. There was something about the high lonesome country that gave a man clarity and brought him closer to himself, and maybe closer to something else. He had never been able to formulate words for that feeling, and he would have been embarrassed to say as much to anyone. However, he felt it, just the same. Something as real as anything he knew and something that called to him.

He thought of a question he had asked his father when he was but a little boy. His father had rarely told tales of his youth and then only when prodded by his wife or children or when the warmth of a good fire on a cold evening loosened his tongue for storytelling. It was during one of those times that Newt had asked him why he had left his home and gone off to the far western mountains trapping and hunting. And his father's answer was as clear to his memory as if it were yesterday, and the words had stuck with him ever since. *Because it was out there, Son, and I needed to see it.*

The creak of saddle leather and the clack of horseshoes on rocky ground pulled Newt's mind fully back to the present. They had been following a clearly defined trail, what Happy Jack said was the Barlow & Sanderson stagecoach run and the trail for pack trains going from Wagon Wheel Gap to points higher in the mountains. Yet, halfway out into the widest part of the valley, he left that trail and led them across the river and followed a narrow stream running down from the north. By then, it was growing dark.

They traveled that way for a mile or more, climbing gradually up from the river. There was little moon to speak of, but enough to cast the mountain ahead in looming shadow as they rode ever closer to it. By the time they had traveled another half hour, Newt sensed they were in the mouth of a canyon. He sensed that by the darker shade of black like the bottom of a pit and by the sound of their travel echoing off rock walls

Happy Jack reined up and dismounted. "We'll camp here and go on up to the claim in the morning."

"I thought you said you were in a hurry to get there," Newt said.

"Only thing I was in a hurry to do was to get out of Wagon Wheel Gap," Happy Jack answered.

The old man tottered around in the dark while the others got down and unsaddled their horses and unloaded the mules. By the time they had finished, he had a fire going. Newt noticed that there was already a pile of wood gathered and that the place where Happy Jack had laid his fire was thick with old ashes and bits of black charcoal. It was obviously a campsite he had used before.

When the flames grew high enough, they reflected off an enormous wall of sheer rock. Newt craned his neck to look upward, but the cliff face was high enough that the top of it disappeared into the darkness. They all hobbled the horses and mules and turned them loose on a small grassy flat beside the creek and went back to the fire.

Jose and the Hudlow brothers shared cooking duties, which consisted of cutting open a few tins of corned beef hash and warming them beside the fire. It was already growing cold enough that they could see their breath, but the fire's heat radiating off the rocks cut some of the chill.

Newt used his saddle for a seat and took out his pistol and began rubbing it down with machine oil and a rag he carried for that purpose. Tandy Hudlow watched him from across the fire and paid close attention to Newt's weapon.

"Fancy pistol," Tandy said.

Newt nodded. The Smith & Wesson no. 3 revolver, chambered for the .44 Russian cartridge, was, indeed, a fine weapon. The blued-steel of it was so dark as to be almost black, and that made the pale blue turquoise crosses inlayed into the walnut grip panels stand out all the more. And those crosses were a match for the same type of blue stones in the hitched horsehair hatband on his broad-brimmed black hat. Newt was a plain-dressing man who in every other part of his person abhorred any kind of flash. The fancy pistol grips and hatband were out of place on him, but both had been gifts from a dear friend, having once belonged to her recently deceased lawman husband.

"It's just a gun," Newt said. "Only as good as the man holding it."

"That man back in Wagon Wheel Gap let on like you're something," Tandy said. "You must be pretty good."

"First thing a man carrying a gun had better learn out here is to carry it quietly and don't hunt trouble, unless you're bulletproof or think there isn't somebody better than you," Newt said. "And let me guarantee you something, nobody's bulletproof and there's always somebody better."

"Tully there is the best rifle shot I ever saw," Tandy said. "We come out here thinking we'd hunt some buffalo."

It was Happy Jack who gave a scoffing grunt this time while he puttered over the coffeepot he was tending. "Well, you're about five or six years too late. Hide hunters done all but killed out the big shaggies."

"Yeah, we already figured that out," Tandy said, and frowned at the old man.

"You two worked with a freight outfit?" Newt asked.

"What ain't we done?" Tandy pushed the can of corned beef he was overseeing away from the flames with a stick to keep from burning his hands. "First there was the flatboat job. That got us far as Paducah. Half starved between there and Springfield. Worked the harvest there until we saved a few dollars, and that bought us a train ride to Wichita. Fellow there hired us to run his wagons down to Fort Reno and the Indian reservations in the Indian Territory. Spent better than a year whacking six-yoke teams of oxen, and let me tell you, that's slow traveling."

"Teach a schoolmarm to cuss, I promise you," Tully threw in. "That's no kind of work for a freeborn man."

Tandy nodded his agreement and went on, "But we saved enough to buy us good horses and outfit ourselves to go on west."

"And then you heard about the job in Lake City?" Newt asked.

"Fellow we were locked up with in Alamosa told us about it." Tandy looked a little sheepish as soon as he said that, like he had let something slip he hadn't intended to reveal.

Newt gave Tandy a pointed look. In truth, it didn't surprise him. The Hudlows had always been the outlaw bunch of the family. They lived farther back in the mountains than almost anyone else and tended to make up their own minds about what laws they would or wouldn't abide by. Not truly bad folks, but too wild and stubborn in their ways for most people. Mother Jones had been fond of telling her children that she was going to send them to live with the Hudlows when they did something bad, though as he recalled, she had always seemed quite fond of her husband's half sister, the woman who was the boys' mother. Miles and miles of steep, up-and-down travel and mountains had been between the homesteads of Newt's family and the one belonging to the Hudlows. Because of that, there had been few occasions when they had gotten together, and that was before Tully and Tandy were ever born. And like the brothers beside the fire, Newt knew little of his distant kin other than what stories he had heard his parents tell of them.

Tandy noticed the way Newt was looking at him and shrugged his shoulders and waved a cloud of smoke out of his face. "Yeah, Tully there got us in a little trouble, but we ain't got nothing to hide. Nothing to be ashamed of."

"All I did was go walking with a girl," Tully said sullenly.

Tandy shook his head and gave a hiss of disgust. "Her pa and his sheriff brother didn't see it that way. Justice of the peace ramrodded us without us even getting to defend ourselves and say our piece. Gave us thirty days filling holes in the streets and cleaning ditches."

Tully muttered something that Newt couldn't understand.

Newt looked at Mr. Smith and gave a jerk of his head at the brothers. "What we've got here are two regular desperados. Hardened criminals and fugitives."

Tandy squinted at Newt, likely trying to weigh if insult was intended. It was hard to tell whether he or his brother were the proudest and touchiest, and neither one of them liked being teased. Finally, he sighed and let it go.

"We've taken our lumps, but we've made it this far," he said. "Been more twists and turns than a mountain creek, but maybe you don't know how that is."

Newt chuckled so loudly that it startled them. Even Mr. Smith's head snapped his way.

Newt took in the two brothers, still boys in some ways, but men in all ways that mattered to the world. Young enough not to realize how young they were, but old enough to pay the consequences. *Sink or swim,* that's how Mother Jones would have put it. Newt knew it because he had lived it—was still living it. They had already undoubtedly learned things, but they wouldn't understand if he told them. Not yet, not until they had some more years and miles on them, if they made it that far.

Still, something made him speak. Maybe it was the touch of home they carried in their accents and their mannerisms or the old memories that familiarity brought forth. "I was

fourteen when my pa died. There were three of us brothers
and a baby sister with my ma on a two-bit, rocky farm that
wouldn't make a living for one person, much less all of us."

Both of the brothers were watching him intently by then.
Maybe they were still green, but their upbringing must have
been hard enough that they related in some way. Mountain
folks, be they young or old, knew a lot about hard living.
And even Mr. Smith was giving him a curious look.

"Our pa said Kinch's heart quit him while he was
plowing on a hot day," Tully said, trying to bait Newt into
continuing his story. "Least that was what we were told."

Newt shrugged. "Who knows? He was lying there in a
furrow like he had simply gotten tired and lain down to take
a nap. Like it was nothing at all."

"Hard way to go, no matter," Tully said.

Newt stared up at the big rock bluff beyond the fire and
at the snake dance of flames and shadow there, remembering as much as he was searching for words. "We all turned
a hand at trying to make a living and make up for Pa being
gone, but none of it amounted to much. My oldest brother
took a job with a logging crew. For a time he sent money
back home, but it wasn't long before we heard he had
drowned walking a log raft on the Mississippi River up in
Minnesota. Sister married a missionary and ran off to the
jungle country down in Nicaragua. My youngest brother
was the best farmer of us, and he was determined to stay
and make a go of it and look after Ma."

"But you left?" Tandy asked.

"I did."

The brothers shared one of their looks between them.
Both of them seemed to want to ask something of him, but
it was equally plain that they were hesitant to do so.

It was Tandy, the talker of the two, who finally worked
himself up to the question. "It was before our time, but folks

tell it that you got into a fight with Old Man Weams and his boys at a dance. They say you hurt ol' Lefty Weams real bad, and that's why he's missing most of his teeth and has got that crooked arm. And that you cut the old man and one of the other boys with a knife. That's why the high sheriff came looking for you. Maybe it ain't so, but if you be Kinch's middle son, then that's why they say you left home, because you were on the scout."

Newt nodded grimly, not looking at either of them. "There was that, too."

"Those Weamses are rough," Tully said. "Especially when they're on the whiskey. We went to school with two of them, younger ones, of course. They used to wait for Tandy and me when we were walking home and jump us. We never could whip them, but we gave them the what-for a time or two."

Tandy gave Tully an irritated look for interrupting Newt's storytelling. "What did you do after that?"

Newt shrugged. "Worked on the railroad some. Worked for a blacksmith long enough to learn I had no knack for the trade. Dug graves for a winter. Fought a little with my fists for prize money here and there, and tried my hand at mining. Placer, hard rock, you know, whatever it took. Feel like I've done everything in between since."

"You ever go back home?"

"No, I never did. Ma passed on years ago."

"We know. We were at her funeral," Tandy said. "You should have seen it. People came from all over. Hacks and buggies all in a line, some walking and some riding to get there. Reckon a lot of folks set store by your ma."

"She was a good woman." Newt pointed at the tinned beef. "Pass me a plate of that."

Tandy raked out a third of the can's contents onto a plate

and handed it over the fire to Newt. "You ain't asked about your brother."

Newt scooped up a forkful of the corned beef and blew on it to cool it off. He looked over the steaming fork at Tandy. "How's he doing?"

"Fine. Got a wife and three kids, but I suppose you know that."

"No, I didn't."

The way Newt said that made Tandy go quiet for a while. Newt busied himself with his meal, not looking up from his plate until he was finished.

"What about this job guarding a claim?" Tandy asked. "You've done this before?"

"Once or twice," Newt answered.

"How's that usually work out?"

"Three dollars a day, that's how it works out."

Tandy let out a low, long whistle. "Three dollars a day? You're kidding me. You hear that, Tully?"

"It isn't much," Newt said.

"Not much?" Tully replied.

"That's the thing about fighting wages. You're either doing someone's dirty work or being done dirty."

"Then why do you do it?" Tandy asked.

"Now there's a question." Newt reached for a mug of coffee Happy Jack handed him.

Tandy mulled that over for a moment, his brow wrinkled. "This fellow paying us, he must be expecting trouble."

"Now you're getting it."

"How would anybody steal a claim? I thought every claim was registered with the government," Tandy went on, obviously not bothered by the amused, condescending looks the older men were giving him.

Newt slurped at the hot coffee, and Happy Jack answered for him when he didn't offer a reply. "Doesn't happen as much as it used to, but it happens. Holding a claim isn't only a matter of driving your stakes or marking your boundaries. You have to make improvements and move it toward production. What we call *proving up*. You run a man off his claim, you keep him from doing that."

"Then the law would step in."

Happy Jack snorted. "By the time any law shows up, the matter is mostly decided. And anybody trying to steal a claim is already planning on muddying things up in the courts. They argue they were there first, or maybe it's an issue of a survey. If they can run you off, they might convince a court that what you thought was yours was actually theirs. Good lawyers and a crooked judge in your pocket have got more to do sometimes with who gets a claim than who drives their claim stakes first."

"I hate a thief," Tully said.

"Of course, in the old days, it sometimes wasn't so complicated," Happy Jack said. "You scare a man off for good or kill him, then there's nobody left to argue the matter. Possession is nine-tenths of the law and all. There were some rough, bloody times back in the mining camps when I was a young man. And that's the reason the claim laws came about."

Newt rose and took his coffee cup away from the fire. He walked far enough away that he was out of the firelight and looked down the hills back the way they had come. Standing there, he noticed a dim light showing miles away to the west.

There came the sound of boots crunching on the gravelly ground near the creek, and Happy Jack appeared beside him. Newt pointed out the light he saw.

"Not somebody following us, if that's what you're thinking," Happy Jack said. "Too far west, I think. Likely some pack train's campfire, making their last run down out of the mountains. Or could it be some hunter, or maybe it belongs to a sheepherder, though I'd have thought they were all down out of the high country by now."

"Nobody else up here?" Newt asked. "I mean that lives up here."

"There's Wason's ranch. We passed it in the dark," Happy Jack said. "He runs a few cattle and operates a pack train business hauling freight between the Gap and Baker's Park. But he's got a new wife and took her down to Del Norte for the winter. I saw them when they came through the Gap."

Newt took another swallow of the hot coffee and continued to watch the flickering point of faint light in the distance.

"You strike me as a worrying sort," Happy Jack said.

"That bothers you?" Newt asked.

"No, probably comes in handy for a man in your line of work."

His line of work. Newt let that statement soak in. He started to walk back to their fire but didn't. "How bad does the snow get here?"

"Not all that bad if you're used to it and prepared," Happy Jack answered. "That's right here, but higher up she can get deep. Of course, some winters are worse than others. Jose's going down to Del Norte with the mules and my horse in the morning. Won't be nothing for them to feed on where we're going. If I was you, I would send your horses back with him, unless you want to turn them loose down along the river and chance finding them come spring. I've got a deal with a man to winter my stock for me. I reckon he'll do the same for you."

"I'll keep my horse with me," Newt said. "I'll ask the others, but I imagine they'll feel the same."

"Suit yourself." Happy Jack said, and headed back to their fire.

Newt started to follow him but cast one more look at the light in the distance. Yes, he was a worrier at times, but there was some other new feeling picking at him that he couldn't quite get a handle on. He couldn't say why that new feeling was there or where it had come from. It was a bad feeling, almost like a premonition, and one that had nothing to do with the Cutter or Saul Barton's claim or the Hudlow brothers or the grouchy old prospector. Nor did it have anything to do with the Ute with the sneaky eyes or Mr. Smith's death wish. Any of those things could get a man killed or cause him to fail. And not for the first time, Newt considered how he had come to live like he did.

CHAPTER TWELVE

The grizzly bear had not eaten any part of Zuri's father. She had no way of knowing whether such a monster would do that or not, but that secret fear had stayed with her as much as the worry that he might not still be alive. But the sight of him lying there, a sight no child should see, was harder than anything she had ever experienced. It was harder than the bear almost killing her and harder than losing her mother to the fever.

In truth, she was fortunate that her father hadn't been eaten, for grizzlies did that, the same as they would eat their own kind. The fact that the crippled old boar had filled its belly on the ewe's meat might have kept it from devouring his two-legged kill, but that knowledge would have been no comfort at all to her. Her father's body was so torn and broken that she would not have recognized him had he not been wearing the clothes she knew and had she not loved him so dearly.

Staring at him that way brought on a sorrow such that she felt herself receding into a dark place that had no bottom. It was as physically painful as it was emotional. It was as if her whole body and her spirit were struck down, and it was the first time ever that she felt utterly defeated. She had no words for the moment, no concrete thoughts.

Her mind was as blank and empty as her sense of loss. She forgot about the bear and stood alone on a plane of nothingness where seconds were an eternity.

She sat on the jenny that way for a long time, refusing to look at her father's body anymore. And when she did look at him again and her mind began to work in stuttering, halting spurts, her first coherent thought was that she wasn't big enough to load him on the mule and that she had no shovel to bury him.

She got down from the mule, wiped her eyes with the back of one hand, then took down the rolled-up blanket from the packsaddle frame. The ladies of the village had not let her help prepare her mother's body, but she would do the best she could for her father.

Before she started with him, she took his belt and sheath knife. The belt was too long for her, but she wrapped it twice around her and buckled it in place with the knife on her right hip.

She spread the blanket beside him and rolled him onto it. She had to stop more than once to take a few breaths and steady herself, but she eventually had him rolled up in the blanket.

His gold pocket watch had been in his vest pocket like he always carried it, and that was good. But she wished she had brought his *trompa*, which is what her people called a Jew's harp. He had so loved to clench it in his teeth, thump the metal tongue with his finger, and play music with it by the fireside of an evening. It would have been fitting to lay it to rest with him.

The ground was far too rocky and hard to dig a grave where he lay, even if she got a shovel. What she needed was some way to move his body to a better place. She wasn't strong enough to load him onto the jenny. There was plenty of rope back in camp, but dragging him was something she didn't think she could bear.

She rose and went to the mule. There was no rock for her to use to help her mount like she had in camp, so she simply took hold of the packsaddle with both hands and jumped and pulled at the same time. She managed to land with her belly across the jenny's back on the first try, but her jumping scared the skittish animal and it took off in a run. She bounced on its back for several strides and almost fell off but then got her leg over its back. In a few more runaway strides she got hold of her improvised rein. They ran down the hill and the jenny wouldn't stop, no matter how hard she pulled. She was almost to the end of the alder thicket by the time she figured out to try and circle the jenny. That technique worked, but not instantly. She pulled hard on the rein on one side and bent the jenny into a big circle. Round and round they went with their curve getting tighter, so tight that she feared the jenny would fall. Eventually, the jenny gave up and slowed to a trot and then a walk.

"Don't you do that again," Zuri said to the jenny when they finally stopped.

She was about to continue her ride down the ridge at a much slower pace than before when she heard something that sounded like pots and pans banging together. And there were other sounds like something was tearing up the camp. When she was past the end of the alder thicket, she saw what was making all the noise. It was the bear. Far below her, she could see it tearing apart the grub boxes beside the tent. It didn't even seem to recognize she was above it on the mountainside. She was out in the open and would have been easily spotted if the bear wasn't so intent on its raiding of their camp.

The jenny saw the bear, too, and whirled and threw another runaway back up the ridge. Like the first time, Zuri had a hard time stopping her mount, but at least she didn't have to circle it. Regardless, they were almost back to her father's body before she managed that feat.

Once the jenny stopped again, Zuri rode the rest of the way to her father. The mule was still beside itself with fright. Zuri leapt down and had to untie one end of the lead rope rein in order to keep hold of the jenny. And it took her longer to search the grass until she had found her father's rifle. The buttstock on the rifle was busted halfway down its length, but the rest of the weapon seemed undamaged as far as she could tell.

Once she had taken up the rifle, she tried to move closer to her father's body, but the jenny was pulling on the lead rope so hard that it was difficult to keep hold of it and almost impossible to make any progress. But she did, and she folded back the blanket she had wrapped him in and searched inside his vest and coat pockets for cartridges to load the gun.

There was only one spare cartridge. The rest of his ammunition was likely in their tent or elsewhere in camp. She had never shot the rifle, although she had asked to once. But her father had said the gun was too big for her and its recoil too much for someone her size. No matter, she had seen her father load it, and it didn't seem too hard.

It would have been no more difficult than she thought if the mule hadn't been pulling against her and tugging her so. She couldn't hold the rifle in both hands and still hold the lead rope tightly enough to keep the jenny from escaping, so she did it differently than the way her father had. He wouldn't have approved, no doubt, but she had no other choice.

She put the end of the barrel against the ground and tried to rest the broken stock against her hip. The rifle's hammer was already at half-cock and the trapdoor block was already flopping open, like her father had been trying to reload the weapon at the time he was struck down by the bear. She fumbled both the gun and the fresh cartridge she held when the jenny jerked against the lead rope, and she barely kept from dropping all three. It took great effort, but she finally poked the cartridge into the rifle's empty chamber and snapped the trapdoor shut. Her father would have told her to lower the hammer back to the safety notch, but she didn't and left the hammer at half-cock.

She tried to get back on the mule with the rifle, but she found that task to be impossible. The gun was long and awkward for her to handle, even with part of the stock broken off. And what's more, the jenny wouldn't be still. So, she solved her problem by sticking the end of the rifle through the forks of the packsaddle. It was loose there, but she hoped it would stay there long enough for her to get on. When she did get on, it was hard to pull the rifle out. That and other difficulties took up far too much time, and riding back down the ridge and trying to control the jenny while holding the rifle was an equally great challenge.

Her eyes were blurry with moisture and tears ran down her cheeks as she rode toward the camp, but her crying wasn't only because she was sad. Anger mixed with all the other emotions swirling inside her, and it grew until it all but smothered out everything else. It was a fury unlike anything she had felt before. That awful bear, that monster, had come into her world and destroyed all that she had. Yes, she was horrified of the bear, but she hated it, as well. Hated it until she was all but in a tantrum like she had thrown when she was much younger, where she wanted to break things and scream and stomp her feet and pull her hair. It was a rage that shook her body and made her want to scream. But she reveled in that feeling because her wrath pushed away the fear and fighting back felt good.

She bit her lip and kept riding, forcing herself to think only of vengeance. She didn't consider that she knew nothing about how to shoot and hit what she aimed at, nor did she consider that the jenny would likely throw her if she fired the rifle from its back. All she thought of was seeing the bear and hurting it like it had hurt her.

Camp was close enough then that she could see it clearly. The jenny balked, stopped in its tracks, and refused to go closer. The bear was no longer at the grub boxes, but she could see how things were scattered all over the ground there. The tent was torn down and other things were strewn about, but there was no sign of the hateful brown killer.

Then she saw it at the very instant she thought it must be gone. It was on the far side of the campground and about to cross the stream and go into the quakies like it was leaving. She tried to aim the rifle, but the broken stock didn't allow for anything to brace against her shoulder. She did the best she could, one hand gripping it like a pistol and the other resting on the forearm. She pointed it at the retreating bear, but the barrel was so long and end-heavy that she could hardly hold it up, much less aim. And she wasn't sure how to use the rifle sights, so she simply ignored the back sight and focused only on the front blade. The bear was already across the stream and almost to the edge of the trees by then. Once inside those close-growing aspens she wouldn't be able to see him anymore.

She tried to will steadiness into her shaking arms. She never thought to aim at a particular place on the bear's body, but simply at the center of its mass. And though the rifle refused to hold steady, there came a point when she couldn't hold the weight any longer. So, she jerked the trigger hard and was shocked that nothing happened.

At first she was surprised, then she was mad at herself when it dawned on her that she hadn't moved the rifle's hammer to full-cock as she had seen her father do when he shot the weapon. She had to lower the rifle back down to her lap to cock it because her hand was so small, then it took several frustrating moments to raise it and aim again. The jenny was being fractious and wouldn't be still, making her aim even less steady than her first attempt. Her front sight finally passed over brown fur at the same instant the bear disappeared into the quakies.

She almost shot, even though there was nothing left to shoot at. She almost fired simply because she needed that release, but she didn't. She let the rifle fall back to her lap, lowered the hammer back to half-cock, and glared at where the bear had gone.

"You come back and I'll get you," she said, though her voice wasn't loud like she intended it to be. Actually, it was barely a whisper because her vocal cords wouldn't work right, perhaps because she was crying and sobbing again.

"You come back, and if you don't I'll come find you anyway," she said. "I'll hunt you when I get bigger, and I'll shoot you."

But the bear didn't show itself again, not even when she rode the mule the rest of the way down to camp. Either it had not seen her or it had simply decided that it was through with that place. Neither Zuri nor any other person could have guessed why it left after so long tormenting her or how it did not see her or smell or hear her. For the mind of a bear and the mind of a human are so far apart as to be impossible to so much as guess why one or the other does what it does.

Zuri's anger and excitement fell away as fast as it had built to a peak, and again she was left drained. She fell off the mule as much as she got down from it, but she kept hold of the rifle. And she was still holding it when she sat down by what was left of her fire and stared at it. She muttered to herself and prayed fervently, but it was the first snowflakes landing on her face that moved her mind back to reality.

Snow. Winter. Bitter cold. She was young, but she knew that she needed to get down out of the mountains. It was daunting to think that she must find her way back to the settlements on her own, but that's what she had to do. She tried to remember how they had traveled back to the low country the year before and to map where she was and where she needed to go in her mind. But her memories of trails and directions was spotty at best, and it dawned on her that she was likely lost.

The river—they had always gone downriver at the end of the season, just like they had gone upriver in the late spring. She was sure she could find the river. All she had to do was keep going downhill. Down, down, and follow the little drainages until she found it.

She looked for the mule, having forgotten it for a time. Instead of running off like she thought it might have, it was not far away and nipping at the tops of a clump of dead grass beside the stream. That was good. She still had the jenny, and she would gather what she could and what she needed, load it on the packsaddle, and then find the river and follow it to someplace safe. But first she needed to bury her father.

She knew she should tend to him right then, but she was tired, very tired. And she was still hungry, but she filled her stomach with cold water from the canteen and made no effort to find more food. By then the snow was falling heavier. At first, it had been scattered, big flakes, but now it was coming down steadily and thick enough on the air that it was hard for her to see as far as the alder thicket up the ridge.

Again, she told herself she should go get her father. Instead, she gathered a blanket and wrapped it around her. The temperature was no colder than it had been that morning, but she was suddenly chilled. She put more wood on the fire and lay down beside it like she had the night before. She did not sleep but lay there on her side with her eyes open and stared at the flames while the snow continued to fall. Already, the ground was turning white, and the blanket over her was soon covered, with the snowflakes lying against the nap of the wool like delicate butterflies that landed on flower stems before they slowly melted away before the fire's heat.

And then she slept.

CHAPTER THIRTEEN

"I'll kill him, I swear it!" Johnny Dial said through the bloody rag he was holding against his broken nose.

He looked at where the Mexican sat in one corner of the saloon at a table. But the Mexican said nothing in return. He was holding his mouth in one hand and rocking back and forth in his chair because of the pain of his broken teeth.

The Cutter, with one boot propped on the brass rail at the foot of the bar, set his glass of whiskey down slowly and carefully, with a grimace of growing frustration. He looked down at Dial at the other end of the bar and laughed. It was not real laughter, only a short, scoffing bark of sarcasm.

"And quite the job of it you did," he said.

"He got lucky, is all," Dial answered without looking at the Cutter.

"Just like he got lucky with your brother?"

"He must have had the drop on Bobby, or got him in the back," Dial said.

"I was there, remember?" the Cutter said. "And let me tell you, Jones gave it to him head-on."

"I'll get him."

The bartender was sitting in a chair over by the stove at the back of the room, trying to pretend like he was reading a copy of the *National Police Gazette* and not paying attention to them.

The Cutter took his boot off the rail and turned to face Dial. "Give me one reason why I shouldn't shoot your sorry ass right now and finish what Jones didn't."

"What?" Dial turned slowly to face the Cutter, the rag still held over his nose. He eyed the pair of Colt Thunderers in the Cutter's shoulder holsters, and it was apparent he was making some calculations about possible outcomes he didn't like and trying to think of what to say that wouldn't get him killed.

"Easy, gentlemen," the bartender said, suddenly upright in his chair. The burlesque, wood-engraved illustrations of hurdy-gurdy girls and crime adventure scenes he had been perusing in the pink paper pages of the magazine were forgotten and dropped into his lap. "Take it outside if you can't act friendly in here."

"Mind your own business," the Cutter said, without even looking at the bartender.

The bartender sat back in his chair with his eyes darting from one man to the other. And he didn't say anything else.

Dial held up a hand to the Cutter. "I know you're mad about something."

"Something?" the Cutter snapped at the skinny Texan.

"Like I said, that was personal business." Dial backed away a half step before his back bumped into the wall behind him. "You and Jones some kind of friends?"

"I don't have any friends, Johnny. What I do have is a job," the Cutter said, "and the people that hired me have certain expectations about how it should be done. If I do it well, I'll get paid, then you get paid. That's how it works.

Maybe you're different, but I don't let anything get in the way of me getting paid."

"You can count on me. You know that." Dial's already swollen, broken nose made him sound like a man with a head cold. "Getting even with Jones has got nothing to do with what you're talking about. Doesn't bother it at all."

"Jones is the job."

"What?"

"You've never even heard of Buckskin Creek, have you? Or maybe Buckskin Joe? Used to be quite the place."

"Well, why don't you cool down and tell me?"

"You listen real close, Johnny, because I'm getting real tired of talking to you," the Cutter said.

"All right. All right," Dial said, and held up his hand again, as if that would ward off the Cutter's anger.

"The Phillips Mine was a dandy when Buckskin Joe was in its prime, but it played out, or at least it looked that way. But Joe Smith and Saul Barton didn't think so. Some years ago they bought that old mine and were starting to make a fortune cleaning up what the Phillips people hadn't been smart enough to find and what they left in their tailings pile," the Cutter said. "But my employers at the time had the same idea, and they offered a higher price for the mine the same day it was sold to Smith and Barton. The Phillips people wanted to accept that offer, but they had already shaken hands with Barton on the deal. Only thing was, though, Barton wasn't as savvy back then as he is now, and his lawyers were sloppy with their paperwork transferring the ownership. The kind of men I was working for notice that kind of thing.

"I was off on other business, but some of the other boys on the payroll were sent one evening to convince Barton and Smith that they didn't own what they thought they owned. In the meantime, Smith had gotten sick and Barton had to go with him over to Leadville to see a doctor. They were working those diggings by themselves, and with them gone it should have been easy to take over the place."

"And what happened?" Dial asked, as carefully and reluctantly as a cat dipping its paw tip in water.

"Those were three hard men sent up to the Phillips Mine. I knew every one of them," the Cutter answered. "But they couldn't get it done. Barton had hired a fool kid to guard the mine while he was gone. Nobody knew that boy from Adam other than some of the men over at Leadville had stuck him in a boxing ring a few times to entertain themselves. Maybe that's why Saul thought he was tough enough to guard the mine, and it turned out he was right. That kid sent those three hard men back the way they had come, except one of them was riding belly-down over his horse's back. Care to guess who that kid was?"

Dial shrugged and gave the Cutter a nervous smirk. "Tell me."

"It was Jones," the Cutter said. "That little stunt he pulled was all the talk for a while. I'd guess that reputation's what got him the job in Shakespeare later on working as a mine guard. You know, shaking down miners after their shifts and trying to catch anybody high-grading. Dragging their sorry asses out of the saloons and making sure they went to work on time and busting heads on anyone who spoke up against the company or the wages it paid. Shakespeare was a company town, and the men who owned the mines were getting rich and expected it to stay that way."

"Never heard of the place," Dial said.

There was a long pause before the Cutter spoke again. "If you had, then you would've heard about what those same miners did when they had their fill, or at least what they tried. Fifty or so of them got roaring drunk one night, and when they got their courage up, they thought it a good idea to burn the whole town down and blast the mines closed. Only they didn't get it done. The same stubborn cuss that stopped those men on Buckskin Creek walked out with a pick handle in his fists and broke that mob. Broke it before it ever got good and started. Earned himself that nickname. The Widowmaker."

"Are you trying to tell me you want Jones for yourself? Wanting a little payback for your friends?" Dial asked.

"What I'm saying is that Jones is likely working for Barton again, and that makes him strictly business."

Dial lowered the rag from his face. His nose was broken badly, and the swelling was already moving to his eyes. There was dried blood all over his chin and down the front of his shirt. "Well then, he's in our way. All the more reason to kill him. I'll do it for you, or I'll help you. Doesn't matter to me, so long as he pays for what he did to my brother."

"You'll do what I tell you and when I tell you. No more and no less," the Cutter answered. "Barton's got himself a claim up in the mountains. And we're going to take it from him. And we're going to do it without anybody being able to say we did it or how we did it."

Dial nodded. "I got you."

"Half the people in this two-bit spot in the road watched you try to kill Jones, and they saw you with me. Our employers don't like that sort of man working for them. They expect a certain . . . how do you say? *Finesse*, that's it."

"All right, I understand. If you had told me this before, I could've waited."

"Do you really understand? I need to hear you say it." The Cutter turned his head and aimed one ear Dial's way. "I'm waiting, Johnny."

"Won't happen again. Not until you say," Dial answered. "It's just that finally meeting Jones set me off wrong. I don't guess I was thinking right. Probably better if we wait until he's up in the mountains and get him then, just like you said. Roll him under a rock and nobody will know.

"You're getting it now."

"Never meant to cross you."

The Cutter glanced at the Mexican sitting over in one corner at a table with his head leaned back against the wall behind him and his eyes closed. "What about you, Cholo? You savvy me and Johnny's little talk we're having?"

The Mexican opened his eyes and nodded, but even so little of a movement of his head caused him to wince. He leaned over and spat blood onto the floor, then put his hand gingerly back to his mouth.

"Damn, if you two aren't a pair," the Cutter said as he looked from one to another of them and shook his head.

"Are we good now?" Dial asked. "You and me?"

The Cutter waited, saying nothing and doing so on purpose. He watched Dial as closely as a hawk looking for the telltale wiggle of the grass to know when a rat was moving.

"I've already apologized," Dial said.

"Quit your chatter, Johnny. Maybe I was going to blow you all over that wall, but I've changed my mind. I guess you're starting to grow on me."

There came the sound of horses outside the saloon, and then the door opened. A short man in a thigh-length blanket capote with red-and-black stripes at the bottom hem of it stepped inside and nodded at the Cutter. That style of coat, made from blankets once used to trade with Indians and worn by some American and French trappers, hadn't been popular since the heyday of the beaver fur trade.

The man flipped the hood of his blanket coat back and revealed the coyote fur cap on his head under that hood. Thin, stringy long hair hung well past his shoulders, and his cat-yellow eyes were as unusual as his coat and that hair.

He glanced at Dial and the Mexican, obviously noticing their condition.

"Are the rest of the boys with you?" the Cutter asked.

The man wearing the capote nodded, then he looked again at Dial and the Mexican. "They look like they tangled with a wildcat. Hate that I missed the show."

"We've just been playing pinochle and waiting for the new to wear off Del Norte's fast women and whiskey enough for you boys to show up."

The man in the capote gave Dial and the Mexican a wry glance. "Remind me not to play cards with you. What now? Are we staying or traveling?"

"Traveling. That old man that went out with Barton this summer left out of here just before dark. Him and five others."

"Five?"

"Nothing we can't handle. We'll push upriver a ways and make camp. You ought to have no trouble tracking them come daylight."

"Shouldn't. That many will leave plenty of sign."

The man in the capote went back outside, and by the lamplight cast through the open door the Cutter could see portions of several horses and their riders waiting. He went to the door and took his coat down from a peg on the wall. It was made of heavy corduroy with a goose-down quilted lining on the inside and beaver fur on the collar and the sleeve cuffs. He shrugged into the coat and looked back into the saloon before he went outside. Neither Dial nor the Mexican showed any signs of moving.

"You staying or going?" the Cutter asked.

"Cholo's mouth is busted bad," Dial said. "There's a dentist in Del Norte."

"Well then, Cholo should have had the sense to do like I said and he would still have a mouth full of teeth," the

Cutter said. "And I suppose you think you need a doctor for that nose of yours."

"I'll be all right."

"You'd best be better than all right. And that goes for you, too, Cholo. Get up and get on your horses, and maybe I'll let you have another chance at Jones and that big Indian of his. Let you show me that you're worth your wages."

"I go with you," the Mexican said as he got up.

Dial waited for the Cutter and the Mexican to pass through the door, then followed them outside into the night. The man wearing the capote and the other new arrivals were on their horses. One of them brought the Cutter's horse over to the saloon, and he swung up in the saddle.

"Getting cold," the man in the capote said.

Another of the newcomers snorted. "Worked with a Canadian one time. No matter how cold it got, he always had to tell you one better about where he came from. Snows there were always the deepest, and the wind blew the hardest, you know. Ice ten feet thick. Only thing he said worth remembering was that the good thing about winter is it lets you know you aren't in hell."

Most of the men laughed at that, all except the Cutter. He looked to where the man who had said that about winter sat on his horse. "Not yet," he said. "Not yet."

Then he reined his horse around and led them toward the gap in the mountains. They were ten tough men, including the Cutter, and every one of them loaded down with gun steel as heavy as their past crimes and sins.

CHAPTER FOURTEEN

Newt woke the next morning to find that the rock cliff face they had slept beneath was bigger and higher than he had guessed in the dark. Happy Jack had camped them in the mouth of a canyon with the cliff on one side and a knob of a mountain on the other. Willow Creek passed down through that narrow gorge, and it was up its course that Happy Jack led them riding single file when they broke camp.

For a short ways, the canyon was so tight and tall-sided that you could only see a thin strip of sky straight overhead and the bottom was cast in shadows. Not too far along, both the creek and the canyon forked. Happy Jack led them up the right-hand branch. The rock bluffs topped with dark timber continued on their right, while the all-but-bald mountainside to their left became a little more gently sloping. Maybe a mile up from their night's camp, they came to a flat along the creek slightly wider than what was behind them. There was a white canvas stretched over a pole frame that served as a tent or cabin and a horse corral back in the aspen trees behind it. That corral was made of two ropes strung in parallel for railing and using some of the trees for posts. Newt could tell that horses or mules had been kept there the past summer, for the beaten ground inside the makeshift pen was littered with old manure and the bark on the trees inside the enclosure was gnawed off up to about head high and the inner portions of the trunks were grooved with teeth marks.

He also noticed the little pile of tailings and stacked stone on the bluff side of the creek and higher up and right against where the ledge went straight up to the sky for fifty or so feet. It was plain that somebody had been working at the foot of the rock face there.

He watered the Circle Dot horse in the shallow trickle of water running over the bed of creek gravel while the others dismounted. There was a thin crust of ice along the edges of the creek bank.

Tully Hudlow was the first off his horse, but he barely had both feet on the ground before a skinny, midsized red dog with a curled tail and of no particular breed came out of the tent, growling and barking.

"Quit that racket," Happy Jack said in a loud voice.

The dog stopped barking but didn't quit growling. The hairs along its spine were standing straight up. Its normally erect ears were tilted back on its head, and its lips were curled enough to show its teeth. It advanced on Tully in slow, halting steps.

"I said quit it!" Happy Jack scolded. "Act like you've had company before."

The dog's tail wagged slightly at the sound of the old prospector's voice, and it quit showing its teeth. However, the arrival of so many strangers still had it on high alert. It circled Tully and his horse, sniffing and glaring, and stopped once to scratch at the ground with all four feet.

"Don't mind old Rufus," Happy Jack said. "He doesn't see so good anymore, but he'll get used to you."

"That dog better leave me alone or he won't get time to get used to me," Tully said. "I'll kick his fool head off."

Happy Jack glared at Tully, but he called to the dog again in a milder tone, "Come on, Rufus. You be a good dog, now."

Happy Jack's dog showed no sign that it heard him, and Newt realized that it was not only nearly blind but also likely almost deaf. The dog circled the rest of them like it had Tully, then it calmed down some. Newt was off his horse by then, and the dog stopped in front of him and stared at him. Newt squatted down and held out a hand to the decrepit old mutt.

"You're going to get yourself bit. I got dog bit bad once . . . one of Pa's hounds. Big old redbone, and he snapped me like a steel trap right here on the lip." Tully said, and pointed at his mouth.

"Hell, that old pot licker couldn't do anything but gum you to death," Tandy said, while he, too, eyed Happy Jack's dog.

Newt ignored the brothers and continued to hold out his hand. The dog came a step closer and then another, with its neck stretched out and taking in his scent. Both of its eyes had a milky blue film over them, and Newt didn't know how it could see at all.

Newt said nothing to the dog and continued to wait it out. It came forward far enough that it put its nose to his hand. After a moment, it sat down and Newt rubbed its head. The dog leaned against his hand as he scratched its neck under its leather collar, and it pushed up closer to his chest and wagged its tail, liking the feel of the attention it was being given.

Happy Jack watched the proceeding and nodded at Newt and the dog. "Wouldn't have believed that if I wasn't looking straight at it. Old Rufus doesn't like many, but he seems to fancy you. Traded for him one winter in a Cheyenne village outside Fort Hays when he was just a pup. Those red heathens were dragging him to the cook pot when I first saw him, and he was whining and fighting for all he was worth, like he knew what was about to happen to him. I've always figured that's why he doesn't trust people."

Newt shrugged and stood back up.

Tully was still keeping a cautious eye on the dog, but Tandy had seen Newt petting it and thought he would do the same when the dog came walking by him. The dog lunged and tried to bite him, and Tandy barely managed to jerk his hand back out of the way.

Tully laughed, and Tandy whirled on him with both fists doubled. "What are you laughing at?"

"I'm laughing at you," Tully said.

Tandy took off in a run right at his brother, and Tully didn't hesitate to charge back at him. They met with grunting impact, fists flying. Tully was the first to land a solid blow, and he planted an overhand right squarely on Tandy's forehead. Tandy staggered back a few steps, shook his head, then kicked Tully in the knee. After that, they grappled again and went to the ground, rolling around and gouging and clubbing each other. The dog, excited by all of the action, darted around the edge of the fray, barking and threatening to dart in and take hold of one of them. By then, both brothers were gasping for air and the fury of their battle tactics was weakened by the exertion.

Happy Jack looked at Newt. "You going to stop them?"

Newt looked at Mr. Smith and jerked his head at the fighting brothers. "Reckon they'll kill each other?"

"They fight hard," Mr. Smith said.

Newt looked back at the brothers on the ground. Both of them were too tired by then, and nothing much was happening, other than Tully had Tandy in a headlock and was trying to squeeze his head in two.

Newt went over to the brothers and kicked a cloud of

dirt and dust over them. "You two want to fight, then you go back where you came from."

Tully didn't let go, and Tandy squirmed and kept rabbit-punching Tully on top of his skull. They wrestled around a little more until Newt reached down and grabbed Tandy by the back of his suspenders and yanked him free of the tangle. Mr. Smith came over and grabbed hold of Tully and hauled him back until there was enough distance between the two brothers that they might have time to cool their tempers.

"You finished?" Newt asked when Tandy quit trying to break free of the grip on his suspenders.

Tandy wiped away a bit of blood leaking from one of his nostrils with his hand and glared at his brother. "I reckon he's had enough."

"I ain't hurt," Tully said. "Come get you some more."

Again, they tried to break loose and go at each other, but Newt and Mr. Smith managed to keep them apart. Tandy quit fighting Newt pretty quickly, but Tully continued to struggle against Mr. Smith. In fact, he was swinging his fists and fighting like a wildcat, though it wasn't doing him much good. Mr. Smith was simply too big.

Newt saw what was about to happen before Mr. Smith even reached inside his coat. He barely managed to yell for the Mohave to stop, keeping Tully from taking another hard rap on the head. Mr. Smith paused with his hand still inside his coat.

"You can't go around knocking everybody on the head like that," Newt said.

Mr. Smith gave Newt an almost apologetic, guilty look that reminded Newt somehow of a kid caught with his hand caught in the cookie jar. That image should not have matched with the fearsome appearance of the Mohave, which made it even funnier and more absurd.

Mr. Smith shoved Tully away and let go of his club.

Tully started to run at him, but he thought about it long enough to change his mind. He pointed at Mr. Smith's coat.

"That would have been the second time you've pulled those sticks on me," Tully said. "And I saw you use them on that Mexican back at the Gap."

Mr. Smith gazed back at the kid without expression, then slowly nodded after a long moment between them. "Guns are good, but any man can aim and pull a trigger. To get close to your enemy and strike him is the mark of a real warrior."

"I'll take a gun, but I admit you're pretty handy with those head knockers," Tully replied. "Wouldn't mind having a look at them."

"Maybe I'll show you how *kwanamis* fight some time, but first you must do as he says and make no more trouble with your brother." Mr. Smith pointed a finger at his mouth and then at one ear. "Mouth closed, ears open. That is the way for the young when they first walk on the war trail."

Tully frowned at him but didn't make an issue of Mr. Smith lecturing him, likely because he was half the Mohave's size and his earlier efforts at battling the giant hadn't gotten him anywhere.

Tandy pulled against Newt's hold again. "Let me go. I ain't going to hurt him no more."

Newt let him go.

Tully snorted his disbelief at Tandy's words. "You couldn't whip me if you wanted to. Never have."

Newt was about to grab hold of Tandy again to keep them apart, but the kid turned to face him.

"Don't you ever lay hands on me again," Tandy said. "You're supposed to be some kind of big-shot boxer or whatever, but don't you do it again. You do and I'll—"

Newt never let Tandy finish whatever else he was going to say. He hit the kid on the chin with his left fist. It was only a half punch, a short straight jab, but enough to knock Tandy down.

Tandy landed on the seat of his pants with a stunned look on his face. He rubbed his chin and then wiggled his jaw to make sure it still worked while he stared up at Newt.

"Get him, Tandy!" Tully called to his brother.

Tandy gave Tully a scowling glance, then muttered, "Don't believe I will."

"You were saying?" Newt asked.

"All right, so you're the toughest," Tandy said. "Are you going to let me back up?"

Newt took a step back to give the kid room. Tandy got up and dusted himself off, still eyeing Newt.

"Go help Jose unpack those mules," Newt said. "Or do you want to fight over that?"

Tandy started toward Jose, but he paused and looked back over his shoulder at Newt before going on, as if he had been about to say something else but had suddenly thought better of it. Tully followed him, and whatever wrath they had shown each other before seemed to disappear as quickly as it had taken hold of them. They helped Jose with nothing more than a few muttered dares and threats at each other but with little sign of real anger in their words. Before long, they were helping with the gear like nothing had happened between them. Newt even heard them laughing a couple of times.

Newt left the Circle Dot horse saddled but loosened its cinch and slipped the bridle off. He let the gelding go to pick at what little grazing it might find. Happy Jack had told him the truth, and there was little for a horse to eat in the canyon.

Happy Jack noticed Newt turning the saddled horse loose without hobbles or a stake rope. "Good way to lose him. I mind the time when losing my horse meant a damned long walk or maybe I didn't make it at all."

"He'll stick around close," Newt said, watching the work Jose and the Hudlow brothers were doing.

They were stowing most of the gear and supplies on the ground beside the tent and under a canvas tarp. Happy Jack saw what Newt was looking at.

"If it was me, I'd store my food up high," Happy Jack said. "Hang it or build you a cache house up on a platform or in a tree. Keep the bears from robbing you."

Newt picked up on the implication that Happy Jack wouldn't be staying in the camp, but let that question lie. "Lots of bears hereabouts?"

Happy Jack nodded. "Lots of black bears. Grizzlies, too, but not so many. Haven't seen one in two or three years, or maybe more."

Tandy heard that bit about the bears, and he stopped what he was doing and looked at Happy Jack. "Did you say grizzlies? Might not get me a buffalo, but I'd like a crack at one of those big bears."

"You tangle with Ol' Ephraim, and you'll wish you hadn't. He's bad business," Happy Jack answered.

Newt had heard many Westerners refer to grizzlies as Ol' Ephraim, although he had never encountered one of the big brown bears himself.

"How big do they get?" Tully asked.

"Big enough," Happy Jack answered.

Tully was carrying his rifle in one hand and his saddle on his other shoulder toward the tent. He stopped and laughed and hefted his rifle and shook it. "Give me a crack at one, and I'll take it."

"You take a shot at one with that pop gun and all that's

left of you is liable to be what we find in his scat pile,"
Happy Jack threw back at him.

Jose was tying the unsaddled pack mules together, string-
ing them out nose to tail. And his horse was still saddled.

"Is he leaving already?" Newt asked Happy Jack.

"Looks like it, but ask him yourself," Happy Jack answered. "Jose don't take to being bossed nor asking him too
many questions, kind of like those fool kids you brought
with you."

Newt didn't bother Jose and instead went to the Circle
Dot horse, took his bedroll off his saddle, and went inside
the tent. There was one camp cot in the room with bedding
already on it. Newt assumed it belonged to Jose or Happy
Jack. Other than that cot, there was no other furnishing in
the room other than a sheet metal sheepherder's stove in the
center with a chimney pipe running up from it through the
peak of the roof.

Newt went to the back wall and laid his bedroll there.
Tully came in behind him and took a spot closer to the door.

"Home sweet home," Newt said.

"All right by me," Tully answered. "We've been mostly
sleeping out on the ground since we left Tennessee."

Newt kept his rifle, which he'd been carrying all along,
and went back outside. Happy Jack had caught his dog and
tied a short length of rope to its collar. The other end of that
rope was tied around Happy Jack's waist. The old prospector was walking away, leading the dog, with his rifle and a
rolled set of blankets thrown over one shoulder.

"Where are you going?" Newt asked.

Happy Jack didn't quit walking. "Don't you worry about
me and old Rufus."

Newt noticed that Happy Jack was heading up the

canyon and not down it. He looked at Jose. "Where's he going?"

"*¿Quien sabe?*" Jose said, as he climbed back on his horse. "He comes sometimes and visits, then he leaves again."

Newt turned back to Happy Jack. "Thought you worked for Saul."

"Oh, I do him a favor here and there and make myself a little grubstake to see me through," Happy Jack called over his shoulder. "But you couldn't pay me to do what you boys do. No sir. Stay up in the high country and mind your own business, that's what I say."

Newt watched him go out of sight. He was an odd old man, and the visage of him leading that blind dog was as unusual as he was.

Tandy came up to stand beside Newt. "What's the matter with him?"

"Nothing other than I think he likes to keep to himself, and that's not a bad way to be."

Jose had gotten the mules in order and was about to set out back down the trail. Newt waved at him to stop him.

"Figure I'll ride back down the trail a ways with you. Might get a chance to shoot some camp meat, and thought I'd look around and get my bearings."

Jose's only reply was a shrug, and he simply led off with his mules and Happy Jack's horse in tow. Newt went to the Circle Dot horse, readied it, and mounted. He followed behind Jose until they passed out of the canyon and into view of the river in the distance. There, Newt stopped his horse, while Jose continued on. Neither of them had said anything to each other on their brief journey. Newt lifted his hand in a gesture of parting, Jose nodded, and that was that.

A flat plain ran a couple of miles to the west, and low

foothills dotted with low pines rose up on the east side of the creek. Newt headed into the hills and found the top of a hogback hump of open ridge that provided him a good vantage point where he could scan to the south toward the river and where it disappeared into the mountains to the west and farther toward its source. He looked for any stirring of game that might provide meat for their cook pots, but it was also in his mind that he might find some grass along the river that could be cut and hauled back to the claim to stockpile and feed their horses. It was only an idea that he hadn't thought fully through, but it was also one that was driven by knowing that Happy Jack had spoken the truth. The immediate area around the claim offered little to no grass for grazing, and how to get the horses through the winter without starving them to death was going to be an issue.

Most of the treeless, open countryside before him was covered in a thin stand of short grass varieties, especially on the higher ground and away from the river, but it wasn't tall enough to cut and gather, even if he had the haying tools, such as a scythe, to do so. They could do as Happy Jack had suggested and turn their horses loose on the range between the canyon mouth and the river. Most horses would manage to paw their way through the snow if it didn't get too deep and get at the old grass beneath to give them some roughage, but he didn't like the possibility of losing them if they drifted or wandered or if they were stolen by some chance passerby.

He knew that many of the Indian tribes used small cottonwood limbs and bark to get their horses through the worst of the winter and did the same with aspens. The inner bark on both trees had some nutritional value, but he also knew that some Indian ponies often starved to death. And the survivors were always weak and thin by the time spring came, no matter how good a winter campground was chosen. That was the very reason the army often raided the tribes' winter camps, because they knew their opponent's horses would be in a weakened condition while their own were fed stockpiled and cured hay that was supplemented with corn and oats. It was also the reason that Indian war parties rarely raided until after the spring's green-up had put flesh and strength back into their war ponies.

It was barely a mile to the river from where he was at. He had seen the tracks and manure piles left by cattle in the hills on his way down, and it seemed they had eaten down whatever lusher, taller growth might have grown in the bottom. Or perhaps it had been a dry summer and a bad year for grass. He turned and rode back to the north, not the same way he had come, but taking a swing to the east and on a course that would curve him back to the mouth of the canyon.

The temperature was dropping. Already, he could see the smoking breath coming out of his and his horse's nostrils, and steam was rising from the edges of his saddle blanket where the horse had worked up a sweat.

Not far above the river, he came in sight of a log cabin. There was a barn and a couple of outbuildings and a corral beside it, the whole layout setting not far out from a steep climb of mountain behind it. No woodsmoke rose from the chimney, nor were there any other signs of current habitation, so he guessed whoever lived there was gone. And he also guessed that the homestead was what Happy Jack had referred to as Wason's ranch. The entire place looked well-built, and it had a beautiful view of the river and the mountains on the far side of the valley.

He made his way back to Willow Creek and followed it toward the canyon. He was almost to the canyon's mouth when he heard a gunshot in the distance.

He stopped and looked back the way he had come, but there was no sign of anyone at all and no speck of movement that caught the eye. But the sound of the gunshot had been plain for what it was, though he thought it had come from farther downriver. Jose had gone that way, but it had been hours since they had parted, and he should have been nearing Wagon Wheel Gap by then.

Newt listened for another gunshot and continued to watch the terrain down-country from him. After several minutes of observation, he turned and rode back up the canyon to the claim. It was starting to snow before he made it there. At first, it was a few scattered and tiny flakes, then a light falling.

Tandy Hudlow was cutting a log into firewood lengths with a single-man crosscut saw, while Tully was splitting the cut pieces with a double-bit axe. Each fall of the axe cracked louder than it should have in the confines of the canyon and in the cold, still air. Mr. Smith was nowhere to be seen.

Newt pulled up near where the Hudlow brothers were working. "Did either of you notice what kind of rifle Jose was carrying?"

It was Tully that rested his axe and gave him a questioning look. "It was a Winchester in .32-20. I saw a box of his cartridges under his cot in the tent."

Newt considered that information. The .32-20, like most of the caliber options in the Model 1873 Winchester, was underpowered and more suitable to pistols or as a small game cartridge. The boom gunshot he had heard sounded more like it had come from a more powerful gun. It was hard to tell sometimes the way sound echoed or carried over the terrain, but he was almost sure that that gunshot sounded more like a big-bore Winchester such as his own '76 Model, or a Sharps or Remington or something.

"Why are you asking about Jose's rifle?" Tully asked.

"Where's Mr. Smith?" Newt asked instead of answering Tully's question.

Tully pointed up the mountain. "Last I saw him he was sitting up there in the rocks staring at the sky and singing or praying or something."

"One of you go fetch him," Newt said, and he took off his hat and slapped it against one thigh to knock some of the snow off of it.

He put his hat back on and yanked his Winchester out of his rifle boot and dismounted. He dropped the reins on the Circle Dot horse and walked a ways back down the creek and stood at the edge of their camp with the rifle held in the crook of one elbow. The snow was coming down harder now—big, slow falling flakes.

Tully had already gone to find Mr. Smith, but Tandy stood at the woodpile behind Newt, watching. "Are you expecting trouble?"

"There's always trouble, it's just a matter of what kind and when it comes."

Chapter Fifteen

The Cutter and his men had camped for the night not far upriver from Wagon Wheel Gap, and the sun was well up when they finally stirred out from under their blankets. And it was even longer before they had fed themselves and saddled their horses. As it was, it was late morning before they finally struck out upriver in search of Saul Barton's claim.

They were strung out in a long line following the stage road when the Cutter decided to ride up on the higher ground to the south of the trail and have a look. The rest of his party rode on, but he was up there looking over the countryside when he noticed that they hadn't gone far before they stopped. Something ahead of them seemed to have their attention.

It didn't take him long to find what they were looking at. A man on a black-and-white paint horse was coming toward them, leading a string of mules with empty packsaddles on their backs. A single saddled and riderless horse was strung in line with the mules.

The Cutter's men ducked off the trail and took cover down in a dry wash. He hoped the fools were merely being cautious until they had a good look at who it was coming their way, but it was just as likely that they were arranging an ambush.

He wanted to ride to them, but there was little chance that the man on the paint horse wouldn't spot him moving along the foot of the mountainside. He decided to sit on his horse in stillness and watch the proceedings. Even though he was farther away, he recognized who was coming by the time the man on the paint horse was within two hundred yards of the gully hiding his men. It was the half-breed Indian he had seen with the old man back in Wagon Wheel Gap. He had been told the old man worked for Saul Barton, and he had seen the old man and the half-breed ride out of the Gap with the Widowmaker and the others.

He wondered if the breed was going back to the Gap for more supplies, or if they were already that near the claim. All he had been told by his employers was that Barton had spent the summer prospecting the San Juans above Wagon Wheel Gap and that he would likely find the claim somewhere along the headwaters of the river. He was supposed to find that claim and take it and hold it.

He was still pondering what the breed's presence might mean when he saw one of his men crawl up to the lip of the gully with a rifle ready. The breed was within a hundred yards of the gully when the rifle boomed. The Cutter knew instantly from the sound of the gun that it was the Mexican they called Cholo who had fired the shot. The Mexican carried a Sharps rifle. The Cutter swore under his breath and spurred his horse down toward the fight.

The heavy fifty-caliber cast-lead bullet spinning out of the Sharps' bore and riding the explosion of a 110-grain black powder charge hit the breed like a hammer and almost knocked him from the saddle. He reeled for a brief instant before he righted himself and reined his horse around and headed back upriver toward the claim. The Cutter could see several of his men with their rifles trying to find a bead on the fleeing, wounded breed, but none of them fired.

The breed laid low over the front of his saddle and lashed the paint horse with a quirt, urging it to run for all it was worth. He was three hundred yards away by then and gaining ground with every stride. No more shots came from the gully, though the Cutter could see some of his men scrambling to get to their horses. He thought he saw the breed sway and wobble in the saddle again like he might fall off just as he and the paint horse topped a low rise, but man and horse soon disappeared from sight.

The Cutter arrived at the gully at the same time his men managed to get on their horses—all of them except Cholo. The Mexican was going up off the bank of the wash carrying his Sharps buffalo rifle. He held his other hand to one cheek, and his mouth was bleeding again. The Cutter slammed his horse to a stop from a run right in front of Cholo.

"What the hell are you doing?" he asked.

"That breed was with them back at the Gap." It was Johnny Dial who spoke, not the Mexican. His whole face was so swollen and his eyes such little slits that it was a wonder he could see at all.

"So you thought you would bust him?" The Cutter asked. "Bust him without my say-so?"

Dial glanced at the Mexican, but the Mexican was still holding his mouth and wasn't looking at either of them.

"Cholo had him dead to rights. Figured we might as well get started now," Dial said.

"Well, he missed," the Cutter said.

The Mexican removed his hand and said something, but his words were too slurred to understand and he didn't finish whatever he was trying to say, but grabbed his mouth instead.

"That Sharps stock punched him in the mouth," Johnny said.

"I no miss," the Mexican said, and then spat blood on the rocks at his feet.

The Cutter started to tell all of them how stupid they were, but he wouldn't have hired them if they were the kind of men you insulted lightly. And there were more of them than him, no matter what kind of bluff he held over some of them. And the breed was getting farther away while they remained there. It wouldn't do for him to make it to the claim and warn any others there. The Cutter spurred his horse toward the stage road, and the others followed him, leaving Cholo to try and catch up.

They first passed the mules and horse that the breed had turned loose in his flight, but they didn't stop or slow and kept riding after him. The breed's retreat led them along the river. The valley was mostly open ground, keeping them in sight of him most of the time, but he had a good head start on them. Accordingly, the race went on for better than half a mile and then more. On they went, beyond the mouth of Willow Creek and then around the bend where the river turned south and the valley began to narrow once more. By then, their horses were starting to falter after such a lengthy sprint. A horse could only run like that for so far, but the Cutter knew that the breed they were chasing was in the same predicament. A little more than two miles into the chase, they finally closed in on their prey. The paint horse had slowed to a trot and was not far ahead—close enough that they saw there was no rider on its back.

They slowed their pursuit, taking care to look for the breed if he had fallen wounded somewhere between the paint horse and them and keeping their eyes on the timbered ridge points hanging out over the river above them in case he had decided to take a stand. It was the man in the blanket capote coat who dismounted and found blood and a few boot prints where the breed had fallen from his horse and then got back on his feet and ran.

"He went up there." The man in the capote squatted over the boot prints and then pointed at the maze of mountain ridges running down to the river. Those ridges were knife-edged and steep-sided and densely timbered. Several of the draws leading up between those ridges consisted of open glades of grass littered with jumbled stones the size of a man's head.

"He's trying to find a place to make a stand," the Cutter said.

"I think he's all but done for, if he ain't already dead," one of the men replied.

"Damned Indians take a lot of killing," another said. "Cholo already knocked the stuffing out of him with his fifty, and that didn't do the trick. Don't like the thought of him up there maybe taking a bead on me."

They followed the tracks of the breed up into one of the draws, riding slowly with their rifles ready. It began to snow, and the farther they rode up the draw, the steeper the climb became. After a while, the Cutter got down off his horse and led it, and those with him did the same. None of them said much, for they were too intent on watching the timberline above and on each side of them. By then, it was snowing hard.

The man in the capote pointed to another blood splatter on the fresh white dusting of snow, then he pointed to the talus slope and rockslide at the head of the draw a couple of hundred yards ahead of them. There were a few scattered and sickly looking trees higher up the worst of that rock pile, and a little lower than that there were several broken ledges that the rockslide had flowed around.

"What do you make of it, Arnie?" the Cutter asked the man in the capote.

"I'd say he's up there," the man in the capote answered.

"No way he climbed that in the shape he's in," Dial said.

The Cutter looked at Dial. "All right. You go ahead of us. Go on up there and show us he isn't there."

Dial didn't make any attempt to ride on ahead, not liking the thought of covering all that open ground and then climbing the rockslide with the breed possibly up there waiting.

"And I supposed you noticed that the rifle boot on that paint horse was empty, didn't you?" the Cutter asked.

Dial gave no reply, and he made a concerted effort not to look at the Cutter, likely not wanting to admit that he hadn't thought to look at the breed's horse to see if the breed might have a rifle with him or not. And Dial, like all of them, knew that a rifle could make all the difference.

The Cutter waited long enough for Dial's foolishness to soak in on him and for the rest of the men to see that before he spoke again. "Good place up there for a man to make a stand, if that's where he's run to. High ground. Good field of fire."

A couple of the men threw curious glances at the Cutter, noticing his use of terms that were more suited to a soldier.

"I heard you were in the army or something back when," Dial said. "That true?"

The Cutter's attention swung back to Dial, but he did not answer the question.

"None of my business, of course. Just asking," Dial said, and then snickered as if he was remembering something. "I joined up once. Spent a whole winter at Fort Griffin, but by the time spring came, I'd had my fill of army life, and I lit out of there without asking anybody's leave. Do this, do that. Those officers thinking they were something special just because some other fool like them pinned rank on them."

Again, the Cutter made no comment, but he was slow to take his gaze off of Dial. When he finally did look away from the Texan, he slapped his mittened hands in an attempt to warm them while he stared up the draw where they thought the breed had gone.

"What do we do now?" the man in the capote asked.

"We could leave a couple of men here, then split up, and one bunch of us get up on that ridge and the rest of us go up the other. Get higher than him in the timber and try to come down on him," the Cutter said.

"He'll see what we're doing if he's up there. And if he isn't hurt as bad as we think he is, he might slip off on us while we're in that dark timber," the man in the capote replied. "And if it snows any harder, we aren't going to see him, anyway."

"He's bleeding like a stuck pig," Dial said.

"All right, we settle down here and wait," the Cutter said. "We'll keep an eye on those rocks and see if he moves. If he's alive he's hurting, and time's on our side."

The snow was already a solid covering of white on the ground by the time they moved over to one side of the draw against the foot of the ridge, where the tree limbs offered them some shelter. They could still see the rockslide from there. A couple of the men built a fire while the rest of them stood around or tended to their horses. The temperature felt like it had dropped ten degrees already.

"You think you can hit him this time?" the Cutter asked the Mexican.

The Mexican nodded.

"Then get you a rest for that cannon, and don't you dare take your eyes off those rocks."

The Mexican jerked his saddle off his horse, stood it on

end on the ground, then sat down behind it and beside the
fire. He rested the heavy single-shot rifle's forearm across
the back end of the upright saddle and flipped up the Vernier
tang peep sight and adjusted the elevation to suit him.

"How far can you hit something with that thing?" one of
the men asked.

The Mexican didn't answer, perhaps because he had
failed to make a killing shot earlier at a lesser distance or
perhaps because his mouth hurt too badly.

"They say Billy Dixon busted an Indian off his horse at
danged near a mile with a Sharps like that," the same man
that had asked the earlier question said.

"Who's Billy Dixon?" another asked.

The Cutter gave them all a look that quieted any more
such conversation about buffalo guns and Indian fighters.
They all stood close to the fire with their hands in their coat
pockets and their shoulders hunched.

"Damn, it's getting cold," Dial said.

By that time, the Mexican had draped a blanket over
his head and shoulders to keep some of the snow off him.
Beyond their names, the Cutter didn't know either of those
two very well and didn't care to, though he believed that the
Mexican had come up from Texas with Dial and that their
acquaintance was longer than a recent one. Both of them
had looked like they were running from something when he
had stumbled across them in a saloon in Las Vegas, New
Mexico Territory, on his way to Colorado. Or perhaps it was
the other way around and they had stumbled across him. In
fact, he didn't even know the Mexican's full name. The man
had introduced himself simply as Cholo, and the Cutter had
asked no questions to find out more.

He looked over all of them as they stood around him
in the snow, seven hardcase killers and thieves and dry-
gulchers, and he liked not one of them. Two he had ridden

with before, but he knew them little better than he did the rest. Nor did he trust any of them, even if they followed his lead. There had been a time when he rode with much better, but that was long behind him, so far back that it might as well have been in a different life.

Again, he looked at them. They were simply tools and voices taking up space in his head for the moment. But that was often the way it went with the kind of work that he was good at. There was no "help wanted" advertisement for such employment and no formal recruitment other than finding yourself among the company of other such men when an opportunity arose. And when that happened, a man's credentials were often nothing more than a hard air about him and a willingness to break the law and to set his strength against whoever he was told to or needed to.

The older he got, the more he came to learn that the world operated by a certain economy where such men had their place. No matter what some would say, every person had a price, and morality or a lack of morality had no part in that transaction or that pricing. Just because a man or woman couldn't be paid to kill didn't mean their life wasn't for sale. Some wouldn't cheat or steal, but there were plenty that would, all for a price of one kind or the other, either their own or someone else's. He had shot the second man he ever killed for thirty dollars. Thirty dollars, that's what a man's life was worth that time, and that's what it cost to buy another man to murder him.

He looked from one to the other of those around him. When this was over, what would it get any of them? Whores, whiskey, a night or two at card tables until the money was all gone? A bullet in the guts? A hangman's noose or a long stint in jail? He admitted that he was no different. Maybe they had come to realize, just like he had, how cheap life really was. That it was better to be the murderer than the murdered and better to ask a price for your worth than to be auctioned off with no say of your own.

Johnny Dial moved under the trees to get his spare shirt out of his saddlebags while the Cutter brooded. It was a thin shirt, but maybe another layer under his coat would help. He shivered and stamped his feet when he got to his horse, and he blew on his bare hands before he tried to unbuckle one of his saddlebags. The man in the capote came walking by, coming from his own horse. The Cutter simply called him Arnie, if he called him any name at all.

He stopped beside Dial and said quietly, without looking at him, "I'd quit that talk about the army if I was you. Kirby won't like that."

"What do you mean?" Dial asked in the same quiet voice

"He was an officer with the Second Dragoons."

"How do you know that?"

"Scouted for him once. That's how I got in on this deal."

"Lots of men have done time in the army."

"Not like him. He was West Point. Real professional, fire-eating type. Spent some time back in the old days at Fort Union and Fort Massachusetts, patrolling and fighting the Indians up and down the valley. Was in the that big fight after the Utes raided Hardscrabble."

"How come he's not still in the army?"

"The big brass didn't like how he operated. They caught him paying his men in whiskey and giving them extra leave for trophies. Wasn't his men who ratted him out, it was a cleaning girl who found them in his quarters."

"Trophies?"

Arnie shrugged and flicked a crust of half-melted snow off the one tip of his mustache. "Indian scalps, fingers and ears strung on strings . . . trinkets and other such."

"Did they court martial him?"

Arnie shrugged again.

"He ran, didn't he? Deserted, just like I did," Dial scoffed, but instantly realized his voice had gotten too loud.

"You tell him that if you want to, but I wouldn't if I was you." Arnie walked back to the fire and left Dial alone.

Dial added a second shirt over the one he was wearing and got back into his coat. He had no gloves like the others were wearing, and especially not a pair of beaver fur mittens like the Cutter had. He was scolding himself for not purchasing something for his hands before they had left the Gap or while he was in Del Norte, and he was blowing on his hands again as he walked back to the fire.

Nobody said anything when he returned. The Cutter was standing apart from the rest of them and staring up the draw.

"How long do we wait?" Dial asked after some time had passed, unable to take the wait in silence like the rest of them.

"Give it a while," the Cutter said, as he wound his wool scarf several times around his neck and covered the lower part of his face. "Maybe he moves, or maybe he bleeds out."

"I think this snow is settling in to be a good one," Arnie observed. "He's going to be one miserable fellow up there."

"Well, he isn't going to be the only one that's cold," Dial muttered. "Wish he would move so Cholo could bust a cap on him and then we could find somewhere better to wait this storm out."

"What'd you say?" the Cutter asked.

Dial shivered and held his hands out over the fire. "I said I wish I had never left Texas."

CHAPTER SIXTEEN

It took Zuri all of the next morning to bury her father, or at least to bury him as best she could. Despite her plans not to, she had ended up having to drag him down the ridge behind the jenny. She had used a shovel to scoop out a shallow trench beside the creek to lay him in, then she covered him with creek stones.

It was well into the afternoon before she had the jenny packed with everything she thought she might need or could manage to find. The bear had busted and splintered the grub boxes, the very same wooden boxes her father had built to perfectly fit inside the packsaddle panniers. He had been a cabinetmaker when they still lived in Spain and had loved working with wood. But she tried not to think about him when she could help it.

Not only had the bear broken the boxes, but it also had torn open their flour sacks and the last bag of beans, as well as biting holes in the only remaining tin of condensed milk. Most of the rest of the larder that had been in the grub boxes also had been ruined or devoured. She raked up what she could of the beans that the bear had left scattered on the ground and put them in a sack, then did the same with a portion of the spilled flour.

She tied the beans and the flour to the packsaddle frame,

along with two rolls of blankets, the axe, and a skillet. Those, along with a few other things she carried on her person, were all that she had decided to take with her.

The snow had quit falling sometime the night before, and that had lasted through most of the morning. But it was snowing again by the time she was almost ready to leave. Not as heavy as before, but the flakes were still big and coming down steadily.

She had not rolled and packed one of the blankets she had taken from the tent, saving it for another purpose. She used her father's sheath knife to cut a slit in the middle of it so that she could pull it over her head and it would cover the front and back of her over the top of her coat. She had seen a Mexican sheepherder down on the desert wearing a wool blanket over his head in a similar fashion, and she improvised her own poncho after what she had observed. She buckled her father's belt and knife over the poncho to hold it in place. She hadn't been able to find his hat, but at least she had her wool stocking cap. It wouldn't do as well to fend off the snow as the brim of her father's hat would have, but it would keep her ears warm.

The last thing she took up was the rifle, and in one of her coat pockets were two more cartridges she had found for it. She led the jenny to the same rock she had used before and mounted. Past experience with guiding the jenny had taught her that she needed both hands free, so she had tied a loop of string to the rifle's trigger guard. She hung the rifle barrel-down from the saddle by that loop.

By the time she was up on the jenny, the pile of rocks covering her father was already nothing more than an indistinct white mound of snow. She didn't let her gaze linger on that mound, for she feared she would never leave there if she did. She pulled the jenny around and started it away from the campsite without another look back.

The stream led down the mountain, and that was where Zuri pointed them. But mostly, she let the jenny choose their way. The snow was already ten inches deep on the ground and getting deeper.

She half expected to encounter the surviving sheep, the sheepdog, or her father's horse, but she didn't. Not even when she was far down the mountain from the camp.

Her mind must have wandered, for she found herself deep in a stand of dark timber without recalling exactly how she had arrived there. It was only a limb slapping her in the shoulder and dumping snow down inside her poncho and coat that startled her out of the daze she had been in.

The forest was so dense and tangled with low limbs that it was difficult to navigate, and she had to guide the jenny to prevent being dragged off its back. But at least the thick conifer limbs offered respite from some of the falling snow and from the wind that had started to gust. Before long, the snow was coming down almost sideways and the treetops were swaying.

It was hard to see anything through the trees, much less with the blowing snow blinding her, and she decided to stop for a while and take shelter under the spreading boughs of a large spruce tree. She dismounted and squatted next to the foot of the tree with the jenny pulled close to her for a windbreak. She wasn't there for very long before she regretted her decision to try and wait for the storm to blow itself out. She was cold, and there was already enough snow on the ground that it would have been hard to find any wood to start a fire. Even if she could have found enough fuel, she wasn't sure she could have lit a fire shivering and shaking like she was and with her fingers stinging and hurting like they were. Her thin wool mittens weren't enough, and she tucked her hands under her armpits and rocked back and forth in an attempt to get warm.

It wasn't much longer before she became fully aware that she was going to have to get back on the jenny and find a better shelter. The little gray mule seemed as miserable as she was, standing with its back humped, its tail tightly tucked, and its head down and both ears pinned. It didn't move at all when she climbed on its back once more. In fact, she had a hard time getting it to set off down the mountain again, and when it did go it kept trying to turn around, not liking having to travel down the mountain with the wind and snow hitting it dead-on in the face. Zuri's legs were already tired from kicking the jenny, the only way to keep it moving. The rein felt like a club in her cold, numb hands.

At first, she tried to face the wind as the jenny was having to do and to pick the best way for them, but the snow was blowing so hard that she could barely see twenty feet in front of her. Soon, she gave up and pulled her stocking cap down to her eyebrows and tucked her chin inside her coat collar. Like the jenny, she leaned into the teeth of the storm with her head bowed and with her only sense of anything being the feeling that they were still going downhill.

How long that went on, she couldn't tell. Time stood still, and there was nothing but a swirling world of white. And it was so cold. She had no thermometer, but if she had, she would have seen that the temperature was already below zero and dropping.

Perhaps she fell asleep, perhaps her body simply became so numb that it felt like sleep. But something shook her from that place she had drifted off to, and it took her a moment to realize that the jenny had stopped. Zuri wiped the snow from her eyelashes, blinked several times, then looked around her. It was hard to tell anything, both because of the limited visibility and because her mind was as numb as her body. But they seemed to be down off the mountain, or at least they had come to some sort of flat or bench among the timber where the slope wasn't as steep.

The snow was already almost up to the jenny's hocks, and the blizzard showed no signs of letting up. Zuri knew that she had to find some kind of shelter or she and the jenny would likely freeze to death.

Then she saw what looked like a snowbank at the foot of another slope that ran down at a diagonal from above and joined the one she had been following off the mountain. What's more, the sight of that snowbank reminded her of something her father had once told her.

She urged the jenny toward the mound of snow. Twice, she lost sight of it, though it was only thirty or forty yards from her. She didn't know that they were crossing the little stream, the same one that had led her down from the sheep camp, until the jenny slipped on a patch of ice and almost went down.

The jenny barely had time to right itself and splash across the stream before it plunged into a drift and sank down until the snow was all the way up to its belly. There it struggled and lunged, trying to break free. Zuri slid off its back, and she too sank, though not so far as the jenny had. The snow was almost up to her waist.

She eyed the drift in front of them, where the mounded snow was the highest. That snowbank had formed there because the wind had blown it against a cluster of boulders at the foot of the slope, and the V of the intersecting ridges and the streambed made a natural place for it to gather. She rubbed the jenny's neck and tried to calm it, and again she thought of what her father had taught her.

Was the snow deep enough for what she needed? No matter, it would have to do. Neither she nor the jenny could go any farther.

She dug with her hands around the jenny, freeing its legs

and making some room for it to stand more comfortably. That done, she began to dig in front of the mule and away from it toward the snowbank, scooping snow and flinging it out of the trench she was making. The snow was powdery dry and moved easily, but her hands soon ached with the cold so badly it brought tears to her eyes. She wished she had brought the shovel with her, then she thought of the frying pan tied to the packsaddle. She went back to the mule and untied the black cast-iron skillet from the packsaddle.

The frying pan made her digging much easier. Using it for a scoop and working down on her hands and knees, she soon had a trench that got deeper the farther she dug her way back into the drift. The walls of the trench soon became a tunnel. She stopped her work several times to tuck her hands under her armpits in an attempt to warm them.

Deeper and deeper into the drift she dug. The farther in she went, the farther she had to carry the pans of snow back to where she had started, pitching the panfuls up on the drift and adding to its height. At the end of her tunnel she shaped a chamber, a little room in a fashion of some animal's burrow.

Little rabbit, dig, dig, dig, she thought. *Dig a warm little hole.*

How much snow did she need around her to insulate her shelter? Her father had said that he had once known a man who had been caught out in the blizzard much like the one torturing her, and the only way he had survived was by digging into a snowbank. According to her father, such a snow cave might not be cozy warm, but it would keep one from freezing to death.

Once she had made enough room in her burrow to sit upright and move around somewhat freely, she went back out to the mule. The poor thing was still standing as it had been when she left it. She hated that it had to suffer such conditions, but there was no way to dig a big enough shelter for both of them. She was already so exhausted and cold that her hands wouldn't work well enough even to remove the packsaddle.

Somehow she managed to get the rolled blankets and the rifle down, and she crawled with them back into her shelter. One blanket she laid on the floor, and the other she covered herself with, wrapping it tightly about her and over her head until she only had a small hole in front of her face to see out of. In that fashion, she faced out into the blizzard. She could not see the jenny, only a faint bit of light at the end of her tunnel.

The burrow felt no warmer than she had been outside, and the blankets didn't even seem to help, but at least her improvised shelter kept the wind off of her. There was that, and she was in better shape because of it. She hugged her arms and the blankets tighter around herself and tried to quit shivering. Her teeth chattered, and during the worst of it she wondered if that's how someone would find her when the summer sun finally melted away the snowbank— some hunter or trapper wandering through the wilderness and stumbling upon her remains curled up in a ball as stiff and brittle as an icicle. They wouldn't even know who she was or where she came from, if anyone came at all.

I have dug myself a grave the same way I dug father's, she thought. *And here I will stay until I am nothing but bones.*

She waited and hoped and listened to the howl of the wind outside. Hours passed, or at least what felt like hours. It was growing darker outside. Was it already night, or was that because the snow was filling in the passageway leading into her shelter? She had not considered that she might be buried and unable to get out. She promised herself that she would pay attention and clear the snow at her tunnel entrance when she had to, but that snow was also keeping some of the outside air from getting to her, and though she didn't realize it, it was also allowing the chamber she sat in to retain some of her body heat.

The fact that she was starting to feel less cold dawned on her slowly. She shivered less and her teeth quit chattering all together. She was cold, but not painfully so. By then, it was so dark inside her burrow that she could see nothing at all.

Again, the fear of being buried came over her, and she was warm enough to move and do something about it. She put her blanket aside and crawled down the tunnel with the frying pan and dug at the snow that had almost totally blocked the opening to her burrow by then. Instead of trying to completely reopen the tunnel entrance, she dug close to the ceiling, pulling the snow back to her and packing it into the floor. When she had an opening the size of her head, she quit and peered out of it. Night had truly come, but she could still make out the jenny, or the shadowed shape of it, through the flurries and the moonless black. The poor little mule had not wandered off, and it stood right where she had left it.

She crawled back to her den and wrapped the blanket about her again. How long could a snowstorm last? Surely, it would quit before the morning. But the snow came down as heavily as ever well into the night, and the wind continued to blow. She could hear it howling and singing strange, wailing songs, although those eerie sounds were muffled by the snow around her.

Alone. She felt more alone then than when she had found her father's body. She would have cried again, but she had no tears left. She would have shouted for help, but she knew there was no one to help her.

CHAPTER SEVENTEEN

It was an icy draft of air that woke Newt from his bedroll. He rose to a sitting position, and his first glance was at the stove, thinking that it had burned out and needed more wood. He rubbed his face in an attempt to come fully awake, and when he took his hand away he saw what had let all the cold in the tent.

The Circle Dot horse had pushed the tent flaps back with its nose and was standing with its head and neck inside the tent. Its eyes were closed as if it was asleep.

"Get that horse out of here!" Tandy Hudlow said, then shivered and pulled his blanket up over his head.

"He always likes a fire." Newt pulled on his boots and got to his feet.

"Smart horse. Can't say as I blame him," Tully said, not sounding as bothered by being woke up as his brother was, but also remaining under his blankets.

"Well, good for him," Tandy said, with his voice muffled by his covered head. "If he's so dad-blamed smart, then he can build his own fire and quit fanning those tent flaps and freezing me half to death. One of you put some more wood in that stove, why don't you?"

Mr. Smith rose from his corner of the tent and put a stick of firewood into the stove. He pitched it into the firebox with enough force to cause a shower of sparks to fly out of the open stove door and land on Tandy.

"Here now!" Tandy come up off the floor slapping at himself and looking for embers that might have landed on him or burned his blankets.

Mr. Smith gave a thin smile at the kid's antics, then his face went serious again. "The horse is marked with the Sacred Circle and the Eye Of Power. It is a symbol of the Run Far People who live to the south in the land of the Mexicans, though there are others who know it as a spirit wheel and shape it differently."

"Don't be filling their heads full of nonsense," Newt said to Mr. Smith while he pushed the horse's head back outside.

"What you're saying is that his horse used to belong to the Indians?" Tully asked.

"Got him from the Comanches and not any Run Far People," Newt said.

"Shut those tent flaps. You're letting all the heat out." Tandy was standing by the stove in nothing but his red long-handle underwear and a blanket thrown over his shoulders. He was hopping from one foot to the other with his arms hugged across his chest.

"I need to pee, but I don't want to get up," Tully said.

Newt continued to stand with his back to them and to hold the tent flaps open so that he could see outside. It was already turning daylight, and he saw that the snow had quit. He rubbed his face again, still half groggy because he hadn't slept long enough or well enough because of the gunshot he had heard. He had waited and watched the canyon until nightfall and then until the cold and the snow drove him to the tent when he could take it no more.

He let the tent flaps fall shut and went to finish dressing. Tully Hudlow darted out from under his blankets and went outside still in his socked feet and without a coat. When he came back to the door, Mr. Smith pitched him a knife.

"Go cut some meat," he said.

When Tully came back the second time, he was still carrying nothing but the knife. "No elk steaks this morning. The hindquarter that Ute left hanging is froze solid. It'll take a saw to cut it."

"There's some beans left in the pot from last night," Tandy said.

"I'm sick of beans."

Mr. Smith shoved between the two of them with a jar of sourdough starter under one arm. He picked up a bowl and began to mix flour and other ingredients in with some of the starter. He shaped the dough he made into little hand-patted balls and put them inside a Dutch oven. He worked as fastidiously and with the same attention to detail as he did when he was making his tea, like some strange alchemist in his workshop fussing over his chemicals and proportions. When he was finished, he set the Dutch oven on top of the stove, then scooped some coals from the firebox with the ash shovel and placed them carefully on top of the oven lid.

"I can take beans again as long as I get one of his biscuits," Tandy said, then looked up at Mr. Smith. "What a fine biscuit you made yesterday morning?"

"He do make a fine biscuit," Tully replied, "but that elk hindquarter's won't last forever. I figure one of us ought to go see if he can scare up some more meat."

"Good luck hunting in this weather," Tandy said. "I doubt much game will be stirring."

"I'll go," Newt said. "Like to look around a little more."

Both of the Hudlows looked disappointed. It was plain they were avid hunters and had looked forward to trying their hand at bigger game than they were used to back in Tennessee. And like the young men they were, camp life, even after only one day, was already boring them. Newt couldn't blame them. He never had liked to sit still for long himself. He wanted to be doing something, working or moving. Waiting was always harder.

"I want one of you down canyon standing guard," Newt said. "You can rotate out, but keep watch. Find a good place up high where you can spot anybody coming up the canyon."

"I reckon we can handle that," Tandy said.

"Make sure they do like they're told," Newt said to Mr. Smith.

Newt waited for a share of breakfast, and when that was done he slung his pistol belt around his waist, put on his sheepskin coat, then his hat. He took a handful of spare cartridges from his saddlebags and put them in one coat pocket, then he took up his rifle. It was a '76 Winchester chambered for .45-75. The gun had originally been an express rifle variation of the model with a shotgun butt plate and folding leaf rear sights, but someone in the past before Newt had acquired the weapon had cut the half-round, half-octagonal barrel down to carbine length. The tube magazine was also trimmed to a half magazine and held only five rounds with one in the chamber.

He went out of the tent and found the Circle Dot horse standing just outside. He saddled the gelding, stuffed his Winchester in the boot, and mounted. The snow was only ankle deep, but enough for him to leave a distinct trail as he rode out of camp.

He went up the canyon instead of down it. It was cold, but not unbearably so. Just enough that he folded up the collar of his coat, buttoned it all the way to his chin, and slipped a pair of elk-skin gloves on his hands. The Circle Dot horse was stepping out, the crisp morning making it spry and full of energy, and he let it trot up the canyon.

The canyon stayed tight, but the slope of the canyon

walls on either side became less steep. He was a quarter of a mile from camp and looking for a way to ride up and out of the canyon when he felt he was being watched.

He stopped his horse and searched the canyon ahead of him and the heights above him, yet saw no threat, but he was a man that had long before learned to trust his gut hunches. He let the Circle Dot horse walk forward a few steps, then stopped as he had before. Farther up, the canyon constricted once more, and a thin stand of timber ran down almost to the creek. And though he couldn't prove it, he felt someone was up in that timber watching him.

He turned the Circle Dot horse and started up the bald mountain on his left, zigzagging to pick the easiest way. He didn't look back as he climbed out of the canyon, but the dog tracks along the creek and the woodsmoke he had smelled were on his mind. He couldn't prove that Happy Jack had been in the timber watching him, but he wasn't about to ride on up that canyon and find out.

He found a saddle across the crest of the mountain and rode down the other side until he hit the west fork of the creek. He went slow, scouting for game for their cook pot, but he saw nothing, not even any fresh game tracks.

He followed that fork of the creek all the way to where the west and east canyons joined back together, then turned and rode back toward camp. He passed Tandy Hudlow on his way. The kid had found a spot behind a blown-down tree up on the canyon side about fifty yards above the creek. It was a decent place to stand watch, but he wasn't concealed as well as he probably thought. Newt saw him easily. That and the fact that Tandy was sound asleep and snoring loudly made him pretty easy to locate.

"Wake up," Newt said as he rode past.

Tandy jerked upright and was about to say something,

but Newt was already too far past him to hold a conversation. Mr. Smith and Tully had built a fire in front of the tent and were sitting on a log that served as a bench when Newt reached camp. He dismounted and came to stand by the fire across from them.

Mr. Smith had his teapot sitting on a thin bed of coals beside the fire, heating his water, and he had removed both his buffalo coat and the dress coat beneath it, despite the temperature being below freezing. He had both his war clubs out and was holding them for Tully to see.

Both war clubs were carved from single pieces of screw beam mesquite, dense and hard as stone, although the weapons were of two different designs. One was short with a straight, thick handle with a leather wrist loop and an enlarged, four-inch-diameter cylinder on its end. Its shape resembled a potato smasher. The cylinder-like knot on the end of that club had been carved out to make it concave, and the edge around that cupped depression had been sharpened. It was painted or dyed a dark red, and the handle was black. The other club was a simple, straight stick about an inch-and-a-half in diameter and about two-and-a-half-feet long, painted all black, and with the same wrist loop built into it.

"*Halyawhai*," Mr. Smith said, and he hefted the potato smasher. After that, he shook the straight club in front of Tully. "*Tokyeta.*"

"Let me see," Tully said. He took hold of the potato smasher and made a downward chopping motion with it.

"Not like that." Mr. Smith took the weapon back and pantomimed an underhanded, upward stroke like a boxer's uppercut. That was obviously a blow meant to take an enemy under the chin, then he made other compact punching and stabbing motions.

"What's this one for?" Tully asked when Mr. Smith let him hold the straight, stick-shaped club.

Mr. Smith mimicked various striking motions, pretending he was holding the club. It was easy to understand that the slim club was meant as a slashing weapon with the advantage of greater reach.

"The warriors of my people usually learn to use one or the other."

"But you use both?" Tully asked.

Mr. Smith nodded, and that nod was the closest thing to pride or bragging Newt had ever seen the big Mohave show. That surprised Newt almost as much as Mr. Smith letting anyone handle his war clubs, especially considering how superstitious the Mohave was.

Mr. Smith, as he sometimes did, seemed to read Newt's mind, and he said, "Young warriors must learn."

Tully didn't like that referral to his age and his lack of experience, but he resisted saying so. He seemed truly interested in Mr. Smith's ancient battle gear.

"Not saying I'm not impressed, but Pa always told us that the good thing about a rifle is that you can keep a fight at a distance when you need to," Tully said.

"A rifle is a powerful weapon," Mr. Smith replied. "But there is little honor in using one, and if you shoot all of your enemies, you will have no prisoners to take back to your people."

"Prisoners?" Tully asked.

Mr. Smith stood and snapped the clubs into the spring steel clips on his shoulder harness, one under each arm. "Yes, scalps are good, but prisoners are better. Take them back to your village so that all can see the enemy you have beaten. Let the children chide them and the women cut them and the old ones sing and dance like when they were young. That is how the people stay strong and brave and fearless. That is how they will be proud and not doubt the true ways."

Mr. Smith folded his dress coat over one arm, then bent and picked up his teapot before walking back to the tent. He left Tully with somewhat of a shocked expression on his face.

"Is he serious?" Tully asked Newt.

Newt nodded. "Serious as can be."

"Where's he going?"

"To make himself a cup of hot tea," Newt replied. "He likes tea."

Tully shook his head in disbelief. "Indians back home dress like us, but I ain't never seen anything like that man. Where the heck did you find him?"

Newt gave that some thought, but he was unwilling to share what little of the Mohave's history he knew

"It's all right. You can tell him," Mr. Smith said from inside the tent, obviously able to still hear them.

"Mr. Smith grew up in the old ways of the Mohaves. Fought the army when he was young, but when his tribe lost out, he thought he would see the world where the white men who had defeated him came from. He wanted to discover the source of their power. Walked to the coast, and a sea captain took him aboard his sailing ship," Newt said.

Mr. Smith came out of the tent carrying a steaming mug of tea and with his suit coat back on. He sat down on the log.

"Is that about right?" Newt asked him.

"It is not exactly the way it was, but close enough to the truth," Mr. Smith said. "The captain was British, and he taught me to speak your tongue and he taught me to be civilized, something he believed in quite strongly. Now there is a word, *civilized*. I have pondered its meaning ever since I first heard it spoken."

"So you were a sailor?" Tully asked.

Mr. Smith nodded. "I have sailed far on strange waters. Seen many lands and tribes, but the strangest to me were the books the captain kept in his cabin. That was a power I did not expect."

"Did you ever see a whale?" Tully asked. "I saw one in a picture book one time."

"Many whales and many other creatures such as I had never seen before," Mr. Smith answered. "At first, I was a common sailor, and at the last, his first mate, though that took me many years. By my second year, I could read. And the things I learned were greater even than fish as big as a ship. Every time we made port, the captain would search for more books to replace those we had already finished, and we would sit and discuss the things we read. And he would answer my questions, for I had many."

"How come you didn't stay at sea?" Tully asked.

"I liked the ship, but I wanted to go home, and I wondered if some of my people still lived or if they were all gone and no more."

"And after that?"

Mr. Smith took a sip of his hot tea and looked away from Tully. "I found it was not the same as when I left."

"What do you mean?"

Newt saw that Mr. Smith did not want to tell any more, but Tandy came walking up behind Newt and that redirected the conversation.

"If I catch you falling asleep again when you're supposed to be on guard, you can pack your gear and leave," Newt said to Tandy.

"Won't happen again," Tandy answered.

"It better not. One of you go back down there."

"I'll take a turn," Tully got up from the log. "You worried about Jose?"

"Maybe," Newt said.

Newt led the Circle Dot horse away from the fire by a bridle rein. He unsaddled it and turned it into the corral with the other horses. Tully or Mr. Smith had cut some aspen limbs and piled them in the corral, and the other horses were already gnawing on them. The brown gelding joined them.

Newt left the corral and started toward the creek and the foot of the high bluff.

"Where you going?" Tandy called after him.

"Going up to look at what work Jose has done for Barton," Newt said.

The creek was shallow but too wide to jump. Newt was careful of the ice along its edges and made it across in two long, lunging strides in an attempt to keep his boots as dry as possible. Once across, he rubbed the leather down with handfuls of snow to absorb what moisture he could.

The place where he had seen sign of somebody chipping away at the bluff was about twenty yards above him. A steep slope of loose earth mixed with gravel and rock led up to it. The leather soles of his boots had a hard time finding purchase on the snow and the treacherous footing beneath it, but he managed to make it.

Somebody, perhaps Jose or perhaps Barton or Happy Jack, had done some work on the rock face, but very little. So little, in truth, that Newt was surprised. What he had thought was rock litter and smaller tailings from the start of major assay work or the beginnings of a mine shaft was actually only pieces that had broken off the bluff naturally and come to rest there. There was a hammer and a pair of old rusty rock drills lying there, but only a few flakes and chunks had been removed from the rock face with those tools. He could also see traces of pick marks on the rock, like the scattershot holes a woodpecker left on a dead tree.

Happy Jack had told him Jose's job was to continue proving up the claim, but from what Newt saw, the Ute had done next to nothing as far as that work. Besides that, Newt would have expected that there would have been far more excavation done in order for Barton to gather what he needed for his original assay of the claim.

He looked up and down the foot of the bluff, searching for signs of other work sites, then turned and looked across the creek to the other side of the canyon. Perhaps what he had found was nothing more than some of Barton's initial prospecting and the site that had made Barton optimistic enough to file a claim was elsewhere.

He took one last look at the rock face beside him. He was no rock hound geologist or even any kind of layman expert when it came to prospecting or analyzing ore veins and the telltale signs of precious metal deposits, but he had worked in several mines and around the business for years. He went back down to camp with lots of questions nagging at him.

Tandy was eating one of Mr. Smith's leftover biscuits when Newt made it back to the fire. It had started to snow again by then.

"There's one more biscuit left," Tandy said around the bread stuffed in one cheek. "Found some cherry jelly in the supplies. You can't beat it."

Newt almost snapped at him but held it in. He tried to sound a little less irritated but didn't quite manage that feat. "You and your brother eat enough for four men. Don't you ever get full?"

"I'm telling you, you've gotta try this jelly," Tandy said, as if Newt's teasing hadn't registered with him at all. Then he grinned.

Newt couldn't find it in himself to stay mad at the kid, even though he had caught him asleep while standing guard and even though he and his brother were perpetually hungry and ate like ravished wolves every chance they got.

Mr. Smith had gone inside the tent, and Newt wanted to talk to him alone.

"You see any game on your ride?" Tandy asked before Newt was halfway to the tent.

Newt shook his head and didn't stop.

"Mind if I give it a try?" Tandy asked.

"No, stick close to camp." Then Newt stopped and looked back at him. "And don't go up the canyon."

A gust of wind blew through the camp and lifted some of the powder off the ground and swirled it about in a white cloud.

"Why not up the canyon?" Tandy asked.

Newt grabbed at his hat and shoved it down tighter on his head to keep it from being blown away when another, slightly stronger gust ripped up the canyon. "'Cause I've got a hunch that old man's pretty serious about being left alone."

CHAPTER EIGHTEEN

Zuri woke in a panic from where she lay curled on her side among her blankets, and it took her a while to fight down the panic and to realize what had jolted her from her slumber. It was the wind. Not blowing and roaring, but silence that was almost as loud as the storm had been. Was it over?

She crawled down the tunnel while groping ahead of her with both hands to feel her way. She realized that the snow had buried her only means of exit long before her hands felt the cold touch of it. She dug at the blockage, thinking that she would easily break through, but she didn't. The snow piled up around her in the tunnel, and she had to use her feet to shove it farther back toward the chamber behind her. How much did she dig away? A foot? Two feet? And still she didn't break through to the outside.

She wasn't as strong as she had been the day before, and twice she had to stop digging and rest. When she had about given up hope, she thought she could see a dim light through the snow, like a lantern held against it from the outside, and she knew she was getting closer. She crawled back into the shelter and retrieved her father's rifle. When she had returned with it, she poked into the snow, probing.

She had pierced the rifle almost as far as she could into the wall of snow when it broke out on the other side. Immediately after pulling the rifle free, a cool draft of air seeped into the hole she had made. She asked herself how close she might have come to suffocating herself while she pressed her face close to the hole and breathed in deeply. The fresh air was so cold it hurt her lungs, but it still felt good. When she felt refreshed, she put her eye to the hole and peered outside. There was daylight, but not bright sunlight.

She used the rifle and her frying pan to dig away enough snow to escape, then wiggled her body out into a world of white and drab gray. She had expected to find the jenny lying frozen to death, but the little mule was nowhere to be seen, and there was not a single track showing which way it had gone. The snow had long since filled in any sign of the jenny's passing.

She looked behind her at the snowbank and discovered that it was twice as tall as it had seemed when she had dug into it the evening before. That was no wonder, because the entire forest floor was now covered in snow, and in places the windward sides of some of the trees were banked up as tall as she was. The limbs of trees were sagging with the weight of the load on them, and while she watched several of them sagged enough or snapped to dump mounds of snow to the ground. It was like small explosions and a cloud of smoke every time one landed.

Fire. She needed a fire, but every bit of wood she might scavenge was buried, and even if she could find some, it might be too frozen or wet to get it to burn. She only had a handful of matches in her coat pocket and could ill afford to waste them, but something had to be done because she was cold and getting colder with every passing moment. To make matters worse, what little food she had was with the jenny, wherever it had gone.

Stay or move on? Winter had come, and it wasn't leaving soon. She needed to get to a town, and she was perfectly capable of walking, the same as she was of riding the mule. It didn't take her long to decide she was going to keep trying to get off of the mountain.

She went back inside the snowbank to get her blankets. When she came out, they were rolled and hanging across her back and one shoulder by a piece of string tied to either end of the roll. The rifle she held in one hand, and before she had taken a few steps, she was using it to probe ahead like a walking stick to help her keep from falling.

After a few hard-fought steps, she stepped off into some kind of a hole or a drift and sank to her waist. She could not go forward or back, no matter how high she lifted her feet.

The snow hiked her skirt up to her hips, and the thin wool long-handled boy's underwear she wore underneath was poor protection against the icy press surrounding her thin legs. She leaned out until she was all but on her belly and flailed and wiggled and pumped her knees. She did not climb out of the drift, but rather pushed her way through it. Luckily, she did not have to go far. The snow on the other side of the drift was only barely above her knees, although that was still tough going. She was already breathing hard and her heart was pounding in her chest, no matter that when she looked back at her shelter she saw that she had only managed to travel a few yards or so.

She reached the stream. It was frozen over and covered in snow in most places, but she found a hole the current had kept open, took off one mitten, and reached down into the weak trickle of current and scooped a handful of water to her mouth. It was so icy that it hurt her teeth, but she scooped another handful and swallowed it before her hand hurt too badly. She doused that hand into the snow to dry it, then quickly put the mitten back on.

She wandered into two more drifts before she found a spine of ground in the center of the ridge where the snow was less deep and managed to move faster. From then on, she looked for higher ground and rocky outcroppings where the snow hadn't accumulated as deeply and where the going was easier. But it was still a struggle.

Her knees were wobbly and shaking, both from weariness and from the cold, when she stopped to rest for a spell, but her hands were the worst of it. Her knitted wool mittens were simply not enough to keep them warm. Her only other pair of long wool socks, or stockings, besides the ones on her feet, was inside one of her coat pockets with all of the other odds and ends she had thought to take from camp. She cut a thumb hole in each of the socks, slipped them over her aching hands, and put the mittens back on over them. Her improvisation offered immediate relief, and she was proud of her idea and wished she had thought of it sooner.

It took her two hours of bucking the snow to pass through the stretch of dark timber. For the first time in two days, the sun was promising to burn through the overcast sky when she came into sight of the alpine meadow through the trees ahead of her. When she broke out into that glade, she almost shouted with joy simply to feel that little promise of sun on her face and because the wind there had blown back some of the snow and made traveling easier. She became even more excited when she caught a view of the river valley below her in the distance. Suddenly, she was not as tired as before.

The long, narrow meadow led down to another stand of timber before dropping off steeply to another larger meadow. The drainage she followed toward the river was simply a long chain of glades and meadows following the bottom of a draw. It turned to canyons in places and then widened again.

She looked back behind her several times at the pair of grooved tracks she left behind. And each time she looked back, she wondered how far she had come, as well as how much farther she must go.

She came to the end of a third meadow, picked her way across the icy bog above an old and long-abandoned beaver dam, and came to a point where it looked as if the mountain dropped away out of sight all at once. A scraggly mix of spruce and pine trees grew there, some of them dead snags, standing like lonely sentinels at the sheer edge of the world. Before she even reached them, she could see an uninhibited view of the river. It was almost right below her, maybe less than a mile.

When she reached the trees, she saw that she was at the top of a steeply sloping rockslide. Rocks of every size and shape formed it, and the flow and movement of those rocks under the force of nature and gravity had only been thwarted by a ledge of even larger stones in the middle of the slide. There, the smaller rocks had parted like a stream, buckling and splitting around some obstacle too strong to yield to the current.

She was so caught up in the view and the sight of the river that it took a while for her to register everything she saw. Then it dawned on her that there was a man kneeling against the uphill base of the rock ledge in the middle of the slide and there were other men coming up toward him from below—several men, scattered in a wide line across almost the entire width of the slide.

Her initial reaction was to want to call out to them, but she hesitated. She had seen men with guns before, but something other than that caused her to close her opened mouth. The shout she was about to give never went beyond a sharp inhale of breath. She stood behind the wind-scoured and beetle-mangled trunk of a dead pine tree and peered around it. That's how she saw what happened.

Before she even had time to decide what so many men on the mountain meant, the man down behind the ledge rose up and fired his rifle at one of the men below him. He fired the rifle one-handed, and there seemed to be something wrong with his other arm, for it hung limply at his side. She saw where his bullet knocked snow and fragments from a rock in front of the man it was meant to hit. Then one of the men coming up the slide, a short man in a white, hooded blanket coat with red-and-black stripes at the bottom, stopped and fired his gun back at the man behind the ledge. The man behind the ledge staggered and fell, but he got back up again. Instead of shooting back at those who had wounded him, he broke into a hobbling run behind the ledge, using it for cover to shield him. A portion of his body must have been revealed to the men attacking him through some crack or hole in the rocks, for another of the men fired at him. The bullet missed and ricocheted and deflected uphill.

She was frightened but unable to keep from watching the fight. The wounded man ran out from behind the cover of the ledge, leaping from the top of one rock to another and angling to cross the rest of the slide and reach the cover of the timber at the edge of it. He had dropped his rifle and was clutching his side as if that was where he had been hit, and his bad arm still hung limp and useless.

He made three or four lunging leaps before they shot at him again. She thought she saw him flinch or hesitate, but he kept going. Then he dove into the trees at the edge of the rockslide. It was hard to tell who fired that shot, but her attention was drawn to the man among them in the little round-topped hat and the coat with the fur at the collar and cuffs. He was bigger than the rest of them, and he was pointing into the trees with his rifle where the wounded man had gone and shouting something at the others.

Zuri knew she should run, but her body wouldn't seem to respond as fast as her mind. She stared down at the men below her, and just before she broke and fled, she locked eyes with the big man. He simply stared back at her, seemingly as shocked by what he saw as she was. Then she was running for the same timber where the wounded man had gone.

She feared they would shoot at her, but they didn't. The trees were close together and the ground was rough and broken, but she didn't stop. At least not until she skidded to a halt at the edge of a little canyon and saw the gray jenny standing in the bottom of it.

The pack mule still had its packsaddle in place. She heard the men behind her. They were coming her way and talking back and forth to each other. She was about to run down to the jenny when the wounded man appeared below her and leapt onto the mule's back. He kicked it and slapped it on the rump with his good hand, and it ran down the bottom of the canyon and was soon out of sight.

The men were still coming through the woods, and they would see her soon if she didn't do something. She scrambled down the side of the canyon, slipping and falling, and finally simply sitting down and sliding down the steep slope. At the bottom, she turned and ran the way the jenny had gone. The mule had broken a clear track for her in the snow, and that aided her speed.

She had no way of knowing if the men were pursuing her or if they were only after the man they had shot. Were they some kind of policemen and the man they had shot an outlaw? None of them had been wearing uniforms, and everything in her warned her that those men were bad. She didn't know why she was so sure of that, but she was. It was as if the bear was chasing her all over again, and she feared to look behind her.

She ran until she could run no more and stopped with her hands on her knees, panting and heaving for air. There was no way those men behind her would be able to get horses down into the canyon, and they would have to choose another route to possibly head her off. If so, she might run right into them.

She straightened and tried to think clearly. If she broke from the jenny's trail, she was going to leave tracks of her own in the snow, and they would find them if they looked hard enough. But what other choice did she have?

She left the jenny's trail and climbed out of the canyon on the opposite side from which she had entered it. The climb was steep enough that she had to use her free hand to grab hold of saplings and bushes as handholds to pull herself up by, and once she dropped the rifle and had to go back down and get it. She fell on her back, exhausted, when she reached the top. She was soaked in sweat, despite the freezing temperature.

When she had rested again, she moved on, side-hilling along the mountain. She was paralleling the river down below and headed upstream, deeper and deeper into the woods. Every step took her farther away from the low country and one of the towns out in the San Luis Valley where she needed to go. She promised herself she would gradually curve her way down to the river, but the farther she walked, the more unsure of her bearings she got, and it was hard to tell how far she had gone since leaving the canyon. And the snow was as deep and as challenging as ever.

She spied a ledge of rock uphill from her through the trees, and at its bottom she thought she saw a dark shape like a cave. She high-kneed it through the snow until she reached the outcropping, but she found that what she thought was a cave turned out to be only some odd shadow. The ledge ran on for a good ways and grew higher until it was more of a cliff, maybe ten or twelve feet high. Before she had gone too much farther along the foot of it, she found a real cave, or at least the closest thing to one she could find. It was an overhang that ran barely eight feet back into and under the solid rock overhead. The ceiling was low, and the floor of it was free of snow except right at the front. She got on her hands and knees and worked herself all the way to the back. There, she turned around and sat looking down at the trail she had left through the trees. If someone came she would see them, or perhaps hear them, and then she would run again.

She wanted to build a fire but was afraid the smoke or the flame would give her away, so she wrapped herself in her blankets as she had in the snow shelter the night before. Now that she wasn't moving, the sweat inside her clothing was beginning to chill, and the outside of her clothing where that sweat had soaked through was already frozen in places. In the course of less than half an hour, she went from sweating to shivering.

The men she feared were following her had not shown themselves, nor did she hear them. Her suffering was such that she could wait no longer, and she went outside and hunted for firewood.

The sun had fully broken through the clouds by then, and the glare of it off the snow was so bright she had to squint to see properly. All that she could find were a few broken limbs and twigs she saw sticking out of the snow and a piece of large deadwood. She made a bundle of the wood on her forearms and carried it back to the overhang. She was young, but her two summers in the mountains with the sheep had taught her to build a fire. Not with the flint and steel like her father sometimes used, but at least she could get one started with matches.

She took the knife and shaved off several splinters from the chunk of deadwood she had found. She was delighted to see that it was a piece of lighter wood pine, or pitch pine, cured in the arid summer heat or after some fire in the past, with nothing left of it but the hard center streaked with yellow resin. The other wood she had found was cold and some of it felt damp, but if she could get the pitch pine burning, it would be no problem to get a real fire started.

She made more pitch pine shavings until she had a little pile of them on the bare dirt floor before her, then she took the box of matches from her coat pocket. She struck one of the matches against the rock ceiling overhead, and it flashed to life. Cupping the tiny flame in her hands, she leaned over and rested on her elbows and held the match tip near to the shavings.

The resin in the shavings came to life almost instantly, and she added little pieces of twigs over the top of the flames, leaning them against each other like the shape of an Indian tepee. When the flames had taken hold of both the shavings and the twigs, she began to carefully place broken bits of the dead limbs and bark she had found over the top of them. The heat from the fire on her face felt heavenly.

Wrapped once more in her blankets with the rifle lying across her thighs, she watched her back trail like she had before. The fire made the overhang smoky, but the tight confinement of the rock around her also helped reflect some of the heat. Soon, she was warm for the first time since she had left the sheep camp, even with such a small fire. Occasionally she looked up at where the smoke was rolling out from under the overhang and where it drifted up through the treetops. Smoke like that could be seen, but from how far away?

The fire soon burned down to nothing, and she knew that she either needed to find more wood or get moving again. She decided to build the fire up one more time. Maybe she could wait a while longer just to make sure the bad men didn't come, then she would go down to the river after nightfall. They wouldn't see her that way, and perhaps she could make it as far as that little train town at the Gap and there would be someone there to help her. She could make it that far if she only stayed strong.

CHAPTER NINETEEN

The snowstorm had forced the Cutter and his men to camp for the night in the draw. None of them were in a good mood when they woke up the next morning. A night of restless sleep in the bitter cold and the blowing snow had seen to that, and the Cutter seemed in even a worse mood than the rest of them. He was sitting on a rock smoking his pipe and squinting up the draw at the rockslide when the rest of them threw off their snow-covered blankets and got up.

The Cutter's tracker, the man in the capote that the Cutter called Arnie, went to check on the horses while the rest of them stood by the fire with their backs to it. He stopped beside the Cutter when he came back.

"One of the horses is in bad shape," he said.

"Will it make it?" the Cutter asked.

"Maybe. We're lucky they all didn't freeze to death, and us, too."

The Cutter nodded. The blizzard had blown most of the night, and it had gotten so cold that he had woke to find that the water in his canteen was frozen solid, even though he had left it within six feet of the campfire. However, the wind had died down with the coming of the morning, and the sun was hinting that it might burn away the clouds.

Johnny Dial was sitting on a wall of stacked rocks they

had put up the night before to serve as a heat reflector for the fire and to block some of the wind where they slept. He was nursing a cup of coffee and speaking in Spanish to the Mexican beside him.

"Hell of a night," Dial said in English when he saw the Cutter watching him. "I'd give ten Yankee dollars for a fire-place and roof over my head right now. Sell my horse and my gun for a fat woman and a blanket to go with her."

Dial had always reminded the Cutter of a rat, but the resemblance was almost uncanny now with the Texan's swollen face pinching his eyes to half their size. The Cutter put his pipe away and walked out in the snow to where he could better see the rockslide. Arnie went with him.

"Who's fixing something to eat?" Dial asked as they walked away.

"Not yet," the Cutter called back to the fire. "Not until we're done with this."

The men reluctantly moved away from the fire and went to stand with the Cutter.

"Come on, Cholo," Dial said, taking up his rifle. "You can't drink that coffee no way without hurting your teeth."

The Cutter waved a hand across the snow between them and the foot of the rockslide. "Spread out and pay attention. We'll make a skirmish line from one side of the draw to the other."

Some of the men looked like they wanted to protest the tactic, but they didn't. With grim expressions, they scattered out in a long line and started a slow walk toward the rock-slide. Most of them believed that the storm had likely killed the breed if his bullet wound hadn't done the job, but the slim chance he was still alive wasn't a pleasant one. If he was, he was going to see them coming, and they all knew that the only reason they were doing it that way was be-cause the Cutter had lost his patience.

Dial took one end of their line with the Mexican beside him. They made it fifty yards up the draw before Dial got some snow inside the top of one of his boots and started cursing. They all looked his way, but none of them said anything or stopped moving. There was still a hundred yards between them and the foot of the rockslide when the Cutter stopped. He was in the middle of the line, right out in the center of the draw. He scanned the rockslide for a few minutes, and those to the right and left of him did the same. The Cutter glanced over at Arnie beside him, nodded, and they started forward again.

"Fool way to do this," Dial muttered under his breath. "But I reckon there's no way he could make it through that storm without a fire."

He barely said that before the breed appeared at one end of the ledge halfway up the rockslide and fired a shot at him. The bullet barely missed him, and he cursed again and made a wild, fumbling attempt to bring his rifle up. Arnie shot at the breed before Dial could manage to aim, and the breed disappeared behind the ledge again.

"Don't stop!" the Cutter said. "Keep him pinned down!"

They waded through the snow faster and started climbing up the jumble of rocks. The Cutter caught a glimpse of the breed somehow and snapped a quick shot at him with one of his pistols. He must have missed because the breed came running out from behind the ledge and leapt from rock to rock across the slide and toward the timbered ridge on Dial's end of the line. One of the breed's arms was flopping uselessly, and he was hunched over like he was hit in the guts.

Dial fired at the breed just as the man disappeared into the timber, and he knew he had missed just like the Cutter had the instant he pulled the trigger. Then he looked up at the top of the rockslide by chance and saw the little girl standing there looking down at them. He forgot about the breed getting away and stared back at her until she, too, disappeared from sight.

The others went past him, pursuing the wounded breed, and only the Cutter remained behind with him.

"Did you see her?" Dial asked.

The Cutter was looking at the top of the rockslide like Dial had been, and he nodded.

"What's a little girl doing up here?" Dial asked.

"I don't know. Maybe there's a homestead close by," the Cutter answered and started after the rest of their gang.

Dial followed him. "She saw us."

The Cutter didn't answer him. When they were not far into the timber, they caught up to the rest of the men. They were standing at the lip of a narrow, steep-sided canyon that ran at an angle before them like it would eventually run into the draw a little farther down the mountain.

"He rode off on a mule," Arnie told the Cutter.

The Cutter could see the tracks the mule had left behind in the bottom of the canyon just like the rest of them could. "Where did he get a mule?"

"Must belong to that girl we saw," Dial said.

The Cutter pointed down into the canyon. "Arnie, take one of the men with you and get down there and follow him. The rest of us will go back and try to head him off at the river."

The Cutter didn't wait to see if his weird little tracker did like he said. Instead, he turned and started back toward their camp. Dial and most of the gang followed him. They got out of the timber and came out into the open draw again barely in time to see the breed whipping a gray mule toward the river. None of them tried a shot at him, for he was moving fast and the range was well past what any of them could hit something at.

They waded their way across the snowy draw to their camp, saddled the horses, and rode down to where the canyon spilled into the draw. Arnie and the one with him met them there and got on their horses.

"Saw something funny back there," Arnie said.

"What?" the Cutter asked.

"Another set of tracks following behind our man. They broke off going west about halfway back up the canyon. At first, I thought he had jumped off or fell off that mule and was trying to give us the slip, but they weren't his tracks. Too small, almost like a child's footprint."

The Cutter didn't say anything to that, but he did glance at Dial before he led them all after the breed. They rode down to the river at a trot, with their horses blowing smoke out their nostrils and flipping white powder up with their hooves. Arnie rode at the front, though it didn't take any kind of tracker to follow the plain gouging line of tracks the mule left in the snow.

The mule's trail led them back down the river and along its south bank until they were once again near the mouth of Willow Creek and close to where they had first ambushed the breed. There, the breed had forded the river, heading toward the mountains on the far side of the valley and the bluffs at the mouth of Willow Creek Canyon visible in the distance. They spurred their horses up to a lope.

Arnie pointed ahead of them. Though wounded, the breed had somehow remained on the mule's back. They saw him for an instant at the foot of the bluff before he vanished into the canyon.

They hit the mouth of the canyon riding almost ten abreast with their rifles in their hands, but they soon had to change to single file when the canyon choked down, though that didn't slow them. Not one bit. In fact, the Cutter spurred his horse up to a dead run, and the rest of them weren't about to get left behind. The chase had their blood up, and they were ready to finally corner their prey.

Not far around the bend in the canyon, past where the creek forked, was a certain mining claim and the camp of the men paid to guard it, the very same camp that the breed on the back of Zuri's mule was trying to reach before he died.

CHAPTER TWENTY

Newt was pouring himself a cup of coffee inside the tent, and he barely had time to make it outside before Jose came riding into camp on the back of a mule, slumped over it and bloody as the devil. He didn't even stop the mule before he fell off in a heap in front of the tent and the campfire there. Then there came the drum of hoof beats on the ground and the clatter of shod hooves on rock that told of riders coming up the canyon. Things might have turned out different if Newt could have gotten to his rifle quicker where he had left it leaning against the log beside the campfire, if Mr. Smith hadn't been in the horse corral doctoring a saddle sore on his horse's back, or if a guard had been in place like Newt wanted. But life is never fair.

Tully hadn't quite made it to where he was supposed to stand guard when the Cutter's men came up the canyon at a dead run. The Cutter put a pistol bullet in him before the kid even had a chance to get his rifle up. Tully's body tumbled down the foot of the bluff, and by then, the Cutter's gang was already past him.

Newt was reaching for his rifle when the riders burst into view. A man in a long, hooded blanket coat shot at him and missed, but the bullet struck the log near the rifle and a sliver of wood pierced Newt's palm. Newt jerked his wounded right hand back and tried to reach across himself with his left to make a grab for his holstered pistol. A horse struck him, and he was vaguely aware of the roar of guns as he went rolling and crashing into the tent wall. He scrambled upright in time to see that Jose was up and staggering toward him. The Ute half-breed looked like he was trying to say something to Newt, but two bullets smashed into his back almost simultaneously and put him down again and silenced him so that those words were lost forever.

Newt caught a glimpse of Tandy ducking and dodging through the milling riders that now surrounded them. The kid had his Merwin & Hulbert pistol in one hand and blew one man off a horse before he took a bullet and crumpled and fell.

Newt's reached again for his revolver, but his holster had spun around behind the small of his back during his tumble. The Mexican Mr. Smith had clubbed back at the Gap spurred his horse at Newt and had his pistol raised as if he was about to chop down with it and shoot Newt in the face, but Newt lunged forward and punched the horse in the nose with his left fist. The horse stopped and reared, and he grabbed the Mexican by one boot and shoved him out of the saddle.

Newt was trying to get at the Mexican when he heard a war cry unlike anything he had ever heard. Mr. Smith charged into the fight. His tattooed face was savage with fury, and he already had one war club raised over his head. A gun boomed and he was hit before he made it two strides from the corral. He spun, tottered, then fell sideways into the creek.

Newt saw none of that because at that very same moment the Cutter appeared out of the mad mix of milling horses and men and churning snow. He stopped his horse broadside to Newt and stretched out a handful of Colt pistol.

Newt dove headfirst in front of the Mexican's horse. The bullet intended for him ripped harmlessly into the tent canvas where he had been. The Cutter swung his gun hand, tracking Newt for another shot, but Tandy Hudlow fired from where he had fallen. He tried to kill the Cutter, but only managed to shoot the Cutter's horse in the head. The brained gelding's legs instantly went lifeless, and it crashed on its side, pinning the Cutter's off leg under its side. The Cutter was trying to shove himself out from under the horse with his free leg when Newt got back to his knees.

The Mexican was also on his knees right in front of Newt. He swung the barrel of his pistol at Newt's head, and Newt blocked the blow with his forearm and grabbed the Mexican by the head with both hands. The splinter in Newt's right hand drove deeper into his flesh, but he ignored the pain and dug a thumb in the Mexican's right eye and felt the soft, wet eyeball give and then burst. The Mexican screamed and flailed at Newt and tore away from his grip, and the Mexican's empty socket was a raw, red wound.

Newt drew his own pistol left-handed, fumbled his grip until he had it cocked, and shot the Mexican in the chest. The distance between them was so close that some of the unburned black powder set the Mexican's shirt on fire. He hit the ground on his side, with smoldering little tendrils of flame dancing on his chest as a hail of bullets ripped past Newt.

Newt lunged to his feet and ran to his right, his pistol ready, trying to spot someone to shoot back at through the confusion. Everything was a blur.

He fired a shot at a passing horseman but missed. For an instant, he thought he saw what was Mr. Smith's body lying half in and half out of the creek. His vision swung across the camp, and he saw someone on top of Tandy clubbing the kid with a pistol. He took careful aim and shot the man between the shoulder blades.

At the very same instant, the Cutter rested his own revolver across the side of his dead horse and shot another hole through Newt's coat, catching nothing but a little of Newt's skin above his hipbone as the bullet passed through the garment. Newt winced and tried to shift his body to shoot the Cutter, but he tripped over something and almost went down again. That stumble likely saved his life because the Cutter's second shot went high.

Someone struck Newt in the back of the head with a rifle butt at the same time he regained his balance and got up. Dazed by the impact, Newt grabbed at the rider's saddle to keep from going back down, and another blow from the rifle stock grazed off one of his shoulders. A hand groped at him, and Newt caught one of those clawing fingers between his teeth and bit down as hard as he could. He tasted blood, then a boot hit him in the chest and spun him away.

Newt shook his head to try and clear it. He was still standing, but only barely. He found himself behind the tent. Tandy and Mr. Smith were down and likely dead, and how many of his attackers still remained was unknown to him, other than there were too many of them. The only thing left was for him to die, but he'd be damned if he'd make it easy. He cursed the Cutter, then he ran up the canyon. A couple of shots were sent his way, but they did nothing other than go past him or kick up snow around him.

He made it fifty yards up the creek before he heard a running horse coming after him. He veered away from the creek and started up the more gentle side of the canyon, legs pumping like steam pistons. Another bullet spanged off a rock in front of him and he tried to stop and turn around, but he went down on one knee and his pistol flew from his grasp in doing so. The rider pursuing him was not twenty feet down the slope. The steep ground slowed the horse some, and it was having a hard time getting traction for its hooves. The man on its back was trying to jack another round in his Winchester while at the same time spurring the horse to keep it going.

Newt's outstretched hand struck something, and when he took hold of it, he saw that it was a dead fir sapling, charred as black as charcoal, that had been left behind after some forest fire in the past. He gave a yank and half of its trunk snapped off. When he came to his feet again, he swung the eight-foot length of trunk and brittle limb spikes at the horse and rider. The sweeping blow went over the horse's ears and took the rider in the side of the head. The horse reared and pivoted on its haunches and ran back down the canyon side with its rider clinging to the saddle horn.

Newt dropped his improvised club, found his pistol, and snatched it up out of the snow. Then he turned back up the mountain and climbed as he had never climbed before. He stopped once, halfway up the side of the canyon, and looked back toward the camp. He could see some of the Cutter's men still milling around, and there were flames and smoke where the tent had caught on fire.

Again, he cursed. He took a last look, then moved on up the mountain, purposefully taking the steepest and roughest course where it would be hard to follow him.

CHAPTER TWENTY-ONE

The old grizzly was still hungry, and little else drove his fevered mind and emaciated body. *Food and pain.* He came back to the camp the evening after Zuri left, hoping to kill another of the sheep as he had before. But the sheep were gone, and the cold made his bad shoulder ache so horribly that, even if there had been sheep, he couldn't have run one of them down in the deep snow.

He rummaged through the camp again, sniffing and making strange grunts and groans, but he found nothing to stave off his hunger. He thought of the lamb he had only partially eaten and left in the thicket, and he lumbered up the ridge to that spot only to find that scavengers had finished what he had left there. Not even the bones of the little lamb were to be found, only bits of wool and bloodstained ground remained beneath the snow.

Frustrated and restless, he made his way back to the camp. It was purely by accident that he passed close to the sheepherder's grave. It was only another mound of snow, and there was nothing there to indicate it should hold any interest to him, but the bear's keen sense of smell caught a faint scent of dead flesh.

He went to the mound and dug into it. The rocks he found beneath, those that Zuri had stacked over her father's body, were no obstacle. He hooked the claws of his good front leg under them and flipped them out of his way as if they were nothing. Then he feasted again. The sheepherder, the first man he had killed, also became the first man he ate.

He lay at the grave until nightfall, then on through the night, alternating eating and sleeping. Even the driving snow and blizzard winds did not make him leave the sheepherder's remains. It was not usual bear behavior, but the old, crippled boar was not the usual grizzly. Especially not now, not after he had partaken of man flesh.

The blizzard blew itself out by the next morning, and the bear went to the fallen tent and lay on top of it and licked his infected shoulder wound and slept some more. The sun finally came out and warmed him, and that was perfect for more napping. By evening, he was already hungry again and went back to the sheepherder's grave, but there was nothing left of the man thing's carcass worth taking.

The bear moved on, going down the mountain less by instinct or some knowledge of the terrain that he had gained during his lifetime in those mountains and more by chance. Though he didn't know it, the course he took led on the same track Zuri had taken. Because of that, he found where she had dug her snow shelter and spent the night. He tore into the snow cave, but found nothing other than a frying pan. The pan smelled delicious, like old grease and fat—fat that he needed more than anything. He gnawed on the skillet, but there was no sustenance to it. All he did was hurt a few of his bad teeth, and he knocked the thing away from him in disgust.

When he moved down the mountain again, it was not by accident that he followed the way Zuri had gone. Not that time. He had caught her smell and recognized her. It was the scent of the little man cub he had chased up the tree. His bear brain did not rationalize or chronologically order the chain of events as they had happened when she had escaped him, nor did he necessarily associate the sore cut on his tender nose with her, but he did remember her in the way that bears remembered things. Above all, she was food and was much easier to find than searching for where the sheep had gone.

CHAPTER TWENTY-TWO

The Cutter dragged his saddle free from his dead horse and turned away from the burning tent that was scorching his face. Somehow, the stovepipe had been shot away and the stove turned over by one turn of events or the other during the fight, and the tent and everything inside it were all but consumed by flames.

He was just out of reach of the heat when one of his men came riding back down the canyon. The man's face was scratched badly and bleeding.

"Did you get him?" the Cutter asked.

"No, I didn't." The man rode on past the Cutter, trying not to show any more of his wounded face than he had to.

It was plain that the Widowmaker had not only gotten away, but that he had also managed to give the man who went after him a beating. The Cutter scowled and gazed over the camp and the results of the fight. Two of his men, including the Mexican, were dead, and another was shot and badly wounded.

Yet, they had only managed to kill the breed and one other. The Widowmaker had escaped them, and the one they had shot coming up the canyon was gone when they went back for him. There was no telling where he had crippled off to or how badly he was hit. Then there was the big Indian. The Cutter was sure that one was badly wounded, but the giant Mohave had somehow gotten across the creek and up into the rocks along the foot of the bluff during the hectic conclusion to the gun battle.

"Some of you start dragging those bodies out of camp," the Cutter said to the men still remaining to him. "This is going to be your home for who knows how long, so get it in order."

Arnie, still on his horse, rode up to the Cutter. The fur cap he usually wore under his coat hood was gone, and his long hair was as wild as his eyes. The Cutter had seen a lot of survivors after a fight and knew that look well. He wondered if his own expression was the same.

"Go up the canyon and see if you can find Jones or any of the others," the Cutter said. "Take some help."

The tracker was thumbing cartridges into the loading gate of his Winchester, and one of his hands was bloody. He didn't rein his horse away until he was finished loading the rifle. He waved at the man with the scratched-up face and another to get their attention, and the three of them rode off up the canyon.

Johnny Dial was sitting in the snow with his back leaned against the log beside the smoldering remains of the scattered campfire. His legs were stretched out before him. One hand held his rifle in his lap, and the other was pressed to his chest.

"How bad are you hit?" the Cutter asked him.

"Missed my boiler house, but I think my collarbone's busted," Dial answered through gritted teeth.

The Cutter stood over Dial, looking down at him. He stood that way for a moment and then reached down and jerked back Dial's coat and shirt so that he could see the wound. Dial tried to protest, but he was hurting too badly to contest the issue. The Cutter pulled him forward and yanked the man's clothing in the opposite direction so that he could see the top of Dial's shoulder blade. The bullet had passed clean through the Texan, little hole in front and bigger hole in the back.

"You'll live if the blood poison doesn't set in or if that wound doesn't get infected," the Cutter said.

He took out a Barlow pocketknife and cut a strip from the tail of the dead breed's shirt, then came back over to Dial and stuffed the bullet hole, front and back, with plugs of the cloth. "That ought to stop the bleeding."

"You got to get me to a doctor," Dial said.

The Cutter gave no reply to that and took another look up at the bluff where the big Indian had to have gone. He didn't like thinking that ink-marked savage was up there in the rocks, possibly aiming a gun at him.

"You turn around and keep a watch on that bluff up there," he said to Dial. "Do it now, and don't you quit watching."

"Fat Richie shot that big Indian good," Dial said. "I don't know how he walked away from that."

The Cutter nodded at the body of the fat man lying not far away. "Well, Fat Richie's dead, and so's your Mexican friend."

"We really stumbled into it, didn't we?"

"Yes, we did."

"I guess you didn't have any idea they were here when we decided to charge up the canyon?"

The Cutter shook his head.

"That damned kid bored a hole in me."

"Wasn't your lucky day."

"A damned kid."

"Well, somebody did for him, too. Guess he was even unluckier than you were."

Dial looked over at Tandy Hudlow's body and gave a grim nod of his head. "That's right."

The Cutter started to move away, but Dial stopped him.

"You really think I'll live?" Dial asked.

"I've seen men pull through who were hit worse. Had a sergeant one time took an arrow right through the middle. We could smell the busted guts on him. Thought he would be dead before I could even get him on an ambulance litter, but I hear he's got a wife and kids and a hardware store up in Denver now."

"That's good. I'm the only boy of our family left. If I die there won't be any more of our name."

"Stack those guns over there," the Cutter said to one of the men carrying several firearms he had gathered. "And somebody see if they can drag some of those supplies back out of the way before they all burn up."

"This is the claim, ain't it?" Dial asked. "Is it silver or gold?"

The Cutter shrugged. "Doesn't matter."

"No, I guess it doesn't." Dial moved wrong and grunted from the pain it caused. "What about that little girl we saw?"

"What about her?"

"I don't know, I just thought about her. She was a pretty little thing, wasn't she?"

CHAPTER TWENTY-THREE

Newt reached the spine of the mountain and followed that backbone to the north for a ways until he was confident that he had likely avoided any immediate pursuit. At that point, he sat down on a rock and took the time to examine his wounds. There was already a growing knot on the back of his head, although the bullet that had grazed his side was little more than a bad scratch and bled little. Shockingly, it was the splinter in his hand that hurt him the worst. Sometime during his struggles, he had broken off some of the splinter, and that violence had driven what remained of the wooden sliver into his flesh even farther and ripped the puncture larger and more ragged than it had been originally. He didn't give himself time to think about it any longer, just took hold of the splinter and yanked it free. He flung it away from him and pounded the rock beside him with his good fist until the worst of the pain left him.

He cleaned his palm with snow as best he could and wrapped it in the neckerchief he had worn about his neck. He took his gloves from his coat pocket and pulled them on, taking special care with his wounded hand.

There was nothing he could do about his head or the headache. Hatless, angry, and hurt in more ways than one, he moved on along the mountaintop, paralleling the canyon

toward where he thought Happy Jack's camp lay. He
needed to warn the old man about what had happened.

Just then, he heard the old man's dog barking from
somewhere up the canyon, then a gunshot. The crack of that
shot rippled and reverberated over the mountains for a long
time, and the dog quit barking. Another shot sounded on the
heels of the first one.

Newt worked his way over some rough terrain, moving
closer to where the gunshots had come from. He was still
high on the mountain when three men on horses came back
down the canyon below him. He had no rifle, and the range
was too great for him to do anything with his pistol except
get himself killed. He kept going in the opposite direction
as they disappeared from his sight.

Happy Jack's camp wasn't far into the timber from
where Newt had stopped earlier that morning when scouting. It lay on a little flat stretch beside the creek much like
the camp farther down the canyon at the claim. The old
man's body was lying in the hoof-torn snow in front of a
tiny dugout cabin built into the foot of the mountain on the
west side of the creek. The dog was standing nearby and
growled when Newt approached its master.

"Easy, boy," Newt said, and knelt before the dog and
held out a hand to it as he had the first time he had met it. "I
mean him no harm."

The dog growled again but lifted its nose and smelled
the air. Perhaps it remembered Newt's scent or his voice
because it did not try to attack him. However, it did not
come to his outstretched hand, either. It sat in the snow and
watched him out of its cloudy eyes, everything about it
showing that it was still unsure of him.

Newt moved to Happy Jack's body, keeping a close
watch on the dog. When he rolled the body over, he was
shocked to find that the old prospector wasn't dead. Perhaps

not far from it, but his chest still rose and fell and he was looking back at him with clear eyes.

"I heard the commotion down your way, but I wasn't quick enough getting out of here," Happy Jack said in a rasping, weak voice.

There was blood all over the old man's shirt, and the bullet that had hit him had taken him through the chest. Another bullet had struck him in the hip. Newt couldn't tell anything about either wound through Happy Jack's clothing, but from the way he was breathing it seemed one of his lungs was punctured. There was no telling what else inside him was broken.

"Let's see if we can get that bleeding stopped." Newt reached to unbutton Happy Jack's coat.

"Leave me be."

"You'll die for sure if I don't try."

"Hell, son, I'm a goner. You know it, and so do I," Happy Jack hissed. "Just let me lie here."

"Never took you for a quitter," Newt said.

"Hmph." Happy Jack scoffed, then coughed hard twice. They were wet, rasping coughs, and pink-tinged foam showed at one corner of his mouth.

"Tough old coot like you ought to be able to take a little lead," Newt said.

Happy Jack grabbed him by the coat lapel. His pull on the coat was weak, but Newt gave to it and leaned closer.

"Got something to tell you," Happy Jack said.

Happy Jack coughed again before he finished what he was going to say, then gasped for air while his eyelids fluttered. Newt thought the old man was gone then, but Happy Jack gathered himself and his breathing came back closer to normal.

"I already looked over the claim," Newt said. "Either

Saul didn't tell me everything or you and that Ute were pulling a fast one on him."

"Ah, I knew you for a crafty one when I first laid eyes on you," Happy Jack said in a voice so quiet Newt had to lean even closer to hear.

Happy Jack's hand fell away from Newt's coat, but even in that condition, the old man was tough enough to try and laugh. He only managed to wheeze and cough again, but that attempt said something about him.

Happy Jack waited until he had caught his wind and after a rigor of pain had subsided. "I showed him the old diggings on Rat Creek first, west of here, but that place has already starved out better men than Saul Barton."

Happy Jack stopped to cough again and strained to suck in enough air to speak. Everything he said became broken, often with long pauses between words. "Then Saul . . . he went off with Jose . . . working their way up . . . towards . . . towards Stony Pass."

"You didn't go with them?" Newt asked when the old man took a long pause.

Happy Jack gave a feeble shake of his head. "All I was paid for was . . . was to show him those diggings on . . . Rat Creek. Went my own . . . way after that."

"And then what?"

"He must not have found anything." Happy Jack was straining so hard to breath that there were tears in his eyes. "Come the end of summer, he showed up . . . camped in the mouth of my canyon one night. Figure he followed my sign . . . snooping after me. Saul never was the . . . the prospector he claimed to be, and . . . he ain't above sss . . . stealing someone's thunder."

"Quit talking and save your breath," Newt said.

Happy Jack didn't heed Newt's wishes, and he seemed determined to finish his story, like it was the most important thing to him in his dying moments. His voice became stronger. "I come down to his camp at daylight and watched him pilfer about for an hour or so. Then he said he was done and he wanted to pack up and head for town."

Newt took off his coat, rolled it up, and placed it under Happy Jack's head. "Saul must have found something here he liked."

"Maybe, but I don't think there's a lick of silver sign on that claim."

"So what's his game?"

"Who knows? But my guess is that Saul's counting on his reputation."

Newt thought about the San Francisco investors Saul had mentioned. They wouldn't be the first to buy a bad claim or a salted mine.

"You mean he doesn't have to make the next big strike as long as someone believes he has?" Newt asked.

Another round of pain hit Happy Jack and his body racked and he arched his back up off the snow and gasped for air. The pink froth that he had spit up before now had more blood in it and was all over his whiskers. His body relaxed, and he lay there quietly for a time. Newt could barely see his chest moving.

The dog growled, then followed that with a short whine. It rose and took a few steps closer to its master, as if it could sense the life ebbing away from Happy Jack.

"Can't get any air," Happy Jack said, then tried to turn his head to see his dog. "How's Rufus? Is he hurt bad?"

"Not a scratch on him."

"Damn them to hell," Happy Jack hissed.

"Let me, at least, get you in the dugout and get you warm," Newt said.

"I ain't cold and I ain't going anywhere." Happy Jack

whispered, then he said something else that Newt couldn't understand.

"What's that?" Newt asked.

"You've got to swear to something before I tell you."

"Tell me what?"

"Promise me first. Promise me you'll kill every one of those drygulching devils."

Happy Jack gave a gasping bark of weak laughter before Newt could answer him. Despite the pain and the bitterness of that laughter, there was also something else in it. It was the way some had when telling a joke, when they couldn't resist laughing at the punch line before they told it.

Happy Jack gave a bloody-mouthed grin and took hold of Newt's coat again. The old man's voice was so quiet by then that Newt had to lean down and put his ear close to that quivering mouth, and even then he barely made out the words.

"No sir, old Saul ain't nearly as smart as he thinks he is," Happy Jack whispered when he finished telling Newt his secret.

Newt straightened and thought about what he had heard. He sat that way for a while, and when he looked back down, Happy Jack was dead. He brushed the old man's eyes closed, and the dog whined again.

Newt was watching the dog when he heard the snow crunching under the footsteps of somebody behind him. His bandaged hand slapped the butt of his pistol and came up with it as he pivoted on the balls of his feet to face whatever attackers were coming for him.

Mr. Smith appeared on the far side of the creek. He looked like one of his legs wasn't working right, but he was still strong enough to be carrying Tully Hudlow over one shoulder. The kid was either unconscious or dead.

"About time you showed up," Newt said to the Mohave.

The dog was standing up on all fours, growling and watching the newest arrivals. Mr. Smith ignored the dog's threats and limped toward the dugout.

"How bad's the kid?" Newt asked.

"His body is weak, but his spirit still fights."

Newt waded through the snow after Mr. Smith, but the dog stayed where it was. Soon, it lay down beside Happy Jack's body with its head resting on its front paws.

CHAPTER TWENTY-FOUR

Zuri left the overhang in the afternoon. The skies had cleared to a pure pale blue and the sun was bright and warm, and if she didn't think about being cold and didn't look at anything but the sky, she could almost pretend it was a nice fall day.

She did not go back the way she had come but headed straight down the mountain. Though the temperature was still hovering somewhere near freezing, the sun had already worked a little magic on the snow. Where it had been powdery before, there was now a little crust forming on the top that crunched slightly when her shoes pressed through it. And she had to squint to fight the glare.

She walked more slowly than before, partially because she was tired and the snow was deep and partially because she was keeping a sharp lookout for the bad men. And there was always the bear in her mind. That evil monster lurked at the back of her consciousness.

By then, her eyes were watering for some reason, and it was harder to fight the glare of the sun off the white snow, but that was the least of her discomforts at the moment. The sole of one of her shoes had torn loose and was flopping from the end of her toes back to the ball of that foot, and it was letting snowpack in around her stocking. She stopped and took the string off the rifle that she had used for a loop to hang it to the packsaddle, then wound it around the shoe several times and tied it. But that did not work well, and the string slipped off and was lost somewhere in the snow behind her and the shoe sole continued to flop. It wasn't long until that foot was aching so fiercely that it was almost more than she could take.

She came to the river sooner than she had expected. The snow was deeper in the valley along its banks, and there was still a lot of daylight left. Her plan had been to travel through the night to avoid the risk of the bad men possibly finding her or her accidentally stumbling into them for a second time, but she decided to keep moving. The open valley allowed her to see farther than before, and she thought she would be able to see any danger to her long before it arrived.

She was almost to the point where Willow Creek dumped into the river when evening came. Other than having to wade the snow, the terrain along the river was relatively easy to travel. She stumbled into a couple of drifts and had to back out of them and choose a way around them, but she told herself she was making it just fine, frozen foot or not.

When she was passing the mouth of Willow Creek, she remembered the ranch she and her father had seen nearby when they were driving the sheep up the previous summer. If she remembered correctly, the ranch lay on the other side of the river. If she could get there, maybe whoever owned it would feed her and give her shelter for the night. Then they could take her down to Wagon Wheel Gap the next morning.

Her father hadn't learned to speak English well and, in truth, almost not at all. He had sent her to a one-room schoolhouse near the sheep rancher's headquarters the previous winter, but that schooling and time around a few English-speaking children had given her only the rudimentary beginnings of taking on the language. Perhaps because of that, and in part because of her father's worry that the Americans didn't like foreigners, they had pretty much stayed away from anyone but each other or fellow Basques and a few sheepherders since their ship had landed on the coast of California and since coming to Colorado. Though she had often fussed at her father for being standoffish and unwilling to meet new people who might be nice, she found herself almost as afraid to try and find that ranch and whoever owned it as she was of crossing the cold river. If her foot hadn't hurt like it did and if she hadn't been so hungry and tired, she wouldn't have tried it.

She found what looked like a crossing, and the river, though shallow, was as cold as she feared it would be. She had taken off her shoes and socks, rolled up the legs of her long johns as high as she could, and hiked her skirt up to her thighs, but the water was still deep enough and cold enough to chill her to the bone. Her teeth were already chattering again before she was halfway across, but at least she didn't step off into a deep hole like she feared she would. She had learned to swim in the ocean on the Bay of Biscay when she was only five, but there was no way anyone could swim for long in river water so icy. Already, her muscles were trying to lock up on her just wading across water only up to her knees, and the shock of it made her have to concentrate to breathe.

Her crossing almost ended in an accident when she was trying to climb out on the far bank. That bank was high and steep and covered in snow, and the edge of the water was iced over. That lacing of ice crumpled under the first foot she put on it, and she almost fell back into the water, but she righted herself and gingerly took another step where the ice was thicker. Twice when trying to scale the snowy riverbank, she slid back to the ice, but she finally made it to the top.

She was soaking wet from the thighs down and trembling and shivering in a terrible way by the time she rolled her underwear legs back down and put on her stockings and shoes. Though she knew nothing about hypothermia or the biological limits of what the human body can take, she knew she was in more trouble than she had been since she had left the sheep camp on the mountain. Wading the river had been a foolish move.

Not for the first time in the recent and past days, she prayed, and either her prayer was heard or she got extremely lucky, for she walked right to the ranch she remembered, even though she hadn't been sure how to get there.

There was no lamplight shining from the cabin, even though the dusky evening light was already turning darker. Nor could she smell woodsmoke from the chimney. It was as if nobody was home.

She paused only briefly, considering that she could already feel the temperature dropping. She clamped her teeth over her lower lip to fight the trembling and her nerves, then walked right up on the cabin's front porch. Maybe somebody was home but they had already gone to bed. And if they weren't home, surely, they wouldn't mind her building a fire and sleeping on the floor in front of it.

She knocked on the door once, then twice, and there came no answer. She waited for what she thought was a reasonable amount of time to be polite, but she couldn't take standing there any longer, even if she might have been rude. She lifted the door latch and went inside. Before long, a light showed in the window because she had lit a lamp, and sometime after that smoke began to lift from the chimney.

CHAPTER TWENTY-FIVE

The Cutter threw a sour glance at what had been a tarped mound of supplies beside the tent. Those supplies had also caught fire when the tent went up in flames, and if they hadn't burned, they would have been more than enough for him to keep men on the claim for as long as he needed them. Now he was going to have to send someone out to Wagon Wheel Gap or Del Norte to bring back something to feed them. That would take at least two days round trip, maybe more if the weather turned for the worse again.

He told himself that such a setback was nothing and that the job had gone faster and easier than it should have. What might have been a bad stroke of misfortune when they chased the breed to the claim had turned out decidedly in his favor. All he had left to do was send the telegram he had been instructed to send once he had physical possession of the claim, and the thousand-dollar bonus promised him for that action was his. A thousand dollars was a healthy sum. Not that he wouldn't have liked to have earned the additional thousand offered him to kill Saul Barton, but Barton had gotten off to California before he could locate him, and that chicken had long since flown the coop.

The fact that Jones, the Indian, and one other had escaped bothered him. Witnesses were something that both he and his employer wished to avoid. Because of that, he fully intended to hunt those survivors down and hide them in a nice dark hole somewhere.

Arnie and those that had gone with him came riding into the camp. The other two unsaddled the horses while the tracker came over to him.

"Heard you shoot. Did you get Jones?" the Cutter asked.

"He's gone over the mountain, but we found another camp and did for the old man."

"No sign of the Indian and the kid?"

Arnie shook his head. "We thought we'd come back here and see how you wanted to play it."

"I'll give you one of the men to help you," the Cutter said. "Go after Jones. He's on foot, and he'll be easy for you to trail in this snow. Keep the pressure on him until you run him in the ground."

"All right."

"We'll stay here and see if we can smoke that Indian out," the Cutter said.

"Might be better just to get some men down towards the gap where they can see anybody coming by," Arnie said. "Might send someone else up towards the high passes to catch them if they go that way."

The Cutter nodded as if that fit with something else he was thinking. "That homestead we passed down by the river might work. Post a couple of men there. Didn't get a good look at it, but the place looked abandoned when we went by it."

Arnie and one other man started preparing their horses and gear to go back out after Jones while the Cutter gathered the rest of the men. He picked two men to remain at the claim and another two to go with him to the homestead near the river.

"I gotta have a doctor," Dial said from where he still sat with his back against the log.

"You're going with me. I'll send you to town with whoever I pick to ride after supplies," the Cutter answered.

They ate and made more plans before leaving, and by then it was growing late into the evening. The sun was almost below the west rim of the canyon by the time the Cutter led Dial and two others out of camp. Dial had one arm in a sling and was so slumped in the saddle that the Cutter wasn't sure he would be able to handle the ride.

Nothing of the day remained but weak gray light by the time they rode into sight of the little ranch they had spotted during their initial pursuit of the breed.

"Somebody's home," the Cutter said when he saw woodsmoke pouring from the cabin's chimney and the lamplight already burning in a window.

"No horses in the corrals that I can see," one of the men beside the Cutter said.

"Maybe they're in that barn," the Cutter replied.

"Are you still of a mind to use the place?" the same man asked him. "Whoever's in there burning that fire might not be partial to us showing up and making ourselves at home."

Dial had stopped his horse a little ways from the rest of them. "Oh, I got an idea who's in that cabin."

The Cutter rode to him and looked down at what he was pointing out. Even in the growing dark he could make out that it was a set of tracks in the snow. What's more, they were the tracks of someone on foot. He peered closer at them and saw that at the bottom of one of those holes in the snow was the clear and unmistakable footprint of a very small shoe—very close together.

"Looks like a kid's tracks," the Cutter said.

Dial nodded his agreement with that observation. "I'd say they're about a match for a little girl like that one we saw."

"What girl?" One of the others with them asked.

Dial never took his eyes off the Cutter when he answered. "The one that saw us up at that rockslide."

Dial didn't wait to see what the Cutter's response to that answer would be. He was already riding toward the cabin and shucking his pistol out of his holster.

"You coming?" Dial asked when he saw that the Cutter hesitated.

The Cutter only waited a moment longer before he yanked his rifle out of his saddle scabbard and spurred his horse after Dial with the other two men following him and doing the same. The Cutter had never killed a child, or an entire family, but he was also a man who didn't like loose ends.

Soon, under the cover of darkness, they found that there were no horses in the barn, nor were there tracks in the yard around the cabin other than the line of little shoeprints in the snow that led straight from the river and up on the front porch.

CHAPTER TWENTY-SIX

Nightfall came before Newt had finished the stretcher to carry Tully Hudlow. It wasn't really a stretcher, simply two long poles he cut and lashed two shorter pieces across to form a frame. A doubled blanket stretched tightly over the framework made a place for Tully to ride, and Newt could pull it along by one end and let the other end drag.

He went inside the dugout to check on the kid and found Mr. Smith stripped to the waist and tending to his own wounds by lantern light. Two buckshot pellets had buried themselves in the Mohave's chest, and he was digging them out with the tip of his knife. It was hard for Newt to tell much about the seriousness of those shotgun wounds because his eyes had a hard time looking away from the tattoos. Like much of his face, Mr. Smith's torso was covered in inked designs. Most were the abstract shapes of his tribe, but mixed in with those were some that were obviously the work of sailors or others he had encountered in his travels—an anchor, some kind of fish, and Polynesian islander marks like Newt had seen sailors fresh off the Pacific and on the ship docks at San Francisco wearing. It all mixed into a wild pattern that you had to concentrate on to pick out any detail.

When Mr. Smith turned away from him, Newt noticed

something else that he had never seen before. There were crisscrossed, long scars across the Mohave's back. They looked like whip scars.

"How's the kid?" Newt asked.

"He sleeps and his spirit comes and goes. I think it will leave him before the night has passed," Mr. Smith answered.

Tully was shot low down on his abdomen and to one side, and another bullet had struck his left wrist. Or perhaps the same bullet had caused both wounds. Neither Newt nor Mr. Smith could detect any of the telltale smell of punctured intestines or other guts, but that wasn't a guarantee that the kid wasn't busted up inside. The bullet hadn't passed all the way through, so it was lodged somewhere inside him. Not to mention that he had lost a lot of blood.

Newt pulled one of the blankets back up on the kid where it had fallen off. Mr. Smith was probably right, but that didn't mean they shouldn't try and do what they could. The only chance the kid had was them getting him down to the settlements and in the care of a doctor.

Mr. Smith had finished digging the buckshot out of his chest and had now rolled up one pant leg and was looking at a nasty cut on his shin. It looked like a ricochet had caught him there, or maybe a chunk of flying rock knocked loose by a bullet. His whole lower leg was swollen badly.

It was cold in the dugout, for they couldn't light a fire in the earth fireplace at the back of the cramped room, not with the men at the claim camp so close by and liable to smell their smoke. Newt could see Mr. Smith's breath floating around him every time he exhaled.

Mr. Smith saw Newt watching him and said, "I do not like this country, either. It does not get so cold in the land of my people."

"We've got to get him to a doctor," Newt said, "and the quicker we leave, the better."

Mr. Smith nodded. "I agree. He needs a healer."

"Maybe we can drag him over the mountain and down into the next canyon. We might stand a chance of slipping past them in the dark that way," Newt said.

"I will help you."

"With that leg of yours like it is, you're going to have your work cut out just walking."

"There is another way," Mr. Smith said.

"What's that?"

"We do not go over the mountain and try to slip past them."

"You mean we go through them."

Mr. Smith gave one of his almost imperceptible smiles. "I'm glad you have made up your mind."

Mr. Smith put his clothes back on and shrugged into his buffalo coat, and they carried Tully outside and laid him on the improvised stretcher. A piece of rope strung under the kid's armpits and tied off to either side of the frame would keep him from rolling or sliding off during their journey.

Once Tully was secured on the stretcher, they carried Happy Jack's body inside the dugout. The dog followed them and sat just outside the door while they laid the old man to rest.

Newt remained in the dugout for a moment after Mr. Smith went back outside. He went to the earth wall at the back of the tiny room and found the burlap sack on the floor where Happy Jack had said it would be. He reached his hand inside the sack, took something from it, and put that something in one coat pocket before he rose and went to the door.

He closed the slabs of log that served as a door for the crude dwelling and started back to the stretcher, leaving Happy Jack in his crude tomb, but he stopped and looked back at the dog.

"Are you coming?" he asked.

The dog stayed where it was. Newt went to the stretcher and gazed out into the darkness and down the canyon. Mr. Smith stood nearby.

"Are you ready?" Newt asked.

"Cry havoc and let slip the dogs of war," Mr. Smith said.

"Is that your man Poe again?"

"No, Shakespeare."

Newt pitched Happy Jack's rifle, which he had found earlier in the snow, to Mr. Smith. "Shakespeare, hmm. Heard of him. Worked in a town once named after him."

"His words are known to many."

"Reckon he must have found himself in a pinch like this a time or two to come up with such."

"He was a playwright and a poet and no warrior, from what the captain told me."

"Shame. I'd say he missed his calling."

Newt took hold of the stretcher and started dragging it down the creek. The poles of the frame creaked at the joints and hissed through the snow. He pulled steadily and didn't look back. Mr. Smith moved across the creek and closer to the foot of the mountain on that side of the canyon. Newt could hear him for a while, moving on a course parallel to his own, but after a time that, too, faded away and the Mohave was not even so much as a ghostly presence.

Behind Newt, the dog scratched at the dugout's door once with a front paw and whimpered.

Chapter Twenty-Seven

There was a little firewood stacked on the hearth, and whoever owned the cabin had already laid the makings for a fire in the stone fireplace. That was good, for Zuri was in such bad shape she might not have managed to build one without that. Even so, her shaking hands had a hard time striking a match. It took all of her remaining matches before she finally managed that simple feat, and she knelt in front of the fireplace with the tiny flame cupped in her shaking hands and held it to the crumpled ball of dead grass beneath the kindling someone had left in the firebox. The ball of grass caught, and she blew gently on the flames to help the kindling burn. Once it was going good enough, she arranged a few sticks of firewood over the flames, careful not to crush or suffocate her infant fire.

She knelt there for a long time and held her palms to the growing flames until the thawing flesh of her fingers began to hurt so badly that the ends of them felt as if they were splitting apart. With her teeth gritted against the pain, she rose and lit an oil lamp, trimmed the wick, and replaced the globe. After that, when she was better able to see what she was doing by the lamplight and the fire's glow, she took off her clothes and shoes and laid them all out before the fire to dry. The poncho had not gotten as wet as the rest of her things, and she put it back on out of modesty to cover her nakedness. She was alone in the cabin, but for some reason she could not help the feeling that someone might be watching her.

She fed more wood on the fire, laid her father's rifle on the table in the center of the room, took the lamp in one hand, and searched the cupboard she found in one corner that served as a kitchen. To her delight, she found a sack of cornmeal. With a little boiling water and a skillet she could make *talo*, the traditional Spanish flatbread she had grown up eating. The cornmeal was coarser and different from the corn flour her mother had taught her to use, and there was no *txistorra* sausage to top it with once it was fried, but she could make do. She placed a bucket of frozen water she found in the room on the hearth. The thought of the bread made her even hungrier than she had been, and she looked in the bucket several times to see if the ice had thawed while she stood with her back to the fire, even though she knew it hadn't had enough time.

Both she and the room were slowly beginning to warm, and she felt much better except for the aching of her hands and one foot. When the fire in the fireplace was too hot for her to stand near it, she went and peered into the back room of the cabin. There she saw an iron bedstead and lace curtains on the window like her mother used to have. She closed the door to the bedroom, feeling like she was trespassing. Then she glanced at the ladder that led to a loft over the opposite end of the main room from the fireplace. She was fighting the temptation to climb the ladder and go have a look up there when she heard the sound of boots thumping on the porch outside the cabin door.

For a brief instant, she saw the big man with the sideburns and the fur collar on his coat appear in the window, but she didn't look long. There was no back door to the cabin, and no time to crawl out a window or seek some other means of escape. Without thinking, she scrambled up the ladder. Her bare feet had barely disappeared over the edge of the loft when the cabin door swung inward.

Unlike the bedroom at the back of the cabin, the loft had no iron-framed bead nor lace curtains, nor any window at all. The roof overhead was so low to the floor that an adult wouldn't have been able to stand fully upright, and the only bed was a narrow one made of peeled poles set against the end wall of the cabin. The crudely fashioned bed's thin tick mattress had been given extra padding by animal furs laid on top of it and several layers of blankets laid over them. At first, she considered hiding under those blankets and furs, but she reconsidered that tactic and chose one equally simple. Her bare feet made almost no noise as she crossed the loft and crawled under the bed. She could hear other men coming inside the cabin as she reached up and pulled down the edges of the blankets and furs to hang down off the bed and screen her in her shadowed hiding place.

She lay on her stomach, staring out the thin slit she had allowed herself between the hanging blanket edge and the floor. She could see the firelight flickering on the far cabin wall, and she heard the creak of someone opening the bedroom door and searching it. Then she heard someone on the ladder.

She closed her eyes for a second, made herself open them again, and saw a hat and then a head appear over the loft edge. It was the man in the fur-collared coat. He did not climb all the way into the loft but stayed there at the top of the ladder, peering into the gloom where she hid. It took a moment for it to dawn on her that he was staring straight at her, even though there was no way he should have been able to see her.

"Come out from wherever you're hiding."

She understood almost none of what he said, the English words lost on her, but knew he was talking to her. Her heart hammered in her chest even harder and faster.

Maybe he was only trying to trick her into revealing where she hid and wasn't sure she was in the loft. She bit her lower lip and concentrated on slowing and quieting her breathing, for it sounded terribly loud to her own ears and she was afraid it would give her away.

"You're not anywhere else, so I know you're up here," the man said.

His voice was as strange as his language to her, and though he was trying to sound nice, she knew it was only an act. She had seen him and his men trying to kill the man on the rockslide on the side of the mountain.

"You can come down on your own, or I can drag you out of there," he said.

She was trembling again, but it had nothing to do with her being cold. She felt the same horror she had felt when the bear was trying to get her out of the tree.

Then the loft's floorboards creaked under his weight, and she saw his boots coming closer to the bed. *Please don't look under the bed. Just go away.*

"I know you're under there. I can see your breath," the man said.

She put a hand over her mouth and nose and didn't breathe. Truly, it was still cold enough inside the cabin for her breath vapors to show like rising steam, and she hadn't thought of that.

The blankets and furs were ripped upward, and he stood there bent at the waist and with his face almost down at eye level with her. She pressed as tightly as she could against the wall, but there was no farther she could retreat.

He motioned at her with his free hand while he continued to hold the blankets out of his way. "Come on out, girl."

Girl was the only word of his she knew, but she did understand the motion of his hand. He backed away and gave her a little space as she crawled back out from under the bed. He was still watching her intently when she reached the better light at the top of the ladder.

Again, he used his hand to motion her to climb down. She saw two other men as she descended, one standing by the fireplace and one sitting at the table. They were both watching her, and the look on their faces was almost as terrifying as when the man in the fur-collared coat had first looked under the bed at her.

Zuri reached the bottom of the ladder and turned to face them. She noticed then that the bucktoothed, skinny man slumping in a chair at the table was somehow wounded and had one arm in a sling. His face was also injured, with his nose being so swollen that it looked like no nose at all, and his eyes were tiny little slits in his bruised and puffy face.

The big man above her was coming down, and she moved to get out of his way. Her eyes cut quickly at the door, but another man swung it open and stepped into the cabin from outside almost as quickly as she thought of trying to make a run for it. He did not go to join the others, but stood there in front of the door even after he had closed it, blocking her way as if he knew what she was thinking.

"Where are your people?" the big man asked.

She was afraid to look at him, but she could tell by his tone that she had somehow angered him.

"Your parents, girl. Where are they?"

Parents. She recognized that word, too, and shook her head.

"You're not here by yourself. Speak up."

"Maybe she is here by herself," the man at the table said. "Look at her clothes by the fire. I'm guessing this isn't even her place, from the look of it."

The big man looked Zuri's clothes drying by the fire. He saw the crude poncho she had made, then glanced at the rifle with the broken stock on the table.

"What would a girl like her be doing out there by herself?" The big man jerked his head at the snow-covered world outside the window and the mountains looming up beyond the river.

"Maybe she belongs to some of them we ran into back at the claim," the man at the table said.

"That it?" the big man asked her.

She looked from one to another of them, knowing that they were asking her questions but unable to understand or answer them.

She said in her native tongue, "Leave me alone!"

The big man slapped her. It was not a hard slap, and the shock and brutality of it was worse than the pain it caused her cheek.

"Talk," the big man said.

She held a hand to the side of her face and fought back the tears she felt forming at the corners of her eyes.

"Don't you speak English?" the big man asked.

"Zuri," she said. "Zuri Altube." *Why were they treating her so? She had done nothing to them.*

"*¿Habla Español?*" the man at the table asked.

She spoke fluent Spanish, as well as a little French, but she did not answer him. For some reason, she suddenly felt that saying anything would put her in even more danger.

"She doesn't understand a thing we're saying," the man at the table said. "Be done with her and quit wasting time. I've got to get to a doctor."

The big man turned and kicked the chair out from under the man, and he lay on the floor moaning and clutching at his chest and his wounded arm in the sling. The other two men made no attempt to help him.

"Shut your mouth, Dial, or I'll shut it for you," the big man said.

"Easy, Kirby," the man by the fireplace said. "He didn't mean anything by it. He was only wondering what we're going to do with the girl."

The big man looked back at her. "Get your clothes on."

She could tell what he wanted by where he pointed, and she scooted past him and picked up her things. She started to go into the bedroom, but he held out a hand to stop her.

Did he expect her to dress in front of them?

The big man turned his back to her and picked up her father's rifle and examined it. The man by the fireplace moved away, intentionally giving her space and making a show of ignoring her, or simply because he wanted to look at the rifle. The man at the door looked off to one side, too. Only the wounded man on the floor looked her way. Sweat dotted his swollen face, though it was far from hot in the room.

"Bashful little thing, ain't you?" he said to her before he, too, looked away.

She turned her back to them and pulled into her long underwear without taking off the poncho. Next came her skirt. Then she took the poncho off and drew her white blouse over her head and into place. The clothing still felt damp, but better than it had been before. She sat on the hearth and put on her stockings and shoes. She hoped she was wrong and they actually meant her no harm.

The big man set her father's rifle on the table and turned again to her. His glance was a brief one before he looked to the man beside him. "Tend to her."

"Let Dial do it," the man answered with a shake of his head.

"Take her for a walk," the big man said. "Do you want her going and telling somebody what she saw up here?"

"I've done a lot of things, but never a kid."

The man in the arm sling picked himself up off the floor, set his chair upright, and eased himself back onto it. The big man watched him for a moment, then shifted his attention back to the man he had been talking to.

"Do like I said."

"Don't believe I will," the man replied. "You pay good, but not that good."

The big man tensed, anger showing in his stance and the livid expression on his face.

"Don't want to cross you, Kirby, but I'm not shooting that girl."

"Count me out, too," the man by the door said.

The man with his arm in a sling leaned back with his head resting against the back of his chair. He closed his eyes and said nothing.

It was all Zuri could do not to run right then, even though there was nowhere to run. She might not speak good English, but she recognized the seriousness of their tone and caught enough bits and pieces of their conversation to understand that that her life hinged on some decision they were making, even if she didn't know exactly why. Her eyes lowered to the poker leaning against the fireplace. It was a length of heavy steel rod used to stir coals and prod burning pieces of wood, with a sharp point on one end.

She tugged into her coat and pulled the poncho over her head before the big man took a step closer to her. He was almost upon her when she could fake calmness no longer. She grabbed the poker and swung it as hard as she could at the big man's knees. It hit him with a solid crack, and he cried out and staggered, giving her a small space to bolt through. He pawed at her as she went by him, but missed. She was almost to the front door when the man stepped in front of her. Without thinking, she stabbed at his face with the sharp end of the poker, a long lunge like a fencer with a rapier in hand thrusting at an opponent. The tip missed the man's eyes and skidded along his jaw, but it was enough to knock him aside and allow her to get a hand on the door latch.

He snatched at her, and for a moment she was almost jerked off her feet before she pulled free and got the door open. She skidded and almost fell on the snowy porch, but she kept going. She ran straight toward the barn at first, but one of the men chasing after her paralleled her and would have headed her off if she kept going that way.

She veered away from him at the same time she heard other running footsteps plowing through the snow behind her. She threw a wild look over her shoulder and saw the shadowed form of the big man hobbling after her. His injured knees might have slowed him, but his long stride and greater size already had him closing on her.

She went wide of the barn, turned a corner of the corral beyond it, and broke out onto the field of snow beyond the homestead. She ran blindly into the night with no specific course in mind. She could tell it was snowing again only because she could feel it hitting her face. She had expected them to shoot at her, but maybe the snow and the darkness made her an impossible target. Even if she were so lucky, she knew she could only outrun them for so long.

"Get her!" the big man shouted.

The man who had turned her away from the barn must have gone around the opposite side of it. He came at her from an angle out of the night and dove at her. She sensed him more than saw him, and she veered her course sharply again, barely managing to dodge him. He landed face-first and came so close to tackling her that she stepped on one of his hands, but she was soon past him and running as fast as she could and as fast as the snow would let her.

It sounded as if the big man was right behind her and coming closer with every stride. But she didn't quit running, not even when her lungs felt like she was breathing cold fire and her legs were refusing to move as fast as they should. She knew that to stop or stumble was to die, just like when the bear had chased her.

Neither her swiftness nor her determination were the reason she got away from them, but rather it was the sound of gunfire not far away to the northwest. The men chasing her stopped at that sound, but she didn't. She ran straight at it because she had no other choice.

CHAPTER TWENTY-EIGHT

The old grizzly reached the river two hours after dark. He had not lost the periodic scent of the small human's passing, and twice he thought he had winded her when the breeze shifted in his favor. However, now that scent trail had become mixed with the smells of other humans, and many of them. Before his injury, the presence of so many of the two-legs would have made him uncomfortable and caused him to leave the area or to keep his distance, but he was not the same bear he had once been. The scent of the blood splatters he found among the rockslide and the manure droppings of horses made him think of only one thing. Food.

He waded the river, shook his hair coat as free of the icy water as he could, and moved on, stopping often with his nose lifted high and sniffing for the smell of prey. The night masked his movement as he prowled and ghosted through the falling snow like some malignant spirit birthed from the hollow, cold tomb of winter.

It was not more man scent or even the promise of horse-flesh that caused him to turn toward Willow Creek, but mere, random chance. That, and because turning in that direction kept the slight breeze at his face.

The dull boom of gunfire came from ahead of him in the

distance—the same gunshots that Zuri and the Cutter had heard. The noise caused the bear only a short moment's pause, the same as it had with the other sporadic shots he had heard earlier in the day. He sat on his haunches with lifted nose and cocked ears, trying to interpret what his senses told him. When the wilderness had gone silent again, the bear moved on, never once diverting from his course and never ceasing to hunt.

CHAPTER TWENTY-NINE

Newt stopped dragging the stretcher a short ways from the outlaws' camp at the claim site. He could see the glow of their campfire ahead and the vague shapes of men passing before the flames. There were four of them, he thought, but it was hard to tell. The bottom of the canyon was too narrow to pass by them undetected, even if he had bothered to try. He set the stretcher down and slid the Smith & Wesson .44 from his holster. When he started forward, the pistol hung beside his right leg.

The men around the campfire were relaxed and enjoying the warmth of the fire on such a cold night. They were telling stories and laughing at each other's jokes as he came nearer, and perhaps that was why they did not hear his approach. Also, they had stared into the flames so much that they were night-blind, even if they had turned and looked into the darkness at him.

Arnie, the Cutter's tracker, along with the other man that was supposed to go with him, had procrastinated and not left camp like the Cutter had told them to do. It was the tracker who was the first one to see Newt step into the edge of the firelight. He dropped the cup of coffee he was holding and reached for the Colt stuffed behind his belt.

Newt never stopped walking, raised the Smith & Wesson

to arm's length, and shot Arnie in the chest. The tracker spun away and fell back out of the firelight in a swirl and flare of his blanket coat, and Newt thumbed his pistol hammer and shot him a second time in the back as he was falling. At the very same moment, Mr. Smith rose up out of the snow on the opposite side of the fire. His buffalo robe and his size made him look like some kind of mythical beast standing in the shadow world at the edge of the light. Perhaps that's what the Cutter's men thought, also, but he gave them no time to get over their surprise, and the rifle he held was no myth. A real bullet from it knocked one of the outlaws off the log where he sat. Then there was a continuous roar of guns as men cursed and fought and died.

Newt was in their midst by then. He backhanded the outlaw nearest him across the mouth with the barrel of his pistol, then shot him twice. He shifted his aim toward the last remaining outlaw, but that one was already down. Mr. Smith had seen to that, and he came to the fire jacking another round into his rifle. So far as Newt could tell, the Cutter's men had never got off a shot in their defense.

"I think that is all of them," Mr. Smith said.

It always took Newt a long while to settle himself after a fight, and he simply stared back at Mr. Smith and said nothing. One of the downed outlaws stirred where he lay, and Mr. Smith shot him again without hesitation. The blast of the gun startled Newt, and he almost laughed at how preposterous that was after what he had just done.

When he finally found his voice, even he could hear the slight quaver in it. "There should have been more of them. Where's the Cutter?"

Mr. Smith gave a slight tilt of his head to one side as he often did in place of a shrug. Newt broke his pistol open to eject the spent brass, then reloaded the empty chambers with fresh cartridges. He holstered the weapon and went to get Tully. He was dragging the stretcher back to the fire when he got the feeling something was behind him.

"Somebody's out there," he said to Mr. Smith once he was back at the fire.

"Is that what you heard?" Mr. Smith asked, and pointed behind Newt.

Newt turned and saw what the Mohave was pointing at. Happy Jack's dog was standing at the edge of the firelight. It did not wag its tail or offer to come closer, and Newt couldn't tell if it was looking at him or seeing anything at all.

Tully was awake, though his mind seemed far from clear. It was obvious that the kid was in shock and that his wound was steadily weakening him more and more. He looked around him as far as he could from the confinement of the stretcher, then his gaze landed on Newt.

"Where's Tandy?" he asked.

Newt looked at Mr. Smith, then back to the kid. "I'm afraid he's gone."

Tully gave a feeble nod of his head. "That's what Mr. Smith said, but I thought maybe I dreamed it."

"It's my fault," Newt said. "I'm sorry."

"Wasn't your fault." Tully closed his eyes.

Newt watched the kid for a while, then said to Mr. Smith, "We've got to get him to Del Norte. The longer we wait, the worse his chances likely are."

Mr. Smith sat down on the log before the fire, picked up a plate of beans one of the outlaws had dropped, and began eating what was left.

"Have you got an opinion on the matter, or are you going to sit there and say nothing?" Newt asked.

"You asked no question. You say he is hurt and we need to take him to Del Norte, and I wait for you to say when we go," Mr. Smith replied between mouthfuls of beans. "You white men are very strange sometimes."

Newt found his Winchester among a stack of firearms not far from the fire and also Mr. Smith's big-bore Marlin lever-action. He pitched the Mohave's rifle to him.

"You might want that," Newt said.

Mr. Smith caught the rifle out of the air and gave it a careful examination. Newt went to the corral and led out the Circle Dot horse and Mr. Smith's black. He handed them over to Mr. Smith and went back in the pen. Neither Tully's horse nor his brother's was in the corral, so Newt chose the first horse he could catch from what was there, a rangy, ugly-headed bay that seemed like it might be gentle enough for what he needed.

After the horses were saddled, they eased Tully off of the stretcher and laid him beside the fire. Mr. Smith tried to get the kid to eat and drink something while Newt reworked the stretcher. When he was done reconfiguring it, the conveyance more closely resembled a triangle-shaped Indian travois. He rigged the narrowest and longest point over the bay's saddle and secured it to the saddle horn, then added two more tie points to each runner and to the saddle's back D-rings. The bay looked askance at the contraption several times and jumped once with fright when Newt set the frame over him, but after that it didn't seem to mind. He led the horse away from the fire and back to see how it would act to the sound and feel of dragging the travois, and though it cocked one or the other ear and kept a look behind it, it didn't panic or try to kick the frame apart.

Newt felt the first scattered snowflake land on his ear, and by the time he led the bay back to the fire it was snowing more steadily. It was a slow, gentle snow, but he knew that could change.

"Did he eat anything?" he asked Mr. Smith.

Mr. Smith shook his head where he knelt over Tully. "He speaks sometimes, but he makes no sense. I think he walks in a land far from here more than he is with us in this place."

Newt stripped the blanket capote from the first man he had shot by the fire, and they put that coat on Tully to better keep him warm. Afterward, they laid him on the travois base and once more tied him down as they had before. Atop him they spread several layers of blankets they scavenged from the gear of the dead men. While Newt was arranging those blankets, Mr. Smith retrieved two more good Winchester rifles and three pistols. He shoved a pistol in each of the pockets of his buffalo coat, then laid the rifles and Tandy's Merwin & Hulbert revolver and gun belt under the blankets with Tully.

Newt followed the Mohave's lead and sought to better arm himself. Surprisingly, no one seemed to have pilfered through his saddlebags or taken anything from them while he was gone, and he pulled out a snub-nosed Webley British Bulldog revolver with ivory grips. He dropped the pistol into his right-hand coat pocket as Mr. Smith had done, then emptied what remained of a box of .45-75 cartridges for his rifle in his other pocket.

Newt noticed that Happy Jack's dog had crawled up on the travois and was lying curled up with its nose to its tail beside Tully in the blankets. Tully's arm was on the dog, either by accident or intentionally.

Mr. Smith found Newt's hat and sailed it to him. Newt caught the hat, set it tightly on his head, then swung up on the Circle Dot horse. He rode over and took up the bay's lead rope while Mr. Smith was scattering the fire and kicking snow over it.

Mr. Smith noticed the dog as Newt had. He looked at Newt with the same hint of humor on his face that passed for irony with him, as if he found everything Newt did highly amusing and predictable.

"I suppose you will let the dog go with us?" Mr. Smith asked.

"Is everybody in your tribe a smart aleck?" Newt tucked his chin down against the slanting snowflakes and started off down the canyon.

Their going was slow, even on horseback. The darkness made it hard to choose the best way for the travois, and several times it struck some obstacle that Newt couldn't see. Tully groaned occasionally at the jarring and beating he was taking, but there was nothing to do but keep moving. The good news was that the travois rode over some of the deeper drifts fairly well, acting more like a sled when its two legs weren't digging into the ground.

Though the wind didn't blow as it had the night before, it was bitter cold and the snow was steadily getting deeper and deeper. Several times, Newt questioned his decision to try and make it to Del Norte during such weather. He had no way of knowing how bad the passage downriver would be or if the snowfall would get stronger as the night went on. His decision might be the end of them, but he shook those thoughts off, reminding himself that Tully wouldn't make it if they had stayed back at the claim. There was no guarantee the kid would pull through, even if they managed to get him to a doctor, but at least there was a fighting chance. And a puncher's chance was all that Newt had ever asked for when it came to anything.

He led them out of the canyon, hugging close to the foothills and ridgeline above the creek to the east where the snow was less deep. As he rode he remembered the homestead overlooking the river, and he considered it as a place to hole up and wait until morning if they couldn't make it downriver to Del Norte, or to Wagon Wheel Gap if they couldn't get that far.

Lost in such thoughts, it took a moment for him to recognize that someone or some *thing* was running through the darkness toward him. The clouds overhead blocked what little moonlight there might have been and the falling snow made it even harder to see, but there was no mistaking that something was out there. A long draw scattered with pines slashed down toward the creek, and through those trees he caught hints of a wispy shadow of movement.

He reined up the Circle Dot horse and snatched at the butt of his rifle, which was sticking up out of his saddle scabbard, but the gelding had sensed whatever was out there and shied and caused him to bobble his hold on the gun. Whatever was coming was now close enough that he could hear its running steps on the snow.

Then something fell in the snow not far from him. He got the Circle Dot horse under control, snaked the rifle from his scabbard, and dismounted. The dark shape on the ground did not move, and after a short wait he left the horses behind him and went toward it. He approached it cautiously, rifle ready. When he leaned over it, he got the distinct impression it was no *thing* at all, but instead it was a child.

That recognition barely had time to register with him before the child, or whatever it was, lunged up at him with the ferocity of a wildcat. Wild blows struck at him, and he barely managed to pivot and shove the flailing little body aside. He dropped his rifle and managed to grab a hold on one arm, but that brought on a whole new onslaught of punches and kicks and thrashing about. Had his coat not been so thick, he was sure he would have had some skin clawed off of him. He spun the child about and pinned it against his waist.

"Easy now! We mean you no harm!" he said.

The child was saying something in a language he had never heard, babbling at him uncontrollably. Then all that savage fright and fury disappeared in an instant, and the child sagged against him in exhaustion or surrender.

Mr. Smith came to them leading the horses. "What is it?"

The little thing sat crumpled at Newt's feet. Newt had felt the long hair sweep against him, and that combined with the voice gave him a distinct impression.

"I think it's a little girl," he said, unable to hide his own surprise.

CHAPTER THIRTY

Mr. Smith held the girl while Newt struck a wad of matches and held them up in front of her face. She made a feeble attempt to break Mr. Smith's hold on her and tried to turn her face away from the light, but not before they had a brief look at her.

She couldn't have been more than ten or so, a petite little thing with long dark hair that was tangled and twisted and matted with snow and balls of ice. A livid welt lay across one of her cheeks where something had struck her, and it would soon turn to a bad bruise. There were other signs of the hard living she had endured, such as the torn and filthy red skirt, the crude poncho made from a blanket, her worn-out shoes. All that, Newt saw at a glance before he had to shake the match flame out, and it was enough to make him wonder about her presence even more than he had before.

"Who are you? Where did you come from?" he asked, and when he got no answers he asked her again and again, the same questions and different ones.

She refused to answer him. She had gone silent, and it was obvious she intended to stay that way, no matter how long he tried to wait her out or wear her down.

The snow was falling heavier by the time Newt got her up on his horse, larger flakes that built up on the brim of his hat and in the folded creases of his coat sleeves. He didn't trust that she would ride on the travois with Tully, no matter how much he tried to assure her that neither he nor Mr. Smith meant her any harm. Only the fact that she seemed so exhausted by whatever trials and tribulations had led her to them allowed him to get her up in the saddle and to climb up behind her without her escaping his grasp. She did not fight as she had before, but he could tell that she was biding her time and would run at the drop of a hat.

Newt tried to determine how far they had come from the claim. They had yet to strike the river, and though it was hard to tell, he guessed they had come little more than a mile or two. So little ground covered after an hour's traveling was disheartening and made him all the more certain that he had made a bad choice leaving the claim site.

"This weather's turning bad," Newt said to Mr. Smith when he was up in the saddle with one arm around the girl and his other on the bridle reins. "We can try to make it back to Happy Jack's dugout, or we can try for a little ranch I saw yesterday down near the river. Either way, I think we need to dig in and wait this out."

Mr. Smith pointed up the draw where the girl had come from, up among the pines. "Maybe we find a place there."

"Whatever she thinks is chasing her might show up."

Mr. Smith took long enough considering an answer that it let Newt know the Mohave was thinking the same thing. He was also likely thinking how hard it was going to be to keep sufficiently warm. They had no axe, only their knives, and they would have to be highly lucky to scavenge enough wood to start a fire under so much snow cover and in such conditions, much less keep one burning for long. Newt had never counted on any kind of luck except bad luck, so he made up his mind that they would try for the cabin.

It took them another hard haul to make it down to the

flat along the river. The snow there was hock-deep on the horses, and the going was even slower. The only sound was the creak of saddle leather and the grind and scrape of the travois poles passing over the rough ground and through the snow. The girl remained quiet in the saddle, but he felt her trembling at times. When that shaking of her body grew worse, he stopped and had Mr. Smith take one of the blankets from the travois so that she could wrap it around her and drape it over her head.

"How's Tully?" Newt asked Mr. Smith when they had done the best they could for the girl.

"Alive, but he does not speak to me," Mr. Smith answered.

"Is the dog still with us?"

"Yes. It is a good thing, I think. I put the blankets over both of them so that he will help keep Tully warm," Mr. Smith said. "I suppose that is why you let the dog come with us."

Newt spit a snowflake off his lips and nodded, even though Mr. Smith likely couldn't see that gesture. "Might all of us need a dog before this night's over."

They moved on, a slow struggle of willpower and trying not to think about the cold. It seemed like they had been riding for far longer than they actually had before they came to the ranch buildings Newt was trying to find. He might have gone past his intended destination if it had not been for the light showing through the cabin window. Newt saw that light when they were still a good ways off, but not before the girl saw it.

He thought she had fallen asleep, so heavily did she sag against him, but she cried out and stiffened when the light in the cabin window appeared, then tried to tear loose from his hold. When her thrashing and squirming gained her no leeway, she began to babble again. Although, like when he had first come across her, he could understand none of what she said.

Mr. Smith stopped his horse beside Newt's. "There is something about the place that she fears."

It was then that Newt caught a word, or maybe a phrase or two he recognized, and the girl must have noticed his recognition. She quit fighting and began to speak in Spanish. She spoke it with a strange accent and odd inflections that were different from what little of that language Newt had learned during his time along the border and in Mexico, but it was definitely some kind of Spanish.

Newt took hold of one of the girl's wrists and pointed her hand toward the cabin in the distance. "*¿Mal hombres?*"

The girl nodded so fiercely that he could feel her body jerk.

He let Mr. Smith question her further, for the Mohave was exceptionally fluent in Spanish. Newt could catch some of what she said, but not all of it. He had to ask Mr. Smith for clarification several times, and at first the girl made little sense to either of them. She was too scared or too cold to think calmly or speak slowly and plainly, and she often broke away from Spanish and went back to whatever language she had been speaking earlier. But with a little patience, and bit by bit, they soon had the general points of the story she was trying to tell them.

It seemed her father was a sheepherder, and they had been on their way back down to the desert with their flock when a bear or some kind of monster, they couldn't tell which, had killed her father and scattered the sheep. Whatever beast had killed her father, it had almost gotten her, too, but somehow she had evaded it.

She had been on her own since then and had made her way down out of the mountains in a blizzard. There was something about bad men and guns and seeing a man shot who had later stolen her mule. Both Newt and Mr. Smith immediately thought of Jose and the gray mule he had ridden into camp right before the Cutter's men had hit them.

She talked more, about coming to the very cabin they were staring at in the distance and the bad men finding her there. How they were going to kill her or something worse, but she had run from them. Ran into the hills and ran until she could run no more. It was then that she had accidentally stumbled upon Newt and Mr. Smith, at first believing them to be more of the same men who were chasing her.

The girl acted calmer after her story was told, and Mr. Smith seemed to have enough information that he wanted to ask no more questions. Newt was still trying to make sense of it all, and he gently tapped the girl on her shoulder.

"What is your name?" he asked. "*¿Como te llamas?*"

Either she didn't understand him or she was reluctant to answer for some reason.

"*Mi nombre es Newt.*" He slapped a hand against his chest, then reached out and tapped Mr. Smith on the shoulder. "*Este hombre se llama Señor Smith.*"

He could feel her twisting in the saddle and turning about to peer through the dark at each of them.

"*¿Su nombre es?*" Newt asked her again.

"Zuri Altube," she finally answered. Then she asked them something that Newt couldn't understand.

"She wants to know if we are men from the sheep ranch sent to find her and her father," Mr. Smith interpreted for him. "She says they were late getting down out of the mountains, and I think she expects someone to come looking for them."

"*No, somos meramente hombres del campo.*" Men of the country. It was the only thing Newt could think to tell her.

"*¿Americanos?*" she asked.

"*Verdad.*"

"*¿Tu no estas con esos hombres?*"

"We are not with those men." Newt answered.

"She wants us to take her to Del Norte," Mr. Smith said.

"I gathered that. Tell her we will, but it is too cold and we must find a place to stay until this weather breaks," Newt said.

Mr. Smith talked with the girl at length, and Newt could tell that she was insistent they kept going downriver and not stop for the night, especially at the homestead they had come to.

"Ask if the Cutter's there," Newt said when he grew impatient.

Mr. Smith seemed unable to convey the question so that the girl could understand who they spoke of.

"Big man with sideburns. Two pistols under his arms," Newt said. "*Hombre grande. Dos pistolas.*"

Again, Newt could feel her nodding in agreement.

"How many are in that cabin?" Newt asked. "*¿Cuantos hombres?*"

"Four," she said in English. "Four men."

Newt could tell by her tone that she wasn't sure of those words, but her trying told him she was beginning to believe that he and Mr. Smith might truly mean her no harm and that they were reaching some kind of accord. Also that she did, at least, speak a little English.

Newt considered the count of the Cutter's men and liked nothing about the conclusions he came to. They needed that cabin, but ousting four armed men from it would be no easy task, especially not with a wounded man and now the girl to take care of.

He was still debating with himself about his next course

of action when Tully stirred under his blankets on the travois.

"Watch her," Newt said to Mr. Smith as he got off his horse and left the girl in the saddle.

He went to the travois and squatted beside it. "Be still or you're going to get those holes in you bleeding again."

"I know how we can get in there," Tully said in a surprisingly lucid way.

"You're out of your head, kid," Newt said.

"Hear me out," Tully answered.

Tully made it through his whole idea without stopping, but Newt could tell when the kid was talking through gritted teeth and fighting through the weakness and pain of his wounds.

"Like I said, you're out of your head," Newt said when the kid was finished with what he had to say.

"It'll work," Tully insisted.

Maybe it was a stupid idea, but Newt had to admit it was a better plan than anything he could come up with. A long shot, but the more he thought about it, the more he thought it might work.

"All right," Newt said, "but I'm going to be the bait. Not you."

"We need both of you on a gun, and it's my plan," Tully said.

"You're in no shape for this. The whole reason we're here is to get you to a doctor," Newt said. "And what if you go wandering off back to the spirit land at the wrong moment?"

"I'll get them outside that cabin, you watch."

Newt went back to the Circle Dot horse and reached for his rifle in his saddle boot. The girl flinched away from him as he slid the rifle out of the scabbard. Mr. Smith said nothing about what he thought of Tully's plan. He simply got off his horse and began to ready himself for war.

Newt laid his Winchester in the crook of his left arm. "Are you ready, Tully?"

It took Tully a moment to answer him, and his voice wasn't as strong as it had been before. Newt wondered if the kid could even make it to the cabin.

"Hell, don't I look ready?" Tully finally answered.

Newt couldn't admonish the kid for his false bravado, for it was a trait common among even the most experienced men before a fight. He turned to Mr. Smith, barely able to make out where the Mohave stood in the driving snow and darkness. "You know what to do if Tully gets them outside."

"I will be ready," the Mohave said.

Newt started to go, but hesitated. "You have any kind of dream about this? You know, one of your power dreams where we win and go on to live happily ever after?"

"No," Mr. Smith said. "I have had no such dream, but if you live, make sure those who sing my deeds tell of this and that I was here and made myself known before my enemies like a true *kwanami*."

"Well, if one of the Cutter's men gets me, then I only want you to do one thing," Newt replied.

"You want me to sing your death song?"

"No, I want you to make sure you kill the sorry devil that did it. That's good enough for me."

"I will avenge you if I can."

"Me, I'd as soon we get this over and we both talk about it sometime over one of your hot cups of tea."

"You do not like tea."

"If we come through this, I promise I'll sit down with you and drink a cup."

"I will hold you to that promise."

"There's something we've got to do," Newt said to the girl in a gruff voice that didn't carry the kindness he intended it to convey. "Mr. Smith will watch over you."

But the Mohave already had taken up the bay's lead rope and was walking toward the cabin, leaving Newt with the girl. He wasn't sure what he should do with her.

He started to lay a hand on her thigh, but feared it would scare her worse than she already was. "Stay here. I won't be far away."

The girl gave no answer, and he couldn't tell in the dark if she was even paying any attention to him. He knew her terror and what it likely meant to her for things to be going on that she couldn't fathom, but there was nothing he could do about that. He thought the odds were good that she would take his horse and run away as soon as he turned his back on her, but he was surprised that she tried to follow him as he walked away. He stopped and turned back to her.

"No, you stay here," he said. He went to Mr. Smith's black and took it by one bridle rein and led it to her. He put the rein against her hand. "You can hold Mr. Smith's horse for him."

The girl took the rein and kept hold of it.

"Good. Steady yourself and this will be over before you know it." Newt's Spanish was too limited to say what needed said, and he didn't know why he kept talking to her in English when she likely couldn't understand him. He stepped closer and rubbed the Circle Dot horse's neck while he looked up at the dark shape of the girl wrapped in the blanket and sitting slumped in the middle of a saddle twice too big for her. "We'll come back for you, but if it goes wrong and we don't, you keep going downriver. I've never given him a name, but he's a good horse, and he won't quit you. He'll take you where you need to go."

Newt made another attempt to walk away, but once

more, he hadn't gone more than five or six steps before he heard the horses walking behind him. Mr. Smith had already disappeared into the night, leading the bay horse and the travois toward the cabin.

There was no time to make the girl understand. Newt walked as fast as he could push through the snow, with the girl riding behind him. His intention was to get part way up the long point of a ridge that came down to the west of the homestead and in a position where he could still have a shot at the front of the cabin. There wasn't a single tree or rock big enough to provide cover, so once he was within sixty or seventy yards of the cabin, he stopped and began to kick up a pile of snow with his feet. He stomped on his pile to pack it and kept building it up until it was thigh-high. Then he went back to the girl, dragged her out of the saddle, and sat her down behind the snow mound so suddenly that she had little time to fight him.

He wrapped the black's rein around his saddle horn but kept hold of one of the Circle Dot horse's reins when he hunkered down beside the girl. He laid his Winchester across the top of his snow pile and adjusted his position until he felt he had a good rest for both himself and the gun.

"You keep your head down," Newt told the girl, and when she sat up too high, he shoved her head back down. He watched the cabin intently, but it wasn't long before he felt the girl rising up again and looking at the same thing he was.

When he reached for her head again, she warded off his hand with an angry shove and an irritated and indignant grunt.

There was no time to argue with her, for the shapes of Mr. Smith leading the horse and Tully's travois appeared in the weak light spilling out of the cabin window. Then Newt thought he saw Mr. Smith running away and leaving the horse and travois with Tully on it in front of the cabin porch, but it was hard to tell. That very lack of visibility and trying to shoot in the dark through the slanting snow was the weakest part of their plan. He needed to get closer to the cabin, but couldn't because of the girl.

She must have understood what they intended, inferring it by their actions and by Newt's Winchester pointed at the cabin, and he felt her blanket quivering where it touched him. He reached a hand out for her again, only slower that time, all the while trying to think of something to say to her. But what did you say to prepare her for what was to come?

His hand found her shoulder, and he gave it a gentle hint of a squeeze. "I wouldn't look if I was you, and you might want to put your fingers in your ears."

CHAPTER THIRTY-ONE

At first, Zuri thought that the big man with the sideburn whiskers and the two pistols from the cabin, or some of his men, had gotten ahead of her. Or maybe she had become confused in the darkness and somehow traveled in a circle that had brought her back to the homestead. Either way, it did not matter. By the time she all but crashed into the two riders and their horses, she was physically spent to the point that there was nothing she could do other than put up a feeble and losing fight.

She listened to their voices while she lay in the snow at their feet, and she hardly fought at all when they pulled her up and held some lit matches before her face. The light seemed overly bright, but that wasn't the only reason she turned her face away from it. The same match light that illuminated her also lit up the two men standing over her.

They were both big men, with one as big or bigger than the man with the two pistols back at the cabin and the other more like a giant than a man at all. But their faces were even worse behind the flickering match flame, especially the giant with the strange marks on his skin and the dark, shining eyes like she had always envisioned the trolls having, the ones who lived in caves and came out to steal children that her grandmother had once told stories about.

Like the men back at the cabin, they asked her questions that she could not decipher, and her heart hammered so that she could not think clearly. She felt her own mouth trying to shape words, but no sound would come out.

Then the one with the scars and a sharp-angled face like a craggy mountainside put her up on his horse and swung up behind her. *Where were they taking her?*

Slowly, some of her panic subsided, and she was overcome with a numbness and a sense of defeat like she had felt when she had found her father's mauled body. She was so tired, and some whispering voice only she could hear, as cold and sluggish and sleepy as the blood within her veins, continually reminded her how easy it would be to curl up in a ball and close her eyes and surrender. No more suffering, no more fear, and nothing but sweet, painless surrender and an eternity of blissful sleep.

Then she was pulled slightly out of her lethargy when the man stopped the horse and placed a blanket over her. The blanket and the gentle yet firm clutch of the man behind her surprised her, and she slowly came to realize, to dare to hope, that the men she was with possibly bore her goodwill.

She considered the litter they were dragging behind the riderless horse. It was impossible to tell who was on that litter, but she assumed it was a wounded person. Could it be the man she had seen shot on the rockslide? If so, that meant the two she was with weren't in alliance with the big man who had come to the cabin. It was hard to think that men who looked as they did could be those who would help her, but her mother had always told her not to judge people by their appearances.

Maybe it was that newfound hope or the added comfort of the blanket and the rock of the horse's stride that brought back the heavy fog of weariness that she had been battling earlier, and before too long she was on the verge of falling asleep. Eventually, she nodded off, but the jerk of her head startled her back awake. She rubbed at her face in an attempt to come fully alert, then she recognized the dim light burning in the distance ahead of them for what it was. They were back at the homestead. *No!* She tried to get off the horse, but the man in the saddle behind her held her as effortlessly as he had before.

"Please, don't take me back there! Let me go!" she cried in out in her native tongue.

Her words had no effect on either of them, and that made her even more frantic. She talked in a breathless rush, but during that frenetic outpouring of words she chanced to say something to them in Spanish. Maybe it was only a phrase or a single word, but it was enough. The scar-faced man holding her relaxed his grip slightly, and she realized that he had understood her.

She took a deep breath to steady her nerves and made an attempt to speak more clearly and coherently and only in Spanish. The man with the scarred face was the first to respond to her, but to her surprise, it was the giant Indian with the designs on his face who did most of the talking.

She told them all that had happened to her, about the bear and losing her father and the long journey down off the big mountain. She begged them to take her to a town, and she questioned them as to whether or not they were men sent by the sheep's owner to find her and her father.

They weren't sent looking for her, and neither man made any attempt to explain their presence. Her next thought was that perhaps the cabin in the distance belonged to them. When they questioned her about the big man with the mean eyes and the two pistols that had accosted her at the cabin, her sense that he and they were enemies was reinforced. When they dismounted and began to ready guns, she was

sure that another bad thing was about to happen and that
she was still caught up in something that she had no control
of, like a snowflake falling from on high and fluttering
about on the wind with no choice in where she landed.

The last place she wanted to be in the whole wide world
was anywhere close to that homestead. If she could only
somehow explain to them how bad those men inside the
cabin were, then surely, they would be just as anxious as
she was to avoid the place and be gone to somewhere else.
But no matter how much she talked to them, they didn't
seem to understand.

The Indian with the tattooed face headed toward the
cabin, on foot and leading the horse dragging the litter with
the wounded man on it. Zuri was shocked to see part of a
dog revealed among the pile of blankets on top of the litter.
The sight of the pet reminded her of her collie sheepdog,
and not for the first time she wondered what had become
of it. Had it been killed by the bear like her father, or was
it still dutifully herding the sheep? Was it confused as to
where its masters had gone and wondering, as she did, why
nothing was as it had been?

The man with the scarred face said something to her in
English that she couldn't fathom, then he started walking
away. It shocked her that he would leave her with his horse,
and she considered that it was her chance to escape. However, that meant once more being by herself and lost, and
that was a terror almost as bad as looking at the cabin.
Without even realizing she was doing it, she made the horse
follow him.

He turned back once again and said something else she
couldn't understand and in a firmer tone. Then he handed
her one of the reins to the Indian's horse. She could tell he
wanted her to hold the animal, and that implied he intended
to come back. She could hear the sound of his rubbing his

horse's neck while he stood close to her, and he talked more. His voice was deep, and there was something in the tone of it that held a kindness and a concern not at all in keeping with what she expected. She wished her English skills were better so that she could understand what he was telling her.

She had come far since leaving the sheep camp, all of it alone, but when he walked away again, the absence of even so little as his presence hit her hard. So, she followed him as she had before, even if that meant going closer to the cabin.

She could tell that he was angry by the way he stopped and began to kick up the snow and how he jerked her off the horse and plopped her down behind the wall that he had made. But even then, he was strangely gentle, like some beast too big and too wild to be good at being kind or delicate, but trying, nonetheless.

What did he say he was called? Newt? The Americans had such strange sounding names.

He sat down beside her with his rifle resting on the snow wall and peered at the cabin. It startled her when he put his hand on her head and shoved her down, and she was about to hit him when another strange thought struck her. He was scary, yes. She could not see him well in the dark, but she could sense his grimness, and the gun he aimed at the cabin told that he was a violent man. So why was it that she somehow felt safer with him than she had at any point since the bear had come and turned her life upside down?

Then anything she thought or felt was startled from her mind and body when he shouldered his rifle and the blast of it washed over her.

CHAPTER THIRTY-TWO

Tully Hudlow almost lost consciousness not long after Mr. Smith left him in front of the cabin. Maybe he even did for a little while, and maybe it was the cold snow falling on his face that woke him up because Mr. Smith had thrown the blankets off him so that most of him could be seen plainly. Either way, he was awake and somewhat alert when the cabin door swung open and spilled more light onto the porch and into the yard in front of it. One man holding a lantern stepped out on the porch and then two others. Tully couldn't see any of them because he was lying on his back on the travois without moving and with the capote's hood pulled up over his head.

"What is it, Kirby?" somebody asked from inside the cabin. "What's out there?"

Tully thought that voice sounded like the skinny Texan Newt had beaten to a pulp back at the Gap.

"Is that Arnie?" one of the men on the porch asked as he apparently recognized the tracker's distinctive blanket coat, just as Tully had hoped he would.

The light spread brighter and reached closer to Tully as the man with the lantern held it higher to better see. Tully could hear the snow crunching under that man's boots as he came down off the porch and closer to the travois.

"Something isn't right." That was the Cutter's voice, and the porch boards creaked under his weight like he was pacing down its length toward the farthest end, away from Tully.

Tully stared out of the little hole left to him by the capote's hood, through slitted eyes meant to appear closed. He waited and watched until the man with the lantern came fully into his field of vision.

"Arnie? Can you hear me?" The man asked as he bent over Tully and touched the hood to push it back.

At that moment, the dog popped its head out from under the pile of blankets beside Tully and growled.

"What the hell?" The man hovering over Tully took a step backward and grabbed for the revolver on his hip.

Tully pulled the Merwin & Hulbert pistol out from under the same blankets that had hid the dog and cocked it and shoved it at the man's chest. "This is for my brother."

The pistol roared and spat flame. Tully would have tried to get another man, but he was too weak to sit up. That, and the bay horse pulling the travois bolted and threw a runaway as soon as he shot.

Less than a hundred yards out from the front of the cabin, Newt watched the whole proceeding. He couldn't tell exactly what happened, but he heard Tully's pistol crack, saw the man with the lantern leaning over Tully go down, and saw the horse running off with the travois bouncing and skidding wildly behind it.

It was harder for Newt to see once the lantern fell to the snow. The men on the porch and in the yard were little more than dim shadows in the weak light thrown from the cabin's open door. Shooting in the dark without the advantage of one's rifle sights was a poor way to fight, but there was no other choice.

Newt swung the Winchester toward the other man down off the porch and a few steps out from it, and he pressed his cheekbone tight to the comb of the buttstock and took a simple aim down the top of the barrel. The break of the trigger was crisp and clean, and the kick of the rifle drove his shoulder back. He thought the man he shot at went down, but then he saw him up and staggering back toward the porch as he was levering a fresh round home. He was about to shoot a second time when a gun flashed from one end of the porch and the man running for the cabin door went down for good. Mr. Smith must have taken a hiding spot on the side of the cabin and was now in the fight. The boom of his .45-70 lever gun was distinct from Tully's pistol fire.

The dog had either jumped off the travois or been thrown from it, and it was barking and darting around in front of the cabin. A gun flamed from the opposite end of the porch, once, twice, then Newt caught a glimpse of someone running for the barn. He threw a hurried shot that way, but it didn't even slow the man.

Another man broke from inside the cabin, and that one, too, ran for the barn. He was slower than the first, but hard to see and hard to hit. Mr. Smith fired at him and seemed to miss. Newt fired at the same man and did no better. The two who had run for the barn were out of the light and gone into the darkness before either Newt or the Mohave could shoot again.

Newt turned his body to better face the barn. He could barely even make it out the shape of it. When he glanced at the cabin again, he thought he saw Mr. Smith duck through the door and disappear inside. He fully expected to hear more gunfire from within the cabin, but none came.

Four. The girl had said there were four of them. *Two down, plus the two that had run for the barn.*

At that very moment, he heard hinges creak and the barn doors swung open. Several horses charged out of the darkness from that direction and passed through the light in front of the cabin. Right behind them came another horse, only that one had a rider on its back. Mr. Smith reappeared in the cabin door, but he had to duck back as the rider tried to gun him down in passing. The darkness and the snow protected whoever had been on that horse's back, and he was swallowed up and gone again before Newt could pull a trigger on him.

Newt hunkered behind his snowbank and thumbed more cartridges in the loading gate of his Winchester while he waited. He wasn't sure if the other man who had run for the barn had been on one of the horses or if that one was still around. He considered working himself closer to the barn, and he wished he had a shotgun. A scattergun was always better for close work in the dark.

It was only then that he remembered the girl. He reached out a hand to touch her and to confirm she was still beside him. His hand found her, and from the feel of her she was lying on her side and curled into a little ball.

He patted her shoulder. "It's all right now. It's all right."

CHAPTER THIRTY-THREE

It was at least another hour before daylight, and Newt sat at the table and studied the girl and Tully Hudlow lying on blanket pallets in front of the fireplace. Both of them seemed to be sleeping, and the dog was curled up between them. It, too, appeared asleep, but any time Newt moved in his chair the dog opened one or both of its milky eyes or cocked an ear at him.

He finished the last of the coffee in his mug and glanced at Mr. Smith, who was sitting in another chair facing the door with his rifle laid across his lap. Though they had managed to take the cabin, the Cutter and another of the outlaws had gotten away. From what they could glean from their conversations with the girl and from her descriptions of the outlaws she had encountered in the cabin, the other survivor was Johnny Dial. The Cutter and Dial could be out there nearby, waiting to get a little payback for the night's events, and both Newt and the Mohave weren't going to sleep much because of that possibility.

They had made a quick search of the barn by lantern light but found nobody hiding there, then sheltered their horses inside. There were so many tracks around the homestead, and the snow was failing so heavily and rapidly covering that sign, that they couldn't determine where the remaining outlaw might have gone. Newt believed Dial might have been on one of the horses and they simply missed seeing him, but Mr. Smith was less convinced of that.

Newt's attention went back to the sleeping forms on the pallets. He had found Tully a hundred yards from the cabin, where the lashings holding the travois together had broken apart and dumped him. Farther along were the busted poles, blankets, and spilled items from the travois, but there was no sign of the bay horse. Newt had put Tully belly-down over the Circle Dot horse's saddle as gently as he could and carried him back to the cabin in that fashion. Such rough handling had caused the wound in Tully's abdomen to start bleeding again, and the kid wasn't conscious when Newt found him.

The girl, Zuri, was in poor shape herself. Besides being exhausted and near starved, her right foot showed signs of frostbite, as did the tips of most of her fingers, though to a lesser degree. The skin of her big toe and the ball of the same foot was a pale gray color and harder than it should be. It was no wonder, for the shoe she had worn over that foot had almost to come apart and was packed full of snow and ice.

He had warmed a bowl of water and had her soak her foot in that while Mr. Smith fed her some beans and one of the cornmeal cakes he had cooked for them from the larder they found in the cabin and among the saddlebags and gear the outlaws had left in the barn. The girl claimed she felt no discomfort, but that had changed after the warm water took effect. The frostbit skin turned to a bright red and began to swell, and though she hadn't cried out, tears rolled down her cheeks and her jaw tendons rippled where she clenched her teeth against the pain as the blood vessels expanded and the possible ice crystals that had formed in her flesh thawed.

Now she slept like she hadn't slept in a long time. He stood and eased across the room to where she lay. The dog raised its head but didn't growl. Newt squatted and lifted the blankets back that covered her feet and saw that the skin on her toe had lost some of the redness, but tiny blisters were beginning to form. He put her covering back in place and looked to Mr. Smith.

"We need to go as soon as it's daylight," Newt said. "Tully's worse than he was, and I'm afraid the girl might lose that toe and maybe one of her fingers if we don't get her to a doctor."

"I will go look for more horses," Mr. Smith said. "I do not think they will run far."

"And you might stumble on to the Cutter and Dial."

Mr. Smith nodded. "There is that."

"We can put Tully on my horse, and then you take him and the girl down to the Gap."

"I will stay here, and you go," Mr. Smith said. "This lodge is a good one and there is plenty of firewood. It is you who will not have it so easy."

"No, you take the girl up with you, and Tully and I will ride double."

"The snow is deep, and I think the cold will get worse. Your horse is not big and may not make it carrying two men," Mr. Smith replied.

"Nobody gets left here," Newt said.

They left their conversation at that, and neither man said anything for the rest of the night.

True to the Mohave's word, it was the coldest it had been when Newt went outside at the first light of dawn, but at least it had quit snowing. He stood in the open doorway for a while with his rifle in hand, scanning everything he could see, then he took a chance and stepped out on the porch. Mr. Smith came out behind him, his Marlin big-bore rifle ready.

"Keep a lookout for me while I go to the barn and get our horses." Newt threw caution aside and went off the porch and trudged toward the barn.

He paid special attention to the little log building that looked like some kind of smokehouse or root cellar and the big barn, the only two things on the flat that might possibly make cover for a marksman looking to ambush him. When he swung one of the barn doors open, he was careful to step aside as soon as he did it, and when he went inside, he did so quickly and then stepped aside again and into a shadowed corner. He waited until his eyes adjusted to the dark interior of the barn and gave it a careful inspection before he began to saddle the Circle Dot horse and Mr. Smith's black gelding.

When both horses were saddled, he led them to the barn door, but paused there again. Mr. Smith was still on the porch and everything seemed fine, but Newt couldn't get over the feeling that he was an awfully easy target.

He led the horses out of the barn and had barely taken five or six steps toward the cabin when he noticed the smokehouse door was partially open. That wasn't a good thing, for he was sure it had been closed when he passed by it the first time.

CHAPTER THIRTY-FOUR

Johnny Dial had spent a long, cold night in the little smokehouse, and when he wasn't shivering and shaking and hugging himself, he was cursing the Cutter for having turned loose their horses and run off and left him. He had tried to make it to the barn with the Cutter, but his injuries slowed him. With nowhere else to go and with bullets flying around him, the smokehouse had looked like as good a place to hide as any.

The Widowmaker, it had to be him and that big Indian. At one point in the night, he could hear them talking and moving around the homestead searching for him. The Cutter had believed both men injured and on the run, but the arrogant, cowardly wretch was wrong.

The ceiling in the smokehouse was so low that Dial had to stand stooped over, if he stood at all. He had spent most of the night sitting huddled in a corner with his pistol in hand, watching the door and expecting them to find him. But the cold must have driven them inside the cabin, and the search for him had ceased.

Several times, he had to stand up and stomp his feet to try and jar some life and feeling into them, and no matter how he tried to put his hands under his armpits or inside his coat, his fingers still hurt. When he moved wrong, he could feel the broken ends of his collarbone grinding together.

The walls of the smokehouse were made of small logs notched at the corners, with mud chinked in between each log. A hole where a bit of that mud had fallen out let him know when morning came. He moved to where he could put one eye against that hole and peered outside. It was still not true daylight, but only that surreal twilight of gray and shadows where no color could yet take hold. It was an uncertain world hung somewhere between darkness and light, between the real and the unreal, like a tintype photograph that reflected a version of the world in negative.

He leaned against the log wall beside him and breathed out of his mouth. His swollen and broken nose wouldn't let him do otherwise. He knew his only chance was to try to make it to the barn and steal a horse from his enemies, but he also knew he should have made that attempt during the night. The thing that bothered him most, besides possibly dying, was not avenging his brother.

He rose and went to the door and was about to open it when he heard voices from the cabin and then someone walking past the smokehouse. He went back to his peephole and peered at the barn. It wasn't long before he saw the Widowmaker appear. He tried to push out more of the chinked mud to allow room for him to see better, but the Widowmaker had gone inside the barn by the time he was finished.

Back at the door, he listened intently for the sound of anyone else moving about but heard nothing. He dared to crack the door open ever so slightly, giving him a better view of the barn doors. One of them stood open, and he could see the Widowmaker saddling horses. He could not see the cabin porch without stepping outside. The Indian would likely come running as soon as the Widowmaker went down, and Dial could wait for him in ambush the same way. Knock them off one by one.

That fool idea vanished almost as instantaneously as it had formed. His brother Bobby had been a hothead like that, who never took the time to think anything through. Johnny, on the other hand, had survived as long as he had less on being tough or skilled with weapons and more by sly cunning and the application of cowardice and caution when it served his needs.

Get close to the Widowmaker, let him finish saddling, and then kill him and take the horse.

He pushed the smokehouse door open a little wider and leaned his head out and around the doorjamb. He had waited too long to cover the ground between him and the barn, and the Widowmaker was already coming out leading two horses. That was a bad stroke of luck. It would have been much better to sneak up behind him and put a bullet in his brainpan, but Dial altered his plan. He would let the Widowmaker keep coming until he passed by the smokehouse. There wouldn't be more than ten yards between them then.

The Widowmaker stopped for some reason, looking right at him, and Dial knew that he had spotted the open door. He stepped out of the smokehouse with his pistol leading the way.

CHAPTER THIRTY-FIVE

Newt's hand dropped for the butt of his revolver, but he had to brush his coat back out of the way to get to it, and the gloves he wore slowed him and made it hard to handle his gun hammer and get a finger in the trigger guard. That took precious time, and Dial got off the first two shots, firing as fast as he could squeeze the heavy trigger on his double-action pistol. Had he been a calmer or better marksman, he might have taken his time and killed Newt with either bullet, but that wasn't the case. The first shot passed by Newt's cheek and splintered the Circle Dot horse's saddle horn, and the second shot kicked up snow in front of him.

Newt dropped to one knee as his revolver came free of his holster and a third bullet passed over him. Dial was moving by then, not to the right or left, but coming straight at him with his pistol barrel flaming. Newt was just bringing up his Smith & Wesson when Mr. Smith fired from the cabin porch.

The heavy .45 caliber rifle bullet from Mr. Smith's Marlin rifle hit Dial and staggered him sideways. The outlaw dropped his pistol and went down on his knees. But he was up almost as quickly as he had fallen, and he took off in a crippled run, doubled over and clutching his stomach.

He fell once again, squirmed and writhed in the snow, then got back up again. Newt couldn't tell what the outlaw was screaming, for it was too high-pitched and shrill.

Dial did not make for the barn, nor did he try to return to the protection of the smokehouse, but instead he ran past Newt and out onto the open plain of white between the cabin and the river. Newt could see the blood trail Dial was leaving in his tracks. Dial fell a third time, but he got back up and kept going as he had before.

Mr. Smith had levered another round home and had his rifle shouldered and was tracking Dial through his gunsights, but he didn't fire, even though Dial was getting farther away with every moment. Newt searched their surroundings for sign of any other enemies besides Dial, but saw nothing.

"I'd say he's done," Newt called to the Mohave.

Mr. Smith lowered his rifle.

"Owe you one," Newt said.

Mr. Smith nodded his head but refused to take his eyes off the retreating figure of the fleeing and wounded outlaw. The horses had shied from the gunfire but had only run back to the barn, and they stood there with their heads high and ears perked. Newt eased his way to them, caught them, and led them to the cabin.

"Help me get Tully up on my horse," Newt said.

Zuri was standing in the far corner of the room when Newt went inside the cabin. Her eyes were wide with fright, and she was holding the broken old Springfield rifle they had found lying on the table in the middle of the room.

"We're going now," Newt said to her.

He had to say it a second time, then he went to her and plucked the rifle from her hands. She gave him one of her disgusted grunts and acted like she was going to try and fight him for the weapon, but she finally went to her pallet to gather her coat, shoes, and other things. She limped badly.

He made her sit in one of the chairs and examined her foot. There were more blisters, and now the end of her big toe was black. He wondered if she could tolerate wearing a shoe on that foot, but she put on both socks and shoes without showing too much discomfort.

"Does it hurt?" he asked.

She must have understood that much English or simply inferred what he was asking, for she shook her head that it didn't. He wondered if she could feel parts of her foot at all, and that worried him even more than the ugly flesh of her frostbite.

He helped her into her coat and then pulled her poncho over her head. She put on a stocking cap she had found somewhere, and he tugged it down until it completely covered her ears and until it reached all the way to her eyebrows. She shoved his hands away and gave him a brief, angry frown before she readjusted the cap to suit her.

He pointed at the door and Mr. Smith standing in it. She grabbed for the broken rifle, and he put a hand back on it.

"Mr. Smith will put you on a horse," he said.

She wouldn't let go of the gun. For some reason it seemed important to her. He pulled it away from her and put a hand between her shoulder blades and started her toward the door. He followed her outside and hung the rifle from his saddle strings while she watched.

"Does that suit you?" he asked.

Again, she understood somehow and nodded.

Mr. Smith helped her get on his horse. She kept looking at his tattooed face with some measure of apprehension but put up no fight. It was apparent that she still didn't fully trust them.

Why should she? Newt thought. He wouldn't if he were her. *What must such a child think of them?*

He caught her staring at him when he looked at her again

and while Mr. Smith went back into the cabin. She did not look away from his gaze, and he could tell that it was some kind of purposeful defiance on her part. He laughed inwardly when he realized that he found himself in some kind of test of wills with a child.

Everyone had a breaking point, and in Newt's experience the urge to quit was far more prevalent than tenacity and fortitude. It simply didn't take much to break most people. He had no clue exactly what she had gone through, but the fact that she still acted as brave as she did said a lot about her.

When he went back inside the cabin, he found that Mr. Smith already had Tully sitting up. The kid was conscious but weak enough that it took both of them supporting him, or practically carrying him, to get him to Newt's horse, and it took even more effort to get him up in the saddle. They tied a rope in front of his waist and to the back D-rings of Newt's double-rigged saddle. It wouldn't keep Tully from falling off, but it might buy them some time to right him if he got off-balance.

"You up to this, Tully?" Newt asked.

Tully didn't answer and simply sat sagging in the saddle with his eyes closed, as if it was taking everything in him to stay there. Newt went to close the cabin door. The dog had been lying close to the fireplace, and it stood when he took one last look into the room.

"You won't get a free ride this time, but come on if you're coming," he said to the dog.

Mostly blind or not, the way the dog stared at him reminded him somehow of the girl. He was about to close the door when the dog trotted across the floor and went past him and out onto the porch.

Leaving the cabin, Newt took his rifle in one hand and one of the Circle Dot horse's bridle reins in the other.

"You lead off," he said to Mr. Smith, who was up in his saddle behind Zuri. The Mohave had his buffalo coat open, and it was big enough that she could almost fit inside with him.

"You will have far to walk," Mr. Smith said.

"I'll make it as far as I can," Newt answered, "and then you can spell me."

Mr. Smith urged his black through the snow, breaking a trail. Even then, it was hard going for Newt, right from the beginning, and he had at least seven or eight more miles to go before they could make it as far as Wagon Wheel Gap.

The dog followed them.

They had almost reached the river when Johnny Dial came up over the bank of the riverbed, coming toward them in a tortured and lumbering run. Newt shouldered his rifle. Dial was a good hundred yards away, and if he was truly trying to attack them again, that would be the craziest thing Newt had ever seen. Then Newt saw that Dial was looking over his shoulder at something behind him . . . something chasing him.

A large bear came out of the riverbed behind Dial. It closed the distance between them with a speed that gave Dial no chance, as if the deep snow didn't hinder it at all. It was a grizzly— the first of its kind Newt had ever seen, but he knew immediately that's what it was.

The grizzly caught Dial, and the Texas outlaw screamed in the same high-pitched way he had when Mr. Smith had shot him back at the homestead. Newt was far enough from the river that he couldn't see every detail of the mauling Dial was taking, but it was plain that the bear was tearing him to pieces.

Then Zuri gave a pitiful cry. Not a scream, but more of a whimper. She tried to kick Mr. Smith's black and make it go, but the big Mohave pressed her close to his chest and kept the horse in place.

The grizzly looked up at them once. Newt's hold on his rifle became tenser, but the bear didn't move toward them. Its stance was threatening and defiant, and at the minimum showed that it had no fear of them at all.

Dial must not have been dead yet, and he did something to return the bear's attention to him, for it quit looking at the people in the distance and returned to mauling him. Zuri hid her face inside Mr. Smith's buffalo hide coat so that she did not have to watch.

Newt and Mr. Smith shared a glance between them before Mr. Smith urged his black gelding downriver toward the Gap so that the girl didn't have to see or hear any more of the mauling. Newt led the Circle Dot horse after him with his rifle ready and his eyes never leaving the grizzly until they were far away from it. The dog behind him growled a few times, either sensing something wrong or hearing or smelling the bear, but did nothing more than that. Apparently, it was just as ready to be as far away from Old Ephraim as the rest of them.

When they stopped again a mile along their way for Newt to rest his legs, he looked back the way they had come and shook his head. "What's a bear doing out this time of year?"

"It is not the normal way of the *mahwat*. The winter is a time where they go to the Dark House and dream," Mr. Smith said somberly, as if giving his answer considerable thought. "But maybe the dreams come no more for the *mahwat,* either, as they do not for me, and they become restless and do not sleep as they once did."

Newt didn't notice until then that Zuri had been crying. Her gray eyes were bloodshot and wet. He considered how hard it had to have been for her to see the grizzly kill Dial after witnessing her own father killed by the same kind of beast. Or was it the same bear? Happy Jack had said there weren't very many grizzlies in the San Juan Mountains.

"*Oso Diablo*," Zuri muttered in Spanish. It was the very name she had called the grizzly when she had first told them of what had happened to her at her father's sheep camp.

Newt couldn't disagree with her. It had truly seemed like a devil bear.

CHAPTER THIRTY-SIX

There were only four men who decided to winter over in Wagon Wheel Gap. Those men and the few scattered homesteaders up and down the river nearby were the only ones who might have witnessed Newt and the others with him come through the Gap an hour before sundown. The snow had been deep in places, and Newt had walked at least half of the way, with he and Mr. Smith taking turns riding the black with Zuri while the other led the Circle Dot horse bearing Tully Hudlow. Tully had not made it far before he could no longer ride upright. They had stopped and built another travois for him, adding to the length and ardor of their journey.

It was to the hotel at the hot springs that they rode instead of stopping at the settlement around the railroad depot, and the caretaker hired to watch over the hotel during the off-season was shocked, to say the least, when they carried Tully inside and laid him down by the woodstove. The caretaker would have protested the dog being allowed inside, but his impression of both Newt and Mr. Smith was one that made him hold back such demands.

According to that caretaker, and as Newt had feared, the nearest doctor was not at Wagon Wheel Gap or at

South Fork, but at Del Norte, roughly thirty miles away. Neither Newt nor Mr. Smith had slept in over thirty-six hours, but they convinced the caretaker to loan them one of the hotel's buggies used to haul customers back and forth from the hotel to the railroad depot. After a hurried meal for themselves and the girl and some time to warm themselves, they placed Tully, the girl, and the dog in the buggy hitched to a fresh horse. Their own mounts they left with the caretaker.

The road through the canyon downriver was never a good one, and the snowfall had done nothing to improve that condition. The bridge below the Gap was slick and treacherous, and the buggy horse fell crossing it. More than once as they moved down the canyon, they had to stop and dig their way through snowdrifts so that the buggy could pass. The trail was better once they got to South Fork and down into the beginning of the San Luis Valley, but it was still a struggle. They lifted the blankets covering their injured passengers to check their condition often.

A farmer between South Fork and Del Norte saw them passing by his farm at dusk while he was outside his house and splitting firewood for his stove. He hailed them to a stop and loaned them a fresh horse and fed them and poured hot coffee into them. They weren't there long and arrived in Del Norte three hours after dark.

It being a bitterly cold night, and there was no one on the streets to meet them. Another half hour passed before Newt and Mr. Smith found the doctor. By the time they carried Tully into the side room in his house that served as his office and hospital, they were both at the end of any reserves of energy that might have possessed them. Newt made sure Zuri was tucked away in a corner chair with a blanket wrapped around her, then he promptly lay down on the floor beside the doctor's stove and went to sleep. Mr. Smith had already done the same thing.

Both men were so tired that they didn't even wake up when someone in town started ringing a fire alarm bell.

CHAPTER THIRTY-SEVEN

The Cutter rode into Del Norte under the cover of night. It didn't take him long to find the place he was looking for, and he left his horse in an alley and climbed a set of exterior stairs that led up to a second-floor office. He noticed that there was lamplight shining through the glass window in the door, considered the implications of his visit, then climbed the steps quietly.

The door glass had wording painted on it that labeled it as the business location of a one-man law firm, something that didn't surprise the Cutter. He did not pause at the door but immediately tested the doorknob under his hand. It wasn't locked, and he pushed inside without knocking.

There was a middle-aged man sitting behind a desk on the far side of the small room. At that moment, his suit coat was draped over the back of his chair and his shirtsleeves were rolled up on his forearms. If he was surprised at the Cutter's unannounced appearance in his office, he hid it well. He took off his reading glasses, shoved away the stack of documents he had been studying, and then pushed his chair back slightly farther from his desk. He stared at the Cutter intently without saying anything.

"We need to talk," the Cutter said as he pushed the door closed behind him.

"It's after business hours. If you are seeking legal counsel, why don't you come back tomorrow at a more suitable time?" The man behind the desk laced the fingers of both hands across his chest.

"You need to tell the people we work for a few things."

"And who do you work for, and why is it you believe they also employ me?"

"Quit whatever game you're playing, and save your lawyer talk for someone else."

The Cutter's voice had a raw edge to it, and the lawyer noticed that. "And you are?"

"Kirby Cutter."

The lawyer inhaled deeply while he considered the Cutter standing before him. After a moment of thought, he gestured at one of the chairs in front of his desk. "Forgive me, but I'm sure you understand my caution."

The Cutter remained standing.

"Very well, then," the lawyer said. "What is it you have to tell me?"

The Cutter told him what had happened, leaving out very little. The lawyer's facial expression didn't change at all except when the Cutter mentioned the girl, and even then, it was only a slight wince. Overall, he took the news with about as much emotion as a bank teller watching someone count money. However, when the Cutter was finished, he did sit up straighter and there was a furrowed crease in the center of his forehead.

"I need to send some messages," he said. "You say there were only three survivors in addition to the girl? Not counting yourself, of course."

"You tell them I can tend to it. No worries. I'll clean it up."

"I will relay the information you have shared with me." The lawyer reached inside a vest pocket and pulled out his pocket watch. "Come find me tomorrow. At, let's say, ten o'clock. No, make it noon. This may take some time to sort out. I would suggest you find some place to lay low until then."

The Cutter nodded but didn't move toward the door.

"You can go now," the lawyer said in case the Cutter hadn't heard him the first time.

The Cutter let out a deep chuckle and didn't move. "Can I now?"

"Rest assured that I will contact the necessary parties and get us clear instruction on how to proceed next," the lawyer added.

The Cutter continued to stand in front of the desk, staring at the man before him and taking in the room. "How many like you work for them? Here and elsewhere?"

The lawyer shrugged. "I don't know. Several, I would guess, but I've found it best not to ask too many questions. I file the papers they ask me to file and serve as their legal counsel on small matters from time to time. I make certain arrangements when they ask me to make them, and that's all."

"I need money to hire more men."

The lawyer's chair squeaked as he shifted his weight on it. He cleared his throat slightly before he spoke again. "As I understand it, you were paid a healthy advance. Considering you failed to achieve either of the jobs you were hired to do, I don't think—"

"I lost nine men. Nine."

"I'm sorry for your loss, but—"

The Cutter gave the little square metal safe behind the man

a glance. "You're sorry? How about you fork over the money so I can find more men to straighten this out? Set it right."

The man behind the desk leaned back again, creating more distance between himself and the Cutter. When he spoke again he was very careful to keep his voice even and reserved. "That is a decision that I can't make, but I promise, I will relay your request for additional funds."

"You do that."

The chair beneath the man behind the desk creaked again. The Cutter remained where he was for a couple of more breaths, then turned and started for the door. He had his hand on the doorknob when the lawyer stopped him.

"Excuse me, but I forgot to ask where you will be staying," the lawyer said.

"I'll be at O'Doul's," the Cutter replied.

"At his house, or at his place of business?"

"He's got a room in the back of his saloon."

"Good, I will know where to find you in case I get word before morning."

The Cutter pulled open the door.

"Oh, and will you please make sure that door is closed when you leave? It sometimes fails to latch properly and lets a terrible draft pass through."

A thin smile formed on the Cutter's mouth that might have only been a tightening of his lips. "I'll close it good and tight. Wouldn't want you to get chilled, now would we?"

The Cutter closed the door behind him and stood outside it for a long moment, as if weighing something in his mind, before he went back down the stairs to his horse. When he was up in the saddle, he stared at the light in the door glass for an equally long time before he finally rode out of the alley and down the dark streets.

* * *

It was nearing midnight when the Cutter walked into the O'Doul's Saloon. Other than the proprietor, who also served dual duty as the bartender, there were only two other men in the place, one of them passed out drunk on the floor in the corner. But that was not surprising. The crude little shack that housed the drinking establishment lay on the edge of town near the train tracks. Most of Del Norte's sporting crowd and more civilized residents preferred the nicer saloons, and the only things O'Doul had going for him were being a handy stop for the trainmen to nab a quick drink and the hard drinkers liking the fact that he served the cheapest liquor in town and tolerated sloppy drunks.

"Look what the devil drug in," O'Doul said when the Cutter approached the bar.

"Is your back room empty?" the Cutter asked.

O'Doul was a short Irishman, with a grimy, unkempt look about him, from the thatches of uncombed hair sticking out every which way on his head to the week's worth of whisker stubble on his face. He stared at the Cutter for a moment with his sagging lower eyelids showing the red in his eyes.

"It's yours if you need to use it," O'Doul said, and then pushed a glass and a whiskey bottle in front of the Cutter. "Care for a drink?"

The Cutter shook his head. "Have you still got that scattergun behind the bar?"

O'Doul instantly took on a cagey air. "I might."

"Get it for me."

O'Doul reached under the bar top and pulled out a Remington double-barreled 12-gauge. "You buying or borrowing?"

The Cutter ignored the question. "What time are you closing up?"

O'Doul looked around the room, as if only then appraising how slow of a night his saloon was having. "I imagine

I'll close up soon. Midnight's my usual, unless business is good. Are you on the run again?"

"You didn't used to ask so many questions."

"You used to give a lot more answers."

The Cutter cracked open the shotgun to make sure it was loaded, pulled out the two paper-hulled cartridges and inspected them, then put them back in the chambers and snapped the weapon's breeches closed. He took the whiskey bottle and the shotgun and started for the back of the room.

"You better take a lamp with you," O'Doul called after him. "It's blacker than a well-digger's ass back there."

The Cutter didn't bother to find a lamp.

"Suit yourself," O'Doul muttered, "but I saw a rat in there this morning as big as jackrabbit."

The Cutter went through a door that led into a small, windowless storeroom. In one corner was a bed, though he had to feel his way to it through the stacked beer crates and other odds and ends of supplies and junk stored in the room. He could smell the dust on the single quilt covering and the thin mattress when he sat down on it. He propped a pillow behind him and leaned back in the corner, brushing away the cobwebs that tickled his face.

There he sat and waited while he sipped from the whiskey bottle. In time, the light showing under the door that led back into the saloon went out, and he was swallowed in total darkness. He heard O'Doul leaving the saloon and closing up for the night, and after that there was no more noise.

An hour passed and then another. It was cold in the storeroom and getting colder. The Cutter was beginning to question his own suspicions when he thought he heard someone jimmying the lock on the saloon's front door and later heard the door hinges squeak. He took up the shotgun and pointed it at the storeroom door. There came the sound of a boot sole scuffing on the wood floor out in the main room. He held down on the shotgun trigger, hooked a thumb over one of the hammers, and didn't let off the trigger until that hammer was eared all the way back in order to avoid the telltale click of a cocking gun. It was a trick he had learned as a boy stalking rabbits, squirrels, and other small game apt to run away at the slightest sound, and one that had proved equally valuable when it came to hunting men.

A floorboard creaked, and whoever had caused that sound was just on the other side of the door. The Cutter sat his whiskey bottle down on the bed beside him and took hold of the shotgun with both hands.

The door swung inward, and because he couldn't see anything, he simply guessed where to fire and when. The shotgun boomed, and something or someone crashed against the doorjamb and then hit the floor. He lunged off the bed and cocked the other barrel as he moved to the other side of the storeroom. A pistol roared and a flash of flame showed through the open doorway, but the bullet struck nowhere close to him.

He shifted behind a stack of crates and used the top of them as a rest for the shotgun. Someone gave a low moan, and he could tell that the man he had shot was lying on the floor near the door.

"Help me," the man on the floor pleaded.

The Cutter knew the wounded man wasn't asking for his help, and he wondered how many of them the lawyer had sent to the saloon. Whoever else was in the saloon wasn't going to wait long. The gunshots had likely drawn the attention of some of the townspeople, and no assassin was going to hang around when there was a high chance that someone was coming to see what all the noise was about.

The Cutter bided his time, taking care to make no noise to help an enemy locate him in the dark. The Indian Wars had taught him some hard lessons, and one was that in a fight, the first one to move was often the first one to die, especially if you were pinned down in an ambush. Though the Cutter was not a patient man, he was one who had long before learned to control his nerves, as well as being a man who intended to live as long as he could.

He had no clue how much time passed. Seconds? A minute? More? No matter, it wasn't long before he heard a man's voice whispering from out in the saloon.

"Did you get him?" that voice asked.

The Cutter made another guess and shifted the shotgun barrel slightly to where he thought the voice had come from. The second shotgun blast was as loud as the first one in the tight confinement of the room, and again, he heard his victim thrashing on the floor.

The Cutter shifted the shotgun to his left hand and drew one of his pistols with his right. He moved out from behind the crates and eased toward the door. The first man he came to was still alive.

"Ahhh, it hurts," the man on the floor groaned.

Whatever else he intended to say was cut off by the sound of the Cutter's pistol going off.

The Cutter moved out into the saloon. The body on the floor there wasn't moving, but he shoved it with the toe of one boot to make sure the man was dead.

When he struck a match and held it against one of the lamp wicks, it was not to see the effects of his handiwork, but rather to find the can of coal oil O'Doul used to refuel all of his lighting. He splashed that kerosene all over the saloon until the can was empty, then set fire to it. By then, he could hear voices down the street and coming closer.

He ducked outside while the gathering crowd coming toward the saloon was still a block away, and to them, he was nothing but a flicker of shadow that passed before the growing flames. The saloon was built with board and bat siding. That old, dry lumber allowed the fire to spread fast.

By the time that crowd reached the saloon, he was already across the street and ducking down an alley that led over to the next street. When he reached that thoroughfare, he threw the shotgun down a well behind someone's house and moved on.

Someone was ringing a fire alarm bell by the time he returned to the lawyer's office. The faulty doorknob that the lawyer had mentioned was easy to get open with the tip of his knife. A pump wagon pulled by two big horses and with several firemen up on the seat and hanging on to the side of it passed down the street at a run just as he ducked inside the office.

As he had in the back room of O'Doul's saloon, he left the office dark, other than the dim glow put off through the cracks in the stove in one corner of the room where what was left of the lawyer's last fire still put off some warmth. He put another shovelful of coal inside it to stoke up the heat, and when he sat down in the lawyer's chair he laid one of his pistols on the desk. Then he leaned back and went to sleep.

CHAPTER THIRTY-EIGHT

Newt was standing at the bar of one of Del Norte's saloons the next day when two men came through the door. It was only a little before the noon hour, and Newt was the only patron in the room.

Newt gave the pair a glance in the mirror behind the bar, then shifted his attention back to his whiskey.

"Are you the man who brought in that shot-up fellow and the girl over at the doctor's office?" the taller and older of the two asked him.

"I am."

"It would please me greatly if you would tell me how those two came to be in the shape they're in."

"And who are you?"

Both men took off their coats and hung them on the coat tree by the door. It was then that Newt saw the badges on their vests.

"I'm Sheriff Pearitter of Rio Grande County," the older man said, then pointed at the short man beside him with the waxed mustache tips. "And this man with me is Del Norte's city marshal, Bill Peck."

Newt tossed down the last of his whiskey and shot the sheriff a perturbed look. "Congratulations."

One of the sheriff's gray eyebrows lifted slightly. "Son, what say you fix the attitude and tell me what happened?"

"Are you a drinking man, Sheriff?"

"Too early in the day for me," the sheriff replied, "but I would take a cup of coffee. I was up most of the night. O'Doul's Saloon caught fire in the wee hours this morning. Burned two men alive when it went. And then the doctor comes and tells me about you."

Newt patted a palm on the bar top to get the bartender's attention. "Suit yourself, but you might want to rethink the whiskey. What I'm about to tell you is going to make your day a whole lot worse."

The bartender poured Newt another drink and brought the lawmen a pot of coffee and two mugs. As briefly and concisely as he could, Newt told the two peace officers what had happened up in the San Juans, about the claim and about Zuri. He had finished another glass of whiskey by the time he was done.

"That's all you know about the girl?" Sheriff Pearitter asked.

"She doesn't speak much English, and she was in a pretty bad way," Newt replied.

The sheriff nodded. "We didn't have any better luck than you when we paid her a call at the doctor's office, but what we did understand from her pretty much matches what you've said she told you."

"And that surprises you?" Newt asked.

"What surprises me is that you and Kirby Cutter decided to turn my county into a damned slaughterhouse."

"You know the Cutter?"

"I know *of him*, just like I've heard of you," the sheriff said. "I asked around, and Saul Barton spread it on pretty thick that he had hired you before he left town, tossing your name around like a twenty-dollar gold piece. Word spreads fast around here, even to these old ears. And let me be frank with you. I've sent a few telegrams out to find out more about you."

"Are you saying you don't believe me?"

"I'm saying you've got reputation enough to make me wonder. Are you sure you haven't left anything out? Something you should tell me now?"

"I've said my piece."

The sheriff sat down his coffee mug and cleaned the wetness from his mustache with his lower lip while he considered whatever he was considering. The city marshal on the other side of him was looking more and more perturbed, and he struck Newt as a hothead.

"You need to come with us," the sheriff said when he stepped back from the bar.

"Are you arresting me?" Newt asked.

"No, what I'm saying is maybe you're telling the truth, but that's got to be worked out. And the way to do that is for you to take us up to Willow Creek so we can have a look around."

"Now?"

"Now."

"I'd like to go check on Tully."

"You do realize that the marshal here has been looking for that kid?" the sheriff asked.

The city marshal nodded. "He and his brother shot up a dance hall here a few nights ago."

"His brother's dead," Newt said, glaring at the city marshal.

The marshal's posture stiffened, and he gave back the cold look Newt was giving him. "As I understand it, you were also involved in that brawl."

The sheriff cleared his throat, trying to break some of the tension between the two men. "Well, the doc says the one he's tending should pull through."

"Still, I'd like to talk to him," Newt replied.

"Talk to him when we get back. We've got horses saddled and ready."

"I left my horse in Wagon Wheel Gap."

"I'll loan you one."

Mr. Smith stepped into the saloon through a back door from where he'd gone to make use of the outhouse. He took in the two lawmen with a lingering, cautious gaze but said nothing and came toward the bar.

Both of the peace officers were obviously taken aback by the sight of the Mohave, like most folks were the first time they encountered him. Newt found their reaction amusing, no matter how many times he'd seen it happen, especially with the warmth of the whiskey beginning to trickle through him.

Sheriff Pearitter looked at Newt and jerked a thumb in Mr. Smith's direction. "I take it this is the Indian you mentioned?"

"Prime detective work, Sheriff," Newt said.

"You don't have to take that kind of sass, Sheriff," the marshal said. He had a hand resting on the butt of his pistol, like he wanted that pistol noticed, or maybe because touching it made him feel better or taller.

The sheriff scowled at the marshal and then at Newt. He rubbed his chin and gave Mr. Smith another look. "I suppose your Indian ought to go with us."

"He's the one you've got to convince, not me," Newt answered. "And I'll warn that I doubt he appreciated you calling him 'my Indian.'"

The sheriff tilted his head back to look up at Mr. Smith.

"Your friend here seems a little reluctant to heed my authority, and he strikes me as a brawler when he's in his cups," the sheriff said to the Mohave. "And I don't mind admitting I'm hoping you're of a lot more gentle disposition."

Mr. Smith looked at Newt, and his expression was a question without words.

"He wants us to take him up to the claim," Newt said, "to make sure I told him the truth about what happened."

Mr. Smith looked back down at the sheriff. "What if you do not like what you see when we get there? Will you put us in jail? I do not like jails. I don't think I will let you put me in one."

The sheriff was still looking at Mr. Smith, and he gave a frustrated, almost comical grimace. "Now why did you have to tell me that?"

The sheriff turned away and went to the coatrack and retrieved his coat. He had to motion to the marshal to get him to do the same, but even then the marshal backpedaled all the way to the coat rack, unwilling to take his eyes off of Newt and Mr. Smith.

"Take it easy, Peck," the sheriff said to the marshal. "They're coming with us nice and peaceful. Let's keep it that way."

"Just being careful, is all." The marshal made an effort to look more relaxed but didn't quite manage the look, and he was still keeping his shooting hand close to his pistol.

The sheriff looked back at the bar once he had his coat on. "Let's get going."

Newt gave Mr. Smith a shrug before he followed on the lawmen's heels and headed outside. The big Mohave was right behind him. The marshal purposely waited to make sure he was at the back of the procession. Newt started to protest that move, but he was sure he had already prodded the two lawmen enough.

Newt stopped just outside the saloon door. As the sheriff had said, he had horses waiting out on the street. What he hadn't mentioned were the men waiting with the horses. There were four of them already up in the saddle, all with rifles propped on their thighs, and two more waiting on the boardwalk to either side of Newt and Mr. Smith. Both men on the boardwalk also had rifles. Their weapons weren't pointed at either him or the Mohave, but they were ready in case the need arose. Then there was the city marshal behind them in the doorway. It was a show of force and a way of delivering a message.

Newt took in the men on the horses, gave a glance to the men to his right and left, then locked eyes with Sheriff Pearitter, who had stepped into the street and then turned back with his hands on his hips and a hint of smug satisfaction on his face. Newt understood then and there why the sheriff hadn't disarmed them in the saloon.

Newt considered the position he suddenly found himself in. There was no way he and Mr. Smith were getting away, should they choose to try. There were too many guns against them and nowhere to go. The sheriff had them cornered like mice in a grain bin. He gave the sly old sheriff a slight nod in appreciation of the cunning move.

"You must think we're dangerous men," Newt said. "Awfully dangerous."

"Did you think I was going up in the mountains with you by myself?" the sheriff asked with a soft chuckle. "Eight years I've served this county, plus seven more wearing a badge here and there. Walked in my house at the end of most every day the same way I left. Hung up my hat and hugged the missus. Maybe I'm not a good peace officer, but I didn't get this far taking chances I don't have to take."

Again, Newt appraised the men blocking him in, looking for a way out.

"You can keep your guns if that's what's worrying you. So far, I don't have reason not to believe what you told me," the sheriff said. "So far."

Newt waved a hand at the men. "Are they all your deputies?"

"Some, but the rest of them are what you might call concerned citizens," the sheriff answered.

"A little too concerned if you ask me," Newt said.

"Put 'em away, boys," the sheriff said to the others.

"I say we disarm them," the marshal protested.

"You heard me," the sheriff said. "Put 'em away."

The marshal didn't look happy about the sheriff not listening to his suggestion, and the men were slow to comply. But eventually, the posse put their rifles back in their saddle boots or handled them in a less threatening manner.

"And a couple of you go down to Knapp's livery and get two more saddle horses. Tell him I said to put the bill on the county," the sheriff added.

After some time, the men the sheriff had sent off returned leading a pair of saddled horses meant for Newt and Mr. Smith. Newt took the horse offered him and began adjusting the stirrup leathers to fit his leg length. Mr. Smith had to do the same, for much shorter men must have ridden both saddles last. Lacing and unlacing the stirrup leathers and resetting them took a good bit of time, and everyone in the posse was already mounted and waiting on them by the time they finished.

Mr. Smith swung up on his horse while Newt was still on the ground. Instead of getting in the saddle, Newt remained where he was, as if he was oblivious to those watching him and in no hurry at all.

The sheriff rode close, and he must have noticed something about the look on Newt's face that troubled him. He frowned and chewed at one corner of his mustache before he spoke. "You got something else you need to tell me? Spill it now, or we'll find out soon enough."

Newt didn't look back at the sheriff and instead looked beyond him at the three packhorses one of the posse men was handling. Only one of those packhorses was loaded, and the other two had nothing on their packsaddle frames but empty panniers and a few long coils of rope.

Newt pointed at the packhorses. "I take it you're intending to haul the dead back here on those?"

"I am," the sheriff said with a hint of trepidation in his voice, as if he fully expected to hear something he wasn't going to like.

"Hate to tell you this," Newt said.

"Tell me what?"

Newt was acutely aware that the sheriff was waiting and staring at him, but rather than immediately answering the lawman, he swung up on his horse, adjusted his split reins to suit him, and rocked his saddle square on the horse's back. The street before him led in a beeline out of town to the west, and the glare of the sun overhead was hitting him straight in the face. He cocked his hat on his head to where the brim was at a better angle to shade his eyes, then squinted at the packhorses again and nodded at them before he answered the sheriff in a quiet voice.

The sheriff leaned out of his saddle closer to Newt to better hear him. "What's that you said?"

"I said you're going to need more packhorses. Two isn't nearly enough."

CHAPTER THIRTY-NINE

The lawyer was late getting to his office. He had been up most of the previous night and had only managed to catch a couple of hours of sleep that morning. There had been discussions to be had with a couple of men in town, telegrams to send, and a long wait for responses, not to mention the need to put certain measures in place.

He had worked for what he liked to think of as *the company* off and on for several years, and though he knew a few others who were also somehow employed or affiliated with that entity, as well as recognizing the names of others, he wasn't exactly sure who truly ran things or who *the company* actually was other than a few pet theories that he never gave voice to. That hadn't bothered him before, because the effort required of him, until then, had never amounted to much. He was perfectly happy being a bit player of no consequence and receiving sporadic deposits in his bank account, but now things had changed and he didn't like having such a volatile situation landing on him.

It was nearing noon when he entered the office and closed the door behind him. Tired and distracted, worried and irritated, he was halfway across the room before he noticed the Cutter sitting in his chair with a cocked pistol pointed at him over the desktop.

"You look surprised to see me here," the Cutter said. "It's almost like you were sure I would miss our appointment."

"I thought—" the lawyer started.

"You thought maybe I was one of those they found in the ashes down at O'Doul's?"

"I don't know what you're talking about."

"What were their names?" the Cutter asked.

"I—"

"What were their names? The men you sent after me?"

The lawyer steadied himself, but his voice still held a hint of shakiness. "I sent no one after you."

"I see that you don't understand the situation you find yourself in," the Cutter said. "Consider me the judge and this a courtroom. That ought to fit your pistol."

The lawyer started to reply but didn't get to.

"Only in this court, you better be careful with your lawyer talk," the Cutter added. "You tell old Judge Colt one more lie or you waste one more damned word instead of getting to the point, and I'm going to blow your guts out. Hear me? Nod your head if you understand."

The lawyer nodded.

"Now, what were their names?"

"Barnhill and Carter."

The Cutter recognized neither name. "You must be higher up the food chain than I thought you were to have such men on hand. Did you give the order, or was it someone above you?"

"I only did what they told me. You know how it is."

"But you found two hardcase killers that fast? Just walked out on the street in the middle of the night and waved some money around and asked who wanted to do a little dirty work for you?"

"I got Barnhill off on a manslaughter charge a couple of years ago. He owed me," the lawyer answered.

"That's some real forward thinking on your part. You never know when such a man will come in handy," the Cutter said. "Says a lot about you. What about the other one, this Carter you mentioned?"

"I don't know him. I was told where to find him and that he could take care of you."

"Did he work for the railroad?"

The lawyer shrugged. "I believe he has been in their employ in the past."

"Well, he wasn't good enough. Neither of them. Damned amateurs. I don't know whether to be madder about you trying to have me killed or insulted by the kind of men you sent."

"Do you intend to kill me?"

"I intend for you to answer all of my questions, and I intend for you to open that safe."

"I assure you, there is not much money inside it. Not enough to matter."

"And I think you're a bald-faced liar. Open it."

The lawyer knelt before the safe, which was on the floor at one end of the desk next to the wall. The Cutter rose from the chair and stood over him. The lawyer bobbled the combination lock on his first attempt.

"It's hard to think with that gun pointing at my head." The lawyer's hands were trembling.

"You get one more chance."

The lawyer finished working the combination and opened the safe door. Even from the Cutter's angle of view, he could see the brass-framed Colt .22 pocket revolver lying on a shelf in the safe. The lawyer was trying to act like it wasn't there, and the hesitation and the turmoil of whether to reach for it showed in everything about him. The Cutter pushed his own pistol barrel against the lawyer's temple, then he yanked the pocket revolver from the safe.

In addition to some miscellaneous documents, inside the safe was a bound stack of greenbacks and three rolls of silver coins. The Cutter dumped the contents from the lawyer's leather business satchel that was lying on the desk and pitched it at him. "Put the money in there."

The lawyer did as he was told, and the Cutter took the satchel back and tossed the little pistol in on top of the money. The lawyer took a slight step backward as he rose.

"You don't have to kill me," he said. "Let me go and I can get you more money if that's what you want."

"How much more?"

"Four hundred, or maybe a little more."

"You've got that much?"

"It's in my bank account," the lawyer said. "I know you think you want revenge, but you also seem like a cunning sort. Why not leave here with enough to make it worth your while? Enough for you to get far enough away that they forget about you?"

"That's your spiel, lawyer? That's your closing argument?"

"I would think a man like you knows how to cut his losses, even to make a profit in defeat sometimes," the lawyer said, and he held out both hands wide of his waist in a gesture of peace and forgiveness.

The Cutter realized that the lawyer had probably used that very same hand gesture in front of more than one jury, and it was either out of desperation or habit that he did so again.

"A man like me?" the Cutter asked.

"If you shoot me, someone's going to hear it. You're smarter than that," the lawyer added.

"I'm not going to shoot you." The Cutter shoved his pistol back in its shoulder holster, and he saw relief and hope flash across the lawyer's face.

The Cutter drew a knife from his waist and stabbed the lawyer in the throat. The knife was not a big one, but he drove it all the way in to the handle and then gave it a hard, sideways yank, using every bit of the edge as he pulled it free.

The lawyer's eyes widened as he clutched at the red wound below his chin with both hands, as if he could hold in the lifeblood pumping out of him. He staggered a few steps and tried to say something before he crumpled to the floor, but his words were garbled and incoherent like a man sinking under water.

The Cutter reached down and wiped the blade clean on the shoulder of the lawyer's coat, careful not to step in the growing pool of blood on the wood floor. Then he took a kerchief from the lawyer's breast pocket and wiped away a few blood flecks that had landed on his face. The nasty thing about knife work was always the spray.

He cleaned his hands and pitched the kerchief away. Taking up the satchel, he went out the door, but he didn't make it halfway down the stairs before he saw the Widowmaker come riding past the mouth of the alleyway. The big Indian and several other men were riding with him, and they had a long train of packhorses in tow behind them. The Cutter recognized one of the men with the Widowmaker as the city marshal.

The Cutter remained still, and neither the Widowmaker nor any of the others looked his way. When the riders had passed, the Cutter moved to the street and peered out around the corner of a building at the retreating posse. If the Widowmaker and the Indian were in town, then they had likely brought the girl with them. And if the wounded man on the travois had lived? That made possibly four witnesses to what had happened on Willow Creek.

His original intention after dealing with the lawyer had

been to get out of Del Norte as fast as he could. He had places he could lay low, let things cool off, and buy himself some time to figure the angles, like what to do next, with the law and the men that had hired him all gunning for him.

Maybe it had been a fool move to kill the lawyer, but his employers had already shown their hand. They wanted their mess cleaned up and to remove anything or anyone that could possibly tie them to their attempt to take the claim. That meant rubbing him out like a cigar butt ground beneath a boot.

Get out of town. He knew that was the smart play, but as he watched the Widowmaker's back receding down the street, the urge for revenge battled against his common sense. He was a proud man, and to run while the Widowmaker remained behind as the winner was hard to take. Nobody disrespected him without a fight. His enemies were few because most of them were dead.

CHAPTER FORTY

The journey back up into the mountains was a far better one than Newt's last trip coming down from them. The snows had passed for the time being, and the sun was shining bright with not a cloud in the sky, though the sunshine and rising temperatures did little to improve his mood. The sheriff and the rest of the posse were surly for the most part, suspicious of everything he said, and they asked entirely too many questions.

He and Mr. Smith found their horses fed and rested at the resort hotel where they had left them. They paid the caretaker for the horses' board, then changed mounts and went on with the posse, continuing upriver and through the gap.

The bodies of the two outlaws Newt and Mr. Smith had killed at the Wason ranch were just where they had told the lawmen they would be. Johnny Dial's body was another matter. After some searching, they found where the bear had dragged him into a clump of willows seventy yards upriver from the kill site.

Sheriff Pearitter dismounted and followed the blood trail and drag marks into the willows alone while the rest of them sat on their horses with rifles ready in case the bear was still around. He was well screened by the brushy tangle, and the others could only catch bits of movement, but all of them heard what sounded like the sheriff gagging or vomiting. When the gruff old lawman came back out of the willows, he was in a hurry and staring at the ground in front of him and shaking his head.

"Did you find him?" Marshal Peck asked.

"I found him." The sheriff took out a handkerchief and dabbed at his mouth.

The city marshal got down off his horse, as did a few of the others, and they started toward the willows.

"Don't be in such a hurry," the sheriff said, and held up a hand to stop them. "Believe me, it isn't a pretty sight."

"Hell of a way to die," the marshal said.

The sheriff ignored the marshal's observation and focused his attention on Newt and Mr. Smith. "Grizzly, you say?"

"Look at those tracks and tell me what you think," Newt answered, gesturing at the proliferation of bear paw prints in the snow.

"Black bears can get pretty big," the sheriff said.

"Black bears don't have claws like that."

"Doesn't make sense," the marshal said.

"Because he says it was a grizzly?" the sheriff asked. "Not as many as there once was, but they're still around."

"Grizzly or black, what's a bear doing out and about this time of year? And when did they start eating people?" one of the men asked. "Scare a sow with cubs or come up on a kill wrong and maybe you get mauled, but not this."

"I've never seen it myself, but I've heard of bears coming out of their dens midwinter," the sheriff replied. "Maybe they do it because something in them isn't working right or because they didn't put enough fat on to get them through the cold. Either way, there's nothing worse than a winter-starved bear, they say. Kill anything. Crazy like a mad dog."

"I'm guessing it's the same bear that killed the girl's daddy," Newt said.

The sheriff nodded. "No guess to it. Has to be."

"Want to load the body up and take it to Wason's place to put with the others so we can pick them up on the way back?" the marshal asked the sheriff.

The sheriff glanced back at the willows. "No, a shovel will do. There ain't enough left of him to carry."

Once they had buried Dial's remains, they rode up Willow Creek toward the claim. They saw more bear tracks in the snow on their way. Newt feared that the grizzly might have found the remains of the dead in the canyon, but that was not the case. Nor, for some reason, had any other scavengers found the bodies. Tandy Hudlow and the others were lying untouched under the snow where the Cutter had put them outside the camp, as were the four outlaws Newt and Mr. Smith had left beside the old fire ring.

Newt and Mr. Smith busied themselves preparing Tandy's body for transport down to the lower country for burial and searching for anything to salvage that might belong to them, while the lawmen and their posse tried to decipher what had happened to their satisfaction. The snow that had fallen since the fight had obliterated most of that sign, and other than the bodies and the burned tent and supply cache beneath the snow, there was nothing much to go by.

Mr. Smith, Marshal Peck, and a few others went to find the stakes that identified the claim boundaries, while Newt and the sheriff remained at the campsite. The sheriff, instead of continuing his investigation of physical evidence, busied himself building a fire.

"I think better with coffee in me," the sheriff said after he went to his horse and came back with a battered, blackened enamelware coffeepot and a mug of similar make.

Newt went and got his own mug out of his saddlebags, and before long the two of them were squatting by their fire and waiting for the water in the coffeepot to boil. The sheriff was noticeably silent.

"What's bothering you?" Newt asked.

"Everything about this bothers me," the sheriff replied. "Days like this make me wish I'd never ran for office. What am I saying? I've never had a day like this. Lord, I'm getting too old for this. My wife's been telling me that for years now, and damned if she isn't right."

"Have you seen enough here?" Newt asked as if he hadn't heard the sheriff's complaints.

The sheriff gave Newt a probing look. "Maybe this looks like you said it happened, but there are still things you need to explain. And I can't help but notice that everybody that might tell a different story is too dead to talk."

"The Cutter—" Newt started.

The sheriff cut him off. "I'll find him if he's still around, but I imagine, even if I can catch him, he'll have an entirely different story to tell."

"You'll work it out."

"I'm trying to, but you tell me how come Arnie Sennett's got a bullet in his back."

"Who's he?"

"That long-haired little man lying over there where you left him." The sheriff jerked his head over one shoulder at the body lying behind him, the man whose blanket capote Newt had robbed to put on Tully Hudlow. "He's been raising hell in this part of the country for a long time. Was a scout at Fort Garland back when, or at least that's what I heard. They say his folks were killed by a Jicarilla Apache and Ute raiding party when he was a boy, and the Jicarillas took him captive and raised him. Supposedly, he had been with them so long before the army bought him back that he had almost forgot how to speak American."

"He and I never talked," Newt said with a wry expression on his face.

The sheriff nodded while he watched the coffeepot. "Arrested him once when I was a city policeman in Denver, or at least I'm pretty sure that's him."

"What did he do in Denver?"

"He and some others robbed a U.P. train up north and came to Denver to relax and spend a little of their haul. Play the high rollers, you know. Sennett roughed up a soiled dove in one of the sporting houses, beat her half to death, and then he went at us when we cornered him. He would have likely been locked away for a good while, but him and two others broke out of jail. Killed a jailer in the process. Stabbed him in the throat with a fork. Can you believe that? A fork?"

"My first one took him in the front," Newt said.

"So you say."

"You know any of the others?"

"Not a one. You?"

"No. All I know is that they came shooting, and I shot back." Newt lifted the lid on the coffeepot and peered down into it with a frown.

"You make that sound as if it were nothing. Like killing men doesn't bother you."

"It was them or me," Newt said. "Pardon the hell out of me if I don't mind being the one left standing."

"Well, tell me something else," the sheriff said. "I talked to that saloon keeper in Wagon Wheel Gap, and he said you and your Indian friend got into a fight with Dial and some Mexican out in front of his place. Probably that dead Mexican lying over there."

"I already told you about that."

"Let me finish. He said after the fight he overhead Dial and Cutter talking about how you had killed Dial's brother." The sheriff waited for a moment and watched Newt closely, looking for whatever impact that statement might have on him.

Newt gave no response to the sheriff's accusation.

The sheriff must have found Newt's face unreadable, and he let out a weary sigh. "I notice you aren't denying that. Care to tell me how that happened?"

"My guess is he picked a fight he shouldn't have and somebody finished what he started."

"Somebody? Meaning you?"

Again, silence was Newt's only answer.

"I'll take that as a yes," the sheriff said, and waved a hand over the campsite before him. "And if you were in my boots, that might make it seem like this was a personal feud more than anybody trying to jump Barton's claim."

Newt contemplated the coffeepot for a moment and then looked back up at the sheriff. "Have you ever been around hunting dogs?"

"No, I haven't," the sheriff answered.

"Well, I used to be partial to night hunting when I was a boy. Let's say you take three dogs and you strike a hot trail on an old boar coon. Those dogs'll set in after him, every one of them bound and determined to trail him down and put him up a tree. But come to the end of the chase, you're liable to have two barking at a tree in one place, while the other dog might be off by himself bawling his head off and thinking the coon went up an entirely different tree. Doesn't matter if you shoot that coon where the two dogs treed him, there's no convincing the other dog he was wrong."

"I don't follow your meaning."

"I guess what I'm saying is that every old hound believes only what his nose tells him."

The sheriff stood, and one of his knees creaked and popped when he did so. He flexed that leg a couple of times, all the while watching Newt carefully. "Well, this old hound isn't done sniffing around."

While the sheriff was making another search, Mr. Smith and the city marshal came back from their wanderings.

"Not any claim stakes that we could find," the marshal said to the sheriff.

"The Cutter's men must have pulled them up," Newt replied, "or else you're missing them in the snow."

The sheriff put his attention back on Newt. "I sent a telegram to Saul Barton before we left town."

"Good luck finding him any time soon," Newt said. "He said he was going to San Francisco."

"He isn't in San Francisco. He's in Denver, or at least that's what I was told," the sheriff answered. "And the more I think on it, the more I think I might need to talk to the government office about Barton's claim papers, as well."

"Are you sure this is in Rio Grande County?" the marshal asked.

"No, I'm not sure," the sheriff answered with an irritated frown. "Granted, that's another problem, but it's the least of my worries right now."

"We camping or headed back tonight?" the marshal asked.

"I'd like to go find that sheepherder's camp when you're done here," Newt interjected.

"And why is that?" the sheriff asked.

"Just would."

"Well, we're going to find it if we can," the sheriff said, "but first we're going to go up this canyon and have a look at Happy Jack's camp."

"All right," Newt answered.

"What about the bodies?" the marshal asked. "You want to load them now? They're still stiff as a board. Won't be easy."

The sheriff looked at Newt. "You say Happy Jack had a dugout he was living in?"

Newt nodded.

"I reckon we can store them there until we come back. Maybe make a sled or something to haul them," the sheriff said while he gave a concerned study of the clouds rolling in from the west. "We'll be lucky if we don't have to leave them in that dugout until spring if we're in for another snow. Damn this country."

CHAPTER FORTY-ONE

Newt, Mr. Smith, and the posse rode back into Del Norte after being out in the mountains for almost three days. Sheriff Pearitter led them into town with the pack horses strung out behind him, plus a few other horses they had rounded up in the mountains, almost every one of them with one or two dead men tied belly-down on its back. It was a sight that caused people along the streets to stop and watch the procession with morbid fascination. By the time they reached the county courthouse, some of the town's citizens were following them.

The county courthouse was a three-story building built of square-cut, stacked stone. Tall, narrow windows with arched tops lined its walls, and a bell tower cupola rose up out of the roof and loomed over the front entrance. It sat on its own little fenced lawn among a grove of shaggy-barked young cottonwood trees.

The sheriff dismounted and tried to stamp some limberness back into his stiff knees while he studied the growing crowd. Newt and Mr. Smith remained on their horses.

"Look at them," the sheriff said quietly as he eyed the group of gawkers that had followed them to the courthouse. "You'd think the circus just came to town."

Newt also watched the growing crowd of townspeople,

both those that had followed them and the others steadily showing up in ones and twos and threes as the word of the posse's arrival spread through the town.

"You wait here," the sheriff said to Newt. "I need to talk to the district attorney, and maybe the judge if he's in."

"You need to talk to them about what?" Newt asked.

The sheriff glanced at the crowd. "You see all those folks behind you? They're going to have nine kinds of questions and demands once they've had time to gossip. Something like this happens, we've got to look like we're taking care of it like we should."

By then, the crowd had grown to maybe thirty people, and they formed a semicircle that arched around the posse and touched the fence at either end of it. Newt could hear their murmured discussions and saw them pointing at the bodies, and also at him and Mr. Smith. He gave Mr. Smith a look.

"We should not have come back here," Mr. Smith said.

"Go get your district attorney," Newt said to the sheriff. "Let's get this over with."

"Want me to take the bodies on to the undertaker?" the city marshal asked the sheriff.

"No, I'll do it when I'm through," the sheriff answered. "See if you can get these people moved back out of our way."

The marshal went to the edge of the crowd with a couple of the county deputies to help him. They tried to convince the gatherers to go back to their normal business with an equal measure of common sense and polite scolding. Some of the crowd took the suggestion, but most remained, although the deputies did manage to move them back some.

The sheriff didn't have to go into the courthouse because someone must have heard the commotion going on outside or seen it out of their office window. Several men in suits came down the courthouse steps. They and the sheriff met, held a brief, private discussion halfway between the horses and the courthouse, then the sheriff led them back to look over the bodies. Even though Newt and Mr. Smith were right there, the group of men all but ignored them. Newt caught some of what they were saying and wasn't entirely pleased with how the sheriff related what Newt had told him had happened up in the mountains.

When they were through talking, the sheriff left them and came back to Newt.

"Are we done here?" Newt asked the sheriff.

The sheriff looked back at the men he had left, and his eyes found one of the men in a business suit standing by the fence. Newt guessed that man was likely the district attorney, or maybe some kind of judge. Whoever it was gave the sheriff a nod of his head, as if they had both somehow agreed to something.

The sheriff shifted his attention back to Newt. "We talked it over, and you're free to go on the condition you don't leave town for a couple of days. The judge and the district attorney are considering an inquest, and if we have one you need to be here for that."

"We've told you we're innocent, and we've spent the last three days proving it. I'd say that's enough."

A skeptical smile as thin as watered down whiskey spread on the sheriff's mouth. "Yeah, I suspect you've been telling the truth about what happened up there in the mountains, but even so, there's one thing I know. You're about the furthest thing from an innocent man I ever saw, so don't go acting like we're the only cause of your troubles. You might go look in a mirror if you're looking for somebody to blame."

Newt and Mr. Smith started away from the courthouse. Newt purposely put his horse to a trot, and the crowd parted and gave them plenty of room to ride through it. He could feel all those judgmental, unfriendly eyes staring at his back as they rode away.

After leaving the courthouse, Newt and Mr. Smith rode straight to the doctor's office. The doctor wasn't there, but they found Tully lying on a bed. Either their entrance woke the kid or he was already awake, for he turned his head on his pillow and looked at them.

"How are you feeling?" Newt asked, noticing how pale Tully's face was and how dull and tired his eyes looked.

"I've been better." Tully's voice sounded as tired and feeble as he looked. He tried to give a feeble smile but didn't quite manage it.

The doctor came into the room through an interior door that must have lead into his house. He must not have heard Newt and Mr. Smith come in, for he was so startled he almost dropped the tray of food he was carrying. He righted his precarious burden, set it on a table at the foot of Tully's bed, then pushed the wire-rimmed glasses he wore back up on the bridge of his nose and tilted his head oddly, as if bringing Newt and Mr. Smith into focus.

"How's your patient, Doc?" Newt asked.

"He's a very lucky young man, considering the chunk of lead I dug out of him and how much blood he lost. He's not out of the woods yet, but I think he'll be up and out of that bed before long if he continues to heal without any further complications. Of course, it will take much longer for him to be fully recovered, and I'm still unsure how good of a job I did setting his broken wrist or if it will mend properly. Only time will tell."

"You hear that, Tully?" Newt asked. "Won't be long until you're right as rain."

Tully didn't answer him and instead stared at the ceiling. The doctor noticed that and cleared his throat before making as if he was about to leave the room. "I'm sure you have some catching up to do and things you would perhaps like to discuss in private."

"Where's the girl?" Newt asked him.

"The church came and got her the day after you left with the posse," the doctor said.

"The church?"

"Yes, the Jesuits have taken her in," the doctor said. "That was after Father Ramirez had a chance to speak with her and learned the details of her situation."

"Her situation?" Newt asked.

"I take it you are not aware that her father's death left her an orphan with no immediate family? The church is going to take care of her and see if any of her family can be located here in the States or abroad. Of course, the Presbyterians offered to help, but it was decided that Father Ramirez is better suited to aid her since he's from Spain and fluent in that tongue."

"But she's all right?"

"Surprisingly, yes, given what she went through. But children are resilient, that way, aren't they?"

"She's a tough girl. What about her frostbite?"

"I had to amputate the tip of one of her fingers, but it was her foot that worried me most. At first glance, I would have bet you anything I would have to take off a few of her toes, as well, but the frostbite wasn't as severe as I feared. I debrided some damaged flesh, but it is nothing that should hinder her in the future. My best guess is, she'll be running and playing like a normal kid before too long."

"That's good to hear."

"Had you not gotten her here when you did, I'm quite sure I wouldn't have such a positive prognosis to give you. She could have very well lost several of her toes, if not her entire foot, if that frostbite had been worse or gone without treatment longer," the doctor said.

"What happens if that priest can't find some of her kin folk?" Newt asked.

"Why then, I guess the church will move her to one of their orphanages, or there might be a chance some family in the valley would be willing to adopt her," the doctor answered.

"She just keeps taking one lick after the other, doesn't she?"

The doctor cleared his throat again, obviously liking where the conversation had gone no more than Newt did. "I'll leave you with your friend."

When the doctor had left the room, Newt took a chair beside Tully's bed while Mr. Smith leaned against a wall with his arms folded across his chest. None of them said anything for a considerable and awkward length of time, and the only sound in the room was the ticking of a clock.

Finally, Tully turned his head on his pillow again to look at Newt. "The doctor told me you and the law went up to get Tandy's body."

Newt nodded. "We brought him back this morning."

Tully looked up at the ceiling again, and his eyes were wet. "Him and me were born only a year apart. Can't remember a time when we weren't together. Did you know he could play a harmonica? You could just name a song or he could hear one, and it wasn't long before he was playing it as easy as somebody humming a tune."

"No, I didn't know that," Newt answered.

"He made me laugh."

"I'm sorry. I never should have let you two get involved."

Tully look back at him, and his glistening eyes were now hard with anger. He glared at Newt and then at Mr. Smith.

"Nothing you did put Tandy in the ground. We were in the right, and it was them that did it."

"Still, I—"

"I'm going to get them," Tully said. "When I'm up out of this bed, I'm going to get them all. Pay them back for what they did to Tandy. I don't care how long it takes to hunt them down."

Newt glanced at Mr. Smith and then looked back at Tully. "We already got them. Got them all except the Cutter, and the law's looking for him. He'll likely hang for his crimes."

"They better beat me to him," Tully said. "But I'm not just talking about him. I'll get those that hired him. They're as guilty as the ones that pulled the trigger."

For a second time, Newt glanced at Mr. Smith while he considered what he could or should say to Tully.

"Tully," Newt started. "If there's one thing I know, it's that killing just leads to more killing. And all the killing in the world won't bring your brother back."

"Turn the other cheek?" Tully said. "You, the Widow-maker, with a name as bloody as they come? Don't tell me if Tandy was your brother you wouldn't do what I'm going to do. An eye for an eye and a tooth for a tooth. You were taught that the same as me."

Newt gave a somber shake of his head. "A man ought to fight when he has to, defend himself and what's his, but the trail you're talking about is one you don't want to ride."

"Somebody paid to have my brother killed."

"And the kind that will do that will get theirs in the end, one way or the other," Newt said.

"What kind of justice is that?" Anguish and anger made Tully's voice ragged and bitter.

"No justice at all, but right now you think the revenge

you want will put out the fire that's eating you up on the inside and make the hurt go away. But it won't. Only time will help. Put it behind you."

"I can't." Tully turned his face back to the ceiling.

Newt pulled the yellow envelope Saul Barton had given him from somewhere inside his coat and took some money from it. He set the greenbacks on the bedside table. "That ought to pay your doctor bill and leave you plenty of traveling money. Me or Mr. Smith will come back and check on you tomorrow. You tell us how you want Tandy's funeral attended to, and we'll do it. And we'll tend to whatever else you need until you're back on your feet."

Tully gave no reply.

Mr. Smith was the first to leave, and Newt followed him. They stopped just outside the doctor's office and watched the folks pass along the street.

"You look like you've got something on your mind," Newt said.

Mr. Smith made him wait for the reply, as he often did. "You said much to him."

"What do you tell a kid like that?" Newt said. "This isn't any kind of life. He can do better."

"He is not a kid. He is a man, no matter how young and foolish you think him. I know you seek to watch over your clan, and the warnings you gave him about the trail we travel were true words. But there is honor and courage in standing against our enemies, even if there is also a price."

"To hell with honor."

"You say that, but what would you do if you were him?" Mr. Smith was staring directly at Newt.

Newt watched a milk delivery wagon pass by and listened to the tinkle of milk jars riding in their shaking crates.

When the wagon was gone, he scowled at the sky and then both ways up and down the street.

"You know what I'd do," he said as he started up the street.

"You are going to find the girl, aren't you?" Mr. Smith asked as Newt walked away.

CHAPTER FORTY-TWO

The Cutter rode into Alamosa after sundown and entered the billiards saloon through a back door. He made sure that his coat was unbuttoned before walking through the door and that his pistols were handy. He put his back to the wall and surveyed the long, narrow room the instant he came inside, giving his eyes time to adjust the shadowed corners and the lamplight.

He took in the two men shooting pool at a table at the far end of the room and another trio standing at the bar drinking beer, and he considered them no immediate threat. The only other occupants of the billiards hall were the proprietor, who was sweeping the floor near the front door, and two men seated at a small table against the right hand wall. He recognized one of them, for it was the man he was looking for. He walked toward them.

"Long time, no see, Dan," he said in a quiet voice.

One of the men seated before him, a short, solid-looking fellow with a bald head, peered up at the Cutter. "Surprised to see you here, Kirby."

"And why is that?" the Cutter asked.

The bald-headed man had his hat off and lying in front of him on the table. He tapped the hat with a finger and played with the brim of it, spinning it while he did his own survey of the room. Not for the first time did the Cutter think how odd the man's eyes were, one bright blue and the other brown. And what the Cutter felt when the man looked back at him was equally odd, like two distinct and different persons staring at him out of the same face.

"I hear the law's hunting for you over something that happened out Del Norte way," the bald man said in an equally quiet voice that wouldn't carry to any of the others in the room.

The Cutter nodded. "I've got some trouble."

"You've got some guts coming here if that's the case," the other man at the table said.

The Cutter didn't know the second man. That one had a cleft lip, making his speech distinctively nasal, and he was the younger of the pair, darker skinned, dark-haired, and skinny, with ears that jutted straight out from his head.

The bald man frowned at his partner, then looked back up at the Cutter. "What brings you here?"

"Looking for you," the Cutter answered.

The bald man pointed at the empty chair between him and his partner. "Have a seat."

The offered chair put the Cutter's back to the room, and he took another look around before sitting down.

The bald man noticed the Cutter's caution and chuckled. "You're getting scary in your old age."

The Cutter didn't laugh with him, nor did he smile. "You're one to talk. I hear the Mormons still want to tack your hide to a barn wall. Surprised they haven't by now."

"What else have you heard, Kirby, since you're the man with the ears to listen?"

"I heard you and some others tried to rob the bank at Telluride and got your asses handed to you in a hat box."

"How'd you know where to find me?" The bald man tapped at the crown of his hat on the table again, as if it was one of his nervous habits and he had to be fiddling with something instead of sitting still.

The Cutter shrugged. "I passed through Lariat on my way here, and a friend of ours said you might be here."

"And what is it you want?"

"I've got a job for you, and your friend here, if he wants one."

"I'm listening. What's the job?"

The Cutter studied the bald man. He had ridden with the old Jack Mormon outlaw more than once in the old days. Mormon Dan, for that's what most called him, could be overly suspicious and unpredictable at times. While he wasn't necessarily the best gun to have on your side, he was seasoned and steady and would pull a trigger without question when you needed him to. Furthermore, he was the only help the Cutter was apt to find on short notice, as most of the old gang had been all hanged or run into the ground long before. And the harelipped fellow with him had to be a salty sort or else he wouldn't be keeping company with Dan.

"There's a man in Del Norte that needs put down," the Cutter said.

"Never knew you to need help when it comes to one man," Mormon Dan answered. "You always were handy with a pistol."

"I just want you to keep anybody else off my back while I get it done."

Mormon Dan took a drink of his beer, his scraggly mustache dipping deep into the froth. He set the mug down, wiped at his mouth, and belched. "What's it pay?"

"A hundred dollars." The Cutter nodded at the harelipped man. "Same for you if you're game."

"Kirby, you must think I work cheap," Mormon Dan said. "You want me to go with you to Del Norte and help kill a man when the law there is on the lookout for you? Those are tall odds. You used to be smarter than that."

"You used to talk softer to me."

"A hundred dollars won't cut it," Dan said with a more cautious tone. "Two hundred, but if we get to Del Norte and things don't look right I'm pulling out. I got a price on my head, and there's not enough money in the world for me to ride into a necktie party waiting for you."

"A hundred, that's what it pays." The Cutter reached inside his coat slowly so that Dan didn't misunderstand his movements and pulled out some of the paper money he had taken from the lawyer's safe. He was more than aware that Dan likely had a pistol hidden under that hat. He laid the stack of greenbacks on the table. "In advance."

Mormon Dan eyed the thin stack of bills dubiously. "You know how much I made off that bank in Telluride?"

"And how much have you got left?"

Dan sighed and leaned back in his chair, at the same time taking his hand off the hat. "Six months ago that wouldn't seem like much, but tonight it looks like a fortune to me."

"Does that mean you're in?" the Cutter asked.

Dan finished his beer while he looked at his partner. "You hear that, Peck? Are you ready to go to work?"

"Peck? Is that your first name or your last?" The Cutter asked.

The harelipped man gave the Cutter a suspicious look but finally answered, "It's my last name. Henry Peck, that's me."

"He's steady and he ain't bothered by the smell of gunpowder," Mormon Dan offered. "Was with me at Telluride, and he did good."

The Cutter didn't act like he even heard Mormon Dan and continued to stare at his partner. "Peck? Are you any kin to that city marshal in Del Norte?"

Peck smiled, showing his yellow teeth, and nodded. "He's my uncle."

"Uncle, huh? You and him wouldn't be close, would you?"

Again, Peck smiled. "Uncle Bill's done me a favor from time to time, and let's just say he's never been one to turn down an extra dollar if it's offered him. Runs in the family, I guess."

"That's good, real good," the Cutter said with a half grin of his own.

"Let's have another beer to seal our bargain," Dan said, "or you can shoot me a game of sixty-one pool and the loser buys."

The Cutter rose from his chair. "I want to ride tonight."

Mormon Dan gave him a sour look but didn't argue. He took his share of the money from the table, tucked it away in a wallet he carried in his vest pocket, then scooted his chair back from the table and stood. When he lifted his hat and put in on his head the Cutter saw the nickel-plated Remington Army lying there on the table.

Mormon Dan gave an almost apologetic shrug as he picked up the revolver and holstered it. "You were always good, Kirby. Too good. Didn't know at first what you were up to, and thought I might need an edge."

"And you said I was the one getting scary in my old age," the Cutter answered.

Mormon Dan grinned. "Just like old times, huh?"

"Just like old times."

Dan looked at Peck. "Are you game for this?"

"Game as a fighting rooster," Peck replied.

"Well, then, let's go have ourselves a bloody Sunday," Dan said.

CHAPTER FORTY-THREE

Newt rode up to the St. Francis of Assisi Mission Church seven miles east of Del Norte in the farming community of Los Valdeses the next morning. He noticed that he must have arrived just before Mass, for a long line of penitents was working its way inside the church. There wasn't a gringo among them, and he thought them mostly farmers and people of the countryside by their appearance. They were a friendly but impoverished-looking lot. It was a cold day, and every one of the congregation carried a stick of firewood in their hands they had brought with them to help feed the church's woodstove.

He stopped the Circle Dot horse under the spreading limbs of a cottonwood tree some twenty yards from the front of the church, and although they couldn't help but occasionally stare at him, the stranger among them, several people nodded greetings to him as a way of friendliness or passed polite small talk in Spanish. Two men near the tree were finishing their cornhusk cigarettes and offered him the makings to roll his own. He declined and used what little Spanish he knew to discuss the weather with them and ask of their crops the past summer and how their families were.

There was no church bell to ring, but some silent signal must have passed among them, and the smokers he had been talking to rubbed out their cigarette butts under their heels, took off their big, sugarloaf sombreros, and followed the last of their friends inside. Newt did not follow them, nor did he dismount. Instead, he waited.

Mass lasted for almost an hour, and he was chilled to the quick by the time the parishioners began to file out of the church and start home. The priest must have been told about him, for he stood in the open door of the church and waved at Newt to join him.

Newt left the Circle Dot horse ground-tied and walked to the door. He stomped the snow from his boots at the threshold, took off his hat, and held it with both hands as he entered the church. He looked over the room he found himself in while the priest closed the door behind him.

The church was built in a simple rectangle shape with high adobe walls almost three feet thick. The inside of it showed similar poverty to those who worshipped there. There were no ornate stained-glass windows, and the floor of the nave was packed earth with ox blood mixed in to give it a hard finish. It was also unlevel and sloped up toward the altar at the far end of the room with the natural lay of the ground. Those who might attend Mass there would sit not on pews, but simple, crude wooden benches. The ornate candleholder in front of the altar was made of brass and not gold, and the large crucifix hanging behind the alter was carved of wood, likely by one of the locals. Whoever made it had done a fine job, except for the painting of it. The blood on Jesus's wrists and ankles was bright red, and the whites of his eyes were equally bright and oddly wrong, with pinpricks of black dabbed in place for pupils. Newt felt restless under the paint-eyed stare of the wooden, tortured

Messiah and turned away from it and looked at the priest behind him.

The priest was younger than Newt, a thin, clean-shaven man with a sharp point of a chin and an Adam's apple even sharper. He stood there in his black cassock, a floor length, loose-fitting robe. A silver cross on a silver chain hung about his neck, and one of his hands rested on that necklace at his chest while he looked askance at Newt.

"What brings you here?" the Jesuit asked. He spoke English very well, but with a cautious approach, as if he did not fully trust his command of the language. "I notice that you did not attend Mass."

"Are you Father Ramirez?" Newt asked.

"I am."

"I understand you are taking care of the girl," Newt said.

"You mean Zuri?"

"Yes."

"Dare I hope that you bring me some news that might help her?"

"No, I just wanted to check on her."

"Are you of some relation to her?"

"I helped her out of the mountains."

The priest nodded his head. "Ah, you are the one who brought her to the doctor."

"Newt Jones." Newt didn't offer to shake the priest's hand, unsure if that was something you did with Catholic priests.

The priest didn't hold out a hand, either, and continued to stand where he was and to keep plenty of distance between them. "It is a pleasure to meet you, Señor Jones."

Newt started to tell the priest that such a lie was not in keeping with the man's position, but he kept it to himself.

"Where is she? I thought she was up and about and on the mend."

"We discussed the matter and thought it best that she be handed over to the Sisters of Loretto at Conejos, at least for the time being."

"We?"

"The sisters and I," the priest answered. "We have also sent a letter to the archbishop at Santa Fe to confer with him."

"This place at Conejos, it's some sort of orphanage?"

"It is a convent, and a school for children, as well. And, yes, there are orphans there. I assure you, she will be taken care of."

"Did you even try to find any of her family or someone who will take her in?"

"Of course we did. She has told me she has no family here in the States, but there is an uncle in Spain. I have written letters. Perhaps in time the uncle will write back and be willing to come and get her or pay for her travel to join him."

"And what if you get no answers to your letters?"

"Then she will remain with the Sisters of Loretto."

"I just wanted to make sure she was being taken care of." Newt looked down at his hat and turned its brim around in his hands while he considered what the priest had told him. He made as if to leave, but the priest stopped him.

"Could you do me a favor?" the priest asked.

"I guess that depends on the favor."

"I wonder if you could take care of something, something that Zuri couldn't take with her?"

Newt looked a question at the priest.

"Come, you will see." The priest took a coat off a peg near the door and donned it, as well as a hat and a wool scarf. Once in proper garb for the cold, he opened the door.

Newt took one last look in the direction of the altar and the crucifix hanging on the wall above and behind it. The Jesus hanging there still seemed as if it were staring at him, the same way the eyes of people in painted portraits sometimes felt like they tracked you as you moved. He followed the priest outside, glad to get away from those eyes.

The priest slipped his scarf up over his chin and grabbed the ends of it inside his coat. He glanced at the Circle Dot Horse. "You can ride or walk with me. It's not far to my home."

Newt went to the Circle Dot horse and picked up the single bridle rein he had left on the ground. Instead of using that rein to lead the gelding, he pitched it up over its neck. When he turned to go back to the priest, the horse stayed where it was. He stopped, looked back at it, and gave a high-pitched whistle through his teeth. The horse came toward him and followed him back to the church.

"You're horse seems well trained," the priest said.

"Oh, he comes with me when he's of a mind to and follows until he decides to do something else," Newt answered.

He fell in beside the priest, with the Circle Dot horse following them like a dog a few feet behind. They followed the bank of the river, passing by two farms and over an irrigation ditch bridge before coming to the little house with the whitewashed adobe walls where the priest lived.

The priest opened the door and looked back at the Circle Dot horse. "You are welcome to come in out of the cold, but I'm afraid your horse will not fit inside."

"Don't give him any ideas," Newt said. He took one of the bridle reins from the horse's neck and dropped it on the ground. Then he went inside the house after the priest and closed the door behind him.

Like most of the houses in the area, the priest's was built *jacal* style, with cedar poles set in the ground and adobe straw mud plastered between them and over them. The earthen walls and roof held heat well. The fire burning in the beehive stove in one corner had the jacal's single, tiny room toasty warm, and it felt good.

The only furniture was a small table and chairs in the center, another chair with a tanned, hair-on goatskin laid over it in front of the fireplace, and the priest's bed with a large storage trunk at the foot of it along one wall. The room's only decorations were the little cross and carved wood saints on an alcove shelf set in the other wall and a couple of woven Mexican or Navajo rugs laid on the tight-packed earth floor.

The priest went to the fireplace and stirred the coals and added a few more sticks of wood. He then crossed to the other side of the room and began taking his coat off. He gestured at the chair before the fireplace. "Please sit and warm yourself."

Newt didn't take the chair, but did move to stand in front of the fireplace with his back to it and with his hands behind him. He was very curious as to why the priest had brought him there, but willed himself to be patient.

The priest opened the trunk at the foot of his bed. From it, he pulled Zuri's broken rifle. He brought the gun to the table and laid it there. "I want you to take this."

Newt studied the rifle with its broken stock. The firearm's steel was rusty with age and recent mistreatment. It was a gun well past its prime, damaged to the point of being all but worthless.

"She insisted that she be allowed to take the gun with her. In fact, we had quite an argument about it," the priest added. "She places great value on it. Perhaps because it belonged to her father, or perhaps for reasons I cannot fathom."

Newt remembered Zuri's attachment to the rifle and how

she had insisted that it not be left behind at the Wason ranch. "What is it you want?"

"If I give the gun to one of my parishioners there will be jealousy," the priest said. "I had thought about disposing of it somehow, but knowing how much it means to her makes me hesitant to do so. If you will take it, then you will solve my problem."

Once again, Newt studied the broken rifle on the table, and he knew it said a lot about the poverty of the community if a firearm in such pitiful condition would be something to make people jealous of anyone owning it.

"So, you want to push your problem on someone else?" Newt asked.

"It's not that."

"Why me?" Newt asked.

The priest shrugged. "Who else? You seem to care for the girl, and you seem . . . well, someone who would know what to do with it. And everyone will assume that you are some relation to Zuri or a friend that has more of a claim on the gun than anybody else."

"And what is it you want me to do with it?"

"Do with it what you think best."

Newt started to refuse but didn't. He took up the rifle from the table. It felt like a burden and a responsibility heavier than its simple weight in his hands. It was as if it required something of him, though he couldn't say what that was or why it made him feel that way.

"So long, Preacher."

The priest stopped Newt just as he reached the door. "You know, she and I talked a great deal about her ordeal."

Newt turned back to face him. "You must have had better luck talking to her than I did."

"She is a Basque, and they have a language of their own. It's not one that I speak, either, but by God's blessing she also happens to speak Spanish, as many of her people do, as well as some French."

Newt paused with his hand on the door latch, and he considered his own lack of education and the fact that the priest spoke of knowing three languages as if it were nothing. Other than his native English, Newt could barely speak a little Spanish, a few phrases in Mohave that Mr. Smith had taught him, and some Apache he had picked up during time spent in Mexico.

"She said you saved her life," the priest added when Newt remained silent too long to suit him.

"I didn't do anything special."

"She thinks you did. She asked me to pray for you," the priest said. "Are you a religious man, Señor Jones? Do you believe in God?"

"I've talked to him from time to time, but never was sure who I was talking to or if he was listening," Newt answered.

The priest gave a sad, slow shake of his head. "The Lord hears all our prayers, and if you talk enough, maybe you will come to hear him."

"Then how come he didn't help her? How come he didn't hear her prayers?"

"How do you know he didn't help her?"

"Have you thought about what she went through? What kind of answer to a prayer is that?"

"And yet, she is still alive despite her hardships, and perhaps against all odds," the priest said. "I'm told the mountains she walked out of are vast and wild, and she has told me about how horrible the snow and the cold were. But somehow, she survived on her own until she found you to help her. Found you to help her in all that expanse. Both of those events are some sorts of miracles when you think about them in that way."

"You saying that reminds me of my mother. She always found the good in things when nobody else could."

"You mother was right. There is good in all of us, just the same as there is sin."

"So you say, but I've seen more bad than good."

"And that is why you came here? Because you think she is something good."

"Maybe so, or maybe it's just that I keep seeing people lose that deserve to win."

"And that bothers you?" the priest asked.

"It does."

"I sense that you believe you aren't a good man."

"Take somebody else's confession, Preacher. I'm not your man."

The priest crossed himself, then looked Newt in the eyes. "I will pray for your soul."

"You look out for her," Newt said. "That's all I ask."

"I will do everything for her I can, but like you, I worry about her. I fear she will be a long time healing."

"The doctor said she was fine."

"There are other issues," the priest said with a sigh.

"What other issues?"

"She does not sleep well. She has bad dreams."

Newt thought of finding Zuri and what he had seen when he and the sheriff's posse had found the remains of the sheep camp where her father had been killed. Not only had they found the scattered and wrecked tent and gear, but her father's torn-up grave as well. The site was like a battle-field. Few of the sheep were left alive, except for a half-starved little bunch of stragglers they discovered a few miles away, and the remains of the dead woolies were scattered through the hills. There was wolf sign everywhere, and the black ravens scavenging the carcasses were as thick as the wolves.

Five miles or more she had come off of that mountain, and most of that journey had taken place in a blizzard, with nothing to help her other than her own wits and toughness.

"She's been through a lot," he said. "The gang that caught her was a bad one. A man like you might not understand just how bad they were."

"It is not those men she dreams of," the priest said.

"The bear?" Newt asked.

"She cries out in her sleep, and when I tried to console her she spoke of nothing but the devil bear and how it is coming after her. Her first morning here, before we traveled to Conejos, she scared me when I went to wake her up and she was not in her bed. I found her outside walking around and looking for bear tracks, and when I questioned her she told me she had heard it stalking round and round the house in the night."

"She's strong. Strong enough that I wouldn't bet against her," Newt said, then opened the door.

"Yes, she is, but I'm afraid she will be a long time getting over what happened to her. And even then, I fear she now has scars that will forever mark her."

The cold touched the skin of Newt's face, and the chill of it seeped down inside his coat collar like a wicked kiss while he thought about Zuri and stared across the valley toward the mountains in the distance.

"Scars?" Newt turned in the doorway and looked once more at the priest. The expression on his battle-marked face and the strange intensity and unblinking nature of his gaze were like the aiming of two gun barrels.

"I meant no offense," the priest said.

"No offense taken," Newt replied. "I imagine you're right. Those that don't show can mark us as much as those that do."

CHAPTER FORTY-FOUR

Newt was barely back in Del Norte when he saw Saul Barton heading toward the Windsor Hotel with a group of three other men, all of them wearing fancy suits and overcoats. He was about to ride over and have a talk with Barton, but he ran into Sheriff Pearitter at a street corner a block away.

The sheriff was on horseback, and there were two county deputies riding with him. All of them had rifles and bedrolls on their saddles.

"Somebody thinks they saw the Cutter in Alamosa last night," the sheriff said. "Mormon Dan's girlfriend has a hurdy-gurdy house and gambling parlor outside town there, real rough joint. The Conejos County deputy thinks the Cutter might be holed up at her place, and we're going there and see if we can help smoke him out."

"Who's Mormon Dan?" Newt asked.

"He showed up around here from the Utah Territory seven or eight years ago. He took to messing around with his neighbor's wife and got caught at it. Killed one of the big shots in their church when they confronted him over his philandering and has been on the run ever since. Got himself a regular little gang now, stealing cattle and holding up a stagecoach here and there . . . the general rough stuff, you know. He and some other owl hoots robbed the San Miguel Valley Bank at Telluride last spring and got themselves shot up in the process. If the Cutter's looking for a place to hide or someone to help warn him if the law's coming, he's liable to run to Dan's bunch."

"Best of luck to you. Hope you catch him." Newt was having a hard time listening to the sheriff while at the same time keeping a watch on Barton.

The sheriff glanced at where Newt kept looking past him, at the Windsor Hotel farther down the street. Saul Barton and the men with him were just then going inside.

"Do you have any idea who those men are with Barton?" the sheriff asked.

"No."

"So I'm supposed to believe you also don't know he sicced the governor on me?" the sheriff said. "How did the telegram I got put it? Something like this: 'I trust you will handle the matter of the attempt to steal Mr. Barton's claim with expediency and with due respect to Mr. Barton's good reputation and his standing in the state.'"

"I haven't talked to Saul since I got back here."

"He's got some gall, I tell you."

"Sounds like he has friends in high places."

"He's sadly mistaken if he thinks his money and his friends in Denver can buy him sway in this county," the sheriff swore.

"The governor seems to think differently."

"The governor can go jump in a lake."

Newt's lips tightened and one corner of his mouth tilted upward in what might have been meant as a smile. "Now who is it that seems to have a problem with authority?"

The sheriff gave him one last irritated look, then spurred his horse down the street with the deputies following him.

Newt shifted his attention back to the hotel when the lawmen were gone.

Sheriff Pearitter wasn't such a bad sort, even if the old lawman was as cranky as a cornered badger, and even if he was so stubborn and unbending as to be almost comical at times. Saul Barton was another story. Newt's eyes went back to the hotel. It was high time he and Barton had a talk.

He left the Circle Dot horse tied at a hitching rail and entered the hotel. The first thing he saw was two of the nattily dressed men who had been with Barton earlier sitting up on a shoeshine stand in what was both a side lobby and a wide hallway that led to the hotel dining room off the entrance foyer. They both had their feet propped up on the brass footrests, and the shoeshiner who ran the stand was cleaning the snow and mud off their calfskin shoes. That said a lot about them and where they came from—men used to walking on clean hardwood floors, cobblestones, and concrete. One of them was smoking a fat cigar, and he squinted at Newt over the red ash of it and through the smoke, while the other man looked at Newt with a bored expression and then snapped a copy of the *San Juan Prospector* newspaper open and covered his face with it.

Newt's gaze shifted to the register desk in front of him, where he saw Saul Barton and the other man with the hotel clerk. He started toward them.

"I'll see you at dinner. Shall we say six? A good meal and then we can talk business over a fine cigar and a glass of bourbon," the man with Barton at the desk said.

"Sounds good to me," Barton answered. He was dressed as well as the others and had done away with his usual workmanlike attire.

The other man followed the bellboy up the stairs that led to the second floor. Only Barton and the hotel clerk were left at the desk when Newt got there.

Barton heard Newt's rapid footsteps sounding behind him and turned around. He must have immediately recognized the look on Newt's face for what it was because he took a guarded step backward.

"Hold up there," Barton said. "Think about it."

"You set us up." Newt kept coming.

"I don't know what you're talking about."

"Like hell you don't." Newt didn't slow down until he was very close to Barton.

Barton held up both hands. "I'm sure this is something we can work out if you'll calm down."

"I say, what's this all about?" the hotel clerk asked. "Should I send for the marshal? Just say the word, Mr. Barton."

Newt pointed a thick finger at the clerk, stabbing it at him like a knife. "This is no business of yours."

Barton glanced at the clerk, obviously embarrassed as well as flustered, and shook his head. The clerk said nothing else and wouldn't look Newt in the eyes.

"How about we go somewhere else and talk about this?" Barton asked Newt.

Newt's breathing had become harsh and his face was tight with anger. Barton eased around him, took a few steps, then looked back and waved for Newt to come with him. Newt went to where Barton waited for him near the hotel's main entrance.

"The sheriff told me what happened at the claim," Barton said in a hushed voice. "I'm sorry."

"You're a poor liar."

The men on the shoeshine stand were likely far enough away that they couldn't hear the conversation, but regardless, they were watching intently, not at all hiding their curiosity or their attempt to eavesdrop.

"Please keep your voice down," Barton said. "From

what I understand from the sheriff's telegram, you had a rough go of it. It's no wonder that you're angry."

"What I want to understand is why you did all you could to make sure everyone knew you had hired us to guard your claim. Practically advertised your find."

"I've come to a point in my life where it is all but impossible to keep the entirety of my business a secret. I thought an open show of force and demonstrating that I'm willing to hold what's mine might prevent any trouble rather than invite it," Barton said.

"You knew we were going to get hit."

"I told you I was followed throughout the summer, yet you act shocked that I should assume someone would try to take what's mine. Why would I hire you in the first place if that weren't the case?" Barton asked. "And if you'll remember, I told you to take on more men."

"You hung us out to dry so you could pull off whatever flimflam game it is you're playing," Newt snapped back at him.

"I'll ask you again to keep your voice down." Barton glanced at the men at the shoeshine stand and then stepped to the door. "Let's go outside."

Newt went out the door behind him, and they stood face-to-face on the sidewalk in front of the hotel.

"Do you have a clue who that man was at the desk?" Barton said in a whispered hiss. "That's Lloyd Tevis's right-hand man. You know, Tevis, the president of Wells Fargo? George Hearst's partner in his mines? The Homestake in Deadwood? The Anaconda Copper Mine in Butte?"

And those two in the hallway?" Newt asked.

"Money men from back East. They've bought themselves a silver mine in Mexico and badly want another one, and I've got a major stockholder in the Bulldog Mine at Silver Cliff coming tomorrow."

"I suppose you're about to sell them a piece of your big strike? Did you show them a little high-grade ore from somewhere else to make their money jump out of their banks, or haven't you got to that point yet?"

"Listen—"

"I wonder if they'd all like to know that you're pulling a fast one on them," Newt said. "I know it, and Happy Jack knew it before you got him killed."

Barton sighed. "You're right."

"What's that?"

"You're right. My claim on Willow Creek Canyon's worthless."

CHAPTER FORTY-FIVE

Newt was about to pounce on Barton's admission when he noticed some hint of something he wasn't expecting on Barton's face.

"Willow Creek is nothing but a decoy," Barton added, "one meant to distract anyone attempting to ride my coat-tails or wreck my plans and to buy the time I need until I can put this deal together."

"A decoy?"

Barton nodded. "I have no intention of proving up my Willow Creek claim. My real ambition is a few miles west on Rat Creek. I am prepared to file a claim on that location. Immediately, if need be, although I would prefer to wait until spring."

"Keep talking," Newt said.

"The problem with much of the silver deposits in this area is that the assays aren't high enough per ton to make a mine pay sufficiently, at least not without a railroad to it or close by. But I have it on good information that the D and RG tracks will be extended on west in the next few years, and that makes any mining operation far more profitable, especially on a large scale. I also believe that the vein I have located is one that not only will assay well above average but is also sufficiently large to produce a profit for a long time."

Newt felt some of his anger leaking away, if not all of it. "And you intend to be ready when the tracks are laid."

"If and when," Barton answered. "These things aren't done overnight, you know. One must gather investors to buy stamp mills and smelters, not to mention possibly contributing to the development of the railroad for shipping. That's the difference between mining and prospecting. One is dreaming and the other is business."

"I still don't see the need for all the trickery. Why not just file where you wanted to and hold it, the devil be damned?"

"As I've told you before, and you've already had the misfortune to learn, I have certain competitors. Some are more than that. Enemies, if you will." Barton paused to clear his throat, or to consider what he would say next. "They will stop at nothing, and not only are they ambitious, they wouldn't mind seeing me ruined in the process. Accordingly, I felt it prudent to make it appear as if I was very confident I had found the next big strike in Willow Creek Canyon. Every day they might be focused on that false lead was one where I had a chance to get myself back in the game in such a way that they can't muscle me out."

"You could have told me."

"What could I have told you that would have mattered? You knew I was hiring fighters . . . what could be required of you," Barton said. "This has never been a game for soft men."

"I like to know what I'm fighting for."

"You fought for money, just like I fight to make my own living. We reach out and grab what we want or need, 'cause nobody's giving us anything," Barton snapped back at him. "You fought because three dollars a day is better than busting your back digging ditches or swinging a hammer and sweating your life away for next to nothing in return. You did it because you can and because you're good at it."

"You don't know me."

Barton took a deep breath. "The people that think the mining in the San Juans is booming already haven't seen anything yet. There's going to be an even bigger boom, and that means opportunities for those strong enough to take action. Either you can hit me like I see you thinking about or you can get over it and we'll talk about the future and how we might both profit from it."

Newt realized that both of his fists were clenched, though he couldn't remember doing that. He inhaled and shook his head. "No, I'm not going to hit you."

"Good," Barton said, then reached inside his coat and pulled forth a wallet. "Now that that's settled, I believe you and the others have more than earned a bonus."

Newt watched as Barton thumbed over a sheaf of greenbacks from out of the wallet. Barton held out what must have been several hundred dollars.

"Take this," Barton said. "Divide it among the others as you see fit."

Newt took the money in his right hand and looked down at it there in his fist with a thoughtful expression on his face, as if pondering how it had come to be there.

"Have you gotten yourself a room?" Barton asked. "If not, we'll get you one here. A hot bath, a good beefsteak, and a few cocktails in your belly will have you feeling like a new man. Give you a chance to think on things."

One of the hotel doors opened. The two men from the shoeshine stand stood in the doorway, and Newt could see the hotel clerk standing behind them.

"Is everything all right?" one of them asked.

"Fine, fine," Barton answered them.

"You're sure?" the same man asked.

"We're just talking."

They were still standing in the open doorway when Newt looked up from the money in his hand.

"I feel bad about Happy Jack. He was a good man," Barton said. "Not many of his kind left. Half crazy, but then again, he was always that way. Did you know he was one of the originals to come across the plains with the Russell Party back in '58? Real nose for prospecting, though not a lick of aptitude for business. Staked one of the first and best finds in Russell Gulch, but later when he thought the placer gold had run thin, he let old John Gregory's Central City friends talk him into selling out for a measly five thousand dollars. He told me once that he stopped in Central City as he was leaving and spent every bit of what they paid him in one night. Hoo-rawed and drank and gambled it all away. Left there with nothing but the shirt on his back and a single pack mule he was leading, and then he went off looking again for the next big strike, no matter that them he sold it to have likely pulled millions from that ground he sold."

Newt hit him with a left fist. It was not an easy punch, and it struck him squarely on one cheekbone with a solid thud. One moment Barton was standing up, and the next he was lying on his back on the brick sidewalk with his eyes rolled back in their sockets and nothing showing but the white of them.

Newt stood over him with both fists doubled and hanging at his sides. The money in one fist fluttered and rustled in the breeze. It wasn't long before Barton's eyelids spasmed, his eyes rolled back to where they belonged, and he let out a groan and rolled onto his side.

Newt took a step back, and Barton got to his knees and then his feet after several shaky tries. Barton put a hand to his split and bloody cheek and glared at Newt, though he was swaying and his vision still didn't seem to be focusing properly.

"What was that for?" Barton asked.

"That's for lying to me," Newt said, "and because I needed to hit somebody."

"I thought you said you weren't going to hit me."

"I changed my mind."

"You're never going to be anything but a bruiser and a thumper. Just a damned animal."

Newt tucked the money away in his coat pocket and walked away.

"Smarten up, Jones," Barton called after him. "Smarten up and see the world for how it is."

"I've seen the world," Newt said without stopping. As he walked, he was thinking that Barton wasn't half as smart as he thought he was, just like Happy Jack had said.

Newt got his horse and rode it to the doctor's office. He wasn't surprised to find Mr. Smith outside the entrance, but he didn't expect to see Tully Hudlow wrapped in a blanket and sitting beside the Mohave on the bench meant as a place for patients to wait their turn to see the doctor in warmer weather. Tully leaned to one side like he was favoring the bandaged wound at his waist, and he rested his splinted arm carefully on his lap.

"Thought you're supposed to be in bed," Newt said as he got down from the saddle.

"I'm still weak as a day-old pup," Tully answered, "but the doctor said some fresh air and sunshine would be good for me."

Newt gave the sky above them a dubious look, and he guessed the dim glow of the sun behind the thin sheet of gray clouds might qualify as sunshine if one was an optimist.

Mr. Smith noticed the red and split knuckles on Newt's left hand. "Did I miss something?"

"Me and Saul Barton just had a little business meeting."

"How did that go?"

"I don't think I convinced him, but I'm pretty sure he got my point."

Mr. Smith nodded his head at the street behind Newt. "Is that why he's coming over here?"

Newt thought the Mohave meant Barton, but when he turned he saw that it was Marshal Peck riding a horse and coming straight toward them.

"Thought I might find you here." The marshal appeared flustered by something, with his usual self-important arrogance seemingly gone for the moment.

"What can we do for you, Marshal?" Newt asked. "Is there something wrong?"

"Damn right there is. This town had two lawyers, now we've got only one."

"What happened?"

"Somebody murdered him. That's what happened," the marshal said. "His landlord found him lying on the floor in his office with his throat cut."

"Uh huh," Newt said because he could think of nothing else to say.

"Looks like robbery," the marshal continued. "The safe door in the office was standing wide open."

"And how come you here telling us about it?" Newt asked.

"Nothing real awful tends to happen here. Not in a long time," the marshal said. "Not since a lynch mob took the Pond Brothers out of jail and hung them five or six years ago for holding up a stage. But all of a sudden there are dead men turning up right and left. Your fight up at Willow Creek, two men burning to death in O'Doul's bar, and now this. They say bad things come in bunches, but I'll be damned if I think it's a coincidence. Something's going on, and it just so happened to start when you showed up."

"You don't actually believe we had something to do with killing that lawyer, do you?" Newt asked.

"No, but even if I was suspicious, that lawyer's been dead for days and you two were with us up in the mountains then."

"Then what is it you want?"

"A man working out back of the grocery store about noon three days ago said he saw a saddled red roan horse standing in the alley below the lawyer's office," the marshal said. "Said he wouldn't have remembered it except for the horse's color being so flashy and him not ever seeing it before."

Newt and Mr. Smith watched Tully out of the corners of their eyes, waiting to see his reaction and wondering how, or if, he would answer.

"Sounds like Tandy's horse," Tully said.

"Your brother?" the marshal asked.

Tully nodded. "He bought him from a Chickasaw horse trader in the Indian Territory. Red roan gelding with two white socks on his back legs and blaze face."

"Sounds like the one. Any brands on him?"

Tully shook his head. "No."

"When was the last time you saw that horse?"

Tully squinted at the marshal. "Before they hit us at the claim and killed Tandy."

"I saw the horse after that," Mr. Smith said. "Saw it when we fought at the ranch."

Newt tried to remember the horse from that night at the Wason ranch, among all the others charging out of the barn, but he couldn't. It had been too dark and everything had happened too fast, but he guessed what else Mr. Smith was about to say, anyway.

"The Cutter was riding him when he got away," Mr. Smith added.

The marshal took that news with a bland face and no show of surprise. They had given him descriptions of the Hudlow brothers' missing horses days earlier, and he knew before he asked who the roan the grocer saw likely belonged to and who might be riding it now. There was also something about his bearing that hinted he might have other suspicions or information that he wasn't sharing with them.

"Say you're right, why would the Cutter have killed the lawyer, if it was him that did it?" Newt asked.

The marshal stared at all of them for a moment. "I'll ask you the same question."

"Your guess is as good as mine," Newt answered. "I saw the sheriff earlier on his way out of town. He said someone had seen the Cutter in Alamosa last night."

"I hope he catches him, but I'm left here in the meantime with a mess on my hands. Right now, half the town is likely over there gawking at the blood and gore and making up stories, and then they'll start asking what I'm doing about it."

"What are you doing about it?" Newt asked.

"I need you to come with me."

"What for?"

"I found what I think is his brother's roan horse, and I want you to tell me if I'm right," the marshal said. "Won't take us long. It isn't far away."

Newt put a boot in his stirrup to mount, and Mr. Smith got up from the bench.

The marshal shook his head. "Not you. Just him. I'd like to do this with as little attention as possible. You've got half the town convinced you're devil spawn with that marked-up face of yours, and the other half thinking there's going to be an Indian massacre and making sure their kids are off the street if they see you coming."

"I ought to be the one to go." Tully sat up straight from where he had been leaning against the wall behind him, and he favored his wounded side and moved gingerly when he started to stand.

"You're in no shape for it. Jones here will be more than enough," the marshal said.

Newt looked at Tully. "You get those holes in you bleeding again and I'll have Mr. Smith whip you with a knotted plow line."

Mr. Smith laid a very large and insistent hand on Tully's shoulder and kept him down on the bench.

The marshal started up Pine Street with Newt riding beside him.

"I take it you didn't find Cutter when you found the horse?" Newt asked.

"Found that roan in a pen behind an abandoned place near the tracks," the marshal answered. "Doesn't look like anybody stayed there. No saddle or gear. It's like somebody just left the horse there."

"Might be whoever was riding him aims to come back for him."

"I've got someone watching just in case, but what I want to know for sure is if the horse belongs to your friend's brother." The marshal looked straight ahead, never once so much as glancing at Newt, as if he was distracted by other thoughts.

"Just how many strawberry roans with a big blaze face and two stocking legs you figure are in this town?" Newt asked.

The marshal's only answer to that was a slight frown, and he turned them down First Street headed west. The wind that had started out that morning as a steady, intermittent breeze had begun to gust and was hitting them head-on. Both they and their horses leaned into it.

They passed in front of a butcher shop, and Newt looked down the alley between it and the building beside it and spotted Happy Jack's dog. It looked thinner than he remembered it and somehow even older and more brittle. It had knocked over a barrel of meat scraps and slaughter offal and was gnawing on a scavenged bone in a manner that was both ferocious and feeble at the same time. It was so intent on feeding its hunger that it never even looked up or cocked an ear when they passed the mouth of the alley.

"The butcher's going to throw a fit," the marshal said over the wind when he saw what Newt was looking at. "He takes those leavings home and feeds them to his fattening hogs."

"I doubt those hogs will miss a scrap or two."

"Maybe the hogs won't, but you don't know the butcher. He was in my office yesterday complaining and raising all kinds of Cain about some stray mutt tearing into his scrap barrels and scattering trash. You would have thought somebody was robbing him blind by the way he was carrying on. If I had time I'd just stop and shoot that fleabag now and save myself the trouble of having to do it later."

"There's no need in it," Newt said. "That dog likely won't make it through winter and he won't be troubling anybody anymore."

"All the more reason to put it out of its misery. Likely be a kindness."

Newt turned his head to look at the marshal. "Maybe, but I doubt the dog would see it that way."

"What do you care? It's just a mongrel stray that nobody wants," the marshal said.

They had ridden on a good ways and several minutes had passed before Newt answered, and his voice was quiet when he did, as if he was talking to himself as much as to the marshal. "Been a time or two where I lived like a dog, and I don't like to see anything or anybody kicked while they're down."

The marshal seemed surprised that Newt still wanted to talk about the dog. "Anybody ever tell you that you're a contrary sort?"

"Once or twice," Newt replied absentmindedly.

He could still picture the dog in that alley gut pile, and the vividness of that image bothered him and settled a sadness on his shoulders.

"How much farther is it?" Newt asked when they were out of town and riding along the south bank of the river and paralleling the railroad tracks.

"Not far now."

What had once been a Barlow & Sanderson stagecoach station appeared on the south edge of the road ahead of them. The station house itself was a little cabin built of spruce logs topped with a gabled dirt roof, and behind and just beyond it was a fenced yard made of upright cedar pickets that had once enclosed teams of horses and parked coaches. The roof of a sizeable barn rose up from the center of that enclosure. Though the layout spoke of better and busier times before the railroad put the stage company out of business, the entire place was run-down and as weathered and unkempt as the sagebrush flat it sat on.

"The horse is around back." The marshal pointed at the set of double gates that led inside the wagon yard. One of those gates had broken off its hinges and was lying on the ground, and the other swayed and creaked in the wind.

Newt turned the Circled Dot horse off the road and went through the gate. The marshal pointed at the old barn, then tucked his chin back in his collar and clenched his coat front with one hand to try and seal it closed against the wind. A loose board on the barn slapped against its frame.

Newt had ridden ahead of the marshal without realizing it, and when he glanced behind him he saw the marshal getting off his horse. Newt did the same, studying the barn as he stepped down from the Circle Dot horse. The tall structure was sided with long boards that had been stood upright and nailed to a timber frame. No batting strips had ever been put in place to cover the cracks between those boards, and over time, the lumber had shrunk and the gaps had widened until the building had an odd effect of alternating bars of light that drew the eyes to try see through it and beyond it—hints and glimpses of what the barn couldn't fully hold or conceal.

The roofing was missing entire patches of shakes, likely blown free in some storm, and a board somewhere had pulled loose from its nails and the wind slapped one end of it loudly and steadily against the framing.

Once more, the marshal indicated the barn with a nod of his head in that direction. Newt didn't wait for him and tucked both hands inside his coat pockets to warm them, hunched his shoulders, and started toward where the marshal pointed. He'd go look at the roan horse and be done with it.

The wagon yard was a thirty-yard square, and he was halfway across it when he saw that there wasn't just one horse inside the old barn, but three. He could see bits of them through the gaps between the board siding, and none of them looked like a roan.

That realization and its possible implications hadn't taken full effect before the Cutter and another man stepped out from behind the station house and blocked his way. A third man came from somewhere on the other side of the yard and stopped some distance away, flanking Newt on the right. At the same time, the marshal veered wide of Newt, taking the other side and slightly behind him.

Newt didn't recognize any of the men with the Cutter. But it didn't matter because every one of them had guns in their hands and their intent to kill him was plain enough.

CHAPTER FORTY-SIX

"I thought you'd never show," the Cutter said with a satisfied smirk and with the pistol in his fist pointed at Newt.

Newt would have expected a man like the Cutter to get right to it and not to run his mouth before a killing, but that talk bought Newt a split second he wouldn't have had otherwise. His right hand was already on the double-action Bulldog revolver in his coat pocket by chance, and he fired it from there and through the sheepskin.

His first shot hit the Cutter and spun him away. The man to the Cutter's left and closest to the station had a pump-action Colt Lightning rifle, and he threw it to his shoulder. Newt shifted his aim and fired another shot from the hip at him. That shot missed its mark, but it was enough to cause the man to flinch and jump for cover behind one corner of the station house.

Newt was running across the wagon yard by then, and the Bulldog pistol was out of his pocket. The double barn doors were open and big enough to drive two wagons through side by side, and he ran for that looming mouth and the shelter it promised him.

A charge of buckshot sprayed the ground just in front of him. He twisted at the waist, extended the snub-nosed revolver to arm's length, and triggered two shots at the man on the far side of the yard so fast that they sounded almost as one. That man went down with a bullet in his chest, but not before the second barrel of the shotgun he held bellowed and smoked. Something hit Newt in the leg with the force of a swung hammer. He sprawled face-first to the ground, and the Bulldog flew from his grasp. He rolled onto his back and caught a glimpse of Marshal Peck behind him with a pistol pointed at him. The marshal fired, and a bullet kicked up dirty snow beside Newt and then a second one passed over Newt and hit the barn behind him.

He yanked the bulky glove off his right hand with his teeth and clawed under the tail of his coat for the Smith & Wesson on his hip. The pistol came free of his holster while he crabbed backward toward the open barn bay behind him.

The Cutter was down on one knee and swaying with pain, but he was still holding a smoking gun and trying to bring it into the fight. Newt fired at him and missed while he continued his mad scramble to make the cover of the barn. He kept firing as fast as he could thumb the hammer back and pull the trigger, not aiming, but simply pointing and shooting at anything that moved. In that moment he was lost among the roar of guns and the buck of the revolver in his fist, and he was empty of any emotion other than the mad lust to survive and a growing fury.

Sensing he had made it to the barn, Newt flopped over on his belly and made a lunge inside it. He rolled to his right behind the barn wall just inside the doorway at the same moment the man hiding behind the corner of the station sent a volley of hot lead through the doorway with his rifle.

Newt waited for a moment, then leaned back out into the doorway with his pistol ready. He took a shot at the man with the rifle that knocked splinters from the notched log corner of the station, and at the same time saw out of the corner of one eye that the Cutter was making a lumbering run toward a pile of cast-off equipment and junk on the other side of the yard. He swung his aim and tried to track the Cutter's course down the top of his pistol barrel, but the gunman was down behind the box of an old wagon missing its running gear before he could pull the trigger.

Newt took a hurried look around the yard. The man with the shotgun was dragging himself on his belly away from the barn and leaving a blood trail behind him in the snake-like furrow his body made in the snow and the sandy ground. Newt saw nothing of Marshal Peck, and he knew the treacherous lawman had taken cover somewhere out of sight.

Newt ducked back behind the wall again, barely in time to avoid a bullet meant for his head. Whoever that was with the pump-action rifle sent several more shots at him, all of them passing through the thin board siding above and around Newt. He hunkered down and made himself as small as he could. All of them out in the yard must have seen which side of the barn he had gone to, for they soon added their pistol fire to the fray. The wall around Newt was perforated with splintered holes, and those bullets kicked off the barn floor beyond him or cracked into other parts of the structure.

One of the horses tied inside the barn was shot in the shoulder, and it reared in pain against the rope it was tied with and broke free. It charged past Newt and ran out into the wagon yard. The other two terrorized horses also made their escape, running out the door behind the first one. He used that moment of confusion and a lapse in the gunfire to move his position to the other side of the barn and farther back. The barn seemed to have been used as a catchall for junk in its recent years, and he wove his way through a diverse collection of refuse and ducked into a horse stall.

There he hunkered down behind the partial shelter of a barn post where he could still lean out and see out the barn door and into the yard.

His wounded leg ached horribly, and when he put a hand to it below his knee he felt the thick, greasy blood seeping out of him and soaking his pants leg. With gritted teeth, he took off the neckerchief around his neck and tied it in place around his knee, hoping to slow the bleeding.

A couple more probing shots were fired into the barn. Then there was silence except for the wind through the barn walls and the racket the loose board was making as it flapped with each gust.

Newt broke open his pistol and replaced the spent hulls with fresh cartridges, frowning at the empty cartridge loops on his belt as he did so. There were only three rounds left on the belt after he reloaded.

"Come out and surrender!" the marshal's voice called across the yard and into the barn. "I'll take you into custody, and I promise no harm will come to you."

Newt grunted at the ludicrous nature of such a demand after the marshal had just tried to kill him. He knew the marshal was only trying to get him to make a target of himself or answer them and give away his location in the barn.

The smart thing to do was to be still and remain silent, but his blood was up and he couldn't resist voicing his defiance. "Come and get me!"

Newt half expected his words to draw fire, but they didn't. He pivoted on his heels and took a look at the barn wall across from him and behind him, wondering if they were already circling around him. There was no other door he could see besides the big opening he had come through, but the cracks in the wall were large enough in places to shoot through. He was going to have to keep a constant watch for that.

"You sound like your feelings are hurt!" the Cutter shouted over the wind, and he sounded both close and far away. "But the good marshal here was real interested when I told him about that Arizona reward on your head."

Newt let out a string of profanity under his breath. The reward the Cutter mentioned was nothing more than a misunderstanding over the robbery of a gold shipment out on the desert west of Phoenix. His only part in that holdup had been riding shotgun on the stagecoach, but a county sheriff down that way and the owners of the Vulture Mine didn't quite believe him. The three-hundred-dollar reward the territorial governor had offered for his capture was half the reason he had decided to come north to Colorado. Trust a man like the Cutter to have learned of it and to figure out how to use it to his advantage.

"Yes sir, we're going to stake you out and tan your hide. And then the good marshal is going to sell you for the bounty and everyone is going to say what a hero he is," the Cutter called out again. "Of course, it'll come out in the wash that not only are you a wanted desperado, but it was you and yours who attacked us up at that claim. He'll say you admitted it before your demise. You know, picking a fight because of the bad blood between you and Johnny Dial, and how you and your friends set upon us with malice and murderous intent when we only rode into your camp peaceful like."

The Cutter's voice had a growl to it that sounded like he was hurting, and Newt wondered how badly the gunman was hit. He took some pleasure in knowing that he had wounded the Cutter, but it was a short-lived and hollow feeling of victory.

"Why, when the marshal gets done telling my version of what happened, all the church folk and honest citizens of this county are going to swoon and go to bed thanking the

Good Lord that a bloodthirsty demon like you is put in the ground and everyone the better for it. Might even clear my good name," the Cutter called to him.

The Cutter had gone half-crazy if he thought he was going to rid himself of his crimes and walk away scot-free. Or he was simply cunning enough to try and distract Newt while his men moved into more advantageous positions around the barn. Newt guessed it was the latter motive that had the Cutter chattering so.

Newt had no desire to talk, but he decided to try and play the cat-and-mouse game better than they could. Also, it wouldn't hurt to put a little worry in them, if he could.

"Too thin!" he called back at the Cutter. "There's a posse out after you right now. I'll bet a ten-dollar silver piece you hang. And they'll string up your marshal buddy and those others with you while they're at it."

"Maybe, but you won't live to see it," the Cutter said.

Newt glanced around him again and tried to determine how they would come at him. His head felt woozy and light, and his heart was beating faster than it should. He wondered how much blood he had lost, and already, the lower half of his pants leg and his boot felt heavy with it.

He watched what he could see of the wagon yard and waited, but their push into the barn didn't come as quickly as he thought it would.

"Dan needs help," somebody shouted.

Newt didn't recognize the voice, but it sounded like it had come from where the man with the rifle hid at the corner of the stage station.

"Dan's bled out and dead!" the Cutter called back to that one. "But you go out and check on him if you don't believe me!"

Newt rested his revolver against the side of the barn post and aimed at a point where anyone coming across the yard from the station house would have to pass in front of him. But the one that had wanted to help the downed outlaw wasn't concerned enough to come out in the open and risk getting shot.

He tried to place the likely locations of his adversaries in his mind. The Cutter sounded like he was still in the junk pile outside the barn door and wide to the left of it. The man with the rifle was just slightly to the opposite side of the door at the corner of the station where he could fire into the barn at an angle. It sounded as if the one with the shotgun was out of the fight, but the marshal's whereabouts was a joker in the deck.

As if in answer to that question, the marshal cried out to the others, "We need to get this over with now!"

The marshal sounded like he was at the opposite end of the little station house from the man with the rifle and near the entrance to the yard. Newt knew what had the marshal worried. They weren't that far from the edge of town, and the gunshots were going to carry there, even with the wind blowing like it was.

Another hail of bullets passed through the barn, and it sounded like it was from two guns. It came fast enough and with so little accuracy that Newt surmised it wasn't searching fire, but instead they were trying to keep his head down or draw his attention away from whatever it was they intended to do.

The shooting stopped as suddenly as it had begun, probably because they had shot themselves dry and were reloading for another go. Then he heard the sound of someone running away from the barn on his left. It wasn't long after that when he smelled smoke. In short order, the smoke got worse and flames were crackling and popping and licking up the walls in the middle of the barn directly across from him. The old, dry lumber of the barn was going to go up in a hurry, and he wouldn't have long to make up his mind. He could stay there and burn or go out fighting.

Newt heard the crash of someone throwing more fuel against the side of the barn, caught a glimpse of movement through the flames and the cracks in the wall, and fired at it three times. That response drew more shots from the front of the barn, and a bullet knocked over a stack of empty paint cans in front of him and busted splinters out of several of the stall boards.

He ducked back farther inside the horse stall. He was more protected from gunfire there but could see less of what might be happening around him.

He peered out of the stall again. The barn was big enough and he was far enough from the flames that the heat wasn't bad, not yet, but the smoke was rolling so thickly that he had a hard time seeing out into the wagon yard. He took a chance that the smoke would mask his movements and hobbled to the other side of the barn and to the far end of it.

If it came down to it, he might kick a board or two loose and get out that way, but he was sure the Cutter had someone around back. Then he saw something in one corner that looked like a way out. So much junk had been piled in front of it that he hadn't seen it at first.

The wind was keeping the worst of the smoke away from him there, but it was still enough to make him cough and to cause his eyes to burn. He worked at the junk pile as fast as he could while trying to make as little noise as possible. In short order, he had torn enough of it down that he saw he had been right. It was a door. Not a big one, but simply a man-sized one that likely had once been used for someone in the barn to have access to the corral on that side of the barn.

He opened the latch and pushed against the door with one hand, not to go out yet, but to test it. The door didn't move. It was made of the same planks that sided the barn, and it had sagged on its rusty iron hinges and was jammed tightly closed. He pushed a little harder, but it still wouldn't budge.

He squatted and put his back against the door and searched the smoke at the other end of the barn. Minutes passed and the fire and the smoke grew in intensity and reach. A flaming bit of wood or shake shingle fell from the roof and fluttered down in front of him.

A pair of waist-high steel cultivator wheels off some long-ago cast-off piece of farm or construction equipment leaned against the wall beside Newt. He peered at the wheels out of watery eyes and coughed again. Then he stood and rolled a wheel in each hand closer to the open end of the barn and closer to the worst of the smoke that had been driven by the wind in a thick cloud across its front.

"You miserable sidewinders !" he yelled, then gave the wheels a hard shove, first one and then the other, sending them rolling down the center of the barn and hopefully out into the yard.

As soon as he finished with the wheels, he went to the door he had found and put his shoulder against it, pistol cocked and ready in his right hand. Gunfire sounded from the wagon yard. None of it came in his direction, and he dared hope his distraction with the wheels had worked.

He threw all his weight and strength against the door and felt it give way to him easier than he had expected. He gritted his teeth as he lost his balance and stumbled into the corral beside the burning barn, fully expecting to be gunned down in an instant.

He staggered two steps and righted himself with his

pistol held before him and his blurry, smoke-burned eyes looking for someone to fight. A rifle roared and he heard the same wild Mohave war cry that he had heard back on Willow Creek. Everything from that point on became a blur of sight and sound, gun smoke and fire smoke, flashes of movement as men tried to kill each other, the groans and cries of the dying, and the howl of the wind and the crackling fire amid the roaring guns.

He ran across the peel-poled corral he found himself in and toward a section in that fence where the top two rails had fallen down. He caught a glimpse of the Cutter rising up from behind the wagon box that had hidden him earlier. He fired at him without stopping, then dove over the gap in the corral fence, rolled on his shoulder, and came up on one knee.

The Cutter was walking straight at him with a revolver in each of his hands belching flames. Newt didn't even feel the Cutter's bullets whipping past him or the one that clipped through the edge of his hat brim. He willed himself to take the time it took to fully extend his gun arm and find his front pistol sight the way he should. He pulled the trigger only once, and the Cutter quit coming and staggered back a step with the impact of the cast-lead bullet tearing through his chest.

Twice more, the Cutter squeezed the triggers on his double-action pistols, but by then he could raise neither of his arms and both rounds went off into the ground in front of him. He stared at Newt for a brief instant with something between pure hatred and shock on his tightly drawn face before his chin dropped and he crumpled to the ground on buckling knees.

Newt rose and moved toward the entrance to the yard, taking care when he passed the Cutter's body. But the outlaw was dead by the time he passed, eyes frozen open and staring blindly up at the sky.

The man with the shotgun Newt had shot earlier was lying facedown a little farther on, and beyond that, he could see the man with the pump-action rifle lying equally dead at the corner of the station house. At the entrance to the yard stood Mr. Smith with his rifle in his hands. He was standing over the marshal, who sat on the ground with his back against the log wall of the station house.

By the time Newt got there, the marshal was slumped at the waist with his chin on his chest and his legs sprawled before him, and he was too weak to even look up. The front of the marshal's clothing was a bloody mess, and it looked as if Mr. Smith had shot him more than once.

Newt started to say something to the Mohave but couldn't find his voice.

"Nice trick." The Mohave pointed at one of the cultivator wheels that had made it out of the barn and lay in the yard.

Newt glanced again at the body of the man with the rifle at the other corner of the building. "You got 'em both."

Mr. Smith nodded. "You're bleeding."

"Yeah," Newt said, then looked down at his wounded leg as if he hadn't known he was hurt or had forgotten about it. "Thought you were back in town."

"This marshal, he has sneaky eyes," Mr. Smith said. "I thought maybe I should follow you and see what he was lying about."

"You could have told me that before I went with him."

"You don't listen so good sometimes, anyway."

The marshal coughed once and tried to raise his head but couldn't manage that feat.

Newt looked at the bullet-riddled marshal and then at

the heavy column of smoke rising up from the barn. "You know, this is going to be hard to explain."

"My horse is tied a little ways down the road," Mr. Smith replied.

Before they could leave, the marshal grabbed at Newt's pant leg. "Don't leave me."

Newt looked down at him. "I'll give you a better chance than you gave me. You hold out a little longer and I imagine you'll have all kinds of help."

Newt pulled away from the marshal's hold, caught the Circle Dot horse, and went out of the wagon yard with Mr. Smith. They walked as fast as Newt's wounded leg would allow and came to where the Mohave had tied his own horse to a fence on the side of the road.

Both of them could see several riders and a crowd of people on foot coming up the road toward them, drawn by the gunfire and the smoke.

"What about the kid?" Newt asked.

Mr. Smith shrugged. "Tully was no part of this, and I told him to meet us in Chama if we did not come back . . . meet us there if he wanted to."

"What if they lock him up?"

"Then we will come back and free him."

"Just like that?"

The Mohave nodded.

Newt gave a bitter chuckle. "Ain't we becoming a pair of outlaws? Why Chama?"

"Because it is the direction I want to go."

Newt didn't ask any more questions, and both of them took another look at the crowd coming toward them. Mr. Smith looked the longest.

"Marshal Peck will die and they may follow us," Mr. Smith

said as he climbed up on his black. "Do you think you're up to a long run?"

It took Newt two tries to get a boot in the stirrup, but once he was up in the saddle he tried to show a straight face. "Try me."

Mr. Smith put his black to a gallop, and Newt spurred the Circle Dot horse after him.

CHAPTER FORTY-SEVEN

Zuri's sore foot kept her from running as fast as she normally could, and the fact that she wore only one shoe was also an impediment to her flight. It was her second attempt at trying to run away from the nuns, and she was frustrated that this time she had gotten even less far up the road than she had before. In fact, she was still close enough that she could see the roofs of Conejos behind her—the tower of Our Lady of Guadalupe Church, the walls of the adobe plaza, as well as the roofs of the convent and the school.

A rock beside the wagon road gave her a place to sit, and she propped her bandaged foot up on it to inspect what damage she might have done to the wrappings or if she had caused her toe to start bleeding again. She still hadn't got used to missing the last joint of the middle finger on her left hand and felt overly clumsy and odd trying to do any-thing with it. Not to mention that she was constantly bump-ing what remained of the sore and reduced digit and the stitches that held her healing skin together. Most strangely of all, it sometimes felt as if that portion of her finger was still in place. She could see that it was gone and that there was nothing when she tried to touch something with it, but a ghost of that former portion of herself wouldn't seem to leave, no matter that the Del Norte doctor had cut it from her.

She tried not to look at that finger or to think about how ugly it made her and simply attended to her foot. While filthy, the bandages where still in place and no blood showed through them, no matter how badly she had limped. That was good because she needed to stay positive in her thinking if she was going to make her escape this time.

How long did she have before they came looking for her? After Mass, the children were allowed an afternoon of rest or play or quiet time to contemplate their faith in their rooms, if they so chose. The nuns took their own personal time before evening rituals and were less likely to notice her absence.

The crude poncho she had made for herself in the mountains was lost to her, but she still had the coat her father had bought for her and her mittens. They had kept her plenty warm while she was still running or walking fast, but now that she was sitting still she was becoming cold.

She was about to get up and get going again when she saw something coming from Conejos toward her along the road. Her eyes were keen, and by the time she got up off the rock she recognized that the something in the distance was a cart pulled by a single little mule. On the seat of that cart was Sister Maria, the mother superior. Zuri could easily make out the black habit she wore, as well as the particular stoop of the old nun's spine and shoulders any time she sat, especially on a jouncing cart over a rough road.

The road ran along the edge of a tableland, and Zuri ducked off it and down the slope toward the Conejos River. There was enough brush and growth there to hide her until the mother superior passed. She didn't go far before she found a clump of alders and willows to conceal her.

Zuri could hear the cart coming closer even though she

couldn't see it anymore. Its cottonwood axle and solid, high wooden wheels thumped and knocked over the ruts and pot-holes. The mule pulling the cart was slow and the mother superior must have been in no hurry, for it took her a long time to pull even with where Zuri hid beside the road. It was there that the nun pulled the mule to a stop, although she didn't look Zuri's way and only stared straight ahead.

Zuri made sure not to move, in case the old woman hadn't seen her and had only stopped there by chance. The mother superior was the same one who had caught her the last time, and though she appeared physically decrepit, there was nothing wrong with her eyes or her mind. What age had taken away from her in bodily prowess over the years, the Lord had replaced with craftiness and unusual wit. The old woman seemed to miss nothing that went on around her.

"Come, child," the nun said in Spanish, still not looking into the brush beside the road. "My old bones have taken about as much of a beating as they can stand."

Zuri hesitated, thinking that her best course might be to run for the river, somehow cross it, and put it between her-self and the mother superior. There was no way that cart was making it across the river, and the old woman wasn't likely to go on foot.

"You're doing nothing other than getting both of us chilled," the nun said. "Come now, let's get back to a warm fire."

Zuri hobbled out of the brush and up the hill to the cart, defeated. She climbed up the side of the cart and joined the nun on the bench seat. The nun still didn't look at her and simply turned the cart around in the road and started the mule back toward Conejos.

They jostled along half the way before the nun spoke

again. "You have no one to run to, so where is it you think to go?"

Zuri clenched her lower lip between her teeth and chanced a glance at the woman beside her. She wanted to hate her but couldn't manage that feeling. The mother superior, as well as the other Sisters of Loretto at the school, had been nothing but kind to her since the day Father Ramirez had brought Zuri to Conejos. The mother superior even seemed to take special watch over her, but it was that hovering, mother hen effort that frustrated Zuri. Why couldn't the mother superior leave her alone? Couldn't she see that Zuri was perfectly capable of taking care of herself?

"You're right. I have no one," Zuri said.

"Then why do you run away?"

"There is something I must do."

The nun nodded, still staring straight ahead and occasionally flicking the length of willow switch she held at the mule to keep it moving. "I've noticed. Yet, you will not say what it is. Will you talk with me today, or will you pout and act as stubborn as this little burro like before?"

"I can't say."

"You can't or you won't?"

"It is something that belongs to me. Private."

"And you think I will take it from you?"

"You would not understand. I can't even explain it to myself."

"Try."

"You would stop me."

"I have already stopped you, and I will continue to do so," the nun said. "Perhaps if you will tell me, we can come to some kind of accord and I can make you understand why you should remain under our care and why you are very fortunate to have been brought to us considering the tragedy you suffered."

"Do you think I do not appreciate the shelter you have given me?" Zuri asked.

"I do not know what to think about you, except that you are a headstrong young girl who has lost both her mother and her father and doesn't know how to deal with that. A little girl who wakes up crying and thinks no one notices how scared she is. A little girl who needs guidance until she can find whatever peace and healing the Lord gives her."

It was Zuri's turn to stare at the mule, though she hardly saw it through her tear-filled eyes. "I can't quit thinking about what happened."

The nun put a hand on Zuri's thigh and patted it. "Give it time. We cannot force such things."

"How much time?"

The nun shrugged. "Only the Lord can say. In the meantime, attend to your studies like the other children and learn and make the best of your situation. Pray."

"I have prayed but the Lord doesn't answer me."

"You mean the Lord doesn't give you back your father?"

"That's not what I've asked for. I know he is gone to me forever."

The nun sighed and took her hand off Zuri's leg. "I will not come after you the next time you do this. I will send one of the other sisters, and they will not be so kind."

"I will not run again."

"Yes you will."

CHAPTER FORTY-EIGHT

Two months later, Chama, Territory of New Mexico

Newt leaned against the corral fence to take some of the load off his still-healing leg and watched Mr. Smith saddling his black and readying the packhorse that he was going to take with him. The Mohave had not even mentioned he was leaving until that very morning, but Newt had sensed something was on his mind for days.

Mr. Smith worked in silence, but when he was finished and led the horses out of the corral, he stood before Newt instead of mounting.

"Where are you going?" Newt asked.

"I go back to my people," Mr. Smith answered. "Many have forgotten the old ways, and I will try my best to remind them of how it used to be and how it can be."

"You said that didn't work out so well the last time you tried it."

"I will try again," Mr. Smith said. "It is a long ride. I will have much to think about and to decide how it can be better this time."

"Well, I guess I will finally get some peace and quiet without you talking all the time."

"You are a strange man, like none I have even met before," Mr. Smith said, "and you usually say one thing when you mean the other."

"See, that's what I'm talking about," Newt answered. "Always wanting to argue."

"I think you would have made a good Mohave," Mr. Smith said as he got up on his horse.

"I'll take that as a compliment. We've rode far together, my friend."

Newt held out a hand, and although those of the Mohave tribe did not shake hands, Mr. Smith shook his.

"Ships that pass may meet again," Mr. Smith said.

"More of your Poe or Shakespeare?" Newt asked.

"No, that is something the captain once said to me."

"You thought a lot of him, didn't you? How many years did you sail with him?"

"I killed him not long after he told me that." Mr. Smith said that without emotion and without his face changing expression. Only his eyes held any hint of anything more than his simple admission.

"Why?"

"He was a trader but also a cruel man when he needed or wanted to be," Mr. Smith said. "We were anchored off the coast of a strange land, and there was a brown-skinned island girl with slanted eyes he fancied and stole from her village. She was young, very young. I did not like to hear her cry, and he did not like it when I cut the ropes he tied her with in his cabin and helped her over the side so that she could swim back to her people."

"He whipped you, didn't he? That's where you got those scars on your back."

Mr. Smith nodded at that. "Forty lashes tied to the mast. I waited a year until we reached San Diego, and then I put a knife in him as he was taking his afternoon tea. He seemed surprised, but I don't know why. Perhaps he didn't understand that I was still uncivilized."

It was then that Tully Hudlow came walking toward them, and his presence interrupted anything else Mr. Smith might have said about himself or his life. Newt was still a little surprised the kid had hunted them down in Chama, even with Mr. Smith telling him they would head that way. He was still trying to decide what to make of the kid's presence.

Tully had healed well, and the splint was gone from his arm, though he still favored it some. Right then he had a suitcase and bedroll hanging in his good hand and a biscuit in the other.

"What will he do?" Mr. Smith asked in a quieter voice. "Are you taking him with you?"

"Taking him where?" Newt asked.

"Wherever it is you go."

"I haven't quit thinking about seeing Montana," Newt said, "but I'll be darned if I'll take him with me. Besides, he says he got a telegram yesterday from his family telling him they're moving to Texas, and he's going to catch the train today so that he can meet them there."

"Yes, that is what he told me, but you could go with him."

"Why?"

"Do not forsake your clan . . . your kin . . . or you will regret it as I do," Mr. Smith said. "Even those of us who can live alone need our people. This is something I have come to know. Teach him your old ways. Teach him how to fight and how to find his power and to worry about little girls and old dogs."

Newt looked away and mumbled something under his breath. Mr. Smith continued to stare at him.

"Mr. Smith, I tell you, that gal over there at that restaurant will give you a run for your money when it comes to making a fine biscuit," Tully said when he made it to them.

"Sourdough?" Mr. Smith asked with a haughty expression.

"Sure enough," Tully answered. "And she's a sight prettier than you are to boot."

"Careful," Newt said. "You remember what you told us about the last time you sparked a girl in a new town."

Tully grinned again, and there were biscuit crumbs on his chin. He jerked his head at Mr. Smith. "Where are you going?"

"Now that is a question for all of us, isn't it?" Mr. Smith answered.

"He was just saying his goodbyes," Newt said.

"I'd have thought you'd be leaving, too," Tully said. "Old Sheriff Pearitter had it worked out pretty good how that city marshal got himself killed when he let me go, but I imagine he's still looking for you. This here little town is a fine place, but I'd say it's way too close to Colorado for a man that doesn't want to have to answer any more questions."

Newt ignored Tully and looked up at Mr. Smith in the saddle. "I never did sit down and have that tea with you."

"Maybe another time," Mr. Smith said.

He bumped his horse with his heels and rode away. Not once did he look back. The train was rolling into the station, and he crossed the tracks in front of it so that it soon blocked him from sight. Even so, Newt stared at where he had gone for a long moment.

"Hate to admit it, but I'm not going to miss him," Tully said.

"There's your train," Newt said.

"Yeah," Tully answered. "I'm about half glad to get to

see my folks, but the other half of me knows I've got to tell them about Tandy."

"It's best they hear it straight from you and not in a letter or from someone else."

"They're going to take it hard. He was always their favorite."

Newt held out a hand as he had with Mr. Smith. "Take care, Tully Hudlow."

Tully shook hands with him. "Sure you don't want to come along? You'd get a chance to be amongst your own for a spell. You know, tell some stories and catch up on what's happened back home. And they tell me there's some fine land where they're going that a man can take for a fair price."

"That sounds good, real good, but I believe I'll pass," Newt said.

"I know you blame yourself for what happened to Tandy, but they'll understand," Tully said.

"It's not that," Newt replied. "I've got some things I need to do."

Newt walked Tully to the train, and Tully took notice of the way Newt was limping.

"You still favor that leg some," Tully said as they walked out onto the depot decking.

"It's all right." Newt dismissed Tully's observation with a wave of his hand. "Doctor said one of those buckshot balls must have hit a nerve. Said he'd seen that before and most times all the feeling will come back in time, or I might always have a little numbness there if my luck ain't good. Either way, I never was much in a footrace, and suspect I'll do just fine."

"Well, you come to Texas and see us when you can," Tully said. "All you've got to do is holler if you need me. Family stand by their own."

"I'll do that."

Newt watched Tully board the train and then headed for the nearest saloon. His intention was to have one drink before he saddled his horse and started his own journey, but like all things with him, it didn't quite work out how he planned it.

Chama was a regular little boomtown since the railroad had come to it a few years before, and the saloon crowd in the late afternoon was a good one, what with the sawmills running night and day and droves of men headed to the mountains to mine for their fortunes. Not to mention that the bar he had picked served an especially good rye. An hour later, he had four whiskeys under his belt and was feeling much better.

He was about to take another drink when he spotted a framed photograph hanging on the wall behind the bar. It was a group of miners standing in front of the opening to a mine shaft. Maybe his eyes were playing tricks on him, but he thought he recognized one of those men.

"Who are they?" Newt asked the bartender.

The bartender glanced at the photograph. "Just some old-timers. I think that picture was taken up north somewhere, but I don't know where. The owner of this place hung it there, and you'd have to ask him."

Newt rubbed his eyes and squinted at the photograph again. He was almost sure that one of the men in it was Happy Jack, though a far younger version of him.

"To the old-timers!" someone down the bar from him said in a voice too loud for the room. "They sure don't make 'em like they used to!"

Newt turned to look at who had said that and saw a man standing at the far end of the bar. That man seemed more than a little drunk, and he was holding up a glass of whiskey in a toast to the photograph.

Newt grinned at him and held up his own glass. "To Happy Jack!"

The man down the bar downed his drink while he stared at Newt out of red-rimmed eyes and a haggard face. He walked over to Newt and asked, "How do you know Happy Jack?"

"I met him this past winter," Newt said, and he realized there was something familiar about the man he was talking to. That feeling was almost as vague as his recognition of a younger Happy Jack in the photograph.

"He's a good one," the man said.

"Was a good one. He's gone now," Newt replied. "Claim jumpers got him."

"Hate to hear he's gone to the worms. Knew him from back when I first started prospecting."

Newt finally placed the man. "Nick Creede, you don't remember me, do you?"

"Can't say as I do."

"I worked for you in Chaffee City for a week after you made that Monarch find. Or have you gotten so old you don't know a friend when you see one?"

"Is that you, Newt Jones?" the man slurred. "Thought I recognized that voice. Well, I'll be. It's been many a year, or has it? Where you been?"

The two of them found a table in a far corner of the saloon and began to tell old stories and share a bottle Creede brought with him. It took Newt a while to realize the man across the table from him wasn't the same man he had known seven or eight years before. Nicholas Creede seemed quieter, or maybe less optimistic and more beaten down. Everything from his disheveled clothes to the rest of him gave Newt the impression that he had been on a long bender.

"I thought you'd be retired by now and fat-catting it

with the rich boys once you sold that Monarch claim," Newt said.

Creede shook his head. "Hit a lick here and there since then, but my luck's run dry."

"Happens to the best," Newt said, "but you'll pull through. Springtime's coming and you can get out and find your next fortune."

Newt started to pour them both another drink from the bottle, but Creede put his hand over his glass. "You look flush and maybe like you've got a good grubstake. How about we go prospecting together? You were always a hard worker and would have made a good mining man if you hadn't let them keep dragging you in a boxing ring to show everybody how tough you were. There's some country up west of Lake City that I looked at a little last summer. We'll find us a good vein and make some real money before somebody beats us to it."

"I know how to handle a muckstick or a hammer, but I'm no prospector. Farthest thing from it. Never caught the bug and don't have the learning it takes."

"You're laughing at me, aren't you?" Creede said. "You think I'm all washed up and looking for handouts."

"I don't think that at all."

Newt tried to remember just what he had once known about Creede. Near as he could remember, the man had once scouted with the Pawnee for the army in the Sioux Wars and turned his hands to prospecting after that. There had been a time when many along the high divide knew that Nick Creede was a man who kept his word and worked with the best of them. The Monarch Mine wasn't the only one he had located over the years.

"If you won't go, then grubstake me if you can. Or point me to somebody that will," Creede said. "Hurts my pride to admit it, but I'm down to my last dollar. And like you said, spring's coming on. I'll cut you in on anything I find. Sign papers or whatever you want."

Newt pointed at the bottle between them. "You ain't nursing that wolf juice regular, are you?"

"No, I just got to feeling sorry for myself yesterday and got a little sideways. You give me time to sober up and clean up and you'll see I'm fit and tight as ever."

Newt made a decision then. It was a calculated gamble, but he could live with that. He looked around once to make sure nobody was paying too much attention to them, then reached inside his coat pocket and took something out. He laid the thing he had on the table, and it landed there with a hard thump. Creede's eyes locked onto what was set before him with an intense stare.

"Where'd you get that?" Creede asked.

"Happy Jack gave it to me before he died. I've got a couple more samples in my saddlebags."

Creede picked up the ore sample, a little chunk of rock barely as big as his fist. He turned it over in his hands, peering at it and examining it with a critical look. "Holy Moses. You know what this is?"

"Silver ore."

"Not just silver ore. High-grade stuff."

"That's what Happy Jack thought."

Creede handed the ore sample back to Newt. "How come you showed me that? If the vein he found is big enough, you could be a rich man."

Newt shook his head. "Happy Jack told me about his find so I could do with it what I pleased. And it pleases me to talk it over with you."

"I'm interested, but you said the claim jumpers got him."

"They got him, but not where that sample came from.

He never even filed on the place. Worked it all last summer and kept it a secret."

"You're kidding me."

"If I tell you were that silver is, I want you to promise me a couple of things."

"You're cutting me in?"

"I'm offering the information to you with only a few demands," Newt said. "First, as soon as you've got the money, you buy Happy Jack a good tombstone, a real high-toned one that you think he would like, then you put it on his grave in Del Norte. The second condition is that ten percent of whatever you find or make from it goes to your partner."

"My partner? Meaning you?"

"No, I'll give you a name. You'll file the claim and make whatever business decisions you think best, but ten percent goes to your partner."

"And what do you get out of it if this find Happy Jack made pans out to be something?" Creede asked.

"You pay me a reasonable finder's fee if and when you get the claim on a paying basis," Newt said. "How about a thousand dollars?"

"You're kidding me, right? It's some kind of joke."

"Take it for what you will, but I'm riding out of here tomorrow. You don't want to check out what he found under my conditions, then I'll find somebody else that does."

Newt started to get up, but Creede held out a hand to stop him.

"Let's shake on it," Creede said.

Newt started to shake the man's hand, but hesitated. "You realize I'm going to hold you to your word."

"You've got a deal. I'll have a contract drawn up in the morning, then me and you can go have a look at this silver ground we're going to file on."

"Oh, I won't be going with you."

"No?"

"You bring me that contract tomorrow and I'll tell you where to go."

"This is damned irregular. What's your angle?"

"That my business. You bring me the papers tomorrow."

They shook hands over the table.

"You aren't the man I remember from back in the day. Course you weren't much more than a kid then," Creede said. "I keep thinking either that I'm an old fool for getting this excited over a bit of rock or that I'm going to wake up sober in the morning and find out this wasn't anything but some kind of dream."

"It's real. All you've got to do is go find out if Happy Jack found what he thought he'd found and make it pay."

"I'll do that."

Newt started to go again but thought of something else. "One more thing. You don't tell Saul Barton a thing about this, and you don't sell to him or let him buy into it in any way."

"Barton. I wouldn't do business with that crook if he was the last man on earth," Creede said.

Newt smiled. "Good. It's sounding more and more like I've picked the right man."

CHAPTER FORTY-NINE

Newt stood before the door of the Conejos schoolhouse run by the Sisters of Loretto on a bright and sunny spring morning. The mother superior stood in the doorway before him as she had been for the past five minutes. She was still looking askance at him like she didn't trust him any farther than she could throw a bull by the tail.

"I will tell Zuri that you wish to speak with her, but couldn't this wait until later in the day?" the old nun said. "She is doing her mathematics right now."

"Oh, I won't bother you nor her long," Newt said. "I just wanted to see how she was getting along and give her something that belongs to her."

"Very well," the nun said. "Sister Monica should be finished with today's math lesson before long if you don't mind waiting."

"Not at all."

Newt expected the nun to go back inside, but she remained there like she feared he might batter down the schoolhouse door. The look she was giving him and the silence between them grew more awkward the longer they waited.

"How's she doing?" he finally asked.

"She is a very bright girl, and her grades are excellent when we can get her to focus on her studies," the nun said.

"That's good, but I wasn't only asking about her school work."

"She has suffered greatly for one so young, but she isn't the only child here to hold that distinction," the nun said. "But nevertheless, she seems better than when she first came here."

"What do you mean by better? Father Ramirez told me she has nightmares."

"She still has those, and her temper and her emotions can sometimes get the best of her. She lashes out when she shouldn't. Gets upset over small things that didn't bother her the day before. But at least she hasn't tried to run away lately."

"Lately?"

"Twice she has tried, but that was back in the winter."

"Doesn't sound like she likes it here."

"No, that's the surprising part. She claims she does like it here but hints that she has some fantastical quest that she must attend to."

"Quest?"

"She will not say what it is she thinks she must do."

"If she stays here, does that mean she will be a nun?"

"That will be her choice when the time comes, but no, most of our children, even the orphans, do not take the vows. We welcome a new sister, but we realize that not all are so called."

"I take it you've had no luck finding any of her family that would take her in?" Newt asked.

"None at all."

Newt reached into a vest pocket and pulled forth a folded paper and handed it to the mother superior.

The old nun unfolded the paper, held aside the stack of

greenbacks contained in the middle of it, and studied both the money and the document. "What is this?"

"The money's for your school. Just a little something I gathered up," Newt said. "That contract is for her. It's to help pay for her schooling or clothes or whatever she needs. And for when she's grown up and leaves here so she'll have a good start at whatever she does."

"This says she owns part of a mine."

"Well, it's just a silver claim right now and not a mine," Newt said. "Not yet, but I think it will be before long. A very rich mine."

"Was this some investment her father made?"

"That's as good a story as any," Newt said. "That other signature on those papers belongs to the man she'll be partnered with. He'll open a bank account in her name when the time comes and deposit her percentage as it's owed to her."

"Myself and the man there whose signature is on those papers. He'll open a bank account in her name when the time comes and deposit her percentage as it's owed her."

"This is most surprising."

"That's part of why I came here. I wanted to tell her about this."

"You've said that you're the one who found her in the mountains, but you're of no family relation?"

Newt shook his head. "Just wanted to help where I could."

"Most unusual." The nun fanned through the greenbacks, making a quick count of them. "And this is for the school?"

"It's not much, but maybe it'll help."

"Your donation is greatly appreciated. The parish and the church support us where they can, but it is a constant struggle to keep the school open," the nun said. "I'm ashamed how I might have misjudged you when you first appeared."

The door opened behind the mother superior, and she tucked away the money and the paperwork. Zuri came to stand beside her, and Newt couldn't interpret the way the little Basque girl was looking at him. What had he expected? He didn't know her, and what little time he had spent with her wasn't likely to leave her with a good impression. It was no wonder she was almost clinging to the old nun at the sight of him.

"Hello, Newt," Zuri said with a soft smile.

"Your English has gotten better," he said because that was all he could think to say.

"Sisters teach me," Zuri replied in halting and accented English.

Newt noticed that she was no longer wearing the red skirt and white blouse she had been wearing when he found her. Somebody had given her a new blue-and-white-checkered gingham dress, and a new pair of shoes and stockings were on her feet. Her face was clean and veritably shining, and her dark hair was combed and tied back loosely with some kind of ribbon.

Again, there was the awkward silence between them, the same as there had been between him and the nun. He wasn't sure what he should say and why he had even come there at all.

"I've brought you something," he said, and half turned and gestured at the Circle Dot horse standing at the edge of the road behind him. "It's on my saddle."

"Another gift?" the Mother Superior asked.

He ignored her and focused on Zuri. "Want to walk over there with me and have a look?"

He had no clue if her English had improved enough for

her to fully understand him, so he gestured at his horse again and motioned for her to walk with him.

"I think you should bring it to her," the nun said. "She can be shy sometimes."

Zuri stepped toward Newt no sooner than the nun had spoken, and he waited until she was beside him so that they could walk together. The mother superior made as if to follow them, but Newt shook his head at her and she stopped where she was.

Newt went to the horse and untied the long thing wrapped in a piece of canvas under one of his stirrup leathers. He was acutely aware of Zuri watching him while he unwrapped what it was that he had brought her.

He held her father's rifle out for her to see. A gunsmith in Chama had replaced the stock and made other repairs, and Newt had given the steel of it a healthy oiling before he wrapped it for travel.

Zuri reached out to touch it with one hand, and he noticed that she kept the other hand purposely hidden slightly behind one hip of her dress. It was something she had been doing since she first came out of the schoolhouse.

"You can hold it if you want to," he said.

Again, she stared at him, but she reached out with both hands and took the rifle after a moment. He saw then what she had been hiding. The stitches in the end of the finger the doctor had partially amputated were gone, but the skin there was still a little red. She must have seen him looking at her hand because she diverted her eyes toward the gun and the ground.

"That's nothing to hide or be ashamed of. It's still a fine-looking hand," he said when she finally looked up at him again. "You can hardly even notice it."

She looked down as she had before, and he struggled to

think of what he could say to smooth over his bumbling talk.

"Pretty little button like you, nobody will notice, 'cause he'll be all moon-eyed staring at you."

He was about to try something in Spanish when she met his gaze.

"Pretty?" she asked.

He pointed at her, but gently, as if she were a flighty young colt or a butterfly that might flitter away from him if he startled it. "Yes, that's you. Pretty. *Muy bonita.*"

Then he smiled his crooked smile and took his other hand and pinched the end of the finger he had pointed with and made an imaginary motion as if he were plucking it off and throwing it away like it were nothing. "A little scar can't cover you up or hide you. Don't be ashamed of the bumps and bruises you take, 'cause they're part of what makes you who you are."

She smiled back at him, either out of politeness or because she actually understood what he had meant or implied.

He could tell the rifle was growing heavy for her to hold before him like she was, and he took it from her. "I know this rifle means something to you, so I thought I would have it fixed."

"What's this about? You can't give a child a weapon like that!"

Newt turned and saw the mother superior coming toward them in a swish of her black habit scraping the ground. "It belonged to her father," he said.

"I don't care who it belonged to. She's a child."

"You can store it away for her," he said. "I didn't intend for her to be packing it to class and plinking targets out the schoolhouse window. All I wanted was for her to know it wasn't lost."

"Come here, Zuri," the nun said.

Zuri ignored the mother superior and looked at him. "Thank you."

"You're welcome."

The old nun was almost to them, and another had appeared in the open door of the schoolhouse.

"Maybe I'll come by and check on you again if I'm passing through," he said to Zuri.

She reached out and tapped the gun, and the expression on her face was as if she wanted to ask something of him.

"What is it?"

Zuri's mouth fought to try and shape the words in English. "Hunt."

"What?"

"Me, you. Hunt."

"You want me to take you hunting?"

Zuri nodded her head and gave the mother superior a frantic glance.

Somehow, he understood what it was she wanted, understood it because it was something he might have wanted himself.

He grabbed her around the waist and swung her up on his horse's back. The mother superior was almost upon them, her weary old legs carrying her even faster.

"Stop!" she said.

By then he was up on the horse behind Zuri, holding her rifle in one hand. "Calm down, old woman. I'll bring her back to you."

Zuri already had hold of the bridle reins, and Newt gave the Circle Dot horse a poke with his spurs. The brown gelding was fresh and feeling good and bolted away with a start like a racehorse.

"Where are you taking her?" the mother superior cried after them.

Newt looked past the old woman and saw children with their faces pressed to the glass in every window along one side of the schoolhouse and more nuns coming out the door.

He doffed his hat and waved it to them all, then gave the same gesture to the mother superior. By then the Circle Dot horse was running hard. The dust of the road clipped away behind his hooves like puffs of smoke, and the schoolhouse faded farther and farther behind them. Yet, Zuri kept urging the horse to run and leaned out over its neck and let the wind of their passing water her eyes and stream the hair back from her head.

He did nothing to slow either her or the horse and simply let them run. He let them run because it felt right and because sometimes the only way to get rid of a nightmare was to leave it behind or chase it down.

CHAPTER FIFTY

The old boar grizzly shouldn't have made it through the winter, but he did. Even so, he was deathly thin and weaker than ever by the time some of the snow began to melt and the new green popped up between the rocks on the grassy slopes he favored to prowl in the early mornings, where the warming sun first struck and felt good to his aching joints.

He was blind in his right eye by then, caused by a cataract that had been worsening over the last two years, and his other eye, suffering from the same affliction, was feeble and dim and growing worse by the day.

He had lain through the night in a thick stand of spruce trees, and he moved slowly out of them and onto the grassy glade below him. He rarely traveled uphill anymore when he could avoid it, but walking at all caused him terrible pain, and not only from his bullet-crippled shoulder. Arthritis inflamed his joints, and an abscessed tooth had caused one side of his muzzle to swell. The pain of it was a constant dull throb in his mouth and head that made it impossible to chew meat.

He had partaken of no meat since early in the winter, and that morning was no different. It was too early for the berries to show, and all that was left to him were what buds he could find and the insects and grubs he could dig up.

He moved a few yards out into the mountain glade and turned over a couple of small rocks with little energy or passion, despite his hunger. His efforts were rewarded with a single fat grub he found under one of them.

Once, even such a meager meal would have driven him harder to find more of them, but he lifted his head and stared across the meadow. On the other side was a dark clump of thick timber, and he recognized that place somehow, even though he could barely see. Within that timber was a little rocky stream, and beside it there was a deep carpet of soft moss growing in the cool, damp shade. It was a place he had known since he was a cub, where his mother often brought him and his sibling to nap away the heat of a hot summer day. Through the years he had come back to it more than once when he was in the area.

Suddenly, the urge to lie down and feel that soft moss beneath him was greater than his hunger, and he forgot the grubs beneath the rocks and moved toward the far timber. As he got closer he thought he could hear the stream rushing clear and clean with snowmelt and splashing off the rocks. Once, many miles of mountains had been his kingdom, his home, but now the little moss-padded canyon before him was the only thing he longed for.

He was almost there when the breeze shifted slightly and his nose caught the scent of something he almost recognized. He stopped and turned his head to better sniff the breeze, and again he caught that scent. It was the smell of the two-legged man creatures.

For a moment, the old hatred of them tried to rekindle itself inside him, and the promise of possible fresh meat caused his ears to perk. But his rage and his hunger moved him no further than that. The scent did not come from close by, and to chase any kind of prey was something beyond him. It was better to rest.

He let out a low growl and shook his head and moved on toward his bed ground. Though he moved ever so slowly, he moved without fear and with arrogance. Ancient or not, dying or not, he was still the biggest thing on the mountain. His pace, like his will, was ever his own.

CHAPTER FIFTY-ONE

Zuri lay on her belly beside Newt atop the rock ledge while he scanned the mountain meadow below and across from them with his binoculars. He lowered the optics once and glanced at her. Weeks in the mountains seemed to have done her well, and each day he could see her becoming stronger and sounder of not only body but also of mind. It was as if the clear, high air and the exercise were somehow healing her, both outside and in.

She hardly limped at all now, something he could not say about himself, and her smile came more often. Sometimes she even laughed and teased him, though he usually couldn't understand what she was teasing him about. At night by their fires, she taught him words in her language and he shared his. Though they weren't able to ask many questions of each other, even if they had wanted to, they had come to some strange understanding that needed few words. The silence around them and that understanding was a conversation itself, a song they both heard, and the hunt bound them into commonality even if nothing else could.

But right then she wasn't smiling, nor was she at peace. Her eyes beneath the brim of the hat he had bought her were as intense as Mr. Smith's had been in a fight, and the look on her face was both fierce and determined.

He took up his binoculars again and hadn't glassed long before he pointed at something in the middle of the glade less than two hundred yards away. "Do you see it?"

She shook her head, and her hair brushed against the up-turned collar of her coat. He handed her the binoculars and pointed again.

She put her eyes to the lenses, adjusted them to fit her face, and looked where he had pointed. He knew when she had spotted the grizzly by the way her hands gripping the binoculars began to tremble.

"That's got to be him," Newt whispered.

She nodded and handed him back the binoculars and took up the rifle that lay between them.

"Take your time," he said. "Do it just like we practiced."

They were far enough away from the bear that there was little chance it would see them, but she stretched the rifle out slowly before her, taking care not to move too fast. When she glanced at him, he nodded at her to praise her for how well she remembered, and he continued to watch as she rested the long forearm of the rifle on his rolled-up coat that he had laid in front of her.

Her hands were still shaking when she pressed the butt-stock to her little shoulder and found her rifle sights.

"Easy now. Breathe," he said.

He heard her shuddering exhale and inhale, then he looked at the grizzly again through the 4x German optics, tinkering with them and bringing their quarry into better focus.

Several times over the past weeks, they had found the old grizzly's tracks and the signs of his passing, but this was the first time they had spotted it. Newt was a little surprised that it was not as big as he remembered, though that could have been because of the distance and the magnification limitations of his lenses. He reminded himself, as Zuri no doubt had as well, of the last time he had seen the bear.

He heard Zuri cock the rifle hammer. "No hurry. Let him come broadside and then make the shot."

The grizzly was moving slowly and stopping often. It would have been an easy shot for Newt at that distance, but he wondered how she would handle it. They had spent a portion of their first few days in the mountains letting her practice shooting the gun. It was too big for her to handle and shoot offhanded, so she practiced shooting off a rest. When he tried to tell her she had practiced enough after the recoil of it had bruised her cheekbone and her shoulder, she wouldn't listen and kept going. After those days of practice were over, she could shoot surprisingly well if the range to the target wasn't too far.

He shifted himself to a more comfortable position where the crick in his neck didn't bother him so badly.

"Ssshhh." She hissed at him to be still and keep quiet.

He almost chuckled at that but didn't. He found equal humor and surprise in the fact that his own heart was pounding faster than it should have been. It took him a moment to realize the nerves he felt were more for her than him.

"Squeeze the trigger. Don't jerk it," he whispered. "Follow through your sights."

"Ssshhh," she hissed a second time.

He looked through the binoculars again, wanting to place her shot when she took it. He watched and waited while the seconds passed, expecting the boom of the gun at any time, but no shot came.

"He'll be in the timber before long," he said.

Zuri still didn't shoot.

He looked at her again and saw the tear roll out of the corner of her eye and slide down her cheek.

"You don't have to shoot unless you want to," he said. "We can find him again, or we can quit hunting him if you've changed your mind."

She made a slight shake of her head and settled behind her rifle sights once more. Her eye that he could see was still tear-wet, and she was biting her lip like she did when she was upset.

"It's just a bear and nothing more," he said. "Just an old bear that'll die whether you do for him or not. Why don't we go back to camp?"

The boom of the rifle startled him, and he jerked his binoculars to his face and strained to find the grizzly in the meadow. It took him a while, and he half expected to see it running for the timber unhurt. But there it was, a brown hump in the short spring grass at the edge of the meadow. It looked like it would go no farther.

He barely had time to get to his knees before Zuri hugged him around the neck and squeezed herself to him. She was crying so that her body shook, and he knew nothing else to do other than to hug her back.

"There now," he said as he patted her back. "It's over."

She clung to him for a long time, and after a while he felt his own eyes blur with moisture, too.

Well, I'll be damned, he thought to himself. *If you ain't getting soft.*

HISTORICAL NOTES

1. **Willow Creek Canyon:** This was the site of what would become one of the biggest silver strikes in Colorado, about three years later than the setting of this novel. Though Nicholas Creede was really the prospector to make the first strike there, he found it on his own and didn't need a fictional Happy Jack or Widowmaker to point it out to him. The discovery and claim he made in the canyon in 1889 became the Holy Moses Mine. According to some folklore accounts, the naming of the mine came from the first bit of ore he discovered, that he picked it up in shock and proclaimed, "Holy Moses!" No matter, in 1890 the Sherman Silver Purchase Act almost doubled the price of silver, and it wasn't long until word of his find got out and prospectors and miners from all over were showing up to stake their own claims.

    Almost overnight, in the grand scheme of things, multiple boom camps and tents cities sprang up. Nicholas Creede sold a portion of the Holy Moses ownership to several partners for $70,000. By 1892, when the place had come to be called Creede, Colorado, the Denver and Rio Grande Railroad had built a spur line there from Wagon Wheel Gap, which took the boom to a whole new level. It is often claimed that six thousand people lived in the little more than half of a square mile that made up the canyon floor and that ten thousand called the mining district home, with two hundred new people arriving daily. The railroad shipped a dozen carloads of silver ore a day. Fortunes were made and lost.

Along with the miners and business people came con artists, gamblers, prostitutes, and outlaws, along with thirty different saloons. Gunmen like Bat Masterson were there, and Robert Ford, the assassin who murdered Jesse James, was gunned down in his tent saloon by Ed O'Kelly with a double blast from both of his shotgun barrels. Calamity Jane graced the streets, and Soapy Smith of later Klondike Gold Rush and Skagway fame ran his usual rackets and flimflam games. The town burned and was rebuilt, this time with brick. It got electric lights.

But as many such towns went, Creede lived fast and hard and died almost as quickly. The boom ended in August 1893 when the Sherman Silver Purchase Act was repealed and the price of silver crashed. Creede was almost deserted compared to what it had been, even though it lived on as a dagger-thin shadow of its former self and still produced more ore over the years and into the twentieth century.

2. **Rat Creek:** Saul Barton is purely a fictional character whom I created as an amalgamation of several of his type of mining "entrepreneurs" who graced the Rocky Mountains in the days of the Old West. But there is a real historical reason I

chose to have him believe that his big find was located at the junction of Rat Creek and Miner's Creek west of Willow Creek Canyon so that he would mistakenly miss getting rich off of the Creede boom. Call it justice if you will. A small mining camp was located there, years before Creede's find, but the silver there didn't work out in sufficient volumes or assay enough to make any large scale mining operations pay. Too bad for crooked Saul Barton, huh?

3. **Grizzly bears in Colorado:** There were still grizzlies in Colorado during the Widowmaker's time. Some will argue that their numbers were dwindling even then, and others might say that at that time Colorado had as many grizzlies as any Western state. By the 1940s, however, they were all but wiped out there due to government hunting for predator control and livestock protection, increased human population, and habitat encroachment, with their last known home being in the San Juan Mountains in the very southwestern corner of the state. Somewhere around 1952, a government trapper killed what was supposedly the last grizzly in Colorado just north of Pagosa Springs. In 1953, wildlife officials and biologists declared them officially gone. Were they right, or might there still be a few such bears roaming the Colorado wilds?

Despite the supposition that the grizzlies were gone, in 1979, bowhunter Ed Wiseman killed a sow grizzly while guiding an elk hunt in the San Juans near Blue Lake. He stumbled upon her and she charged him and knocked him down, and in a feat that would do the mightiest and nerviest of the old mountain men proud, he somehow stabbed her with an arrow from his quiver and killed her before she mauled him almost to death. Scientific study of her remains revealed that she was very old and in a bad nutritional and physical state, with most of her teeth bad or worn out. More interestingly, she showed signs having nursed cubs sometime in the previous years.

Today, many will argue that there are no grizzlies left in Colorado, despite the yearly claims of grizzly sightings by various tourists, hunters, hikers, or outdoorsy types. Of course, the "official" verdict is that those sightings are the result of the misidentification of black bears, which are quite numerous in the state, no matter that Wyoming and Montana to the north both have grizzly populations. But it was the real story of that grizzly Wiseman killed that gave me an idea. That old sow grizzly, maybe the last of her kind and fighting against the ravages of time and a changing wilderness, became the inspiration for the bear in this novel, even though I changed her to an old boar. Regardless, I hope I did her justice, and whether or not there are still grizzlies in Colorado, I like to think a few of them might exist. Sheepherders, ranchers, and those who live there might not agree with my romantic notion.